THE FACTS OF LIFE

Seven extraordinary sisters live together under the shadow of war, bound by loyalty, love, fear and hope. Then comes one hallucinatory night when the Luftwaffe level the city of Coventry. Among the firestorms that rage across the city, the youngest daughter experiences a magical awakening that, years later, will result in the birth of a son. Following the war, the sisters' paths diverge but they are all still drawn back to this extraordinary child. As the boy grows up, circumstances conspire to test their loyalty to each other while opening up a world of truly spectacular events.

THE FACTS OF LIFE

THE FACTS OF LIFE

by

Graham Joyce

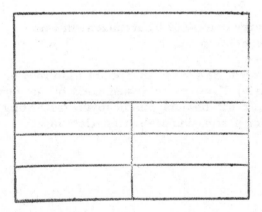

Magna Large Print Books
Long Preston, North Yorkshire,
BD23 4ND, England.

British Library Cataloguing in Publication Data.

Joyce, Graham
    The facts of life.

    A catalogue record of this book is
    available from the British Library

    ISBN   978-0-7505-2639-5

First published in Great Britain in 2002 by Gollancz

Copyright © Graham Joyce 2002

Cover illustration © Mary Evans Picture Library

Published in Large Print 2007 by arrangement with
Orion Publishing Group

Magna Large Print is an imprint of Library Magna Books Ltd.

Printed and bound in Great Britain by
T.J. (International) Ltd., Cornwall, PL28 8RW

To my Mother and Father, who endured the Coventry blitz, and to all people who look at the rubble and start again

1

If she's not here, thinks Cassie, if she's not coming. If she's not here, then what? Then what?

Cassie Vine, just turned twenty-one but dry-eyed, holds the unnamed baby inside her coat and squints into the wind. It is twelve noon, three weeks after Victory in Europe day, and she stands on the white stone steps under the portico of the National Provincial Bank waiting to make the hand-over. Before her groans the blitzed and broken city of Coventry. Opposite, the hollowed shell of Owen & Owen departmental store; to the right the burned out mediaeval cathedral, its shattered gothic arches and spire like the ribs and neck of a colossal excavated creature; in between, the flattened, scooped-out wastelands and the fractured departmental stores awaiting demolition. Cassie hugs her baby.

She's done this before. Four years ago, on these same steps, under the same neo-classical roof, but before the rubble and the twisted metal tramlines were cleared, while broken water pipes still gurgled and fizzed under the toppled bricks. Before this line of inadequate, temporary shops was erected along Broadgate. That time a girl. This time a boy. And if she doesn't come, thinks Cassie, then what?

I'll damn and bloody well keep it, that's what. They can say what they like. They can bloody damned well bugger off. She opens her coat and parts the blanket from the sleeping baby's face, and her heart squeezes. Because she knows it should be different. Because after the last time her girlish heart felt like a bombed-out cathedral, smoking ash, twisted altar, smashed stained glass, father forgive. Five past twelve and still no sign. I'll give her until the quarter past thinks Cassie. That's all. Until the quarter past.

She can't be trusted, you see, Cassie can't be trusted. What kind of a mother would Cassie make? So her sisters said, so they whispered in beseeching, kindly voices, but with a hardness of heart underneath all their good intentions, no Cassie, it's not right. You know you can't manage. What are you going to do when you have one of your episodes, Cassie, what will you do? Think of the mite. Poor little thing, think about him. Give him a straight chance, Cassie, where there's a need and there's one calling for him.

Beatie it was, her sister, punching rivets into the fuselage of Lancaster bombers, who'd found one willing. Just like the last time. Seems with the shortage of men these days there is always one woman willing. She'll be there at twelve o'clock sharp, Cassie, mind you're not late. You don't want to be seen hanging around, and neither does she. And last time that's how it was, the clean hand-over at twelve noon, with no words said, not a syllable and not a breath. No questions, no name, no pack-drill, the hand-over made and the girl gone. But this time, late.

Ten past twelve and still not come. Cassie rocks her weight from foot to foot, staring every approaching woman in the eye, freezing them in the cross-hair of her gaze, but none come to claim the bundle of boy. The child she hasn't yet named. No, don't name him Cassie, that will only make it harder when the time comes. A name will make him real to you. As if this parcel of gurgles and wails and vomit and infinite fleshy sweetness were not already real, as if it were not part of her, as if her liver or gut were not part of her, as if she could give it up without the sound of skin ripping and sensation of bone cracking.

This is a place where prostitutes stand of an evening, sister Una had told her, raising a single eyebrow. On the bank steps. Ladies of the night. Trollops. Cheap perfume and American nylons. Why give it away when you can get good money? Cassie wonders if those women stood in the exact spot she now stands. Spraying their scents, like alley-cats.

She looks up. The blasted cathedral spire of St Michael's pricks the blue clouds, and her heart skips, count of one. At the second spire of the Holy Trinity and it skips again, two. And she thinks of the slender tower of St John's behind her, three. And keeps counting in this city of the three spires: one, two, three. Because on three you jump. And at any moment she feels she might.

Twelve-twelve and Cassie feels a thrill, a flush of possibility in the idea that the woman is not coming. Then through the crowd she sees an upright figure in a navy-blue coat and black scarf making a direct line toward her, a pinched face and a jaw like cathedral rubble, mouth pursed, brittle eyes. At that moment – but only for Cassie, who sees what others refuse to see – a lance of golden light hurtles from each of the three city spires, intersecting at a point of fire in the bundle in her arms. No, thinks Cassie, it's not going to happen this time and she counts one, two, three and she leaps through the triangle of light into blue space, taking the baby with her and leaving the woman in the navy-blue coat standing on the steps of the bank, arms outstretched, open-mouthed, appalled.

Cassie is wayward, Cassie is fey, Cassie is the last girl on earth fit to raise a child. Everyone is agreed. But when Cassie returns to the family home adjacent to the closed sewing-machine shop, they see her with the infant bundle and they stop talking.

For they are all there, the sisters. Gathered for support. This is what the Vines do at times of crisis, moments of import. They regroup, circle the wagons, take up position. All six of her sisters, plus mother Martha large in her chair under the loud-ticking mahogany wall clock, by the coal fire, smoking her pipe. Martha's yellow teeth clack on the pipe-stem in the explosive quiet. It is Martha's hooded eyes Cassie meets first. Then everyone talks at once.

'Her's brought him back, her has,' Aida declares, as if what is required at that moment is a brilliant statement of the obvious. 'Well our Cassie!' says Olive. Damp-eyed Beatie asks, 'She's not turned up then?' 'Don't tell me,' goes Ina. 'What's a-goin' on?' Una wants to know. 'Here's a fine pass,' says Evelyn.

And Cassie sighs. She stands and sighs, a lovely rose flush brought to her cheeks by the warmth of the fire in the grate. It's as if she isn't there amid these noisy, questioning, caring sisters; Cassie with her soft, lustrous gypsy-black curls and candid blue eyes, dreaming, hugging her unravelling bundle while everyone shouts, argues, gesticulates and wrings their hands.

It is Martha who brings her back and all of the other sisters to order by rapping her walking stick on the side of the coal scuttle. 'Hush up! Hush up! Let's have us a bit of peace in the house. Cassie, take off your coat. Olive, give the girl a cup of tea will you? And Cassie you give me the babby while you sort yourself out. And everyone else just hush up!'

Martha accepts the baby from Cassie and sits back in her chair. Olive pours tea. Una helps Cassie off with her coat, and stands, feet together, with the coat folded over her arm, as if Cassie might at any moment be instructed to put it back on again. Beatie pulls a chair from under the gate-legged table. Cassie sits gratefully. She sips her tea, composing herself while the others wait.

'Now then.' Martha says, knocking out her pipe into a bowl on the arm of the chair. 'Tell us what's passed.'

'Nobody came. That's it. That's all.'

'I'm surprised at that,' Beatie says. 'I'm more than surprised.'

'Where have you been all this time?' Martha wants to know. It was gone four in the afternoon. 'Not waiting, surely?'

'Wandering.'

The sisters exchange looks at this. Looks of confirmation. This, after all, is why Cassie can't be trusted to rear a child. She is given to wandering. Martha turns to quiz Beatie on her contact at the Armstrong-Whitworth bomber factory. 'Are you sure it was all above board?'

'Of course I'm sure. It was Joan Philpot's sister. She can't have children on account she–'

'On account she hasn't got a husband!' Una puts in.

'She did have one in the navy but he went down with the *Hood*. But it isn't that, I mean she could always find another sailor couldn't she? No, she had her womb took away when she was only twenty. And Joan said she was distracted for it. Painted the room up herself she had. Though she really wanted a girl, she was still mad to have him she was.'

'You didn't give her the wrong time?'

'Midday, today, steps of the bank! I'm not bloody stupid. I can't believe she didn't come. How long did you wait, Cassie?'

'I waited plenty.'

'How long?'

'I gave her until quarter past the hour.'

'Quarter past!' Beatie cries. 'She might have been delayed! You could have at least waited the half-hour!'

'At the very least!' Olive says.

That gets them all shouting again, discussing how long it is reasonable for a woman to wait before passing on her baby to a stranger. Aida protests that for a thing like that she would see out the hour. Beatie too. Ina says Cassie must

16

have turned around the moment she'd got there. Only Una and Evelyn seem to think a quarter of an hour long enough to wait.

Martha bangs her stick on the coal scuttle again. 'We'll have to set up another hand-over. That's all there is for it.'

'No,' Cassie says.

'Well you can't keep it, girl, we've been through all that.'

'No.'

The sisters remind Cassie of why she can't keep it. There was that time when she had gone missing for a week and no one knew where or why to this day. There was the time the policeman brought her back at three o'clock in the morning when she'd been found wandering the blitzed shell of Owen & Owen. There had been the episode with the American GIs, and look where that had got her. And the time the fire brigade had had to get her down off the roof. And the time she'd drunk that whisky Olive's husband had looted from Watson's cellars. Not to mention the fearful night of the Coventry blitz itself. Not to mention that. And on and on.

What sort of a mother are you going to make, Cassie?

Cassie cries. She puts her head on the table and cries.

'I'll see if I can't set up another hand-over,' Beatie says softly.

Martha holds the baby boy, just seven days old, and regards her own youngest daughter steadily. Tears have no record of working their way with Martha. But to everyone's surprise she says, 'No.

Maybe the moment has passed.'

'What do you mean?' says Evelyn.

'I mean,' Martha says, 'that sometimes when people are late they are late for a reason. Sometimes things have a way of telling you they're not right.'

'But her can't keep him,' Aida says. Aida is the eldest daughter, already in her mid-thirties and thereby entitled to front opposition to Martha's will. 'It wouldn't be fair to the boy. And you know none of us are in a position to have him. And you're too old, what with your stick and one thing and another.'

'I know none of you wants him.' Martha agrees. 'We've been through all that. And I don't see why any of you should have the burden of the child. She's had the pleasure, and she has to have some of the gall. But listen to this. There's every single one of you feels rotten about how we give the other away. Every single one of you. And I do, too. There isn't a day goes by when it hasn't played on my mind. So maybe we can put it half right.'

'How we going to do that?' says Aida. 'And here's me with my asthma.'

'We'll share him,' said Martha. 'Turn and turn about.'

'Share him?' Olive shrieks. 'We can't share him!'

'We can and we will,' Martha avows. And she hugs the boy and chucks his chin.

The sisters all start arguing at once. The room is an aviary of voices raised in competition. Cassie looks up as into this pandemonium walks Arthur Vine, Martha's husband, father to all the girls. Cassie was always his favourite, but he can't find

18

a smile for her this time. He nods briefly at her, and ignores the others. It is a moment of sanction. Cassie lifts her head and mouths a silent thank you to the old man. But he can't stand the commotion. He waves an arm through the air and leaves the room. It is, after all, a woman's thing.

Martha clacks her stick against the coal scuttle, silencing everyone for a third time. 'Hark!' she says. 'Hark! Was that someone at the door?'

Martha often 'hears' someone at the door. The sisters are accustomed to it. They pretend to listen hard for a moment. 'No one there, Mam,' says Beatie.

'It's nobody, Mam,' Una says. 'Nobody.'

Martha slumps back in her chair under the ticking clock. For with the arrival of nobody at the door, it seems a decision has been reached.

2

No one there. The question of whether or not there was ever anyone there would come to vex Frank all of his life. For so was the boy named by Cassie, and very quickly after the aborted handover, because Cassie knew that once Frank was named he might be loved or hated, but he wouldn't be given away. Frank Arthur Vine. Frank for reasons Cassie wasn't giving, though Martha and all the sisters could guess, since the only Frank any of them knew was a retired and incontinent rat-catcher still living in the half-bombed cottage at the end of the street; and Arthur after Cassie's father.

'Arthur, is it to be?' Martha had sniffed at that.

On the matter of names, Martha might not sniff at anyone. When she'd commenced the sport of naming her daughters, Aida, the twins Evelyn and Ina, Olive, and Una it had never occurred to her that she might run out of vowels. So when the next came along, she pitched into the consonants with Beatrice. Cassie came later, the result of a night of careless and rough passion after the celebrations over the election of the first ever Labour government of 1924.

'That's it,' Arthur Vine said, shocked by his wife's fecundity. 'I'm not working my way through the whole bloody alphabet.' It seemed to him that he only had to look at Martha with vague intent and she would fall pregnant. Whatever it was, he never went near his wife again after Cassie was born. 'I shall have the end hammered o'er,' he told his drinking cronies down at the Salutation Inn.

That was of course a joke, but the crack about the alphabet might not have been. After Cassie's birth, Arthur, always a reticent man, almost retired himself from speech altogether. He spoke the minimum to his wife, less to his daughters, and what conversational needs he did have were satisfied by a trip to the pub. When challenged by Martha he retorted that a house full of the clamour of eight noisy women was enough to condemn any man to silence. Challenged a second time he said that what with the house being so full of foolishness he didn't want to open his mouth to add to it.

20

If that's what he wants, Martha decided, that's what he shall get. With Arthur close to what might be called an elective mute, a whole year might pass without thirty or forty words exchanged between the two of them.

Martha, with seven daughters to think about, had enough discourse to be going on with. While Arthur was out working at the Daimler car factory he so detested, she had all the making, mending, cleaning and feeding that goes into running a crowded household.

So when Frank came along, and though she had tried to harden her heart to the boy, it had seemed like a resumption of the flow, the flux of life returning to the household, a return to that which had been denied her by Arthur's withdrawal. And though her joints creaked every time she held the child, and though her arthritis raged, and though it was difficult to get up without the aid of her stick, she looked at him and his cloudless blue eyes gazing back at her and what could she do? He was, after all, the son she'd never had.

Or the son who had never thrived. There had been three boys. One who had died in his cradle, and two stillborn.

At times it did seem to Martha that there was, in her once teeming house, no one there. Only Beatrice and Cassie still lived at home, what with all the sisters marrying or moving out before the war. Beatie had her war-work and her night classes. Cassie was fey and from her it was occasionally impossible to get a sensible conversation. The more empty the house, the more it rattled, and the more it rattled the more Martha dreamed.

It was always the dream of the knock at the door.

Five years before Frank was born, and with the nation facing its darkest moment, Martha sat in her chair thinking what she might do if the Germans overran the country. At that time it looked likely. They had pressed the professional army back to Dunkirk and invasion seemed inevitable. She had a fighter's instinct to take to the hills and resist, but she also had young daughters to think about. Cassie was then fifteen and Beatie seventeen. Both old enough to fight, she concluded, draining her daily glass of stout, when there came a knocking at the door. A muffled thumping. Three knocks.

When she opened the door, Olive's husband, William, stood to military attention. Martha was astonished. His army uniform was black with soot and hanging in rags. A filthy toe protruded through one of his torn boots. He looked exhausted, and his head was bandaged. Near his right temple was a tiny rose, a flowering of fresh blood.

After she'd recovered from the shock she was overjoyed. 'You're supposed to be in Dunkirk!' she shouted. 'They got you out then? Come in, come in, don't just stand there.'

His uniform – his torn shirt and khaki trousers – reeked. She could smell salt water and sand and diesel fuel and stale sweat on him. And something else. A dirty smell she couldn't identify, perhaps a spiritual odour. It made her gag slightly.

She ushered William inside. 'Olive's not here. I'll send our Cassie to go and get her. She'll fall

22

over when she sees you. Cassie! Cassie! Come and look who it is. Cassie! Where's that girl? She's never there when you want her! Shall I pour you a drink? Are you shivering William? However did they get you off? They never told us! What are you doing William?'

William was rooting through drawers. He opened the top drawer of the sideboard and ran his hands through tea towels and cake doilies and tablecloths, searching, searching. Then he opened the next drawer down, scrabbling his fingers at the back of the drawer. Finding nothing there, he crossed to the oak chest on the other side of the room, and began making a similar search of the drawers.

William still hadn't spoken. 'What on earth are you looking for?' said Martha. 'Cassie? Where are you?'

William opened his mouth, but no sound came out. Not until he'd resumed his meticulous search did Martha hear the delayed word, 'Germans.'

Martha laughed, but it was a frightened laugh. 'Well you won't find any in my tablecloths.'

Martha suddenly went cold. She stepped from the lounge into the kitchen parlour, where the fire had gone out. The ash in the hearth seemed wet. The clock on the wall ticked too loudly. There was no sign of Cassie so Martha returned to the lounge. The door from that room opened directly on to the street, and William was already leaving. 'Where are you going William? I want to fetch our Olive!'

William turned. His face was half-shaded by the door. Then he was gone, jogging down the

23

street, breathing hard, and his breathing seemed to come louder the further away he got. Martha called after him until he disappeared in the distance. She looked up and down the street. It was empty. There was no traffic, and no people.

Martha closed the door quietly. Bewildered, she looked at the drawers William had ransacked. Leaving the drawers open she returned to the sitting room, where she slumped into her chair under the wall clock. She stared hard at the cold, wet ash in the grate. After a while she put her head back and fell asleep.

When she awoke, someone had lit the fire again. The coal had sunk to a bed of bright hot embers. It shifted in the grate. Martha blinked at the fifteen-year-old Cassie, her darling fool-headed pretty scrap of a thing, who was drying the dishes at the kitchen sink. 'William was just here.'

'Mam?'

'Olive's William. He was just here. Did you see him?'

'Mam?'

'Where did you go Cassie? I was shouting for you.'

'I didn't go anywhere. I've been here. Washing the dishes. And drying them, Mam, and drying them.'

Martha got to her feet – she hadn't needed the stick then – and moved through to the lounge. All the drawers had been closed again. She felt dizzy. She had to return to her seat under the clock. 'Fetch me a bottle of stout, Cassie. That's proper turned me over, it has.'

'What has, Mam?'

'Seeing Olive's William like that with his head all bandaged. Must-a dreamed it. Where's that glass of stout got to?'

'Here you are Mam, that'll perk you up. You know what you are? You're fey, that's what!'

Fey. This was the word all the sisters and Martha herself used to describe Cassie's excesses. 'Throw that back at me would you? Proper turned me over it has.'

Within the week, William was back again. He was one of the last of the rearguard pulled from the smoking carnage and disaster of Dunkirk beach. And when he did arrive, it was in a filthy, torn and putrid army uniform. Unlike his phantom, which had visited Martha six days earlier, he came through the back door, interrupting a tea of buttered bread and blackcurrant jam. Martha, Cassie and Beatie were there as always. As was Olive, his wife. They were enjoying a joke as he walked through the door. They all turned, surprised by this intruder, and not one of them recognised him.

He was unshaved and his cropped hair was plastered to his head by the rain. His stinking uniform was blackened and oil-stained. Saltwater stains from the hours he'd spent standing in the sea had left tide marks on his trousers. His boots were cracked and the leather stitching had dissolved. A blackened toe poked through.

Olive got to her feet, stammered, fainted.

Troops evacuated from Dunkirk were not allowed to return home in this condition. It was too damaging to morale for the public to see. After disembarking from the rescue fleet the

25

soldiers were transported to processing camps where they were cleaned up, given fresh uniforms and briefed on what to say about the expeditionary disaster. But the train taking William to his processing camp had slowed on its way through Rugby. Defying his sergeant, William had leapt on to the platform, bent on finding his own way to Coventry. From Rugby, a pig-farmer in a truck gave William a lift all the way to the door.

When Olive fainted, everyone identified William inside the dishevelled wraith hesitating at the back door. Martha immediately looked for a wound, and though there was no bandage any longer, she saw the lesion instantly. A patch of hair had been cut away at the side of his head and there was a congealed blot of blood, like a pressed flower against the white page of a book.

William ran to pick up his wife. She came to, murmuring his name. The sisters gathered round, bombarding him with questions. 'Air,' Martha said, 'give them some air.'

'God your uniform stinks, William!' said Beatie.

'Stinks of piss!' said Cassie excitedly.

Cradling Olive in his arms, William said, 'Yes, well I did piss myself a few times.'

This got a laugh until the women realised he wasn't joking. Olive blinked at him. Beatie tried to put a cup of tea under his nose. Martha said he didn't want tea, coming back from Dunkirk like that, he wanted whisky.

'Hell's bells, you do stink!' said Martha. 'Let's have that uniform off your back. Beatie, get those pans a-boiling. This lad is for the bath.'

'Can I have my whisky first?' William wanted to

know, settling himself on to a hard chair.

Olive still hadn't spoken. She continued to stare at her husband as if he might fade before her eyes. Cassie sat at his feet, holding her nose. Martha put her hand on his neck; Beatie brought him his whisky. He knocked it back in one, holding his glass out for a refill.

'But however did you get here?' Beatie thought to ask him.

William told his story of the train slowing through Rugby. 'So I sees as the train is nearly stopping, so it is, and I says this is Rugby, I'm off here. No you ain't says my sergeant, you keep your arse warm. No says I, this is 'ome for me and I gets up, and he roars siddown you little sod or you're on a charge! On a charge I says, what they gonna do, send me back to bleedin' Dunkirk? And the boys all laugh, so I'm up and I open the train door and it's just pickin' up speed and I'm out on the platform and me legs are a-goin' and I'm thinking I'm going to fall on me face here and the boys are cheering and the sergeant is mouthing off out the window and me legs are a-going and then the train's gone and I'm in Rugby, and I think, well, that's it then.'

'Well,' said Martha, drying tears of laughter.

'Well,' said Beatie.

'You told that sergeant!' Cassie laughed.

William did an imitation of the sergeant's face, rubberised and mobile and mouthing obscenities at him as the train pulled away, and they all laughed again.

'Was it bad?' Cassie asked. 'In Dunkirk, was it bad?'

27

'Bad?' William reached down and stroked Cassie's lustrous black hair. 'Bad? Sweet little Cassie.'

Then William lifted his hand from Cassie's hair and covered his eyes. His shoulders trembled. Then his breath came in short gasps, as if he couldn't take in enough breath, and though he made no other sound the hot tears burned through his fingers and dripped from his hand on to his filthy khakis. The women looked at each other. Except for Martha, who looked at the fire.

'It's all right,' William said at length. 'It's just the relief. It's just the blessed relief of coming home.'

Olive snapped out of her silence. 'Come on William. Let's get you out of these rags. Is that water boiled? See to it, eh?' She tried to unbutton his tunic, but she couldn't shift the buttons. The tunic was stiff with dirt and the fabric around the buttonholes had rotted on to the buttons. Cassie fetched the zinc bath from outside and placed it before the fire. Beatie got the pans of boiling water. Cassie was sent to get a pair of pinking shears to hack off the tunic. Olive wouldn't trust her sister and grabbed the shears herself. It was hard work. They all had a go, their eyes gleaming, the now recovered William saying, 'Watch it! Watch it! Careful of the wedding tackle!' until they had him stripped down to his underwear. This he removed himself, slightly ashamed, as Beatie and Martha turned their backs, busying themselves. Cassie continued to stare at her brother-in-law, a glistening seed, naked and white, popped from the husk of war.

'Cassie,' Martha barked. 'Run down to Olive's and fetch a full set of clothes for William.'

'That girl,' Martha said after Cassie had gone.

Olive wanted to take off his metal dog-tag, but he wouldn't let her. 'I'll need it,' he said. 'It ain't over yet.'

William climbed into the bath. Olive washed his hair and bathed him from head to toe. If Beatie and Martha made themselves scarce or busied themselves with other activities it was not merely through modesty; the sudden proximity to war, invasion and death induced another kind of shyness. The brother-in-law had returned where many hadn't, and that was what mattered most.

As William dried himself, Olive took his uniform out into the backyard. Emptying the pockets, she found a plundered Nazi armband and an Iron Cross. There was a notebook and a tiny wallet. These things she kept. She made a pile of the military rags, dousing them with paraffin and setting them alight.

While she did that, Cassie returned with the civilian clothes she'd been dispatched to collect from her sister's house in the next street. William climbed into them. The others were busy with emptying the bath and rustling up something for him to eat, when Martha said, 'I got a message from you last week.'

'Oh?' said William, tapping the end of a cigarette on the packet before lighting up.

'Yes. You came here. You were looking for Germans in the other room.'

'Oh?'

'Well then,' said Martha. 'You're home. That's

all that's important. Isn't it?'

Later, when William and the sisters were drinking whisky and stout and making light of it all again, Cassie slipped outside. There she found her father watching over the dying embers of the burning army uniform. 'Dad, did you know William is home? He's home from Dunkirk! Really he is!'

As was his custom Arthur said nothing. He smiled thinly and wafted a hand through the bonfire smoke before turning his head to the sky, to the stars.

3

The question of how, exactly, the care and succour of Frank would be shared around the sisters went unresolved. Martha had spoken, and anyway she had also declared that none of them would be expected to take on what she called the 'nappy years'. She herself was fit enough to take care of that, and if the sisters were to continue to visit as they always had done, then they might be expected to help out.

'Help out and make and mend and the odd bit of washing and doing,' was how Martha put it.

Cassie was there, after all, when she was on song, and Beatie still lived at home. Though Martha was careful not to overburden Beatie, who had a full-time job plus night school to think about. Though the war was over Armstrong-Whitworth was still on a war footing. Beatie pumped rivets. Thousands of them, drilling the holes, dollying and doming the rivets; and in addition to manufacturing bomber aeroplanes Beatie, who according to Martha was 'afflicted with too much brain', was studying at the Workers' Education Association.

Trade Unionists at the bomber factory had spotted Beatie's affliction and had prevailed on her to have it treated by attending courses in science, history and philosophy. Beatie had lined up for it like a volunteer at a drugs testing clinic, but this therapy only seemed to inflame the original symptoms. She came home with her head punched full of ideas, and every one of these ideas generated another hole crying out to be filled.

'I don't know who's stuffing your head with all these notions,' Martha said, stirring the coal fire with an iron poker. 'I don't know what it shall come to.'

'I love it,' Cassie said. 'I love to hear Beatie talk about these things, even when I don't understand a word she says.' Cassie stepped back and forth with Frank hanging limply over her shoulder. Her dress was unbuttoned after breastfeeding and she was trying to wind him, drumming her fingers on his back.

'No one is stuffing my head,' Beatie protested, lighting a spill from the fire for her cigarette. 'It's just going to be different now the war's over. It will be what we make of it. And if we make nothing of it, who will we blame?'

Beatie spoke in general but she thought in particular; and the particular in this case was that persons at the WEA had unveiled before her a silver chalice of learning. It was a cup brimming with liquor, which on being sipped seemed to replenish itself immediately. A person might want to go on drinking for eternity.

Martha slumped back in her chair under the ticking mahogany clock. 'Well I don't see how it works or how you find the wherewithal, I don't.'

'It's a special college for Trade Unionists, Mam. Workers. People like us. If you show aptitude in your examinations, you can get a grant. A special workers' college. Oxford it is.'

'Another place full of foreigners and thieves.'

'Coventry has its own thieves,' Cassie put in gaily. Baby Frank burped a hearty agreement.

'And when would we see you?' Martha asked, because there was the rub. Martha was all for self-improvement, *and couldn't we do with a bit more of it, but don't take my girls, my little foxes and my leverets for they be all that I am.*

'Why I'd come home every weekend, Mam. Every weekend. It's not far away. Not so far as London.'

'Not so far as Timbuktu neither.'

'Where's Timbuktu?' Cassie wanted to know.

It didn't matter that Oxford was a mere fifty miles from Coventry. It was outwith Martha's immediate constellation, and she did so love to see her satellite daughters keeping close orbit. All of the others lived, through choice, a short walk from the family home, with the exception of Una who had married a farmer and even then the farm was easily reached by bicycle. Beatie was the first daughter to show any inclination to make the long leap.

There was more to it, and Martha always knew when there was more to it. And more to it in Martha's experience was invariably a man. Martha could sense the invisible and unstated presence of a man as easily as she could interview ghosts at the door. They moved behind her daughters like another kind of phantom, making them capricious and unpredictable and prone to staring into the fire. She'd seen it when Aida was young before she married her bloke; and in the thing that had happened to confirm Evelyn and Ina as spinsters; in Olive with William and in Una with her hairy farmer; and of course in Cassie whenever a military uniform filed by the house.

The wonderful thing about it, Martha reasoned, was that men never saw it. They missed it all, too busy puffing themselves up and listening to themselves speak. Women on the other hand saw men's everything. A man with a yen suddenly grew a giant set of antlers too damned big for the room; and there they went, blundering about, cracking their horns in the doorway, tangling them up with the next chap. She felt a little sorry for the way a dignified man could become a buffoon once he'd got the scent in his nostrils.

And they never saw how they were being twisted about. How easy it was for a woman to turn a man in circles, spraying the room with a word here or a gesture there. How she'd seen her daughters at it: no less silly, but somehow it was all missed by the men.

Beatie however had been the most reserved. A good-enough looking girl, but a little too slim around the hips for Martha's liking. She'd held herself back, looking for the thing that was going to be better. And while better was good, it was also more difficult to hold on to. Maybe Aida had done the right thing with her plain but upright Scotsman. Or Olive with her jolly but dependable William and his modest ambitions to become a greengrocer. Or Una with a husband reeking of the milking shed. Better, Martha knew, tended to trail with it a mighty set of antlers for such a small shop.

What Martha wanted to say to Beatie was, 'And what about this chap? Will this chap be going to Trade Union college along with you?' But she couldn't ask that because officially there was no chap. No chap had ever been mentioned, and the surest way to get the least information about a chap was to ask a girl before she's ready to tell. So what Martha said was, 'I just hates to think of you all alone in such a place, I do.'

'I'll not be alone, Mam.'

'Oh?'

'There'll be lots of folk just like me.'

'Oh?'

'And there are one or two from the WEA class as are talking of going, too.'

Here it comes, thought Martha. 'One or two, you say?'

'There's Jennie, who I've told you about before. She's so clever Jennie is. And then there's a chap called Bernard. You should hear him, Mam. He's bright as a button.'

'Why's he not been fighting in the war?'

'He offered himself two years back, Mam. But they rejected him on account of a pigeon toe and

34

poor eyesight. But he's been a messenger and a fireman since he was thirteen and he got a commendation that night Hertford Street burned down. Burned all his arm he did.'

'Half-blind, burned and pigeon-toed? He does sound a crock.'

'Ha!' went Cassie.

'He's not a crock, and I never met such a talker.'

'Well,' Martha said, 'perhaps if he's such a good talker we should have him round for tea if that's what you want.'

Beatie looked up at that, but said nothing. She knew her mother well enough to know that the burned, pigeon-toed, half-blind cat was out of the bag. She just didn't quite know how it had been managed.

'I mean,' Martha said, 'we could certainly do with a bit of male company around here, couldn't we Cassie?'

'Oh yes!'

'I don't want fuss, Mam.'

'Fuss? Who said anything about fuss? He'll have a spam sandwich and a cup of tea and he'll be grateful. There'll be no fuss. We're not ones for fussing.'

'I mean,' Beatie begged, 'that I don't want all the girls here. You know.'

'There'll be me and thee, and Cassie, and baby Frank of course. And that will be all.'

'I'll ask him,' said Beatie.

'Wheeeeeeee!' Cassie, excited by this prospect, jumped in the air. Baby Frank, still draped across her shoulder, slithered from her grasp. Martha lunged forward to catch him and missed. Beatie got an arm outstretched to him but also missed.

Frank hit the rug nose first.

4

Bernard Stokes had been a little flushed with embarrassment at first. Initially slow to hold court, he was warming to it. There were spam and pickle sandwiches, and tea as Martha had promised; there was fresh lettuce and tomatoes from Olive's greenhouse, not to mention the presence of Olive herself. Aida too had taken a chair at the table. Meanwhile the spinsters, Evelyn and Ina, had by miraculous coincidence, dropped by with a dish of beetroot sliced and steeped in vinegar. When Una arrived with half a dozen eggs from the farm, Beatie took them from her without a word and set them to boil, just so she could growl at Martha who was filling the kettle for another round of tea.

'For God's sake Mam!'

'I didn't tell them!' Martha mouthed, her broad back shielding the exchange from the other women. 'It must have been Cassie.'

Cassie hadn't blabbed. She didn't need to. Olive had simply seen Beatie starching a blouse. Una had seen Martha dusting off the best plates. They might just as well have issued invitations printed on embossed cards. Aida, Evelyn and Ina had been informed as a matter of course. After all, it was a question of whether this was going to be the

36

one for our Beatie.

Bernard had arrived with his shoes shined and his face scrubbed up to an acute kind of pinkness. His walnut coloured hair was parted on one side with vicious precision and plastered down with water and zealous combing. He'd been ushered in off the street, and bustled through the lounge with no time for more than a glance at the news-paper-reading figure in the high-winged arm-chair. The old man motioned a hand through the air without looking up from his paper. Thence into the back room to be seated centre table, a guest of honour, waited on by numerous pairs of female hands.

It was true; there hadn't been a young man in the house since William returned in charred rags from Dunkirk that day and Olive had fainted. But needs were strong and leave was short, and it was not long before William was recalled for duty. Exactly five years later William was still in Germany as part of the victorious occupying army. Nevertheless, he hadn't gone back to the ranks before leaving Olive with a present from Dunkirk: a bonny little girl called Joy, now four years and three months old.

Meanwhile Bernard was having to get used to eight pairs of eyes trained on him as he spoke. Martha's kindly but indifferent; Aida's squinting and critical; Evelyn's and Ina's swimming; Olive's moist with sincerity; Una's humorous, mocking even; Cassie's fawning; and Beatie's crestfallen and apologetic. He coped by talking a great deal.

'The rebuilding, you see, the rebuilding. We have to look on it as an opportunity. I mean it's terrible what's happened to this city, but look at the slums that have been cleared. Now we have to think about building decent homes for working people.'

'More bread and butter, Bernard?'

'Have a little more lettuce Bernard. Did Beatie say you are going to be an archie-tec?'

'This is delicious Mrs Vine. Yes, it's my great ambition to become an architect. We've a lot of building to do in this city.'

'Haven't we just,' said Aida. 'Haven't you got to pass lots of exams?'

'Indeed you have. And I hope to go off and study.'

'Just like that, Bernard?' Aida wanted to know. 'I didn't know it was so easy.'

'Spot more tea, Bernard?'

'Thank you, yes. But the opportunities are going to be there for ordinary people now. You'll see. You must have heard all the demobbed soldiers talking. They're going to elect a Labour government. We've got to build a land fit not just for heroes but the children of heroes.'

'First we've got to throw out this lot,' said Una.

'You can't get rid of Mr Churchill after everything he's done,' put in Aida.

'We bloody will!' Beatie cried, with shining eyes. 'We'll chase the bloody old toad off the compost heap, we will!'

'Language!' Martha said. 'Bernard hasn't come here to listen to bad language. But Beatie is correct. We need a new lot, so we do.'

'Quite all right Mrs Vine. I like a woman who can swear.'

'I don't,' Evelyn said.

'Nor me,' went Ina.

'Well the thing is that there *will* be opportunities for people like us. Look at this family. No more spam, thank you Mrs Vine. The salt of the earth if I might say so. And young women like Beatie deserve their chance along with everyone else. She's capable of great things.'

'An archie-tec,' Olive said again. 'I think that's wonderful.'

'An archie-tec.' Cassie shuddered in admiration. 'Just imagine if you married him Beatie, and he was an archie-tec!'

There was a silence in which Bernard could be heard to stop munching his lettuce leaf. Martha dug him out. 'Cassie you nitwit, he hasn't come here to get wed; he's come round for a sandwich. More beetroot, Bernard?'

Then Una dug him in again. 'He don't need any beetroot judging by the colour of him, Mam.'

Cassie laughed like a hyena, and started all the others off: all except for Beatie who gritted her teeth and said, 'Christ!' but went unheard. The laughter became more hysterical, even reaching a slightly dangerous pitch. Bernard meanwhile grinned and looked from one to the other of the six, laughing sisters. Martha meanwhile gestured to him with hands held wide, as if to say, this is what you'd be getting. Bernard took out a handkerchief and wiped his brow, finally smiling at his own predicament. You'll do, is what Martha thought. Yes, you'll do.

The tea things were cleared away, the tablecloth was folded. Perhaps they had sensed Martha's conclusion on the matter, but the company of the sisters broke decisively, almost ritualistically, without anyone having to say a word. Beatie smiled at Bernard, and Bernard smiled back, and he knew that he'd reached the appropriate moment in which to take his leave. But it was at the moment that Beatie was helping him on with his jacket and while the other sisters bustled in clearing the table that events took a turn.

'Thank you for a delightful tea, Mrs Vine,' Bernard said. There was a certain formality to his manner he'd learned from political meetings. 'I'm only sorry I didn't get to meet the gentleman in the lounge.'

The sisters all stopped what they were doing and regarded him steadily.

'I assume it's Mr Vine in there,' Bernard went on, dusting his shoulders free of the plague of dandruff.

Still they said nothing, until Martha said, 'You'll be hard put to get a word out of Mr Vine.'

'He waved at me when I came in, at least.'

'He did, did he?'

'I assume that *was* Mr Vine?'

Martha Vine fixed him with such a piercing look that Bernard shivered.

'You see!' Cassie wailed unhappily. 'You see!' Then she impulsively rushed over to Bernard, took his hand and pressed a kiss on his mouth.

Beatie rescued him, pulling him to the door. 'Come on Bernard, if you're to catch that bus!' She had to shout. He'd been mesmerised. 'Bernard!'

Bernard was bundled out of the door, leaving Martha with six of her seven daughters, who would tidy up, wash and dry dishes, sweep the floor, return chairs to their correct positions and take their leave with no review whatsoever of the foregoing. They never did discuss these things.

They couldn't.

The only remark was made by Una as she wiped down the kitchen table. 'And it was going so well,' she said.

5

'It was supposed to get better.' Cassie winced slightly as baby Frank dragged on her nipple. 'Now that it's all ended. We were supposed to get cod liver oil and orange juice, but I don't see it.'

Martha hunched over the sink, peeling carrots. 'They'll keep us on ration for ten years if it suits 'em. And it might get worse afore it gets better.'

'We should have a party when William comes home, Mam. Do you think he'll make another cousin for Frank? Like he made Joy when he come home from Dunkirk?'

'You're a nitwit Cassie. That's not for me to say, now is it?'

'Ouch! Frankie! Mam, my nipples are cracked and sore! Maybe I'm going to go over to the bottle.'

'I didn't give up on you so easy. Seven of you. I should have had nipples of iron. And mastitis with the twins. Never gave up. That's what God made 'em for, and not for poking men's eyes out in the dance hall, which is what you lot seem to think.'

'That Bernard was looking at my bosom, Mam. Couldn't keep his eyes off 'em.'

'Well, they are the biggest thing of you, and you being a scrap of a thing.'

'I wouldn't have minded his hands on 'em.'

'You're shameless, Cassie. Shameless.'

'Oh Mam! I wouldn't do it! Not to Beatie! Not to my lovely sister and you know it. But doesn't it make you feel good to walk down the street and know you could pick and choose, any one of 'em you want, just with a wink, just with a little flick of your finger, and know they have to follow you. That they're so easy. Doesn't it make you feel powerful!'

Martha turned and jabbed her carrot knife in the direction of Frank. 'And that's where it gets you.'

'Worth it, it is Mam. I love my baby Frank. He's a special one. You see it, don't you Mam?'

'Cassie, you're soft in the head. You'm plain dense. You'm odd.'

'Odd family I come from, Mam.'

Odd family indeed, starting with Martha and her phantom visitors. Then Aida, the eldest, married to a man who by common consent looked like a walking corpse; and then the spinster twins Evelyn and Ina, pillars of the spiritualist church, permanently organising and documenting the visits of mediums, psychics, clairvoyants, rappers, howlers and peepers; Olive who could cry for everything and Una who wouldn't squeeze a tear for anything; and Beatie who would put up her fists to defend the sanctity of an intellectual idea; and Cassie who thought it passing strange that human beings were not equipped with wings to fly.

Bernard, and all the other men who were drawn towards the perfumes and the pleasant wiles of the girl Vines, might have cause to step back and wonder before they jumped the broom. Because they would indeed be marrying into an odd lot. Though Martha dismissed such talk. All families are odd, she asserted, and some odder than others. They all have their rum histories when you looked close enough, and their mad women in the attic and bones in the cellars. That's what families are: queer histories. But even as she would say this, the Vine girls all sensed that there was something about their own family which wouldn't square, wouldn't stack and fold away neatly like those untroubled Jacksons across the Street or the mild-mannered Carpenter family next door. Until war came along, they had to admit. That did send everyone out of kilter, and for a long time the Vines could appear normal, even strong. But now that peace was reasserting its position in the skies and the shadows of war were in retreat, the strange angle and the crooked gate would all look conspicuous again.

And, it had to be said, the strangest angle and the most crooked gate was Cassie.

'It's a pity you didn't keep some record of his name and number,' Martha said, referring to Frank's father. Cassie had conceived after a dance night, given one balmy August evening for American soldiers going into action to support General Patton's Third Army and the push towards Paris.

'He's dead, Mam. I told you before. I felt him go.'

'You can't know that. No one can know that.'

'I know it.'

Cassie had certainly felt something. It had hit her in the midriff, like a mailed fist, in the middle of ironing her pretty blue dress. It was the dress she'd worn the night she'd met Frank's father, also Frank, with whom she'd laid down in a field. The impact had caused her to double up over the ironing table, and though she hadn't known she was carrying Frank junior at that time, she knew with razor-edged certainty that Frank senior had taken a bullet in the gut and had thought of her and her blue dress and that one sweet night in an English meadow. She knew it as clearly as if she'd heard it on the radio, or as if she'd been sent a War Office telegram. And though she'd twiddled with the dials on the radio trying to collect news, the information was of course too imprecise, declaring only that the River Seine had been cut above and below Paris almost simultaneously, like an umbilical cord.

And of course there would be no War Office telegram. Emotional attachments unconsecrated by matrimony didn't count in the War Office. They didn't stretch to telegrams for boyfriends and they certainly didn't run messages for one-night stands with gum-chewing GIs. It wasn't that Cassie *needed* confirmation. Rather, she felt she *deserved* it.

Frank senior, a little drunk, had cried after making love to her in a field. It wasn't his first time; though he was about the same age as Cassie, he'd had girls back home in Brooklyn. He was a passionate lover, sucking and licking Cassie's breasts just as Frank junior did, though without the sting of the cracked nipple. But after ejaculating inside her he'd cried because he thought he would never see Cassie again, or even because he was afraid he might never make love to a girl again. Cassie would always wonder if Frank, too, had known.

Because of what had happened with Frank, and more specifically because of what had happened to Cassie on the night of the blitz four years prior to that, when Coventry had been destroyed by the German luftwaffe, Cassie came to associate sex with magic. The fact that it could produce babies, was, to her, a wonderfully potent example of magic in itself. Where everyone else threw up their hands at what they saw as another unwanted pregnancy, Cassie saw in it only confirmation of spectacular powers, another beam of light in a dark universe. She had no thought of fending for the child, nor of the economic implications of her fertility. But then unlike her sisters, she seemed to live in a guilt- and anxiety-free world where the past and the future were mere details hovering outside the iridescent bubble of the moment.

Sex and magic were mixed up, that was certain. The question, which Cassie had never been able to answer to her own satisfaction, was whether she controlled the magic or the magic controlled her. She couldn't discuss these things with either her mother or her sisters. She'd tried to, but they only looked at her as if she had two heads. It was her great hope that baby Frank would grow up to be clever enough to explain it to her. When he was old enough, she would tell him as much as he needed to know about Frank senior. And she would also tell him about what had happened to her on the night of the blitz. He would believe her, and he would explain it to her. He would know the answer to these difficult questions because he himself was a child of magic. His spirit, if not his conception, had passed into her womb on the exact moment that his father had taken a bullet in his belly somewhere near the River Seine in France. In the same way that her other baby – the baby she had given away on the steps of the bank – had passed into her womb on the night of the blitz.

It was all so simple until it was made complicated.

The child Frank had special powers. It was already clear to her. He looked back at her like one who knew something. Like he was an old soul. Cassie had looked hard at other babies to see if they were bathed in the same golden and violet light, and they were not. She examined them, under cover of fussing and kissing and tickling, to see if they bore Frank's spectral knowledge. They did not. She peered hard into their eyes to see if they sparkled with anything like his insight. Not even the prettiest ones did.

She was careful of course never to mention this to other mothers lest they suspect her of her superiority. After all, which mother did not think her offspring exceptionally talented or gifted? But that was all so different from the *know*. Frank had powers. He had already demonstrated as much. There was nothing more to be said. When entertaining these thoughts, Cassie did so only briefly, and with conviction. Then she pushed them aside.

'Mam, what did you think of Bernard? What did you really, really think of him? I saw you looking at him when everyone else was talking. I saw you reckoning up.'

Martha dried her hands on a towel and lowered herself carefully into her chair by the fire and beneath the clock. 'Have you done? Give me Frank for a while. I'll have him while you pour me a glass of stout.'

Martha drank one small bottle of creamy black stout every day. She drank no liquor other than this single constitutional gold label ale. Cassie popped off the cap and poured the stout very carefully to effect exactly the right head. Holding the contented baby Frank in her left arm, Martha accepted the stout and sipped, smacking lips in satisfaction. 'I thought he will do nicely, though I did see a shadow. First, he's bright as a button and what with Beatie having too much going on her head he's got to be clever, hasn't he? Her shall never put up with a dense one. He's not too bad on the eye, neither, but not so good looking that he'll have every little minx like you scratching on his door.'

'Mam!'

'But he's the sort as will chase and worry away to the end of the earth if he's fixed with an idea. He's too neat. He's too well sorted. He knows what he wants and he's got his life planned out all the way to knowing what gravestone he wants.'

'And what's wrong with that?'

'Life won't let you make all those plans, Cassie,

is what's wrong with that. Life gets under your feet and turns the table over, just when you've got it all laid out, and people like Bernard, well, they can't see that. They've almost got too much good in them.'

'I thought he was a good man.'

Martha drained her glass. 'Yes. I hope as he's not too good for Beatie.'

'Can I sit at your feet, Mam?'

'How old are you now, gal? Come on then, come over.'

Cassie hunkered down on the rug, leaning in against Martha's knees. She lit two cigarettes, passing one of them to her mother. Frank had drifted off to sleep in Martha's arms. The fire in the grate glowed a brilliant orange. The two women smoked in silence, staring into the fire, and the embers shifted, but slightly.

'You know our Frank is a special one, don't you, Mam?'

'All babies are special, Cassie. All babies. And all mothers think so.'

'I'm not just talking about that, Mam. You know what I mean. I mean he's special.'

'Cassie, don't be wishing too much special on the lad. Don't be doing that.'

'I won't, Mam.'

The embers shifted again in the grate.

6

Cassie was not a bad mother. That is to say she was never short of patience, was never willfully neglectful, never knowingly put her own interests above those of baby Frank. Love flowed from her as freely as mother's milk, and was greedily drunk. Indeed Martha remarked that Cassie was too keen to show Frank the nipple, even when the child was clearly surfeited.

In an age in which the spectacle of a mother breastfeeding was considered a breach of the peace, Cassie would happily spill her wondrously lactating breasts in the direction of Frank's shaping lips any place any time. In the park, on the bus, in the café full of wounded soldiers and airmen. Out with the rosy aureole, on with the clamping mouth of the suckling babe without ever breaking conversation. It caused a stir. While she was enjoying a cup of tea with Beatie in the Lyons Corner House at the top of the town an elderly gentleman had complained to the proprietor. Soldiers returning from the front shouldn't have to see that, he protested.

Cassie couldn't see what the fuss was all about, and said so. 'Here we are in a city smashed down to its last brick and you're all upset by a little bit of tit.'

The proprietor wrung his hands in a tea-towel and gave Beatie a beseeching look.

Beatie drained her cup. 'We were just leaving,' she muttered.

'Were we?' Cassie said.

Cassie's problem, if that's what it was, was that she didn't care about what other people thought of her. Not in the normal sense in which someone might be described as without feelings, or overly confident or selfish. The fact is that Cassie didn't have an ounce of judgement in her soul with which to salt her life. If someone did some scandalous thing, she regarded it with interest but without criticism. That was just the way things were. Behaviour was not subject to personal regulation, but at the mercy of forces like wind and war.

But it wasn't all funny. She might 'pop out' for cigarettes and be distracted by a conversation, leaving Frank unattended for a few hours. She might forget to change his nappies. She might arrange to go dancing with no thought of who might take charge of Frank. She might otherwise be careless.

'Cassie! Cassie, come 'ere!' Martha said fiercely to her on one. occasion. 'What's this burn-mark on the child's leg?'

Cassie burst into tears. 'Oh Mam! I was sitting with him, that's all. And what with he kept me awake all night with his teething, I was so tired and I was smoking a cigarette and I nodded off and dropped the cigarette on his leg...' She put her head on the table and sobbed.

'You want a belting, girl, you really do.'

'I know I do, I know it.' And she would sob her

heart out.

Cassie could not be trusted.

Martha had had twenty years to recognise that Cassie had no bad in her. She was just wayward and inept. A free spirit, and ungrounded, and with six sisters all with their heads screwed on so tight they might get a stiff neck apiece it was a wonder how Cassie came about. Though Cassie was not the slightest of the sisters – that rank belonged to Olive – Martha always thought of Cassie as the runt. The brain runt, she'd often thought but never expressed.

So the early years were not without difficulty. Cassie couldn't be relied on to keep what Martha called proper watch. She was away with the fairies and had herself to be watched. That was it: Cassie had herself never lost something of the child. Thus more care of Frank devolved to Martha than she would have liked. Though she was wise enough to allow Cassie her flights, her dance halls, her wanderings because she knew that when a certain demon in her had been addressed then Cassie would be more dependable – at least until the next time.

Beatie was a stalwart help, too, until the time for her to move on came around. Though the one who had originally arranged for Frank to be given away on the steps of the Provincial Bank, Beatie fell in love with baby Frank and took on more than her share of the chores. She and Bernard were happy to spend much of their courting time baby-sitting. Neither was flush with money, and if Cassie should want to go out dancing, and Martha to her whist drive or more rarely to the ladies' snug at the

Salutation Inn, they were happy to be alone together as Frank slept upstairs.

Bernard was a revelation. He changed nappies. He didn't seem to mind it or find it at all unmanly. 'More unmanly to be squeamish about little things like that,' he said, scraping ochre-coloured shit off Frank's cherubic buttocks, patting him down with talcum powder and expertly pinning back the fresh clean nappy. 'Anyway, I want to know all about it in case we ever go in for it.

'It's all going to have to change,' Bernard avowed. 'If we're going to have women working – and we have to with the manpower shortage – then we can't have women going to work and doing all the chores at home now can we? We men have got to step in and take a fair share. It's all got to change. All of it.'

Beatie blushed. Martha raised an eyebrow, because here was a piece of work in a man.

'Is he a communist?' Una once asked Martha after hearing Bernard launch into one of his speeches.

'I don't know what he is,' she replied, 'but he's neither fish nor fowl, this one.'

Una with her farming husband and rustic lifestyle understood that remark.

'Is he an atheist?' the spiritualist twins Evelyn and Ina wanted to know.

'He's of a very strong soul whatever he is,' Martha said, to satisfy them. She also reported to Olive that he was sensible with his money, and to the serious-minded Aida that he was very keen on education. To Cassie she didn't have to report anything, because quite apart from the fact that she never judged anyone she'd adored Bernard from the very outset. Cassie wanted little Frank to grow up like Bernard.

But whatever he was, fish, fowl, communist, atheist, he went off to Trade Union College and Beatie followed him. They had both studied hard through their baby-sitting years, and they had both earned a place at Ruskin in Oxford. Bernard was to pursue his architectural interests, in which he was already partly qualified, and Beatie was to study English.

And Martha missed them both terribly.

Frank was by this time almost three years old, and without Beatie to help her, Martha found it a strain. She had good seasons and bad seasons with her arthritis and when Cassie was not all that she might be, Martha decided it was time to call in the promise. Martha summoned.

When Martha summoned, all answered. All other appointments were put off for what Martha termed a 'gathering in'. A 'gathering in' was little different to a standard Sunday collection of the sisters, who spent far too much time at the family home as it was, except that husbands – and intended husbands – were expected along, too. None had ever ignored or tested resistance to a gathering in.

Catering for the high Sunday tea of the gathering in was easily taken care of by the expedient of each sister bringing one dish. Aida would bake two large corned-beef pies; Olive would bring boiled potatoes, fresh lettuce, tomatoes, celery, and spring onions from the thriving greengrocery she ran with William; Una, hard-boiled eggs, cream and cheese from the farm, and the twins would bake cakes. Cassie in matters culinary was trusted little further than buttering the bread. It was, in these still-rationed times, quite a spread.

The problem, as with each previous gathering in, lay in seating everyone. In addition to the sisters, space had to be found for Aida's husband Gordon, Olive's William and Una's Tom. In addition to Joy, Olive's present from Dunkirk, was a second daughter Grace, a year junior to Frank, and the recently arrived Hope. Girls everywhere, in a country that, it was said, needed men. Then there was Cassie and Frank. Beatie in Oxford had been given special dispensation not to attend the gathering in, but came anyway with Bernard in tow. Hard-backed chairs were borrowed from Mrs Carpenter next door. The dining table was moved into the kitchen to be loaded with food, from where everyone might take up a plate and fend for themselves, eating from their laps in the sitting room.

Three-year-old Frank drifted through the bustle and chaos of the gathering like one whose town has been invaded, subjugated and colonised in a matter of under five minutes. Most particularly he stared at the men; and not uncritically.

Uncle William was a man with permanently levitated eyebrows, who blinked at domestic events with sleepy incredulity. Whatever horrors he'd experienced at Dunkirk, it was nothing to the trauma of finding himself home with three little girls, a grocery business and an emotionally dependent wife. Meanwhile Una's farmer husband Tom winked at Frank, and offered a

54

convincing repertoire of bird whistles. He would also produce striped humbugs or sherbet lemons from his pocket or from behind Frank's ear. Tom had the touch with kiddies, whereas Bernard tried hard to find winning ways with children but failed. Bernard would sit Frank on his lap and ask questions such as, 'And what do you think the future holds for this fine city, young man?'

But it didn't matter that Bernard was inept with children, because Frank was always drawn to and intoxicated by the presence of men in the house. He was delighted by and unafraid of their louder voices. He was intrigued that they didn't smile so frequently as the women. He loved the way their voices crackled and broke up when they laughed. He also liked the way they smelled.

Except for Uncle Gordon, it has to be said. Frank did not like the way Uncle Gordon smelled at all. Indeed Gordon existed in a category of his own.

'Gordon looks closer to a corpse every day I see him,' Martha once confided to Cassie.

It was true. Gordon's sallow skin seemed pasted to his skull like Chinese ricepaper: it showed up every ridge and cranial bump and it collapsed into his hollow cheekbones. This death's-head resemblance was exaggerated by an almost complete loss of hair. Frank, who was learning to count at the time, amused everyone by trying to number the hairs on Gordon's head. There were nine thick grey strands plastered from somewhere below and behind the right ear, across the crown, and curtailing just above the left eyebrow. During the counting, Gordon affected a grin, which was unfortunate, since it exposed a double row of yellowing pegs from which his red gums were in serious retreat. This nervous grin made Frank step back and desist from counting.

Gordon was apt to display his lack of gums every time he spoke; and whatever words he spoke were preceded by a long drawn-out whine, in which he appeared to be locked in heroic or merely constipated struggle with himself while he shaped whatever it was he was about to say.

'Another slice of corn-beef pie, Gordon?'

'Eeeeeeeeeeeeeeeeeeeeeeee, well, no, I'm not much mithered, but...'

He also had an infuriating habit of not completing his sentences.

'A cheese and pickle sandwich then?'

'Eeeeeeeeeeeeeeee, well, aye, that would quite the er...'

A newcomer into the family, like Bernard, or William before him, might lean in expectantly, politely waiting for Gordon to conclude his statement. And they might wait. And wait. And Gordon would widen his eyes at them in a kind of terror and draw his lips back over his disappearing gums, as if this predicament they both found themselves in – the predicament of Gordon not completing his sentences – was just as astonishing to himself as to anyone. Martha and the sisters however would simply leap the chasm and shove a plate or a cup into his cold fingers and move on.

'Cup of tea. Gordon?'

'Eeeeeeeeeeeeeeeeeeeee, aye, well, I'll no say no to...'

'There you are then. Cut another slice or two of

56

that brown bread, now Cassie.'

But it wasn't the skull, or the trailing clauses, or even the gums retreating from around Gordon's teeth, which most unsettled Frank. It was the smell. Gordon smelled funny.

It was embalming fluid, that and something less precise. Perhaps caught up in the embalming fluid was a whiff of carrion. Gordon had been called upon to help out at an undertaker's parlour in the aftermath of the November 1940 Coventry blitz when several hundred were killed and more than a thousand were injured. A lockstitcher before the outbreak of war, he'd found, in clearing up after the blitz, work he rather enjoyed. The lockstitching business increasingly went over to recruiting women, and though he retained a supervisory role in the fabrics yard where he had worked, he divided his professional time between that and the apparently sunnier enterprise of preparing the dead for the city crematorium.

Martha had, early, ruled out Aida and Gordon as first custodians of Frank. They might have to take their turn eventually, but she hadn't got the heart to hand Frank over to the serious-minded and somewhat soured Aida (her own childless condition being a source of some bitterness to her) and the fresh cadaver who was her husband. No, the solution would have to be found elsewhere.

After the meal had been demolished, Martha, as was her custom, sat in her chair and waited for a silence to descend. Only the children seemed astonished that this happened without anyone making a signal.

'You all know why I called you in,' Martha said.

They did. Some looked at Martha. Others amongst them, without need for divination, peered at the tea leaves in the bottom of their cups. Frank had no idea he was the subject of the discussion. Cassie looked downcast.

'Now I did say to you some time ago that on the question of himself we must all be good enough to take him turn and turn about. It's far from ideal, but we're a close enough family' – there were murmurs of assent to that – 'and all things being equal we s'll continue to be and to see much of one another' – more murmurings of assent – 'but now I find as I'm having a very trying time with my joints, and with Beatie gone off to study, well, I need some help, and that's the top and bottom of it.

'The question is, who must it be? And before you all say as you're too busy with this and that, let me say so much. You shall all take a turn, whatever the condition, because that was what was promised. But as I see it, Frank should go somewhere where there's a chap. You can all see how he's drawn to the men and he's had three years or more of petticoats and one thing and another. So I start by saying that the twins might be considered later, but not now.'

Evelyn and Ina looked guilty and relieved at the same time.

Bernard stood up. He dug his thumb under his lapel, much as he might when he got to his feet at a political rally. 'I've talked about this with Beatie, Mrs Vine,' he said with a delivery that might have been offered to a small crowd from a soapbox. 'And she and I are prepared to take him on at any time. Any time you like.'

'But that's plain daft,' Martha said. 'You live in separate digs with one room apiece.'

Bernard coloured. 'We've thought about it. There's a chance of another place coming up for us. It's in a commune just outside Oxford.'

'A commune!' Aida said. 'I don't like the sound of that.'

'What's a commune?' said Tom to Una, who shrugged in turn.

'It's full of good people,' Beatie said, her eyes shining. 'There are other children, too. It would be ideal.'

Martha held her hand up in the air. 'You're very good, both of you,' she said. 'But you've got your scholarship to be thinking of. Your time will come if and when you get settled, on that you may depend. But for now I'm ruling you out of consideration. William and Olive have got their hands full with these lovely girls. That leaves Una and Tom, and Aida and Gordon.'

Aida and Gordon, Una and Tom all looked hard at the floor.

'But, but, but,' Bernard could hardly contain himself, 'shouldn't Cassie have a say in this?'

All heads turned towards Bernard. Martha, un-phased, looked at her youngest daughter. 'Cassie?'

Evidently Cassie did have a say in this, but she wasn't forthcoming. Eyes damp, bottom lip thrust out like a child's, Cassie shook her head.

'It seems to me,' Martha went on, 'that Una and Tom are carrying a great burden at the farm, and can't be expected to find the extra love as is required for this. Farm has to yield its best, and

59

there isn't the room for love of a child just yet. Too much to do. And I should never put a child where there was no love, even when that would be no fault of either Una or Tom. So it's to Aida I'm looking.'

Aida scratched her knee. Gordon drew back his lips and widened his eyes in panic, offering the assembly his most cadaverous smile.

Tom cleared his throat three times before speaking. 'Hold your horses, now Martha. Where's all this talk of no love in our house? Who says so?'

Una was red in the face. 'Why say that, Mam? We've never been short of love at the farm.'

'It's the work you've got on, the pair of you. Milking and feeding and all the things as go with a farm. I've no intention of putting more labours on to you. It's the labour I fear.'

Tom was indignant. 'It's only one more mouth among many.'

'The boy's not a farmyard animal, Tom,' put in Olive.

'Tom knows that,' Una blazed. 'He's saying that it would be no extra labour, that's what he's saying. And at the farm there would be fresh air for the boy and soap and water, and as for short of love there would be no better anywhere and no worse than anywhere. And there's room! And Cassie could come and live with us or stay here, or come to the farm at weekends, she could please herself.'

Martha shook her head. She turned to Aida. 'Well Aida, what with you being the eldest I'd more or less set on you taking first turn. Now if I give in to Una, I shall be disappointing you. What do you say to that?'

Aida made a poor job of disguising her relief. 'Well, if Una's so strong on it, we should have to step back, shouldn't we Gordon?'

Gordon nodded his head judiciously. 'Ayyeeeeeeeeee, that would errr...'

'Well,' Martha said, 'it's not what I had in mind when I summoned you all here, but it looks as if everybody's mind is made up. Fetch me that glass of stout would you Cassie?'

And with the top taken off the bottle, that was that.

The men, and the younger women, all had a bottle of brown ale, too. The tension had passed from the room now that the decision had been made. Young Frank sat on Tom's knee, and both looked happy. Bernard ventured the opinion that the result was the right one.

'Yes,' Tom said quietly in reply. 'We've been played like a bloody banjo.'

Cassie had cheered up considerably. She helped everyone on with their coats. Arrangements had been made for Cassie to take Frank out to the farm at the weekend. As they left, the door was held open for them by Arthur Vine. Though Cassie knew he'd been present in the house throughout the gathering, he'd stayed out of sight in the front parlour. None of them acknowledged him as they left. Cassie, though, blew the old man a kiss after the last of the family had departed. She was happy enough, and she knew that would make her father happy too. After all, in the matter of apportioning Frank, she'd been given exactly what Martha had promised her.

7

On the Wednesday of that same week, Cassie took Frank out in his pushchair. Martha's determination to let one of the sisters take some of the load was well founded. She was struggling. Her breath came shorter every year and she could do less. The autumn chill in the air excited her arthritic joints. Keeping Cassie on the straight and narrow was as demanding as the task of looking after little Frank. Getting Cassie out of the house with the boy occasionally was a relief. She needed to be alone for a few minutes to pull her unravelling self together.

She slumped into her chair and lit a cigarette from the fire, but she'd taken no more than her first puff of tobacco before there came a thumping at the front door. Martha put her smoking cigarette in the ashtray, hauled herself out of the chair and moved slowly towards the door on her stick. The thumping on the door got louder.

'All right, I'm a-coming! I'm a-coming!' She drew aside the draught curtain shrouding the door and threw back the bolt. 'Are you trying to wake the dead?' she asked before she had the door half open.

She instantly regretted the remark. Before her stood a motorcyclist swathed in black and tan leather. He wore knee-length boots, a brown jacket and leather gloves. Martha couldn't see his eyes or indeed any of his face because the man wore a motorcycling helmet and goggles. Hanging from straps at his ears a leather mask covered his mouth.

Martha peered over his shoulder into the street. The motorbike was parked in the road: not at the side of the road as might be expected, but exactly in the middle. The street was quiet.

'You've not bought me bad news?' Martha said.

The motorcyclist didn't answer. Instead he fumbled at the mouth mask, trying to remove it. He seemed unable to grasp the flimsy straps in the thick padded fingers of his leather gloves, so instead he pulled off one of his gloves. Martha noticed his hand trembled. He still seemed unable to remove the mouth mask, until finally, with a desperately scrabbling hand he was able to tear it aside.

Having succeeded, he leaned in to Martha and breathed softly on her face. Martha felt the breath on her cheek. 'What? What is it?' she cried.

But the motorcyclist only seemed to swallow painfully, touching his throat. At last, and with great difficulty, he managed to croak a word sounding very much like 'Frank'. Before Martha could say any more the man was already retreating down the path, fixing the leather mask at his mouth. Without a glance back at Martha he climbed on his motorcycle, kickstarted the machine into life, and roared away.

Martha hobbled out into the street to look after him, but he was already out of sight. She looked up and down the street. There was no one to confirm what she'd just seen. Back inside and with the door firmly bolted behind her, she moved through to the sitting room. The cigarette she'd left burning in the ashtray had gone out. She looked at the red coals of the fire. She looked at the pendulum of the clock swinging back and forth.

Cassie came back at around four-thirty, having walked all the way into the town centre and back again. Broadgate was lined with temporary shops and Cassie was full of the New Look. For the past year or so Christian Dior's hourglass femininity had swept the country. Bust, hips, thighs. Cassie had swooned over the soft shoulders, the handspan waists and the billowing skirts. The junior government trade minister Harold Wilson had gone on radio describing the new fashions as irresponsible, frivolous and wasteful because they used yards of material. But as Cassie pointed out, who the hell would want to dance with the junior government trade minister?

Things were changing, however, and if the government were being stuffy about swirling skirts they were progressive in other fields. Bread rationing had ended. The National Heath Service had been introduced. 'Look, Mam!'

Cassie had collected her free orange juice and cod liver oil for Frank. The state was doing its best for post-war babies on ration diets.

Martha glanced at the juice and the cod liver oil. 'Well and good,' she said. 'Well and good.'

'You all right, Mam?'

'Cassie, you know how we said we was going to visit Great Aunt Bertha? Well you shall not go, you and Frank.'

'Why? Has something happened?'

'I shall go, but you shall stay home.'

'I was looking forward to that, Mam. And it might be Frank's last chance to see Aunt Bertha before she pops it.'

'Don't give me an argument Cassie; I'm tired and I haven't the head for it. You'll not go, and there's an end to it.'

Martha didn't get an argument.

Slam! went the bottle of cod liver oil on the table. Slam! went the bottle of orange juice. Slam! went Cassie's handbag on the chair, and slam! went the door as she thumped upstairs. Plenty of slamming and plenty of pouting too, but no argument.

Great Aunt Bertha had showed Cassie many small kindnesses over the years, and now, approaching eighty, Bertha had taken sick. She lay on her bed with an undiagnosed illness and word had gone out to various relatives that they might come and visit Bertha, because one never knew. And you couldn't argue with that: one never did know. It was because Martha understood that one never knew that she'd arranged to pay a visit to Bertha's sickbed along with Cassie and Frank. The visit from the leather-clad motorcyclist had changed all that.

It was with some anxiety that Martha pulled on her coat the following day. She was anxious about leaving Cassie alone for a few hours with Frank; she was anxious about the condition in which she might find Aunt Bertha; and she was anxious about the journey across the city to Bertha's house in Foleshill. If that wasn't enough she was vexed by a further matter.

Meanwhile she had to take a corporation bus into the town centre, and then another out to Foleshill. She was out and about less and less these days, and though not a complete agoraphobic, any travelling made her nervous. It would have been better to go in company with Cassie, but now that wasn't possible.

The buses were running regularly again, and she was helped on to the one into town by a chirpy and kind young conductor. Rebuilding was going on all over the city. The immediate post-war years had been busy with clearing the rubble and demolition rather than building, but now the reconstruction was happening everywhere. Martha was particularly interested in seeing what they had done with Broadgate. In May of that year, the young Princess Elizabeth had visited the city to lay a commemoration stone to mark the first phase of the rebuilding of the city centre. The reshaping of the city was the inspiration of the architect Donald Gibson, and Bernard was a disciple.

'A genius, Mrs Vine. The man is a genius. You really have to go and see it. Coventry is going to be the City of the Phoenix.'

'That's a bird that flies up out of its own ashes, Mam,' Beatie said helpfully.

'You knew that didn't you Martha?' Tom had said, teasing. Everyone had come for tea at Martha's house after the visit of the princess. Some of the sisters had flocked to join the crowds, to get a glimpse. Martha had stayed at home. She had little time for royalty, she said, after their cowardly behaviour during the war, and what with Edward being a Nazi sympathiser. But the girls had all gone, and the newly laid out Broadgate had thronged with people eager to wave flags at the princess.

'I didn't know that,' Cassie put in. 'A phoebix. That's beautiful.'

'Phoenix Cassie, phoenix,' said Bernard. He continued to address Martha directly. 'And Broadgate is all laid out in a lawn and the plan is to make it a garden.'

'Shops,' William said gruffly. 'That's what people want in a town centre. Shops. Not a bloody bowling green.'

'And shops they shall have. But gardens, too, and a traffic-free precinct in which to do their shopping. I tell you Donald Gibson is an inspired man. You won't have seen the like of it when he's finished.'

'And how are the shops going to get their stock delivered if there's to be no traffic? He hasn't thought it through.'

'William's got a point there,' Tom said. 'A good point.'

'Design!' Bernard said. 'It's all in the design. I've seen the plans. The deliveries will all be made to the rear of the shops so that the shoppers can move in peace in the precinct.'

'They'll be snarled up and fighting for parking. It can't work.'

'You've not looked at the plans, William! I've looked at them, just as you can look at them, if you go to the Council House.'

'Council House!'

'Well, if you can't be bothered.'

67

A slight animosity existed between William the greengrocer and Bernard the possible communist-anarchist-syndicalist – and what with his suspicious enthusiasm for changing nappies and doing the washing up, possibly a member of the fairy folk. Tom, who took no side in the exchanges, said, 'I just hope he's going to build one or two new pubs, that's all.'

'Eeeeeeeeeeeeeee, that would be err...' Gordon possibly agreed.

'He's a great man,' Beatie said, coming to Bernard's aid. 'And all eyes are on him.'

'But what about his strange mark?' Cassie wanted to know.

'Strange mark?' Martha asked.

On the reverse of the commemoration stone laid by the princess was an odd, perhaps Masonic signature, Gibson's own. It was a hieroglyph with an ankh, taken from an Egyptian pharaoh.

'It was the mark of Akhnaton,' Bernard explained. 'He built himself a new capital in the fourth Century BC.'

'This architect, Donald Gibson,' Tom said. 'Does he wear a fez?'

That got a laugh all round, although Bernard and Beatie exchanged an old-fashioned look.

Now as Martha walked up Trinity Street to the top o' town, she marvelled at the work that had been done. Broadgate had been cleared of rubble and twisted metal, and had been paved flat with a huge central lawn. This was what Bernard meant by a garden centre. It seemed an astonishing open space after the busy, narrow streets, the overhanging gables and squeezed buildings of before the air raids. She crossed the paved area with a sprightly step, making her way over to the commemorative stone.

As she did so she looked about her, and it astonished her that so many people were bustling about their business. Women hurried back and forth in the new fashions and there was hardly a military uniform to be seen. This place, this heart of the town that had been smashed into a plot of rainwater and dust, was being made new again. An involuntary smile crossed her lips, as it occurred to her how strong, how resourceful the people were. It was all being made new.

What a testament to the people who had seen so much suffering! You could blink and almost make yourself forget that they had come through a terrible war. She looked back at the twin spires of the Holy Trinity and of St Michael's and a line came to her, perhaps from the bible: *He maketh the sun to rise on the evil and on the good, and sendeth rain on the just and the unjust.* Though not a religious woman under any terms, what she saw here impressed her, and she hoped that she could number herself and all her daughters among the good and the just.

Martha read the inscription on the commemorative stone. Then she went behind it to examine the architect's marks. It was indeed a strange thing. It seemed to be a planet, or perhaps the sun, from which radiated seven lines, but all from one side. And on the sixth line was an Egyptian ankh. Martha wondered why an architect would choose such an unusual sign.

But again she had something other on her mind

at the time. Something other than unusual signs. It concerned Frank.

After paying her visit to Aunt Bertha, Martha took a bus back into town, and a second one home. On the journey she watched from the window, thinking of Bertha, and of her own husband Arthur, and of her own daughters. At one point she had to take her handkerchief from her handbag to dab at her eye. The visit had upset her. Bertha had been very poorly, but Martha had refused to proceed any further than the bedroom door, from where she'd conducted an unsatisfactory conversation with the old woman. The bus jolted along the thoroughfare, and a lemon-grey dusk was already falling on the rebuilding of Coventry before she reached home.

But what concerned her above all things was Frank. What if Cassie had been correct for once? What if Frank was special? Martha thought that the Vines didn't need any more of this kind of special. They just didn't need it.

8

'Rum, that's what it is,' said Tom. 'It's rum.'

Rum. Farmer Tom Tufnall was the kind of countryman who could use the word 'rum' to refer to the cow taking its time in calving or the bull breaking its neck in covering the cow. It could mean odd, strange, difficult, dangerous, obscure or unorthodox; but the real purpose of the word was to stop all profitless enquiry into the unexplained. Often when using the word he would lift his eyes to the point on the horizon where the grey sky met the reddish-brown Warwickshire land, listen for no more than a moment, and then turn back to his work.

What he turned back to at that moment was his tractor. The coupling pin for his trailer had sheered off, and he was making a new one out of a huge bolt and some of the vexatious discarded scrap metal that seemed to litter his fields. Cassie and Una, in headscarves and wellington boots, stood in the yard watching him. Frank was in and out of the barn, chasing kittens through the haystacks.

'Are you sure?' Una said.

'Diphtheria,' Cassie said firmly. 'And the doctor thought she had the flu.'

'Bloody horse-doctor more like,' Una said.

'And now Aunt Megan is down with it, badly, and a good thing Mam didn't go near her, and now she says that was why she kept me and Frank back, though she didn't say anything, and I know she had a knock on the door that day cos I saw it in her face.'

'Knock-knock,' said Frank, swinging on the barn door.

A post-mortem on Great Aunt Bertha had indeed established diphtheria. Bertha had died not a full day past Martha's reluctant visit, and though nothing was said, Cassie and all the other daughters understood the injunction against Cassie taking the boy along that day. They all

71

knew about the knock on the door, and they respected the way it often delivered a skewed prophecy or warning. The pure fact of it went unchallenged among the sisters.

Tom knew about it, too. All of the men knew that by marrying into the Vine family they had also given their hand into some strange shadow play. There it was. And Megan was ill while Martha, Frank and Cassie were all well. 'Rum,' Tom said again. 'Now then one o' you: get a hold of the other end of this while I hit it with a hammer.'

Una grabbed and Tom swung his hammer, and a mighty clonk sent a vibration through the metal so that Una dropped the bar she was holding. There came a giggle from on high. They all looked back. Frank had managed to climb to the very top of the eighteen-foot haystack.

'How the bloody hell have you got up there?' Tom shouted. Cassie shrieked. Frank giggled again.

Only Una laughed, and made as if to catch Frank.

Cassie liked it at the farm – for a while. At first she settled in happily with Frank and they shared a room above the old dairy. Together they fed the ducks and the chickens. Cassie roused Frank in the middle of the night one time to watch a cow calf, though she herself lost the stomach for spectating any longer when Tom had to pull the calf out with a rope. They tickled the pigs behind the ears and gave names to each of Tom's small herd of Friesians.

But the weather took a turn for the worse, and

as the days grew shorter Cassie found herself confined to the sitting room where sometimes the smoke from the fire blew back into the room if the wind gusted the wrong way. After dinner, Tom would gaze into the hearth, stupefied by the long day of his labours. Una would knit or crochet or read a book. Cassie would fidget or play with her hands or twist in her seat.

'Whatever's the matter with you, Cassie?' Una said. 'Can't you keep still for a minute?'

'Can't we go to a pub, Una? Didn't you say there's a pub? The Red Lion or The Blue Pig or something?'

'The Blue Bell. And who's going to listen for Frank if we all go to the pub?'

'I hadn't thought of that. Perhaps you and me shall go, Tom? What do you say? Get your coat.'

'I'll not. I haven't got the legs for it tonight.'

The Blue Bell was two miles away, but Cassie was not to be put off. 'You and me then, Una. Tom will listen out, won't you Tom?'

'Two women going in a pub!' Una said. 'What sort of girls would they take us for?'

'Ach, you're no fun. Neither of you. No fun!'

'That's right,' Tom said, 'I'm a stick in the soggy mud, I am.'

Una laughed. 'A stick in the smelly farty oozy stinking mud. Happy as a pig in shite.'

Cassie got to her feet and moved to look out of the window. Her image in the dark glass stared back. She hung by the window for a while then stepped back alongside Tom, making a dive for his midriff. 'Goose!' she shouted, pulling his shirt loose. 'Let's see your belly for spots!'

Tom grabbed her wrist and held it. 'Get off, daftie!' he laughed.

Cassie drifted back to the window again. Then she stamped her foot. 'Well I'm off to the pub!' She grabbed her coat and her scarf and she was out of the door before the other two had time to answer.

The door slammed. 'Do we let her go?' Tom said.

Una shrugged. 'We have to.'

'Is this how it happens?'

'Yes.'

'Will she be all right?'

Una sucked air through her teeth. 'Yes.'

'Poor little Frank,' Tom said.

The next day Tom drove Cassie in his truck to the bus stop, from where she could ride to Coventry. Frank was told that Cassie was going back to his grandmother's for a while, and he seemed blissfully unconcerned at the prospect of staying at the farm. Cassie was given eggs, milk and a chicken to take back to Martha's. The short ride to the bus stop was a silent one.

After she'd climbed out of the truck Cassie said, 'It's not that I don't love you and Una.'

'I know that,' Tom said shyly.

'It's just that I feel a bit like I'm going crazy in the country. I feel like I want to scratch my skin off, you know? I feel like I want to shout and stamp my feet.'

'It don't suit everyone.'

'But it's not that I don't love you.'

'I know, Cassie, I know. I have to go now.

Things to do.'

'I know you'll look after my little fellow. I know you will. Bye Tom, bye!'

Frank took to life around the farm. To say he adapted would make it sound more difficult for him than it was. He behaved as if he'd always been there. He got dirty, he got wet. He slipped in the cow slurry, and another time Una had to pull him, wailing, out of the duck pond. But like she'd said, there was plenty of soap and water.

Particularly water. The farm was a wonderfully wet place. Water fell from the sky and bubbled from the ground and the water was cupped and delivered in ponds, springs, streams and brooks in a way that it never did in the city. The earth oozed and flowed and flooded. The land spoke to Frank in the language of water, and his favourite place was the footbridge across the brook. Though to designate it a footbridge was to glorify the solid planks of wood Tom's father had lodged firm in the mud years before so that he might step from the top field to the bottom. But the swift-flowing brook was only inches deep, so Frank was allowed to play there in safety. The brambles and thistle patches had gathered in dense clumps around the undersides of the footbridge, and Frank found he could crawl into the cavity underneath the planks and be hidden from the world.

Frank could make dens and fox-holes all over the farm. There were mouldering stables and rickety barns and rusting, abandoned pieces of farm machinery and, by the hedgerow in the field below the stream, fragments of the twisted wreckage of a German bomber that had come down on the night of the Coventry blitz.

One day Una asked Frank if he would help her pluck a chicken. Frank was a great helper by watching. The chicken was a special treat for him, she said, since he was such a good boy. It seemed like an interesting prospect so he followed Una to the hen-coop. There she grabbed a broiler. The fowl squawked and kicked its legs and exercised its wings in a way that suggested these birds might be able to take to the air after all. Then as Una walked back to the house she tucked it under her arm and twisted the bird's neck in her two hands, and chose that moment to look at Frank.

He would remember the expression on her face at that moment for the rest of his life. The bird's head was hanging down. Frank was aware that she had just killed the creature with her bare hands, but her gaze seemed at odds with her actions. In her eyes was not violence or even grim determination. On the contrary, she looked at Frank with great tenderness, even with pity, as if it had been his neck that had been snapped. There was a semblance of a smile on her face and a terrible sheen to her eye. Una suddenly seemed large, and menacing, and powerful in his presence, and the dead fowl was like an offering to her peculiar strength, something that she might wear in her belt.

'Come on Frank,' Una said, breaking the spell. 'Let's get on with these feathers.'

Frank took some of the feathers to the foot-bridge, where he floated them in the bright stream. Then he decided to decorate his fox-hole under the footbridge. He wriggled underneath, where it was dry, and lay listening to the sound of his own breathing. Then he began to plant the feathers in the mound of earth supporting the plank over his head. Some of the feathers went in easily. The sharp quill of others wouldn't puncture the dirt. Frank scraped at the earth with his fingers. He hit a hard object. Something glinted.

Frank had made a discovery which would not only shadow his entire life but which, for many years, he managed to keep secret.

9

If Frank took to the farm, the farm took to him. Almost too well, it seemed. Una and Tom enjoyed having the boy around. Tom said that a farm needed a boy like it needed the dog in the yard and the cock on the hayrick. A boy completed the picture. After six months of having the lad around, they stopped using contraception; lazily, and without debate.

Here's how Una announced developments to her husband: 'Tom, what would you say if I told you your wife was in calf?'

This news was greeted with joy and a little consternation back at the Vine household. While things were going well at the farm, events elsewhere were less even. Frank hadn't seen his mother for some weeks because she was in a place called Hatton.

Hatton, when it was mentioned, was done so in

a kind of underbreath, more a tut of disapproval than an enunciation. Otherwise it was referred to as 'that place' or 'the hill'. It was another kind of farm, a so-called funny-farm: a psychiatric hospital nestling in large grounds filled with blue and pink flowering rhododendron bushes. Cassie was there on the recommendation of a young doctor. Martha had agonised, but as Cassie's condition became more acute, she had finally agreed.

One Sunday, Tom and Una had driven Frank into Coventry, picking up Martha before setting off to visit Cassie in hospital. They took with them black grapes from Olive's shop, and a bottle of Lucozade, just as if Cassie's complaint had been jaundice or a fractured tibia. Cassie was allowed to come outside to see them, because no one seemed to want Frank to go into the ward. As it was Frank was fascinated by a man who stalked the grounds adopting statuesque postures, 'freezing' for a few moments before moving on and striking another attitude.

Cassie was weepy and talkative. 'Don't like it!' she said, wiping her eyes with a tiny handkerchief and looking at Frank, who meanwhile shrank back into Una's lap. 'You don't know what it's like here! You don't know what they're like. You should hear the sounds they make at night!'

'Hush,' Martha said, 'it's only for a while. Until you feel better.'

'I feel better bloody hell goddamnit bastard better! I do! I do! There was a full moon two nights ago. Do you know what that means in a place like this? Do you know, Tom?'

'I think you're going to tell me.'

'I shouldn't be here, Mam! There are lots of girls who shouldn't be here! There's one girl who's here because she had a baby, that's all. She says they took the baby away and brought her here. Now she has a bed between an old woman who bites the skin off her own hands and another who sits in her own piss!'

'You're making it up, our Cassie,' Una said. 'Tell me you're making it up.'

Cassie burst into tears again.

The drive home had been grim. Back at her house Martha made a pot of tea before Una and Tom took Frank back to the farm. 'Those bloody doctors have had the better of me. I've done wrong, letting her go there. I know I have.'

Una didn't think so. 'Mam, the doctor said as she must go in for treatment. How can you go against the doctor? Neither you nor me knows what the doctor knows, now do we?'

'I'm sure I've done wrong by her.'

'You can always fetch her out again,' Tom said, biting into a slice of Dundee cake. 'But then she'll start running round again, won't she?'

'I don't know which is worse.'

'Mam!' said Una.

They went again the following week. This time Cassie was brought out to them in a wheelchair. Cassie recognised them – just. She had little interest in their visit. Una looked away and winced. Martha was shocked. She left Cassie with the others and went off to find a doctor. The first nurse she spoke to was unhelpful and told her that there was no one who could see her at that particular time.

'Listen young madam,' Martha told the nurse, 'you're barely older than the youngest of my seven daughters, and I've never been challenged by any of them yet. And if you want to be standing on your feet when you finish here today, you'll go and fetch me someone as will give me a straight answer.'

The nurse blushed, but went in search of a doctor. She returned with the plump, bespectacled registrar, a man with early jowls and apple-red cheeks. His collar was dirty and his bow tie had turned forty-five degrees. He wasn't Cassie's doctor, he said, but he would take Martha to his office so they could have a chat.

'She's twenty-three years old,' the registrar began, flicking through Cassie's file. 'She's delivered two healthy children.'

'I know that,' Martha said brusquely.

The registrar looked up. 'Quite. She's been with us a very short time.'

'I know that, too. What I want to know is why she looks the way she does today.'

'And how is that, in your opinion, Mrs Vine?'

'In my opinion? In my opinion she looks like someone has sucked the soul out of her. That's how. Like the soul has been taken out of her.'

The registrar perused his notes. 'It appears we've been giving her ECT treatment.'

'And what's that, in plain English?'

'Electro-convulsive therapy. We pass a mild electrical current into her brain. To help with the depression.'

'Depression? No one said anything about depression!'

'No,' the registrar corrected himself hurriedly. 'We occasionally use it for schizophrenia.'

'No one said anything about that, either.'

'I'm not saying–'

'Then what are you saying?'

'Mrs Vine, I'm not your daughter's doctor, but we are giving her the best possible treatment.'

'It doesn't look like it. It doesn't look like passing any current has done any good, does it? Have you looked at her? Have you? There's no sheen in her eye.'

The registrar held up a plump hand to try to stop her from saying more. 'I want to be honest with you Mrs Vine and I need you to be honest with me.'

'I've never had a problem being honest.'

'I'm sure. So perhaps you can answer me this. Has there ever been any history of mental illness in the family?'

Martha paused for a long time before answering. 'We've never had anyone locked up before, to my knowledge.'

'That's not what I asked.'

Martha thought for a long time again. 'I'd have to know whereof you're asking.'

'Mrs Vine, your daughter gets herself into a state of ... some excitement. You can't stop her and she can't stop herself. We are trying to help, you know. And there's this other matter of her talking to her father. You know, my colleague is very enthusiastic about the benefits of ECT.'

'Enthusiastic! Admit it to me – you don't know what you're doing, do you?'

'Mrs Vine–'

'That's it. You bloody demons! Buggers! You're bloody well experimenting! I know what you're doing!' She got up.

'Mrs Vine—'

'You tell your colleague if I see him I'll have his guts for garters! So I will!' Martha bustled out of the registrar's office, down the corridor, past the nurse she'd chastised earlier, and out into the spring sunshine.

'Push her in that thing!' she said to Tom. 'We're taking Cassie home!'

'Can we do that?' Una wanted to know.

'We're bloody well doing it. Come on Frank, look lively.'

'What about her stuff?' said Tom, wheeling the bath chair – and Cassie in it – in the direction of his truck.

But her stuff didn't seem to matter to Martha. They escaped the manicured grounds of Hatton, Cassie in her dressing gown and black hair flying, wheeled by Tom. Frank, trotting to keep up, half dragged by his Aunt Una. Up front and outstripping them all, even though dependent upon her stick, was Martha Vine.

The Hatton funny-farm had seen the very last of her children.

10

Frank noticed how often that – should their paths cross in the yard – Tom would stop his wife so that he could put his hand on her belly, and he would kiss her. Una meanwhile made sure that the mystery was unfolded to Frank in the quivering soil and the rough straw and the water. The reeking pond bubbled with frog spawn, rabbits conjured more rabbits overnight, chicks pecked through shells, the cows lowed and calved. Even the dunghill gave birth to thistles and livid yellow-headed flowers. It was unstoppable. Every sooty nook and damp crevice of the farmyard teemed with fecundity.

And Una's belly swelled.

If the extra pressure on her bladder caused her to be taken short she would squat and piss in the straw in the barn, or by the rabbit hutch. Seeing Frank's gaze, Una would smile at him mid-stream before hoisting up her knickers and proceeding with her chores. Frank tried to imitate her whenever he felt the urge to piss. He would squat over the straw.

'Get out of it lad!' Tom chuckled when he saw the boy squatting. 'You've spent too much time wi' girlies! Come on here!' Tom unbuttoned his flies and took out a heavy handful of fat, pale cock and pissed heartily into the straw. 'You'll take all the fun out o'pissing, you will!'

Tom pissed like the bull. Frank watched the stream of it bubbling and puddling in the mud, and the steam rising from the straw. He stood up and waddled alongside Tom, took his little cock in his hand and found he could still join in.

'That's the ticket, Frank! God gave boys the best toys. You don't want to squat down there with a cold arse!'

'What are you telling that lad?' Una said.

'Quick, Frank, put it away now. We don't let the girls see, do we?'

Carefully copying his uncle, Frank put his away. 'Doesn't it make the mud dirty, Uncle Tom?'

'You're a beauty! What do you think the mud is? Muck and dead things, son, muck and dead things. And if it wasn't there, then the earth would be clean and nothing would grow, and if nothing would grow, I'd be a good farmer wouldn't I? And if I can't farm how am I going to get you that bike for Christmas?'

Tom had promised Frank a tricycle, which they could ill afford. Una had protested, but Tom had said he wanted smiling faces on Christmas Day. And anyway, it was some weeks off and the people had other things to divert them. Like a nude lady on a horse.

In late October of that year, Una and Tom took Frank to see the unveiling of the new statue of Lady Godiva in Broadgate. Beatie and Bernard were back in town to go along with them. Cassie was still considered to be in an excitable state of mind, and so was not asked.

Since the town had recently been blessed with

84

a visit from the Royal Family, the city fathers had to cast around for someone of appropriate stature to perform the ceremonial honours. They asked the American Ambassador. The American Ambassador, finding himself busy on that particular day, had suggested that his wife would stand in. So a lady who was only ever known as The American Ambassador's Wife to the hundreds of schoolchildren watching the event divested the equestrian statue of its Stars and Stripes and Union Jack and offered thrilling nudity to Coventry's young and old.

Tea at Martha's had been arranged for after the event. And though Olive and William had been no more invited than was the American Ambassador's Wife, they came along too. As did the twins, who, incidentally, had strong views on the statue on the basis of what they'd heard about it. Only Aida and Gordon stayed away, on account of Gordon's haemorrhoids. Cassie, sulking because she'd not been asked to go to the unveiling, had gone into the lounge and closed the door behind her. Martha suggested they leave her, and that she'd come round soon enough.

'Disgusting,' Evelyn opined as Una passed her a ham sandwich.

'Who wants to see that on a working day?' Ina agreed. 'And in the middle of town.'

The full-breasted nudity of the unveiled statue had come as a surprise to some of the citizens of Coventry.

'That is the story, ma,' said Beatie. 'Lady Godiva took her clothes off and rode through the streets naked. I mean, what statue are you going to have?'

'No need for it,' Eve said.

'Not completely naked,' said ma. 'Showing everything she's got.'

'Does she show everything, like?' William wanted to know.

'What's the price of melons in your shop, William?' said Tom.

Una dug Tom in the ribs. 'It's a beautiful statue, though.'

'A fitting monument,' Bernard said solemnly.

'Disgusting,' Evelyn said, swallowing a morsel of ham sandwich with evident distaste.

Beatie, since her move to Ruskin, was more inclined to show impatience with her older sisters. 'You *can't* have a nude statue with clothes on!'

William changed the subject. 'I see your bloody precinct turned out to be a pig's ear,' he said to Bernard, trying to recruit Tom with a wink.

'It's not my precinct, William. And it will still work fine. The problem is it's been compromised by greedy councillors. Backhanders and bribes. Local politicians on the make, feeding their cronies in the building industry, that's what it is. Corrupt business interests.'

'You don't know the first thing about business.'

'We know why they put that bloody road through the pedestrian precinct, though don't we!' Beatie blazed.

'We do,' William said. 'So the shelves in the shops ain't empty!' He tapped Tom's foot with his own shoe, and looked, smiling, from face to face.

'Nothing to do with who made a million out of

it,' Bernard said, slurping his tea.

While this was going on the sound of Cassie conversing in the next room grew louder and louder. The door between the kitchen parlour and the lounge was closed. 'Mam,' Una said. 'Who is our Cassie talking to?'

'To your father,' Martha said.

This remark stopped all conversation about traffic-free shopping precincts, business interests and corrupt politicians. The clock above Martha's head ticked solemnly. A log shifted in the grate.

'You'd think,' said Ina, 'that they could have draped a robe around her shoulders. Or even a scarf.'

Is there an office, Cassie was saying to her father, that you can write to? A place in Coventry where you can go and perhaps put yourself forward? There should be. There should be a room. Perhaps in St Mary's Hall, or what's left of it, where all the young girls could go and take off their clothes and parade by. A place of stained-glass windows and old furniture gleaming and polished and smelling of beeswax, and huge velvet curtains and drapes, scarlet-red, bright red, you know, like blood; a place where all the unmarried girls of the city could go on a certain day of the year and that would be Godiva Day. And you would walk across plush carpets with a pile so deep it would be like wading through warm water, and you would be chosen. That's how they should do it. A place where I could go and say I would like to be Lady Godiva this year.

But who would do the choosing? Yes, there

would be young men, seven young men all full of juice and they would have to sit naked themselves, sit on their hands as the girls walked slowly by, and the first girl who could get a stand from all seven all at the same time, that would be the sign, wouldn't it? That's how she would be chosen. She would be Lady Godiva for the day, for the year even. And in the afternoon the procession through the town, on a white horse, no clothes, no saddle, just a crimson rug tossed over the back of the horse.

But how would you choose the boys, that's a good question, how would you choose the seven? It would have to be seven young men who had never done it, now wouldn't it? Perhaps seven apprentice boys, or even schoolboys, what about that? But how would you know they haven't done it? They're such liars about things like that. They'll say they have if they haven't, and they'll make out they haven't if they have.

But the chosen girl, Lady Godiva, now she would have not to be a virgin. You couldn't have a Lady Godiva virgin, no, not with what she is going to have to do, because it wouldn't be fair. No, it has to be a young woman with just a little experience, and she wouldn't necessarily be the prettiest, no, but she would be so full of juice they would all have a St Michael's bobbing in the air the moment she slipped by. She'd walk on her toes and they'd die just to have her.

Don't you think it was so unfair of them, going off to the town without me? Wasn't as if I would have let them down. Wasn't as if I was going to climb on the back of the statue or embarrass the

American Ambassador's Wife. But I *would* have spoken to the mayor. I would have said, I'm your Lady Godiva!

And I would choose the route through town. From the courtyard at St Mary's Hall we would trot out, and down Bayley Lane and back up Earl Street and into Broadgate where there would be thousands watching me. Twice around Broadgate and every inch of my skin stroked by thousands upon thousands of pairs of eyes. And the gentle sway of the horse between my legs, so that I press up near the withers, and down Trinity Street and out of town through the mediaeval gate of Cook Street, and from there I would gallop out of the city and on and on until I reached my lover's arms. And who is he? And who is he?

It was two weeks later, in November, when the pink rose-hips were plump on the branch and the blue-black sloes and the blood-red haw berries were everywhere. Frank was hiding under the footbridge, visiting the Man-Behind-The-Glass. He regularly took small gifts to the Man-Behind-The-Glass: bantam feathers, a chicken's claw, a piece of cow horn, a rubber teat for hand-feeding lambs. If the Man-Behind-The-Glass was pleased with the gift, he would dispense oracles.

The Man-Behind-The-Glass made no sound when he imparted this wisdom. He merely shaped his mouth. Frank would have to peer through the misty glass and guess at the words. But it wasn't difficult. The words took shape in his head and then he heard them like everyday words. That day Frank had delivered a snail shell, embedding it in the moist earth along with all the other trophies. Frank put his eye to the glass and the Man looked back at him steadily from under a leather cap. The Man mouthed something, and Frank thought he understood. After a while Frank began to feel cold, so he said goodbye to the Man-Behind-The-Glass and made his way back to the farm buildings.

There Una greeted him. She trailed Frank through the cowshed so as to let a calf into its mother. After clanging the metal gate shut behind her, she stopped abruptly.

'Are you all right Auntie Una? Are you all right?' Frank was already a sympathetic boy.

'It was a kick, Frank. The baby kicked me, inside.'

Three-year-old Frank stepped over to where Una leaned against the gate and reached up to stroke Una's belly, just as he had seen Tom do. Una pulled his head closer to her belly. She ran a hand through his brown hair. 'You're a sweet boy, Frank, such a sweet boy. I hope my baby is sweet like you are.'

Frank stood back a little and pressed gently on Una's stomach. 'Two babies, Aunt Una. There are two babies in there.'

'Hey?' Una shrieked, laughing. 'I bloody 'ope not!'

Frank didn't want to tell Una that the Man-Behind-The-Glass had assured him that Una was going to have two babies, so he said, 'They spoke, they did. Yes they did.'

Una laughed again, but less heartily. Then they

were both distracted by a large bird, perhaps a kestrel or a hawk, that swooped at them from the rafters of the barn, and then away above the field.

Later, before a roaring, sparking log fire, Una told the story to Tom.

'He must have heard someone else say the same thing,' Tom said. 'Twins, that'd be a double handful, wouldn't it girl? That's it. The lad's heard someone else say it, I'll be bound.'

Una stared into the fire, massaging her swollen belly, wondering.

11

'Twins?' said Martha.

'Twins!' went Cassie.

'Twins!' exclaimed the twins.

'That's what the midwife says,' Una said. 'Certain of it. And I'll tell you of somebody else who knew a long time before the bloody midwife did.'

'Who?' said Evelyn. 'Who was that?'

Una nodded at Frank. He was under the table, pushing his toy car across the linoleum floor. Cassie blushed with a strange pride. This was not news to her.

It was Christmas Eve of 1949. Martha had stuck sprigs of holly and mistletoe behind the pictures and the flying ducks on her wall. She wasn't a great one for ornament, though she did enjoy the festive spirit brought about by the extra seasonal visits from her daughters. It took a woman councillor, it was noted, to come up with a common sense idea to boot out the gloom. Councillor Pearl Hyde had arranged for the city to borrow the lights from Blackpool seafront, and Una had brought Frank into Coventry to see the Christmas illuminations.

Meanwhile Evelyn glanced at Ina, before both heads turned with interest towards the boy. Martha noticed this sudden extra attention, and shuddered. Hitherto the little boy Frank had been an object of mystery and no little vexation to the twin sisters. They thought him loud and aggressive, and recoiled from a small nose that was in permanent stream. Moreover he was given to exhibiting testosterone-fuelled fizzes of excitement in which he was likely to display his affection for his maiden aunts in bruising thumps or kicks to the shins, or in pinches to the thigh and tiny slaps to the face. Frank was slugs and snails sure enough, and though the twin aunts would never express the notion and had demonstrated nothing but kindness to their nephew, a pretty little girl would have been a much more welcome, because pliable, addition to the Vine clan.

But this was an attitude about to change. Frank, it was being suggested, had possibilities. Though he didn't know it, two hawkish pairs of eyes were already measuring him up for a ride strapped to the spiritual wheel. 'When you say he knew...' Ina asked.

'Yes,' said Eve, 'what did you mean by that? When you say he knew.'

'If it's twins you'd better be ready for 'em,' Martha said pointedly. 'You won't know what's hit you.'

'I'm sure we weren't a trouble to you,' Eve said indignantly, putting down her teacup.

'Ha!' went Martha. 'They say double the trouble but each twin is twice the trouble makes four times the trouble!'

'But you always said as we entertained each other,' Ina said.

'Yes, when you didn't want to be contrary. If one didn't want exactly what the other had got, she wanted exactly different.'

Ina wasn't to be ruffled any further. 'So, our Una, what did you mean when you said as Frank knew there was to be twins?'

'Got a good midwife out there, have you Una?' Martha wanted to know. 'You'll need a good 'un.'

'She's a bit strange looking,' Una admitted, 'but they say she's good. Raggie Annie they call her.'

'Raggie Annie? Oh you'll be in good hands.'

'You know her?'

'I'll say. She delivered Ina and Evelyn, and your sister Aida, when we lived over Withybrook. She was just a gal then.'

'Why is she Raggie?' said Cassie.

'On account she brings this big bundle of rags with her,' Una said. 'You should see her. She's a tiny scrap of a thing and she's got a squint and bad teeth, but she's got a good touch.'

'She has that. And what of young master here, when those twins come along. You'll not be wanting him under your feet.'

'Oh no Mam, he'll be no bother. Tom loves having him around the farm. A good little helper, ain't you Frank? And Cassie's there more often, ain't you Cass, now you've taken up hoss-riding.'

A neighbouring farmer had given Tom a mild-mannered grey cob he couldn't keep. The horse had once pulled a coal-cart. It had a wall eye and it dished in the trot, but it was said to be bomb-proof. Tom had saddled him up with Frank in mind, but Cassie had suddenly shown a great interest in riding. She came and stayed at the farm more and more frequently and soon knew her way around the animal enough to take him out alone. Sometimes for several hours.

'We'll have to wait and see how you feel about Frank,' Martha suggested, 'after these twins have arrived.'

'I daresay someone will have him,' Ina said, polishing her spectacles on the hem of her skirt.

In the spring, one morning while Frank was playing on his new tricycle in the yard, Tom emerged from the house fighting his way into a pullover. Cassie was around somewhere, but out on the horse. Tom jumped into his truck, switched on the engine and reversed out of the drive at high speed. Then he stopped, got out of the truck and ran back to Frank, kneeling beside the boy and grabbing him by his arms.

'I'll only be gone ten minutes,' he told Frank. 'Will you go down the field and look for your Mam? And if she's not there, go into the house and be a help to your Aunt Una.'

The boy nodded. Tom sprinted back to the truck, climbed in, toed the accelerator and was gone.

Frank did as he was told and walked across the

94

farmyard towards the fields in search of Cassie. On the way he found a stick, which he tossed into the duckpond. The stick lodged in the mud at the edge of the pond. Frank was wary of the pond, but he knew he could retrieve the stick with the aid of the clothes-line prop, so he went back up to the farm and grabbed the prop. He heard a low groaning from inside the house. He was about to investigate when he remembered that he was supposed to look for his mother in the field, so he abandoned the line-prop, and the stick in the mud, and headed for the field. As he passed the barn, Ruben, an aggressive goose, flew at him.

Ruben had pecked Frank on other occasions, and Frank had a healthy respect for the animal. Tom however had showed him how to intimidate Ruben by the simple expedient of waving a stick, so Frank went back up to the house to get the line-prop so that he could retrieve the stick from the mud. Once he'd done this he returned to the barn ready to brandish the stick at Ruben, but by this time Ruben had gone. Frank climbed the five-bar gate at the end of the yard and looked across the fields for his mother.

There was no sign of Cassie, so Frank sat on the gate for a while, banging his stick on the fence-post. His mother didn't come. Then Frank remembered that he was to go back into the house and be a help to his Aunt Una. But Ruben had returned to block his passage, so Frank went back to the gate to retrieve his stick. This time he was able to wave the stick at Ruben and the goose, who knew the power of the stick, continued to make noisy complaint but allowed the boy to pass.

When Frank reached the house, the sound of groaning from within had become louder. Leaving the stick at the door, he kicked off his boots and traced the source of the groans to his aunt's bedroom.

A fire had been lit in the bedroom hearth. Una, slightly propped up by pillows and with her enormous, distended belly exposed, lay sweating in bed. Her hair seemed to be wet. Another groan started. It started as a deep, low moan, like the sound the wind made around the farmhouse in the depths of winter, almost a humorous song, but building and becoming louder in a steady rhythm.

'You all right Aunt Una? You all right?'

'Frank,' moaned Una. 'Wooooooooooo.'

'You all right Aunt Una?'

'Where's your Uncle Tom? Wooooooooooo-oooooooooo.'

'He's gone in the truck. Yes he has. He said Frankie help Aunt Una, he did. He did.'

'Wooooooooooooooo. Christ it's coming, I'm sure of it. Frank hold my hand will you darlin'?'

Frank hastened to his aunt's side. He grabbed her outstretched hand and she squeezed until it hurt him. He could see pea-sized balls of sweat running from her face.

'WOOOOOOO! Talk to me Frank,' Una said. 'Talk to me. Tell me a story.'

So Frank told Aunt Una the story of the stick. About throwing it into the pond, about Ruben, about the gate. It was a long story in the telling, and between groans Una managed to look into Frank's eyes and nod and listen with rapt attention.

Finally Frank had finished his tale. 'Do you want to see the stick, Aunt Una?'

Una laughed out loud. She laughed long and hard. Then she groaned again. 'Christ! It's coming!'

She pressed herself into the bed and drew back her knees. Frank was presented with his aunt's distended vulva, and there, in the middle of the stretched tissue, was something purple, the size of a walnut. Frank didn't know it but he was looking at the top of the first baby's head.

He saw no more after that because the bedroom door burst open, and there was Tom with the strangest looking lady Frank had ever seen. It was Raggie Annie, the midwife, and she was tiny.

Raggie Annie scuttled across the room carrying a leather bag, and a second string bag stuffed with scraps of torn cloth. 'Now then, what's a doing?' She wore a skirt down to her ankles and a baggy black cardigan. Her jet-black hair was pushed up and pinned in an unfashionable bun. One of her eyes was almost closed, but the other sparkled with fire as it looked about the room taking everything in. Limited to the use of this one good eye, her head jerked about like a bird's.

'Woooooooooooooooooooo,' went Una.

Raggie Annie put her huge, glittering eye dangerously near to the scene of the action. 'Close,' she said. 'But not so close as we can't get sorted. Now then my flower, you scream all you like, for it's a help, it is, yes.'

'Wahhhhhhhhhhhhhhhhhhhhh!' went Una.

'That's more like it my flower!' Raggie Annie whisked off her cardigan and opened a window.

She thrust the bag of torn cloths into Tom's hands. 'You get and boil these up in a big pan. Quick about it, flower!' Tom went off to do as told.

Then the midwife stopped suddenly, bent over and put her bright, hawk-like eye next to Frank's. 'And who be you?'

Frank trembled. He tried to say his name, but he couldn't speak. It seemed to him that this creature had been called from another world. She was already unpacking Lysol, equipment, bottles, instruments from her leather bag, laying them rapidly on the cleared dresser. He could smell on her clothes the odours of wood-smoke and meat stews and antiseptic lotion commingled. Then she pulled out a rubber sheet, stood back and flapped it at the boy. 'There's some as says little boys shouldn't see this, but I says different. Let 'em look. Then they'll know. But stay or go my little flower, if you gets under my feet I'll fetch you one round the ear, so please yourself.'

'Go down to your Uncle Tom,' Una managed to say before another deep, tidal groan took possession of her.

Raggie Annie had set about fixing the rubber sheet on the bed and Frank was only too relieved to be discharged from the presence of this dark spirit from the forest. He descended the stairs slowly. Finding Tom in the kitchen boiling a pan of rags, he burst into tears.

'Whoa there lovely lad!' Tom swept him up. 'What's that for? Your Auntie Una shall be all right, son! She's having a baby! All ladies make that noise when they're having a baby. Helps it come out into the world. You'll see.'

But Frank wasn't crying because of what he'd seen or heard of Aunt Una. It was the encounter with the nightfall hobgoblin upstairs that had terrified him. Meanwhile overhead, Una was putting more effort into helping the baby come out into the world, as her groans changed to screams. Frank could hear the midwife encouraging more noise.

Frank went outside to resume play on his tricycle. He pedalled around the yard, under the open window through which he heard his aunt's cries of distress. He pedalled to the pond and back again. 'Tell that bastard he's not coming near me again!' he heard his aunt shout. Then Raggie Annie's face appeared at the window, squinting down at him before she banged the window shut.

Then there was calm.

Some time later, and with the dusk falling, the door opened and Raggie Annie called Frank over. 'Come along my flower, come on and have a look, yes.'

Cautiously Frank went in. The rags were still bubbling softly on the stove. The midwife went up ahead of him and opened the bedroom door. Una sat up in bed holding a swaddled baby. Tom sat on the bed holding another. 'Cousins,' Raggie Annie said proudly. 'Two lovely little gals. Mark you look after them and be a big help to them always.'

Frank gaped at the pink heads protruding from the swaddling. Tom smiled stupidly. His eyes were wet. Una smiled exhaustedly.

'Now then,' Raggie Annie said to Frank, 'you can come and help me with a job I has to do.' She was wrapping something in newspaper. It looked like a lump of chopped liver the size of a small football. It soaked the newspaper so that she had to take more sheets and wrap it like a parcel from the butcher's. 'Come along, my flower,' she said, carrying the parcel before her. 'Follow me, yes.'

They went outside, Frank nervous but scurrying to keep up with the little woman. 'Do you know where I can find a spade? Good lad. That'll do.' He followed her to the bottom of the vegetable patch, where Tom grew leeks and rhubarb and redcurrants. 'We has to tell the bees, we has to. Must be done, yes. Shall we tell 'em? Tell 'em of your two cousins?'

'Yes,' Frank said.

The midwife found a spot under the redcurrant bushes and laid down her parcel. Then she dug a shallow hole in the soil. After she'd placed the wrapped afterbirth in the hole she turned to Frank, fixing him with her one good eye. 'Tell it to the birds, tell it to the trees, tell it to the wind and tell it to the bees. Can you say that, my flower?' Raggie Annie helped him repeat the rhyme. 'It's done.' Then she covered the earth over the parcel, and her joints cracked as she straightened her back.

She and Frank were making their way back to the house when a horse and rider trotted into the yard. 'Who be this?' Raggie Annie asked Frank.

'Mam!' said Frank. 'Two twins!'

'She's never had them!' Cassie said, springing from the grey cob. She smacked the horse about the flanks and it trotted obediently into the stable.

'She has,' Raggie Annie avowed. 'And you get

your boots off and scrub your hands before you go in there to her.'

After obeying Annie's interdiction Cassie went up to her sister, and Tom came down. He wanted to pay the midwife for her services. It was an unofficial arrangement. She didn't, and wouldn't, work for the health authority, but everyone around said she was the very best in the business. Still, she wouldn't take a penny from him until she was finished. There was, she said, still a lot of clearing up to do.

'What were these rags for?' Tom said, indicating the bubbling stove.

'Oh, that's nothing. That's just to keep the likes of you busy and out from under my feet. Though I shall have them back, if you please. Cup of tea, now, it is. If you please.'

Tom stroked his chin, and thought about a banjo.

Frank meanwhile was running down the field. Never mind the wind and the trees and the birds and bees: he wanted to tell it to the Man-Behind-The-Glass.

12

While all this excitement was happening at the farm, Olive was expressing to Martha fears over the solidity of her own nest. The problem was William. In every sense he was a good husband and father. He worked diligently to build up his greengrocer's business. He was kind and solicitous to his children. He wasn't a big drinker, or a gambler or a gadabout. But there seemed to be something playing on his mind.

'Distracted,' Olive said. 'He seems distracted all the time. And if you speak to him it's like popping a balloon behind his back. He looks at me as if he don't know who I am for a minute. I'm sure something's bothering him.'

'Is it his business? Has he got money problems he's not telling you about?'

'I do his book-keeping, don't I? I sees where every penny goes, Mam. We're doing all right.'

'Have you asked him straight out?'

'He's about as good as our father for talking. You know what men are like for talking.'

Martha took a sip of her stout, swishing the creamy black ale inside her mouth as she thought about that. When Arthur had chosen to retreat into silence she had wondered if she'd been to blame. Perhaps she'd talked the man into silence, chased the soul out of him with her sharp tongue. But Martha wasn't a scold. She'd seen women who could peck at a man until they were broken. Broken and useless. It wasn't difficult to break a man. You just had to choose when he was tired, and not stop, and whine and wheedle and scold and nag and fret and cry until there were only two things a man could do: leave, or stay and be broken. Those who stayed in such circumstances were either pale husks of men or smouldering bundles of rage who clamped their teeth together and who would look askance rather than speak up and start the battle all over again.

Had she done that to Arthur? No, Arthur had other difficulties. He'd not blamed her. Arthur had claimed he'd gone into a quiet world to silence the babble of voices. And when he'd said that, Arthur knew that he was talking about more voices than were raised in the corporeal household. 'If you stop talking to them, they stop talking to you,' he'd said once.

Martha suspected, however, that Olive was one of those women who could indeed break a man with her incessant fussing. Olive was disposed to tears and a stream of interrogative chatter that, after a while, began to sound like the rain falling softly on the roof of an Anderson shelter. Martha wondered whether William would prove to be one of those who left. She hoped not, but feared he would be.

'Anyway,' Olive said glumly, 'he's not the man I married.'

'Perhaps it's the war,' Martha said. 'Perhaps something happened back then that's a-playing on his mind.'

'These carrots are blighted,' one of William's customers complained as he tipped them into the stainless steel weighing pan.

'A little. How about taking the swede instead?'

'I haven't come here for swede.'

'Turnip?'

'If I'd wanted turnip I would have asked for it.'

'Right-ho Mrs Stevenson, how about a nice big parsnip? You can saddle it up and ride it home.'

Mrs Stevenson looked him in the eye. Detecting no humour there she gathered up her vegetables, paid, and left the shop without another word. William bolted the door behind her and turned around the dangling sign so that it read 'Closed, even for Jaffa Oranges'. He pulled down the shutter.

He passed through to the shadowy storeroom behind the shop. There amid the piled-high cardboard boxes was an old armchair with springs and horsehair exploding through the upholstery. Slumping into the chair, he took out his pack of Senior Service cigarettes and lit one up. Then he took out his wallet, where between the leather and the silk lining he kept a small photograph.

The picture was of a woman he had never met. All he knew about the woman was that her name was Rita Carson, and that her husband had died in the war. Her address had been written on the reverse side of the photograph by her husband. William took a nip of smoke from his cigarette and studied the picture. Rita had her head tilted low to one side. She had beautiful arched eyebrows, architecturally proportioned. A long curtain of wavy hair fell across her bared shoulder.

'Gawd! I don't know about Rita! You know who she looks like, doncha?'

'Everybody as sees her says that,' Archie said, snatching the photo out of William's hands and sticking it back in his wallet. 'She's a redhead, too. Fuck it, I'm taking my helmet off. It's too hot to sit round here in a tin hat.'

'Don't let that corporal see you,' William said. He peeled his own picture of Olive out of his wallet. It showed her in a pretty summer dress

104

standing in the back yard of the Vines' house.

'Not bad, my son, not bad at all,' Archie said. 'Got yourself a lovely one there.'

But William knew that Archie was only being generous, seeing as how his own wife was such a scorcher.

It was August of 1944. The Allied advance had become bogged down in hard infantry fighting. With German panzer divisions just a few miles away, William – by now a quartermaster – and Archie had been detailed to guard a shelled château to the north of Falaise. Why they'd been sent to do this job wasn't clear to them until after two hours, when an officer's batman arrived in a car to take away half a dozen cases of wine from the château's massive cellars.

'Is that it?' Archie had ranted. 'We're guarding this gaff so that a few officers can swill claret with their bully beef? Is that it?'

William, who'd seen action now in Dunkirk, North Africa and the Normandy beaches said, 'Don't you know when to shut your mouth? This is the cushiest end of the war I've been, and I ain't in a hurry to change it.'

By the next day they wondered if they'd been forgotten. Archie went down into the cellars and came back with two bottles of wine. William wasn't sure. They'd been told that they'd face a court martial if they touched anything. They had to push the corks through the necks of the bottles and they drank the wine from their mess tins in case anyone should be watching them.

'Seen that cellar? It's a fucking cavern! You could get fucking lost down there. Thousands of

105

bottles and 'undreds of barrels.'

They drank wine in the afternoon sun. For long stretches there was nothing to be heard but the hum of insects in the dry grass, or the sudden rasp of a cricket in a tree. Then the crump of guns and the sporadic chatter of machine-gun fire would remind them of why they were there. They talked about what they would do when they got home. William told Archie the story of when he got back from Dunkirk and jumped from the train. Archie was impressed. He went off in easy search of a couple more bottles.

'I'd like to do that,' he said, putting the bottles on the makeshift table they'd set up in front of the château's ornate wooden doors. 'Go back and make a baby with Rita.'

'You will,' William said. 'You'll be on the nest for three days.'

Archie shook his head. 'Naw. I ain't going back.'

'How do you mean?'

'I mean it ain't on my number is it? I don't get back from this war.'

William shook his head, not understanding.

'I mean,' Archie said, 'that there's a fucking kraut over there and he's got his v-sight trained here.' Archie jabbed the middle of his own forehead with a stiff forefinger. 'Or his tank shell, or his mortar or his fucking doodlebug, I don't know what, it's just that I know I don't get back.'

'You can't say that. No one knows that.'

William told him about some close shaves. About the time on Dunkirk beach when a shell exploded just a few feet away and the sand was taken from under him; about how he felt the sand flying at him like a million tiny golden insects, until it buried him, and until he was eating sand. Three men had dug him out.

'I thought I was gone. It was the worst thing in my life. But you never know. I got out. You just can't say.'

Then he told Archie about how Martha had somehow known about his ordeal. He told Archie that the shrapnel from the blast had taken off a small piece of his scalp, and Martha had seen it.

'There are women like that,' Archie said. 'No disrespect to your mother-in-law, Will, but they're like witches. They see and they know.'

'She can be a witch all right.'

'Well, maybe I'm one too. I see and I know. I don't get to go home.'

They sipped wine and smoked cigarettes late into the night; wine that might have been destined for the Savoy or the Ritz in London if the war hadn't broken out. Archie was choosing, by accident, bottles that would have cost them a week's wages. They did an uncommon amount of talking, and they found they liked each other enormously. Archie made William laugh and they both listened hard when the other wanted to be serious. They remarked frequently that they must have been forgotten. Oh well, they concluded happily, we can wait here until the wine runs out...

At the back of the shop, William stared at the photograph of Rita Carson until the cigarette he held began to burn his fingers. He had a message for Rita, from Archie, and he'd failed to deliver it.

107

The message was five years overdue.

Archie had been right, he hadn't come back. Maybe he had seen it. But each man had made a promise to the other, that if they didn't get back they would deliver a particular message to the other's wife. William's message to Olive was unimaginative but sincere: Archie was to tell her that William had always loved her. Archie's message to Rita was rather different. So different that when William returned home he found himself unable to deliver it.

But he was preparing himself. He was making ready to find Rita, to look her in the eye and repeat what Archie had told him to say.

On returning from the war the idea of delivering such a message had seemed ridiculous. Men under steady fire could say anything to each other; or they could say nothing and, horribly, it all seemed the same. When William returned to Coventry in his demob suit and saw the wreckage of the city, he went around slowly making a personal index of who had come through and who hadn't, and everything that happened in the war, though vivid, seemed to exist on an island in time. You couldn't make what happened on that island fit in with the world you had come back to, and it was best not to try. Even a promise to a friend, a fellow soldier who had died, no longer made sense or purchase.

For a while.

But five years on, and as the memories of war, the long periods of boredom and inactivity and the insane, terrifying moments of action could be assimilated, William began to feel differently. He had come back to a family, to a beautiful daughter who was already four years old, and to a city that didn't want to talk – thank God! – about the war but which wanted people who could roll up their sleeves and set to work.

He'd worked. He'd set up his business and his quartermaster's experience helped him in that. He'd put the hours in and made a go of it. Before he'd even looked up from his work, he had two more children. Then after all this time he started to dream.

For a long time there had been no dreams since the war. Then the same one. He was back at Dunkirk, on the beach. He looked up in the sky and a seagull turned into a German Heinkel, which turned again into a red balloon. He could do nothing but watch the balloon fall slowly to the ground, and when it did it exploded with a soft thump. Then the sand became golden insects spinning around his head, settling, burying him until he was choking. And then he would wake up. He never told Olive about this recurring nightmare. He would get up early and set about his business.

William was an intelligent man. He knew why he was having these dreams. He knew, too, why he was so effective and energetic a businessman. It was because if you worked hard and got your head down you didn't have to think about the war. There was too much to do.

But as the stress of being a soldier retreated from him, so he could begin to relax, and reflect even, upon his recent past. He knew that by flinging himself into business and into family life, he had been fleeing from his experiences.

Now his life after the war, as a husband and as a father, as a dedicated greengrocer – a life unexamined – was threatening to bury him. The last five years had been a kind of amnesia. He was up to his neck in something that had taken him by surprise. He was choking.

And then there was the promise made to Archie, about his wife Rita.

On the fourth morning of guarding the château near Falaise the sun came up like a blood-red balloon and the day seemed too hot even for the crickets in the grass. Archie woke and staggered to the yard, dousing his head with water from the mechanical pump. William was already cooking fresh eggs. The chickens scratching the earth behind the château had decided to start laying. They'd found a larder stocked with tins, and they were eating better meals than the British army could provide.

'I ain't getting dressed today,' Archie said. 'I ain't bothering.'

'You'll get bollocks if you're caught.'

'Listen,' Archie said. William listened. Apart from the spit of the eggs frying in his mess tin, he couldn't hear anything, and he said so. 'Exactly. When did you last hear a gun? Eh? I tell you, they've forgotten us, mate. The war's moved on. We can stay here and live like lords until someone tells us it's all done. We're in clover here, mate!'

'We should be so lucky.'

'Never mind that. I ain't getting dressed and I'm going to start as I mean to go on. That means sitting here in my underpants like Lord fucking

Snooty and getting pissed. Now, would his lordship appreciate a glass of 1932 Claret with his chucky-eggs?'

'His lordship would,' said William.

So they hit the juice early and by midday they were both half-blind. William, sweating in his uniform, took his shirt off. Archie sat sweltering in his long, army-issue underpants, swigging from a bottle. He drained the bottle and tossed it over his shoulder. It landed with a soft thump on the grass. His rheumy, unfocused gaze settled on William. 'I tell you mate, we've been forgotten.'

'No such luck. The army don't forget. They know it if you owe 'em a pair of bootlaces.'

'Why are we here, then? Look round you. This place ain't *strategic*. It's no use to anybody. We've been left to look after the fucking wine cellars for the fucking officer who found it. Now he's some place else with two more blokes looking after another wine cellar for him. Then two more and two more all the bleeding way to Berlin. Or he's dead. Either way we've been left behind, mate. We could desert. No one would know.'

'I've done Dunkirk, Tobruk and Gold Beach. I ain't deserting now that it's going our way. In fact I'm just beginning to enjoy the war. Cheers!'

'All right for you. You're going home at the end of it.'

'Don't start all that again.'

Archie sat bolt upright. 'Here, William. Will you do something for me when you get back. Give my Rita a message will you?'

'Sure,' William said, looking to humour him.

'I mean it. Will you give her an exact message?'

111

'I said yes didn't I?'

'Right then. Are you ready for the message?'

'Go on.'

'The message is this. You're to say: "Archie told me to come and tell you you're to let him give you one."'

William laughed. He took a gulp of red wine, and laughed again.

Archie wasn't laughing. 'I'm serious. That's the message.'

'Yes. Lovely. I'll knock on her door and tell her that.'

But Archie was staring at William strangely. A peculiar cast had come across his eye. 'Likes it, does Rita. Likes it a lot. Likes me to kiss her neck. Likes me to catch her nipple between my teeth, like you might have a grape between your teeth without breaking the skin. Likes me to lick her belly and between her thighs. And her clit. Drives her mad, that does, when I put my tongue to her clit.'

'Fucking hell, Archie! I don't want to hear this.' William had never put his tongue to Olive's clitoris. Mainly because he didn't know what a clitoris was.

'I have to tell you all this just in case she needs convincing. The message. Likes it from behind, doggy style. Loves that does Rita.'

'Put a cork in it, Archie!'

'But here's the one that will convince her, if you have to. She likes me to lick the little fold at the back of her knee. She's the only woman I know it sends wild. Our secret, that one. And if you do it right, then it will remind Rita of me, won't it? I'll

112

be there for her, won't I? So, you're clear about the message, are you?'

William looked him in the eye. He *was* serious. 'Don't talk knickers.'

Archie nodded his head. Then he got up out of his chair, swayed unsteadily and picked up his Lee-Enfield rifle, which was leaning against the wall. He cycled the bolt action on the rifle and levelled it at William.

William scowled. 'Don't fuck around.'

'Tell me you'll do it.'

'Put that fucker down. I don't like it.'

'You already promised. Tell me you'll do it or I'll drill you. I mean it.'

Though William knew Archie was drunk, some deep instinct told him that Archie wasn't fooling. William blinked first. 'I've told you I'll do it, damn you. Now put that bleeding weapon down.'

Archie smiled, and leaned his Lee-Enfield back against the wall. Then he moved off into the shade of the château. William glugged from a bottle of claret and lit himself another cigarette. He noticed his hands were trembling. In all of the war, through all the considerable action he'd seen, this was the first time that a soldier had put a gun to his chest. After he'd smoked the cigarette he decided to go and give Archie a piece of his mind. He followed him inside, but a noise from the wine cellars brought him up short.

It was Archie, and he was roaring. Incomprehensibly. He roared Rita's name and he bellowed things William couldn't make out. Between the words William heard the sounds of glass breaking, wine bottles smashing against the brick walls of

113

the cellar. It was as if a wounded animal was crashing about in there, and the drunken howling did not abate.

But before he'd decided what to do, William heard another noise. It was a buzzing sound, rather near. He turned his head towards the source of the sound. 'Bugger me!' he said and jogged back to the table where the neglected weapons lay. It was a jeep, kicking up dust as it accelerated towards the château. William grabbed his shirt from where it hung on the back of his chair, hurriedly buttoning it. Then he grabbed his rifle.

The jeep stopped a few yards away. The driver behind the wheel stared glumly at William as a British officer got out of the jeep. 'Good day, Corporal,' said the officer.

'Sah!' William shouted, at attention.

The young captain glanced at Archie's Lee-Enfield leaning against the whitewashed wall. Then he looked at William's bare feet. 'All in order, Corporal?'

'Sah!'

'Relax, Corporal. You look a bloody state. Good thing for you I'm in no mood to put you on a charge.'

William went at ease, and quickly pulled on his socks and boots. 'Sah.'

'Time we moved you along, Corporal. Where's your mucker?'

'Nature call. Sah.'

'Get your things together. But I want to pick up a couple of cases before we go. Keep the war, oiled, eh Corporal?'

'Right sah!' William was already jumping to it. 'I'll go and fetch you up a couple of cases from the cellar.'

'I'll come with you, Corporal. Wouldn't want the footwash by mistake, now would we?'

William ignored the implied insult. 'Very messy down there, sah. Lots of broken glass. No lights. Dangerous, sah. I'll go.'

'Don't talk bollocks, Corporal. I want to come and choose a couple of cases for myself. Now lead the way.'

'Sah!' William led the way to the cellar, failing to think how he might get Archie out of this. Then there was the sound of another bottle smashing, and more bellowing and roaring from the cellar.

'What the devil?'

William inclined his head confidentially. He'd seen more of the war in one afternoon than this young captain would for the rest of his life, and they both knew it. 'Sah. When a man is roaring in a wine cellar, you have to let him work it out. Sah.'

Listening again to the animal noises from the cellar, the captain looked at William and nodded. It was as if he was he was being equipped with a piece of wisdom that his education at an expensive private school had failed to offer. As if every man, at some time, has to have his moment in a French wine cellar; and that he himself might have to experience such a moment, too; and that he would appreciate the discretion of other men. 'Corporal, I'm going to inspect the château. In exactly half an hour you'll both be ready to leave. Understood?'

'Sah! Thank you sir.'

115

And in half an hour both William and Archie stood in full battledress, shaved, helmeted and with rifles slung over their shoulders, waiting to climb into the jeep. Archie's eyes were sore and red from crying, and he had a slight glass-cut on the side of his face, but he stood to rigid attention. Meanwhile the officer and his driver had loaded up the jeep with half a dozen cases of wine. 'Splendid,' said the captain, motioning them to jump in. 'Let's get back to the war.'

Now, as he sat at the back of his greengrocer's shop amid the cardboard boxes gazing at the photo, William knew he was going to have to go and see Rita. There was no way out.

At first he'd thought the matter was buried. It had never been mentioned again by Archie after that drunken episode at the château outside Falaise. Not until Archie was dying, that is; at which time he revealed other sexual secrets and made William reaffirm his promise.

Yet that was a promise William had buried along with a lot of other wartime experience. A lot of things he'd preferred to forget. Even though it had never quite been forgotten. And what had woken it all over again was the strangest thing of all. It was the four-year-old Frank. Cassie's little boy.

William had been standing in the backyard at Martha's house one afternoon, having a quiet smoke and a respite from the hurly-burly and laughter and quarrelsome chatter of the Vine sisters. Frank had come outside, clutching a toy rifle Tom had carved for him from a length of oak. Frank had pointed the rifle at him. William had stuck his cigarette between his lips and raised his hands in surrender. Then the boy clearly said, 'Rita.'

The cigarette had fallen from William's lips. It lay smoking on the blue cobblestones of the back yard. William had looked at the cigarette and then at the boy. Then Frank went back indoors. How had he done that? Conjured that name from nowhere? William was shaken to the core. He'd reached in and pulled it, like a child playing on the beach pulls a grenade or a land-mine from the sand.

And since that moment William had been unable to stop himself from thinking about Rita.

13

Una was having a thin time of it. The early weeks of double motherhood of twins Judith and Megan, were not easy for her. Though the twins were hale they were poor sleepers at night, and though poor sleepers they were hearty eaters, and pulled hard at the breast in instinctive competition for at least the half share. Una's nipples were cracked and sore. The newly prevailing wisdom suggested that powdered formula milk prepared in bottles was the answer; and it was certainly easier on the mother.

But Una had become a farm girl and some nagging common sense, much older than prevailing wisdom, warned her that there was more at stake than the simple matter of squirting milk into those beak-hard mouths. So she persisted and sucked in air and cursed in an underbreath, saying true love was a cracked nipple. Eventually her mammary extremities became as hard as iron, such that she told Tom it would take a farrier to bend them. Tom smiled thinly, winced inwardly, and admired his wife.

But after she'd toughened to that, Una contracted mastitis in her left breast and became very poorly, just as the last of the sensational maternal hormones were draining away. The mastitis stole her energy and, worse, she became depressed.

'Baby blues,' Olive said. 'I got weepy with every one of mine.'

'And me,' Cassie put in. Cassie loved to join in the sharing of general wisdom, which was poured as freely as tea in the Vine household. It gave her a new status; and one that excluded the elder sisters Aida, Evelyn and Ina. Of these last two, Evelyn was also present as they discussed Una's problems. She swallowed her tea with spinsterish gulps as her sisters discussed these raw maternal issues. Meanwhile Frank played under the kitchen table with his toy train.

'Maybe it's more,' Martha said. She looked at Evelyn, wanting to include her in. 'Something about having you and Ina together made a big difference to me. I got in the dumps.'

'Did you?' Evelyn said.

'Several weeks. Not the same as the blues at all. Not like a bit of weepiness as your bloom falls off you. More like a dead hand comes on your shoulder and holds you down. Can't see straight. These tiny mouths at you and you don't know if you've got the wherewithal to carry 'em across the river.'

'What river?' said Cassie.

'I don't know what river,' Martha said, nettled. 'It's just how I seen it. For the first year you just think of getting them across this river and then when you get them on to dry land, well, you can breathe a bit.'

Martha's daughters tended to forget that their mother had lost three boys in early infancy. Evelyn said, 'I know what you mean, Mam.'

'Tom's very upset,' Cassie reported.

'Not like our Una to be down,' Olive put in. 'She's the last one to be dragged down.'

This was exactly what had Martha worried. Una had the strongest and sunniest constitution of all of them. 'If she's got the dumps it's going to be very hard for her. Very hard. I know how I felt.' She was looking at Cassie. Then she glanced at Frank playing, under the table, and Cassie knew exactly what that glance meant.

'We've got to help out a bit,' Martha said. 'I'm thinking of Frank with Beatie and Bernard.'

Evelyn put down her cup at that, and it clinked on her saucer. Olive pressed air between her teeth. Only Cassie sat up with enthusiasm at the notion, because it meant that she too might spend time staying with Beatie and Bernard at their large, shared house near Oxford.

It was the large, shared house near Oxford that caused the negative response from Evelyn and Olive. The large, shared house near Oxford carried too much of the whiff of scandal for their liking.

Indeed of all the sisters, only Una and Cassie had failed to voice any concern to Martha about the matter of the large, shared house near Oxford.

It was into this house, known as Ravenscraig Lodge, that Beatie and Bernard had moved while they were studying. Convenience and economy had settled the matter in those days. A senior professor at one of the Oxford colleges owned the property, letting out rooms to students at peppercorn rents in return for certain commitments to an experiment in communal living. The implications of communal living were mysterious to the Vines and could only be grasped through notions of shared cooking and cleaning, and the arrangement initially provoked no objection. It was only after the studying was over and both Bernard and Beatie emerged with respectable degrees, that this living arrangement, which was expected to break up on conclusion of study, became questioned.

Beatie and Bernard found it very comfortable at Ravenscraig, it seemed. No, they had no immediate plans for making other arrangements. The experiment with communal living was proceeding well, they reported, and they wanted to continue with it for a little while longer. The sisters began to realise that all these fancy phrases such as 'communal living' and 'experimental arrangements' concealed the fact that Beatie and Bernard were cheerfully living in sin.

'It sounds wonderful,' Cassie had breathed on one occasion when Beatie and Bernard had visited.

Most of the other sisters didn't think it sounded wonderful at all. Aida certainly didn't.

'Are they intending to get married?'

Aida was asking a question no one could answer. Gordon, grinning, cadaverous, tried to make a joke no one found funny. 'Eeeeeeee ... a free-love colony, perhaps the...' Aida had silenced him with a poisonous glance. Gordon got up to go and stand outside in the yard with the other men.

'Sounds like an odd set-up,' Olive opined.

'Scandalous, more like!' Ina had said that day.

'Scandalous' was the word used because Beatie had made the mistake of not wanting to patronise her sisters. She'd been a little too free with some of the details when she revealed that Peregrine Feek, the Marxist firebrand and Professor of Philosophy who owned Ravenscraig, had at that time children by two mothers living at the house with him; and that both of those mothers continued to live under the same roof; and that the first of those mothers was expecting another child by a colleague of Feek's who also lived in the 'commune'. It was a good thing Beatie pulled up on the information when she did.

'So let me get this straight,' Martha said more than once, trying to get a clear picture of life at Ravenscraig.

'And you all sit down to dinner together?' Aida had asked.

'Well,' was about all Olive could manage.

Outside, the men discussed it differently. 'So then Bernard,' Tom asked mischievously, 'everyone is married to everyone, sort of thing.'

'It's not like that,' Bernard said. He often didn't know when he was having his leg pulled. 'Not at all.'

'Eeeeeeeeeeee ... a free ... love ... errrr colony, that would...' Gordon wasn't going to miss out on the ribbing either.

'No not free love. It's not as if people are sleeping with each other's partners. It's not like that. Just a loose arrangement regarding marriage, that's all.'

'Loose arrangement?' William said, blowing smoke. 'You don't want to let Martha in there here you say that. She'd skin you alive!'

'Sounds like the beasts in the yard.' Tom winked at William. 'One good bull to cover the lot.'

Bernard gave a good-natured laugh. 'Not at all, Tom. You've got the wrong end of the stick.'

'Eeeeeeeeeeee a Roman ... orgy ... you might call...'

'You have to shake your head at these young ones,' William said. 'Well, good luck to you I say.'

Which was why, several weeks after these conversations, when Martha mentioned that Frank might be placed in the tender care of Beatie and Bernard at Ravenscraig, Evelyn clinked her cup and Olive hissed.

'We've got to relieve Una, and that's it,' Martha said. 'And where's the lad to go? Now I've nothing against Aida and Gordon but they're very set in their ways. Olive, you've got your hands full with your three.' (Martha omitted to mention Olive's anxieties over William's distractedness of late.) 'And the last thing Evelyn and Ina want is a little boy running around the parlour, however gifted he is, eh Cassie?'

'He is gifted. He is.' Cassie said.

122

Evelyn cleared her throat. Martha looked at her. Olive and Cassie looked at Martha, whose gaze seemed unnecessarily fixed on Evelyn. 'We've had a discussion. Ina and me. We've discussed it. Perhaps for a little while.'

Martha let a smile steal across her lips, almost as if she were trying to hold it back. 'What, you and Ina? Don't be soft! What do you and Ina know about loving a little boy? Look at him there!'

They all turned to regard Frank, who, squatting beneath the table, suddenly realised he was the subject of their discussion. He looked up at Martha with large brown eyes so unlike any of the Vines' they had come to call his eyes 'American'.

'Well,' said Evelyn, 'you said as everyone should take on their turn, and we're prepared. We've discussed it. Ina and me.'

'No, Evelyn, you've got enough on with the spiritualist church and one thing and another. I can't see it. Let the younger ones to take it on.'

Evelyn's eyes flashed. She was not quick to anger, but she did have a temper. 'Yes, and you'd sooner see him go that nest of vipers in Oxford, wouldn't you? That would suit you, wouldn't it? A fine thing to want for him!'

'What's a nest of vipers?' Frank wanted to know.

Cassie was upset. 'You shouldn't talk about our Beatie like that. You shouldn't.'

'Let it be said,' Olive chimed in. 'It needs to be said.'

'I don't know about any nest of anything,' Martha said. 'But Evelyn, if your mind is set on it then I won't try to talk you out of it. But you mark he's a flesh and blood little chap and he needs a kiss and a hug and his nose wiped.'

'We know all that, Mother.'

Martha modelled a facial cast to suggest that she'd somehow been outfoxed in the voting. 'Well it looks like it's decided then. Though I don't see how it will work.'

'It will work plain and simple,' Evelyn said, warming to what she was already thinking of as a victory.

Then Martha said, 'Hark! Is that someone at the door?'

It *was* someone at the door. This time they all heard the knock. It was the Cooperative Company insurance collector, who called every Friday afternoon. Martha gave Cassie her purse, to pay the man, because the other matter, once again, had been settled.

14

'Does this mean I can't come to the farm any more?' Frank was in tears about the new arrangement. Cassie had gone out to the farm to collect his things. Tom waited patiently, pouches of bruised flesh under his eyes caused by nights without sleep. He was going to drive them to Evelyn's and Ina's house in his truck.

'Not at all Frank,' Cassie said. She was tearful, too. The move meant her transferring to her sisters' house in Avon Street, along with Frank.

She knew it would also curtail her own visits to the farm and her horse riding.

'You'll come to see us every weekend if you want to. Your mammy will bring you, won't you Cassie?'

'I'm NOT GOING!' Frank screamed. 'NOT!'

Cassie tried to hug him but he broke away. 'Just until Auntie Una gets better. Then you can come back again.'

Frank ran from them, out of the house and across the yard. Tom sighed. 'Give him a minute then I'll go and fetch him.'

'Is Una coming to see him off?'

'No Cassie. She feels too bad about it. Let's just slip off, shall we?'

Frank ran behind the barn, across the field and down to the footbridge over the ditch. He hunkered in the hollow under the wooden planks and pulled the foliage behind him, knowing he wouldn't be found. He put his eye to the smeared, webbed glass. The Man-Behind-The-Glass grimaced.

'I'm going to have to live with my aunts,' Frank said. 'So I won't see you for a while. But I will come back and talk soon. I don't want to live with my stupid aunts. They're stupid. But it's all right, because I won't tell anyone that you're hiding here. I still haven't told anyone, and I'm not going to. You don't want me to, do you?'

The Man-Behind-The-Glass grinned.

'No. And I won't. You can hide here as long as you want. But if you want anything to eat, or any gifts, you'll have to wait until the weekends, is that all right?'

The Man-Behind-The-Glass continued to grin.

'Frank! Frankie! Where are you, son?' It was Tom's voice. Frank could hear him approaching up the field.

'Warmer weather is coming,' Frank said. 'You'll be all right.' He edged out of the hollow backwards, carefully replacing the foliage behind him, then scuttled along the ditch so as to emerge several yards from his hiding place. Tom had gone the other way. Frank came up behind him.

'Well now, son, are you ready to get in the truck?' Tom said. 'Or do I have to carry you over my shoulder?'

'No,' said Frank. 'It's all right.'

The house at Avon Street was very different to the farm. Though it was only a few hundred yards away from Martha's house, it seemed to exist on another plane altogether. For one thing the twins kept it in a condition of immaculate tidiness. Its surfaces were polished to a military gleam and its corners squeaked with spotless pride. It also smelled differently, of beeswax and of pot-pourri from the hallway. And there were potted plants where plants had long gone out of fashion, tall aspidistras and sentry palms and ferns so large one might suspect them of carnivorousness.

But Ina and Evelyn had gone to considerable trouble to make the boxroom conform to their notion of a little boy's Utopia. They'd had Frank's toys sent over so that they were placed around the room waiting for him. Ina had picked

126

up a collection of comics and books from a jumble sale and had advertised them on a small bookcase in the corner of the room. Evelyn had salvaged from somewhere a framed photograph of a football team from the pre-war years; one in which the footballers all sported mammoth handlebar moustaches and wore 'shorts' of extraordinary length. And when Frank arrived, they ushered him inside the room with feelings of excitement and immense self-satisfaction.

'Yes,' said Tom, coming in behind him along with Cassie. 'You'll soon have this nice and messed up, won't you Frank?' It was supposed to be a joke. Sensing it had missed the mark Tom looked up at the footballing picture on the wall. 'By the heck!' he said. 'That's a good 'un! What team would that be then?'

Evelyn and Ina looked at each other. Then Ina said, 'Don't be silly, Tom. It's a football team.'

Tom scratched the back of his neck, and decided to take himself away before he could do any more damage with his remarks, leaving Cassie and Frank to wilt under the overweening gaze of the spinster sisters. No one seemed to know what to do next. But since Cassie was expected to stay, at least for the first few nights, she suggested that she and Frank unpack while the sisters put the kettle on for a nice cup of tea. That seemed a sensible way to proceed, so off the twins went, as if this task would require the efforts of both of them.

That nervousness around the boy, the inability ever to determine exactly what might be done next with him, came to exemplify the character of

127

their entire relationship for the period he spent with Ina and Evelyn. But in the oppressively tidy, scrupulously ordered and obsessively resolved room provided by the twin aunts it fell to Cassie to remind Frank that both Ina and Evelyn were enormously kind.

'Ever so kind they are, Frank. You'll see. Ever so.'

Frank was already missing the rough and tumble and stinking fertility of the farm. Bewildered, he looked at the meticulous placing of each of his toys, at the neat configuration of comics and books, and at the framed football team photograph on the wall, and burst into tears. Cassie gathered the boy to her.

'Whatever is the matter?' she said. Then she burst into tears, too.

Ina and Evelyn were, like their newly born nieces at the farm, not identical twins. Evelyn was the taller of the two and had a long, angular and horse-shaped face. Ina was of a somewhat squat build, and she occasionally wore tortoiseshell-framed spectacles so ineptly prescribed that they made her squint and furrow her brow whenever she put them on. They both tended to wear shapeless dresses with floral seed-packet designs, and both reeked of lavender. But one feature they carried in common was something of a transcendent sweetness; and that was the beauty of their eyes, which were like glittering sequins sewn on the pale, flat faces of a pair of rag-dolls. With both of them, the eyes were in constant search, never settling, ever alert, which created an impression of brightness and vigour. The sisters were always wide awake.

Cassie, who didn't mind turning her hand to the day's chores just so long as the daydreaming hadn't taken her, felt a slattern. The pair wandered around the house each grasping a duster, and no conversation was ever conducted in repose, since there was always a surface or an upright or an angle that might be improved by a good gruelling and a generous smear of elbow grease.

'And we'd like to take Frank up to Ansty Road on Sunday evening,' Ina said, lifting a candlestick and polishing the already-gleaming spot beneath where it stood. 'Has he got a Sunday suit?'

'No,' Cassie said, wanting to resist the Ansty Road thing, but not knowing how.

'Well now, our Cassie.' Evelyn had found a speck of dust on the hall mirror and was exorcising it with spit and gusto until the mirror squeaked in protest. 'We thought to take him up town and get him one.'

'Lovely,' Cassie said, making a mental note to ensure that she had some say in however it was they were planning to dress Frank.

It was the strict regime of the twins' household that both Cassie and Frank were finding hard. Breakfast appeared on the table at seven forty-five a.m. and disappeared from the table at eight a.m., and usually consisted of either a boiled egg or two slices of toast with choice of either blackcurrant jam or honey, but not both. This in itself was no hardship but for the fact that the sisters, having finished their own earlier, umpired breakfast. They presided over the boiled egg. The egg would

129

be slipped into Frank's eggcup and the sisters would take half a step back from the table while his engagement with the egg was monitored. If Frank dropped his spoon, Ina would happily retrieve it. If Frank let the crust from his bread slide to the table, Evelyn would cheerfully restore it to his plate. These smiling attendants would wait until the stroke of the hour and then clear away with an air of barely disguised relief that no great calamity had occurred during the breakfasting quarter hour.

It was not that the aunts were harsh or sour with this regime. On the contrary they were sweet and solicitous at all times. Cassie wanted to scream.

Frank felt too paralysed by it all to want to scream. More than anything he missed the farm. That too was a place with its routines and its timetables, but they were operated within a completely different set of values, directed by the recurring need to milk the cows or open the pasture gates. No one studied you at breakfast time and if you mashed your egg with a fork it went unremarked. At the farm his toys were never tidied away the minute his back was turned.

In the aunts' house, life was a constant patrol to keep the forces of spiralling disorder in constant check. At the farm no one ever tried to keep order, because you couldn't. Life wouldn't let you. It was enough just to keep the animals fed and watered and in the right place. Meanwhile life burst through everyone's best efforts. The farm was full of holes in the ground, wet holes and dry holes where life poked through and infected everything with a flitting disorder. There were frogs and spawn, rabbits, mice and rats, birds and badgers; and if you dug in the ground you found the skulls of stoats and the rusting metal of aeroplanes. That, it seemed to Frank, was what a farm was. You didn't go from place to place with a duster; you carried a stick to poke things with.

The aunts could not, in their abode of polish and pot-pourri, compete with all that. Indeed they had very little to offer a small boy. There was just one thing, a single issue to intrigue him. A matter which his mother had mentioned, and which he thought he partially understood.

The aunts spoke with dead people.

On his first Saturday in Avon Street Frank was dragged into town and into the tailor's and trussed up in an off-the-peg 'Sunday suit'. Cassie had been there to ensure that enormous error was avoided, but even so Frank didn't much like the bottle-green outfit his aunts had bought for him. He didn't like the texture of the cloth and he didn't like the way it smelled. He didn't like the white stockings and garters that seemed so inevitably to come with it. And he didn't like the scrupulous manner in which Ina, watched over by Evelyn, had withdrawn a crisp five-pound note from her purse and laid it on the shop counter as if it were a map of heaven to be studied by all present. He was rather relieved when he was told to take off the suit, since he wasn't allowed to wear it until Sunday.

On Sunday afternoon he was trussed up in the suit once again. The white stockings reached to his knees and to the hem of his short trousers, and the elasticised garters holding up the stockings pinched his skin. Cassie put water on his hair, brushing it over-vigorously in an effort to make it lie flat. Thus in an uncomfortable suit, with pinched legs and a sore scalp, Frank was brought for the first time to the Free Evangelical Spiritualist Church on Ansty Road.

Cassie sat next to Frank, holding his hand throughout the service as Frank realised that his aunts Ina and Evelyn were both 'something' in the church. They welcomed people in and seemed to know everyone. The church was actually a very plain place, with a table at the front bearing a vase of lilies and a varnished wooden cross. The rows of chairs were full, mostly with elderly ladies with large hats bearing artificial fruit, beads, lethal pins and other items, all of whom kept their coats on throughout the service.

There was some singing that Frank mouthed along to: something or other so high you couldn't get over it. And there were prayers, during which Frank took his cue from Cassie and closed his eyes. Then the big moment came when Evelyn got up and said a few words, welcoming Frank to his first service. Several of the ladies in large hats craned their necks to get a good look at him. A lady with what looked like a dead bird pinned to her hat nodded at him and smiled broadly. Then Evelyn introduced the special guest for the evening, Mrs Connie Humbert.

Mrs Humbert was an exceptionally large lady whose hand fluttered nervously at her throat. She had a large hairy mole on her neck and a rather breathless air. She began by saying how glad she was finally to be able to come back to Coventry – which she referred to as the city of the covenant – after all this time. Frank lost interest, but his ears pricked up when he heard a kind of argument about someone called Harry. Mrs Humbert wanted to know who he was, and a lady in the second row started crying. Mrs Humbert said that Harry said there was no need to cry because he was in a better place than she was, but this made the other lady cry even more until a lady from the third row put a hand on her shoulder.

Mrs Humbert stopped talking about Harry and said more things that made another lady cry. At the end of the service three or four of the ladies in the congregation had been in tears and Frank still wasn't sure what was being said that upset them so much.

Then the service was over and everyone was putting on his or her coat. Evelyn came up to Cassie. 'Wasn't Mrs Humbert just wonderful!' Evelyn said, her eyes twinkling.

'She was,' Cassie agreed brightly. Frank noted a gleam in his mother's eye. It was the gleam that meant she said one thing but thought another.

Everyone seemed to think Mrs Humbert was wonderful, just because she'd made people cry. 'And the good news,' Evelyn whispered to Cassie, 'is that she's agreed to tea at Avon Street!'

'She's coming back to the house?' Cassie said. 'Gosh!'

Evelyn's beautiful, sequin eyes scintillated.

An air of nervous excitement came back to Avon Street along with Connie Humbert. Two other

133

members of the church, both of them ladies, were invited to the tea party given in honour of Mrs Humbert's visit, and they filed into the house with the certain sense of special privilege. Evelyn and Ina made tea and cut sandwiches in a state of tremulous anxiety, so that when Cassie volunteered to take Frank upstairs and out of the way, both aunts readily agreed; only to call Cassie and Frank down again a short time later.

'I'm firmly of the opinion,' said Mrs Humbert, swallowing the last of a salmon-paste sandwich with a gesture of unnecessary effort, 'that if we do anything not fit for children to witness then we should desist in doing it immediately, and since I'm fierce proud of my spiritual nature, I see nothing of which to be ashamed.'

'Quite,' Evelyn said, clearing away the sandwich plates and the tea things.

'Indeed,' said Ina, folding the white tablecloth and replacing it with the embroidered, decorative one.

'Do you think we might have the curtains drawn? I don't like to think of people looking in at us. Do you have any objection to the boy joining us?'

One of the visiting ladies from the church jumped up smartly and drew the curtains and it was only after a moment Cassie realised she was being addressed directly by Mrs Humbert. 'No,' Cassie said.

Frank looked at his mother. By now he recognised all the signs indicating she was having difficulty in concentrating.

'Not as if there's anything unnatural in it,' Mrs

134

Humbert avowed, spreading her liver-spotted hands across the tablecloth. 'Let's get down to it then, shall we?' Her large eyes settled on Cassie, who then took the hint to pull up chairs for herself and for Frank. Ina covered a table lamp with a silk scarf and turned off the overhead light before taking her own seat around the table. Frank looked at his mother; Cassie pressed a finger to her lips.

They all linked hands, and without preliminaries, Mrs Humbert went straight off. Her eyes closed and her head lolled at an uncomfortable angle, revealing rolls of her neck fat. Frank couldn't take his eyes off her.

An absolute stillness descended on the company; a silence buoyed up by expectation. Frank felt a breath on his own neck. Then a sound seemed to come from the bowels of the silence itself, somewhere between a low groan and a sigh. It was Mrs Humbert. Her head rolled slowly until it lolled on the other side, and she sighed again. Her closed eyelids flickered. It was possible to detect the whites of her eyes through the narrow slits.

Mrs Humbert 'woke up'. She looked accusingly at all members of the company. 'Is someone blocking me? Well?'

No one owned up. Frank stole a nervous glance at Cassie. 'We'll call to mind the seven principles of our faith and try again, shall we? Now come along, please, do try.' Mrs Humbert let her head loll again. Another low, deep groan came from her, uncomfortably reminding Frank of the sounds of his Aunt Una in the early moments of

135

labour. Then it changed to a sound like a long, slow release of gas. Mrs Humbert lifted her head slowly and opened her eyes, seeming to look for something just above her ear. 'Beloved, ah yes, to the one, will you be welcome, no, no, not you my dear I've told you before, do you, do you, no we all understand and we are among friends but you must wait your turn, and then in the right, can you wait your turn there's a dear, no dear I won't, that's right in the fullness of time now here's one and what's your name my beloved, Bert? No Bertha, is it? Bertha? Are you come to us?'

There was a frisson around the table. Ina and Evelyn stiffened.

'Only recently gone over, I know, Bertha, I know my love, so new so new and such a, no, not you dear, I'm talking to Bertha and no I'm not having it. Bertha are you come? Good and will you? I shall, and must I tell them? Bertha is in good hope and wants you to know that there is so much love, so much love and light and the wonder of a loving family is treasured beyond gold and wants you to tell Martha and a special message for Frank who is a lovely boy–'

'What's the message?' Cassie said.

'Shhhhh!' went Ina. 'Hush!' went Evelyn.

'Bertha says you are surrounded by love and light and yes dear, they know you do, yes my beloved they do know that...'

Frank looked at his mother and was disturbed to see that although her eyes blazed open her lips were compressed shut, as if she was stifling an instinct to laugh out loud. And in that moment Frank heard his mother's voice, but inside his own head, saying, *She's making it up, Mrs Humbert is a fake.*

'Yes my dear, I will pass on your blessings to the church, Ina and Evelyn will be so pleased to hear–' Mrs Humbert stopped abruptly. She coughed, and then gagged slightly as if a fishbone were stuck in her throat. Then in a guttural tone not at all like her earlier voice she rasped, *'Wir, die wir einst herrlich waren. Wir fallen immernoch aus den Wolken.'* The colour drained from Mrs Humbert's face. She sat bolt upright in her chair, her splayed fingers indenting the tablecloth.

'Sounded foreign,' said one of the ladies from the church.

'Are you all right Mrs Humbert?' Evelyn asked.

'You look very pale,' said Ina.

'Guttural and foreign,' the lady from the church said again.

'A glass of water please,' said Mrs Humbert. 'Might we draw back the curtains?'

The session was clearly over. Mrs Humbert, massaging her temples with her forefingers, was led away to the lounge where she might recover. No one seemed unduly worried that Mrs Humbert had taken a turn for the worse: this seemed to be the standard sacrifice entailed by mediumship. At any rate, and despite the sudden end to proceedings, Evelyn, Ina and the other ladies seemed to regard the session as a great success. They stroked Frank's hair and congratulated him on being spoken to by his Great-great Aunt Bertha who had brought him an inspirational message. Frank, who didn't know what he had done exactly to earn such approbation, nevertheless showed no

137

disinclination to bask in it.

During this chorus of approval Frank looked to Cassie, but she was elsewhere. He shifted uncomfortably. Though he was only five years old he knew that this could be the beginning of something bad. He knew the early signs, like the first moments in a recurring nightmare where the floor might drop away and an unavoidable sequence of events might be set in motion. These were early days, but there was something wakening in his mother all over again, and he knew they would have to ride the tiger once more.

But other eyes were not on Cassie, as Mrs Humbert left the house in a state of mild distress. Though she did so without lashings of sympathy from the appreciative twins. The twins, and the other ladies of the spiritualist church, would have given their eye-teeth to have the connection, the mediumship, the capacities of Mrs Humbert. But this peculiar potency, it seemed, could not be achieved through hard work or enthusiasm. It was bestowed by higher powers, and if an occasional migraine, weariness or other indisposition was the consequence of communicating with the hereafter, then this was only evidence surely of the immensity of the privilege, the thumbprint of God's touch. Evelyn and Ina were believers. They had seen those very powers demonstrated time and again by their own mother Martha. It was a matter of some chagrin to them that neither had inherited the special ability, and that Martha declined to open herself further at the church or otherwise. Having first-hand evidence of the existence of these powers had, however, doomed

138

them to spend their lives examining the mystery behind them, and too often in the wrong place.

Martha had told them that she would never come to their spiritualist church. Martha had enough of such stuff without going looking for it. Only those who don't know how big a hole it punches in the world will go looking for it, Martha had said.

'Wasn't Mrs Humbert splendid?' Ina trilled as Cassie prepared Frank for bed that evening. 'And you too Frank, you were splendid too.'

'I have a feeling,' Evelyn said, crowding into his bedroom, 'that Frank is going to prove to be more gifted in that direction than any of us. What do you say, Cassie?'

'I say that Frank ought to jump into his bed,' Cassie said in an unusual exhibition of maternal practicality, 'because it's very very late!'

Later, after the twins had gone back downstairs, Cassie closed the door and kneeled besides the boy's bed, stroking his hair.

'It was just like a game, tonight, Frank. With Mrs Humbert. It was a game, like playing Snakes and Ladders.'

'Can Mrs Humbert speak to dead people?' Frank said.

'No, she can't.'

'How do you know?'

'No one can speak to the dead. They can't hear you. You can *hear* them *speak* to *you*, Frank, but you can't speak to them. And Mrs Humbert was pretending they could hear her. That's how I knew. You can listen to the dead. They have plenty to say. But they won't listen to us.'

139

'Why not?'

'They just can't.'

'Why did Mrs Humbert stop talking?'

Cassie didn't know what to say. She had an idea. She had an idea that she'd been blocking Mrs Humbert as soon as she'd sensed the woman was faking. And then something odd had happened. 'I don't know. I didn't hear the last thing she said. It was like a foreign language. Like German. *We who were once glorious...*'

Frank sat up in bed. '*We are still falling from the clouds.* That's what she said, Mam.'

Cassie felt her skin flush. 'How do you know that?'

'You told me, Mam.'

'I did? I don't remember that.'

'Yes, you did.'

'Oh Frank. Go to sleep now my darlin' boy.' We're going to have to tell your grandmother about you, Cassie thought, and suddenly, irrationally, felt afraid for the boy. As Frank snuggled down Cassie kissed his forehead, and on rising she opened the window to let a little fresh air into the stuffy house. 'I'll be back in just a moment.'

Cassie went downstairs and raided the kitchen cupboard for candles. The twins kept candles in great supply as some of the visiting mediums preferred a softer light for the invitation of shadows. She returned to Frank's room with an armful, placing them everywhere around the boy, along the windowsill, on his bedside cabinet, on the ottoman at the foot of the bed and on the shelf above his head. Then she turned off the electric light and settled herself into a chair to watch over him. 'I'm here, Frankie,' she murmured, 'I'm here to watch over you.'

The boy looked so beautiful in his bed, his eyes closing as he drifted to sleep, Cassie had to wipe a tear from her eye. She didn't know why the tear had squeezed from her. Perhaps it was that Frank was too beautiful. She felt sure that the world wouldn't allow such a beautiful boy to thrive; that black forces would muster, willing him to perish; that the world wouldn't allow the pure and the beautiful to put a seed of light in a dark place.

As she began to drift towards sleep herself she began to dream of a splendid city of three fine, tall spires; and the city was aflame. Fire rained down from a sky full of demons, and then someone was shouting her name.

It was Evelyn, bustling into the room and flapping at the curtains. 'Cassie! Cassie! Whatever are you thinking of! Cassie!' The net curtains at the window were alight. Frank was sitting up rubbing his eyes. A breeze from the window had blown the netting on to a naked flame. Evelyn flapped again at the curtains with the heavy drapes, managing to put the fire out. Then Ina appeared at the door, her face in her hands, shrieking at Cassie.

'If I hadn't looked at that moment!' Evelyn cried, pressing her heaving bosom with the palm of her hand. 'To think if I hadn't!'

Cassie retreated behind her chair, hiding. Frank started to cry.

15

'You'd better come in, then,' Rita said, and she left William to close the door behind him as she moved through to the sitting room. 'Cup of tea is it?'

'No,' William said. His hands were trembling. He didn't want the china to rattle in his grip.

'I'll put the kettle on anyway,' Rita said. 'In case you change your mind.'

William sat down uneasily on the sofa. The sofa springs creaked. There was a photograph of Archie on the mantelpiece, one taken in uniform, grinning down. Though the furniture in the room was a little threadbare, it was all tidy and spotlessly clean. There was nothing to suggest the presence of a man; nor a child. Though his nose had told him as much the moment he'd walked through the door, he was relieved to see no coat on the hook nor pipe on the mantelpiece.

Rita came back from the kitchen and sat down on the sofa opposite. Her nylons hissed as she crossed her legs, and William sat upright. She looked exactly as she did in the photograph Archie had shown him in Falaise. Her chestnut hair was pinned back but a rogue curl tumbled across one eye, and she hooked it back behind her ear with her little finger. She sat with her legs crossed and her hands on her large hips. 'Took your time didn't you?'

'I have a family. I tried to forget about the war. That's what you do. You try to forget it.'

'Not criticising you. Just saying. Five years nearly isn't it? Smoke?'

William accepted a cigarette. He flicked his lighter for her and fought to stop his hands shaking. She hadn't taken her eyes off him. She took a deep drag of her cigarette, exhaled a long thin plume of smoke, and sank back into the sofa. William hid a sigh of relief inside a stream of smoke.

'Like I said on the doorstep, I promised Archie I'd look you up. It was playing on my mind that I hadn't done it.'

'I'm glad you did. I've never heard anything about how it happened, or what it was like. They just said an infection.'

'That was the hell of it,' he said too quickly. 'All the fighting over and everything. But then they had us cleaning out that camp. An hour on, an hour off, it was so bad. The poor blighters were skin and bone, that's all they were. Skin and bone. You had to wear a mask. We had to burn most of it. Bodies. And the disease, you see. Well, a lot of the blokes got dysentery though they didn't die of it. But that's what happened with Archie. Which was stupid, after all the action he'd seen. Dysentery. Stupid.'

Rita got up and went to the sideboard where she rooted through some papers. She handed him the letter she'd received from the War Office. The note was brief. It stated that Archie had fatally contracted an infectious disease at Belsen, and that he'd served his country with great distinction. William turned the paper over, as if looking for more information on its blank side.

'Don't give you much, does it?' she said, standing over him. 'They don't want you to know anything Rita. Believe me, you don't *want* to know.'

William gazed down at the carpet under his feet. For a moment he was but dimly aware of Rita. He sensed only her proximity. Her slender, white forearm hanging across her thigh. He could smell her scent. Her female body-scent.

The whistle on the kettle sounded. 'I think you need that cup of tea,' she said.

William told her as much as he could, though he quickly got off the subject of the concentration camp at Belsen. He told her about their days at the château at Falaise. She laughed when he told her how much wine they'd drunk. 'That was Archie,' she said. 'That was him all right.' He told her how they'd been lucky not to be court-martialled, and how they'd become good pals, looking out for each other. For some reason he chose not to mention Archie's conviction that he would not return home.

'You never remarried then?' William asked after a pause.

Rita touched the back of her neck with her long fingers. 'First year I spent crying mostly. Didn't even think about blokes. After three years I started thinking about it. That's all I've done, think about it.' She laughed, lightly.

'Can't imagine you staying alone. Woman like you.'

Rita held his gaze. 'What did you come here for William?'

He blushed. 'Settle a promise, that's all. Told

144

Archie I would. I'll be on my way if you like.'

'Suffer, don't you?' Rita said.

'What?'

You're suffering, aren't you William? Not happy. Bothers you, doesn't it?'

William felt flustered, wrong-footed. 'What does?'

'All of it.'

The woman was able to see right through him. He could see why Archie was so in love with her. She knew everything. She was the kind of woman who knew. She didn't have to say anything to prove it. She was the kind of woman who understood, and who could deal with it with a look or a caress, or in bed. She could make it right. And she didn't even know what she'd got. No wonder Archie was crazy about her. She could take complicated things and make them uncomplicated. 'Archie gave me a message to give to you.'

'Oh?'

William took a breath and told her. For a moment she looked confused. William thought she might be angry. Then she laughed, loud. It was a kind of cackle and she slapped her hand against her thigh. 'You dirty bugger!'

'It's what Archie said!' William protested.

'Yes. I'll bet he would. I'll bet he would. That's just like him, that is.' She looked up at the photograph on the mantelpiece, nodding.

There was a silence. William dug his hand under his collar.

'You must be mad, coming here,' she said.

'I must be. Barking bloody mad.' Please take your eyes off me, he thought.

'Married, are you?'

'Yes. Three kids.'

She picked up a pack of cigarettes and slid open the box. Delicately extracting another cigarette, she slipped it between her lips, lit up, inhaled and blew out a thin jet of smoke the same colour as her eyes, never once looking away from him. Then she shook her head, very slightly, as if amused at some internal monologue, and the rogue curl fell over her eye again. Again she recovered it with her little finger. 'It would only be the once,' Rita said. 'Just the once. You've got a family to think about. I couldn't have you coming back.'

William shaped his mouth to say something, but remained silent.

'Mad,' she said. 'It's completely mad.' She got up and opened a door in the corner of the room. William watched her set foot on the flight of stairs. He made no attempt to follow as she went up. He dug his hand under his collar again.

William lit himself a second cigarette and smoked it, during which time Rita showed no sign of coming back downstairs. William glanced at the grinning photograph of Archie. Then he stubbed out his cigarette and went upstairs.

Rita was already naked and between the sheets. 'Take your time over everything, don't you?' she said.

'No point rushing.' It sounded more confident than he felt. After quickly undressing he slipped into the bed next to Rita. Her skin felt like oriental silk.

'You're a shy one,' Rita said.

146

'Always have been. Not used to this.'

Rita laughed. 'Hell! Do you think I am? What I told you is true. Archie was the last man I went to bed with. First and last. I'm just as shy as you are but better at hiding it. And I'm not scared of you. I was scared of you when you came to the door. You looked a bit fierce. But then you relaxed a bit.'

'So why are you letting me do this?'

'Shut up. Kiss me.'

William kissed her, and along with the mild savour of tobacco her soft mouth had a slightly saline taste, which he liked and which inflamed him to kiss her again. After he drew back she compressed her lips, as if examining the residue of the kiss. Something about Rita lived entirely in the moment. She received the kiss. She looked into his eyes. She was immersed in the moment, whereas he was outside of time, and the back of his brain was swirling with thoughts of Olive and Archie, and of losing business in his closed greengrocer's shop and of shovelling corpses into an open grave at Belsen. He felt that this woman could help him. Rita could help him to get back inside time.

He pulled away the sheets and looked at her breasts. Large and soft, they had unusually large aureoles, surrounded by tiny satellite duct pimples. William leaned over and licked a nipple. She gasped and responded by closing her long fingers around the shaft of his cock. He licked her nipple again and moved his mouth to the undercarriage of her breast, where it joined the rib, nibbling at her before moving on to her belly.

William was after something exotic. It was all Archie's fault, that time in Falaise. Late one

147

evening, wine-soaked, Archie had asked William to nominate his favourite smell in all the world. William had said grapefruit. Archie had mocked and told him that a woman's smell was unbeatable and there was nothing like the honest smell of muff when you were blowing the pink kazoo. William didn't know what he was talking about. He didn't know what a clitoris was either. He'd known about oral sex, but he'd never done it with Olive or anyone else. Archie had told him that you could drive a woman wild by licking her clitoris. Archie guaranteed it. When William expressed the thought that Archie was just making a fool of him, Archie had educated him.

William had been unable to stop his shoulders from shaking with mirth at the idea that anyone should want to put their mouth to a woman's private parts. Archie was laughing, too. Then he said, 'Think about how you play a kazoo.'

The consequence of Archie's musical education, and the promise that he'd made to Archie that day in Falaise, was that William had spent five years fighting back thoughts of muff, of the smell of a woman, of the clitoris and of playing the pink kazoo. On more than one occasion he'd wanted to try it with Olive, but he couldn't bring himself to do it. It was just too absurd. She would be disgusted, he was sure of it. It would end their marriage if he tried, he was convinced.

'It's the vibration, see,' Archie had said between howls of laughter, holding his ribs with one hand and a wine bottle in the other. 'It drives 'em crazy. It's the bleedin' vibration.'

So for five years William had thought, from

148

time to time, of Rita's muff. The thought might come to him in the middle of weighing parsnips, or stacking grapefruit; or it might come to him while reading the football results; or last thing at night in the moments before sleep. And his reflex every time had been to push the degenerate – for so he considered them to be – thoughts aside. For five years.

And now here he was, kissing Rita's belly, running south. Her skin was so unlike Olive's. Rita's skin was the colour of the white sand in the African desert. And when he drew closer to her the smell was not unlike the odour of the spice market in Cairo. It was complex, rich, exotic and threatening. It was so strong he thought it might make him faint. He pushed his fingers inside her and Rita moaned. He found her clitoris, just where Archie had told him he would. He teased it with his forefinger and Rita pushed her pubic mound up at him, towards his mouth. And when he buried his face in her muff the smell of her was like musk. He pushed his tongue at her clitoris and she whipped her body. When he lapped gently at her, she called him by her husband's name.

'Archie.'

William heard it, but was not distracted. Then he heard her say it again and became impatient. He lifted his head from her and turned Rita over on to her belly, and pushed into her, hard, from behind. 'Slow down,' Rita said, 'slow down.' When he ejaculated inside her, William felt the sweat freeze on his back; the hairs on the back of his neck and his arms stood erect as he emptied himself into her.

They lay together, staring at the ceiling. After a while Rita said, 'God, you were like a man just let out of prison.'

'Sorry.'

'Don't say sorry. It was good.'

Yes, thought William, but *who* was good? He was about to speak when he noticed that she was crying. He reached out and held her and she sobbed in his arms for a long time, until she cried herself to sleep. Normally after sex William would close his eyes and drift off to sleep himself, but his heart was hammering. His eyes searched all four corners of the darkened room. At last he slipped out of bed. He had a stupid notion that someone was hiding in the wardrobe. He moved slowly over to the oak wardrobe, turned the small key and opened the door. Inside he found Archie's suits and jackets draped neatly over coathangers. The odour of the man was on the clothes. Archie's shoes rested at the foot of the wardrobe.

After closing the wardrobe door he got down on his hands and knees and looked under the bed. Then he got up and went to the chest of drawers. The top drawer opened with a whisper. It contained Rita's things: socks, underwear. He closed it and opened the second drawer, running his hands through the clothes he found there.

'What are you looking for?' Rita asked softly.

William jumped, and for a second time felt the sweat cold on his back. He closed the drawer. 'I don't know,' he said. He felt strange, dislocated.

'Come back here to me.'

'I have to go,' William said, grabbing his shirt.

'Yes. I'll see you out.'

'No!' he said, too loud. Then, 'Stay there. Relax.'

He dressed hurriedly, kissed Rita and thumped down the stairs. In the lounge he paused only to look at Archie's photograph grinning at him from the mantelshelf. William muttered something under his breath before letting himself out, slamming the door behind him.

He looked back up at the bedroom he'd just left. The curtain twitched.

16

Cassie had to tell Martha about young Frank's abilities, even though Martha was not wholly given to open discussion about matters fey. Martha noted how Cassie spoke without finishing her sentences; how she expressed herself rapidly and seemed to take a breath in the wrong place, halfway through a word sometimes. Frankie had it, Cassie told her; Frankie was an old soul; Frankie was this; he was that; he was the other. Martha gave Cassie a good listening to. She didn't know what to say in response, and was wise enough to know that was the very best time in which to say nothing.

Martha's reluctance to talk had nothing at all to do with scepticism, and everything to do with conviction. Didn't she herself experience visitations and dreams and receive inspirational messages, all of them unasked for? Each of her children – and her grandchildren – she dearly hoped would not be cursed with any 'gift' of second sight.

With most of them her hopes had been answered. Aida was as untroubled as a fence-post. Evelyn and Ina, though they wished for nothing more in their lives, had no such spiritual capacities, and were reduced to listening at shells scooped out by the sea. Olive was too fussy and too concerned with the small commerce of life; while Una was a child of the earth and that was why she'd chosen her farmer husband. As for Beatie, she had too much cleverness to be at all sensitive. And just when Martha had got to the end of her childbearing and thought to have got away with it, along came Cassie, who carried it for sure, and now Frank, of whom she had never had any doubt.

And maybe that was why she'd turned around that day, insisting that they keep the child. Because he'd have enough trouble if he was to have this burden and be around folk who didn't understand.

There was also a protection in Martha's reluctance to talk the matter up. It was a very old instinct, cradled in fear and self-preservation. It made no difference over the years whether they came for you with their white coats and their electric shocks or whether they came with bell, book and candle. Still they came.

Martha had hoped that in steering Frank up to Avon Street the quiet atmosphere there might have done Cassie some good. In Martha's experience not much answer was given to those who spend all their days knocking on the wall. Moreover the twins were spectacularly dense, and so were the spooks and spirit-rappers who came to their church. It had seemed clever to hide Cassie and Frank in the place where it was all talk and no action, but now Martha was thinking that perhaps she'd made a mistake. Cassie would make a hole in the wall for all of them.

'It might pass,' she said to Cassie about Frank. 'Often it does. As they grow.'

'He's made a stir up at Avon Street.'

For so he had. Mrs Humbert's upset at the Avon Street household was not ascribed, as it might be elsewhere, to anything as mundane as a headache or tiredness or the onset of a cold. Her difficulties had to be seen as psychic in origin. And when another spiritualist visitor to Avon Street, a Mr Abrahams with his face half para-lysed from a stroke, pronounced the house quivering with psychic energy he'd not noticed on a previous visit, Frank's presence began to attract comment. Not that everyone was ready to recog-nise Frank as especially empowered; it was more that the presence of a child in the house was seen as a beacon attracting new and positive spirits, as if the boy were a row of lights on the angelic landing strip. This was a notion encouraged at every turn by Cassie, who herself stepped back from the attention of the visiting spiritualists.

Martha said, 'Tell me something, Cassie, have you seen your father?'

'I'm not talking about that any more, I'm telling you about Frankie–'

'Just answer me, gal!' Martha could be sharp with her daughter when she needed to be. 'Have you seen him today?'

'He's in the other room, reading the newspaper.'

'When did you start seeing him again?'

'Last week.'

Martha sighed. 'Cassie, your father is dead. He's been long dead.' She tapped the side of her head. 'When are you going to get that notion fixed here?'

'Can't help it if I see him.' Cassie pouted.

'Yes you can, gal! Look at me when I speak to you. You can stop it if you want to!'

'For God's sake Mam, can it be doing the boy any good to grow up in that atmosphere?' Beatie was making a visit home from Oxford after getting a letter from her mother. Beatie and Bernard still appeared to be living together – unofficially – and there was no mention of marriage.

Beatie had already been told of the incident with the candles and the fire in Frank's bedroom. Evelyn and Ina were blameless, but as usual everyone looked for a way to excuse Cassie. 'They help Cassie keep him clean and fed and looked after. What more can you want?'

'He's well loved, Beatie.' Cassie was loyal to her sisters, who had never stinted in their efforts to do right by the boy. 'Really he is.'

'I don't doubt it, but what's all this about the boy sitting in on seances? Filling his head with mumbo-jumbo?'

'They don't call it seances,' Cassie said.

'Don't much matter what they call it. It's all tripe.'

154

'Tripe? Yes, it is tripe.' Martha lit her pipe, and sighed. A toughness had come into Beatie's manner of talking. Not an unkindness, but an impatience, as if she always knew better. Martha took up her purse from the mantelpiece and found a few coins. 'Run me an errand, Cassie. Get me an ounce of tobacco, would you?'

'You've got a packet there, Mam!'

'Well get me *another* packet would you.' Cassie wasn't stupid. She knew she was being sent out so that Martha could talk to Beatie behind her back. But she went anyway. 'And come back afore nightfall!' Martha shouted after her.

'He's an intelligent little boy,' Beatie said when Cassie had gone. 'What he needs is a scientific grounding. Not a lot of trash filling his head. A scientific direction.'

Scientific was Beatie's favourite word. Bernard tended to use the word a great deal, too, whenever he was visiting. Socialism, they said, was scientific. This or that person's argument was dismissed because it wasn't scientific. The future was going to be scientific. Children should be raised on a scientific basis. No one in the family ever asked what was meant by this term, for fear of a long explanation. But Beatie was highly animated by the notion that the sphere of Frank's influence had it in short supply.

'Starts school next month, Frank does,' Martha told Beatie. 'Eve and Ina have promised to kit him out.'

'Child-minding,' Beatie said. 'That's not a proper education. It's just child-minding so that women can go to work.'

155

'I thought we were all for that,' Martha said dryly.

'We are!' Beatie flashed. 'But for proper wages, and equal rights with the men. Not just so as capitalism can destroy a generation with its wars and then fill its boots with the women! They say shoulders to the wheel everybody, but they mean *our* shoulders to *their* bloody wheel!' Beatie had a habit of folding her arms and sitting back after making such a point.

Martha didn't really disagree with any of it, but it was not a speech she hadn't heard from Beatie before.

'We're still willing to have Frankie in Oxford, you know. Any time. We could teach him in the commune. Everybody could take a turn. Frankie would be taught by some of the finest minds in the country.'

Martha bit on her pipe. 'If you're so keen to have the lad, why don't you get on with making babbies of your own?'

There was a moment of hostile silence. Then Beatie said, 'Cassie's going into one of her clouds, isn't she? Is that why you asked me to come?'

'Yes Beatie, it's starting again. And the older the lad gets, the more I worry for him. She could become a menace to him.'

'Just say the word and we shall have him in Oxford. That's why you called me here, isn't it?'

'No,' Martha said. 'It's not.'

Beatie was not happy with Martha's proposed solution. It was not often she dug in and resisted her mother, but the independence of mind and the

156

spirit of vigorous oppositional debate engendered by her time in the commune at Oxford had stirred her to think that in some matters she might know better. And so in her heart began a quiet struggle to rescue Frank – and for Beatie the boy needed rescuing – from the forces of un-science gathering around him like dark birds. It was a struggle which might cause a deep rift in the family, a rift Beatie would never have wanted; but then she could never have predicted the power of as-yet-undefined but dynamic forces competing to shape the soul of the young Frank.

Beatie was motivated by nothing other than good intentions and notions of progress and self-improvement. It grieved her to see Frank passed about the family as if it all didn't matter. It vexed her to think of his education and upbringing running to the default of a bit of *this* and a bit of *that*. She knew that everything lay in a state of potential, and that potential could only become actual if you took a firm grip of the events of life and forced them along a desirable route. She'd proved it with her own life, from factory worker to an exalted place of learning where she had earned a first class degree. She knew now that it was only a matter of opportunity; and that opportunities had always been excluded from people like herself, her family and young Frank. The danger was that her sisters didn't always see things that way. They assumed their own lives to have worked out for the best simply because that was the way they *had* worked out. Which was not the same thing.

Fate. Her sisters lived in the jaws of the idea of fate, pecking around those monumental teeth for scraps of meat.

But Beatie had studied fate at university. She had looked it in the throat. She knew that it was a Greek word meaning 'that which has been written'. And Beatie had figured out that that which was written was all determined by he who controlled the pen. In legislation. In the recording of history. In the dissemination of ideas and the propagation of values. And Beatie had decided to set her own quill to the blank page of Frank's life.

'Well we didn't expect you here today!' Evelyn said, genuinely pleased to see Beatie and Cassie on the doorstep. 'No Bernard?'

Beatie and Cassie passed through to the hall, where Cassie was hugged by Frank. Beatie sniffed at the beeswax and potpourri. 'He's got work in Oxford. I'm just here for the weekend. Cassie and I thought we'd take Frank up town to see what's new.'

'Won't you have a cup of tea first?' Ina squinted painfully through her tortoiseshell spectacles.

'When we get back we'll all have a cup together. Is it all right if we take him along?'

Evelyn and Ina looked at each other. In truth they were glad to have Frank from under their feet for a couple of hours. They made a huge fuss of discussing whether he would need his coat.

Frank felt hot in his coat as Cassie and Beatie marched him up Trinity Street towards Broadgate. Beatie always seemed to walk incredibly fast. Frank had to make two steps and a skip to keep pace with her. His mother had difficulty in keeping up with her too. Another thing he

158

noticed was that Beatie did almost all of the talking, while his mother mostly smiled, and nodded, but wasn't really listening at all.

Frank knew his mother loved and admired Beatie. In fact Beatie was his mother's favourite sister, just as she, perhaps next to Una, was his favourite aunt. It was just that Beatie was difficult to listen to. Frank tried to catch what it was she was saying, but missed most of it. Beatie seemed pretty mad about something; not mad enough to let it spoil her day, or to get cross with anyone, or even to stop her laughing, or offering her beautiful smile that was like a match bursting into flame; but cross in a general sort of way; cross with the weather and cross with the sky.

'Can you believe they let the Old Toad back in? Can you believe it Cassie? Wasn't it worse that we got the largest share of the vote and they got the most seats? And can you believe that Aida and Olive actually voted for the Old Toad.'

Frank had heard some of this before. Toad had gone back to Toad Hall and some of his aunts thought that was a good thing. His mother, Beatie and his grandmother thought it was a bad thing. Meanwhile Una, Ina and Evelyn all thought it made no difference. Frank had witnessed passionate arguments about Toad of Toad Hall, and at one time, if it hadn't been for Uncle Tom, it seemed that Uncle William and Uncle Bernard were going to fight about it. His grandmother had banged the coal scuttle with the poker and no one had taken any notice.

This was about the Toad in Downing Street, London, but there were other toads here in

Coventry who seemed to upset Aunt Beatie too.

'Look at this! Five years on and we're still looking at cardboard shops this side of Broadgate. Five years on! And you know why, don't you? Because palms are waiting to be greased up at Town Hall, that's why Cassie.'

Sometimes Beatie said Town Hall and sometimes she said Toad Hall. Frank wasn't sure if they were the same place.

'The garden looks nice,' Cassie said, referring to Broadgate island, turfed and almost sacred, planted with flowers and circled by a moat of easy traffic.

'Yes, but they're doing their best to bugger it up pardon my French. More kickbacks. More bloody fixes and backhanders. This was going to be a great new city. Be a dog's dinner before they're through. Now we're to have a great big cathedral before we've even rebuilt the public amenities. Where's the sense in that?'

'Be nice,' Cassie said dreamily. 'New cathedral.'

'Nice! We don't need a new cathedral! We need dwellings and factories and libraries and schools. That's what we need.'

But Cassie wasn't listening. She stopped suddenly and called to Frank. He went to her and she stooped down to hug him. Her perfume almost made his eyes water, and some of the orange powder from her face transferred itself to his cheek. She pointed up at the portico of the bank behind her. 'This is where I saw how special you were, Frankie. Right here.'

She let him go and Frank ran up the white steps and swung round one of the pillars under the

160

portico. Frank saw Beatie squinting at Cassie. 'I remember the night this was all on fire,' he heard his mother say.

If Frank half closed his eyes and looked across the island garden of Broadgate, towards the spire of the Holy Trinity and the shell of St Michael's, he could easily imagine the demon flame and the yellow sparks cascading against a sable sky.

'One day,' Beatie said. 'One day, our Cassie, you're going to tell me all about that night.'

'Not yet,' Cassie said, softly, almost inaudibly.

Frank rubbed his back against the pillar and pretended he couldn't hear them talking.

'Would you like to come to Oxford for a bit, Cassie? Live with me and Bernard at the commune?'

'Oh Beatie! I'd love that! I'd love it! Eve and Ina are good to us and I don't deserve it but I'm going mad there, so I am.'

'Mam wants you to leave Frank with them and come to Oxford on your own.'

'Oh!' Cassie's eyes watered. 'Oh!'

'Come with me Cassie. Work with me. If we work together we'll come back and get Frank. Very soon. They don't approve of how me and Bernard live. But if you work with me we'll come back and get Frank.'

'Don't abandon me Beatie!'

'I'd never do that. Never. I'll be honest with you Cassie, you're going into a blue patch again. That's why they want you away from Frank for a while. You'll have to work with me. Let people help you. But I'll never let you down, never ever.'

Frank listened from behind the pillar, hugging the white stone.

17

So Cassie was whisked away to Oxford, so that in her 'blue patch' she might only be a harm to the intellectuals, the socialists and the anarchists, and not to Frank. Martha didn't like to separate her from the boy, but she feared a return to Hatton with their flapping white coats and electro-convulsive therapy. Beatie had said that there were at the Oxford commune great minds that could help her: psychologists and counsellors of the first order.

The other sisters, or some of them, looked down their noses. They didn't like the sound of this place where unmarried and even divorced couples mixed and matched under the same roof. They would never have approved of Frank going there, but when it came to it Cassie was the greater burden. Aida was too old and too rigid; the twins hadn't recovered from the moment when Cassie almost burned the house down with them all in it; Una was worn out with her own double handful of babies; and Olive was going through a bad patch with William where they weren't on speaking terms and no one knew why.

'Mend it,' Martha told Olive. 'Or you shall end up like me and your father, not speaking for years and years.'

'He's just so moody,' Olive fretted. 'Sour and moody all the time.'

Frank started school in Stoke Aldermoor infants' class. As promised, the twins rigged him out and together one September morning they proudly took him to school and left him, in a state of perplexed silence, in his classroom. Awed and speechless, Frank watched the class teacher hold two boys by the hair as their legs moved underneath them without traction. The boys screamed, they cried, they lashed out. The teacher patiently held them by their scalps until they calmed down and, weeping, were forced into places each behind a tiny desk. Small wonder that Frank thought school was punishment for some wrongdoing. His attendance at school coincided with Cassie's disappearance. No one had explained to him what school was for. He looked at the weeping, red-faced boys and concluded that whatever it was he'd done wrong, it must have been very bad to have earned him this kind of correction.

He accepted his punishment manfully. At lunchtime as he stood alone in the playground a boy with a terrible squint passed by, and caught Frank's glance.

'What are you looking at?' the boy said.

Even though Frank tried to remain silent, a word opened his jaws and forced its way out. 'Squint.'

The boy fetched Frank a vicious blow to the mouth, knocking him off his feet. When he stood up again the squinting boy had gone, and no one even seemed to have noticed the assault. Frank put his finger to a bloody lip.

On his second day at school another boy twice his size approached him in the playground and said, 'Your mother's a basket case. She's been in

Hatton. She's got a screw loose.' Frank flushed with anger. His fist clenched. His hand involuntarily shot to the scab formed on his lip after the previous day's altercation. After some further derision his tormentor moved on.

On the third day in the playground Frank noticed a small group of boys and girls jeering at another lad. One of the persecutors was jabbing a stiff finger at the boy's face and leading a chant: 'GI brat, American sprat, GI brat, American sprat.' Over and over.

Frank walked away, then turned on his heels and ran full pelt at the main persecutor, pushing him over. The boy went down hard, thumping his head on the ground. Frank stood over him. The tormentors stood back. The boy Frank had felled rubbed his sore head, scrambled to his feet and ran to the other side of the playground. Frank saw lots of eyes looking him up and down. From a short distance he saw the boy with the squint, his assailant on the first day, coolly appraising him.

'Why did you do that?' asked the boy he'd rescued.

'American brat,' Frank said. 'Me too.'

'You?'

Frank smiled. 'Yep. My dad was an American soldier.' Frank walked away and sat on a step. The boy followed and sat next to him. He fumbled with something in his pocket and held it out for Frank. It was a cigarette card showing a man in a war helmet and pyjamas swinging a long stick.

'What is it?' Frank asked.

'American,' said the boy. 'Americans are no good at real sports so they have to play this instead. This man is called Babe Ruth. He was pretty good.' Frank made to give back the card. 'You can keep it.'

'Hey thanks. I'll put it on my shelf in my bedroom.'

'Was your dad a hero?'

'He was. He got killed. A soldier hero.'

'So was mine. A hero.' The handbell was rung in the yard, recalling them to class. The boys were in different groups, so they arranged to see each other again. Frank's new friend was called Clayton.

After school Frank was customarily met at the school gates by his aunt Ina, smiling and squinting at him through her spectacles. As he made his way to the gates he was joined by Clayton, who said, 'Still got the card?'

Frank flashed him a smile and the card together. Then someone grabbed the card from his hand. It was the boy with the squint. Frank froze. The boy looked over the card with his good eye, before handing it back, unimpressed. 'I saw you today,' said the interloper. 'I saw you run at that lad. Whack! Pretty good that. Pretty good.' Clayton stood still beside him. Frank said nothing, expecting another blow to the mouth. 'Do you want to be in my gang?'

Frank looked at Clayton, then back at the squinting boy. 'Who's in it? Who's in your gang?'

The boy gave him a toothy grin. 'Just you and me. So far.'

Frank pointed at Clayton. 'And him.'

The boy fobbed a little white ball of spittle on the ground. 'Yeh. You, me and him.' Then he smiled again.

'Right,' said Frank.

'Right,' said the boy. 'See you tomorrow.'

Then he was gone, and Aunt Ina was at the gates. 'Another nice day at school?' she asked.

The boy with the squint was called Chaz, short for Charles, this fuller version too ridiculous a name for anyone to support through school life without risk of a daily playground beating. Being a member of Chaz's gang was uneventful, though, and consisted mostly of leaning against the railings at the edge of the playground with hands thrust in pockets. But it did have the advantage, Chaz looking so fierce, of discouraging tormentors and detractors. No one took an unprovoked swing, at any rate, and the chant about being an American brat was not heard again for a long time.

Clayton meanwhile had a ready supply of Americana: cigarette cards, trading cards, comics and bubblegum which he readily shared with Frank and Chaz. Clayton had relatives in the United States who sent packages over on a monthly basis. He had met his grandfather and grandmother, who had come over to England especially to meet him, and who had tried to prevail on his mother to move back with them to Pennsylvania. Everyone had cried, and no one more than his grandmother, who said that Clayton was the image of the son who had died on Omaha Beach. But Clayton's mother couldn't bear to be parted from her own family. Frank accepted Clayton's largesse with gratitude, but he wondered if there were relations of his own somewhere in

America who might send him bubblegum. He gladly accepted Clayton's cards, but felt bereft.

Chaz was amazed at Clayton's generosity. He'd never met anyone who gave things away so freely, mainly because he came from a family who only acquired things of their own when other people's backs were turned. His clothes were hand-me-downs, several sizes too large, and after seeing the improvised clogs he'd turned up to school in one day, the headteacher had invoked a government scheme to provide him with a proper pair of shoes. But his loyalty to his new 'gang' was passionate, impressive and vicious.

'What are you looking at?' he would challenge anyone he thought had so much as glanced at Clayton or Frank in what he considered to be a disrespectful manner. No one ever responded to the challenge.

One day Chaz produced a bubblegum trading card and gave it back to Clayton.

'What's this?' Clayton said.

'I stole it from your pocket,' Chaz said. 'I didn't mean to take it. I just stole it.'

'It's OK. You can have it.'

'It was sticking out of your pocket!' Chaz was highly agitated. 'You don't let things stick out of your pocket!'

'Keep it.'

'I didn't mean to take it!'

'I don't mind,' Clayton said blithely.

'I can't keep it! I didn't mean it!'

Frank saw that something was going to go wrong, and that Chaz was about to blow his top. Chaz looked confused and angry and hurt.

167

'Swop it with one of mine,' Frank said, snatching the card from Chaz. 'Here, you take this one.'

Chaz took the card. Then he walked away and stood on his own in the far corner of the playground. When the bell went to summon them back to class he returned and said, 'You can come egging on Saturday. With my brothers. We go egging.'

But when home time came around, Chaz and Frank approached Ina and asked if he might go egging. Ina said Frank was busy. She didn't say what he would be doing, but she said they had plans for that day. Clayton's mother said the same. Chaz, not too disappointed, skipped off to find his older sister.

'Where are we going? Tomorrow? Where?' Frank wanted to know that evening.

'What's that?' Evelyn said, on her knees with a dustpan and brush.

'Aunt Ina said we're going somewhere tomorrow.'

Evelyn peered quizzically at Ina and Ina mouthed something in return. Evelyn put away her dustpan and brush and sat Frank down at the dining table. Then the twins sat down. Ina took off her spectacles and looked hard at Frank. 'This boy,' she said.

'The one you've been playing with.'

'At school. The one you've been chummy with.'

Frank knew they meant Chaz, so he said, 'Clayton?'

'No, not Clayton.'

'Clayton is a lovely lad. No, the other one.'

They waited, but Frank gave them no sign of recognition. Then Evelyn said, 'Your Aunt Ina and me. We know his family—'

'We know *of* his family—'

'And though the Lord says you should love everyone, well it is hard sometimes and we know they're not a very nice family—'

'Not the sort of family you would want to mix with—'

'Or have round for tea—'

'No, or have round for tea, and we don't think that you should play with this boy or be quite so chummy with him—'

'Just a little bit less chummy.'

Frank looked from one to the other of his aunts. They stared down at him with wide-open, slightly moist beautiful blue eyes. Ina put her glasses back on, now that she'd said what needed to be said without them. Frank looked down at the table. Then he looked up and with tears beginning to fill his eyes he heard himself screaming, 'STUPID OLD WOMEN! THE FARM! I WANT TO GO TO THE FARM!'

Still screaming he ran from the room and hid himself in his bedroom.

Perhaps an hour later there was a light knock on his door and his Aunt Evelyn appeared with a plate of sandwiches and a glass of milk on a tray. Frank was lying on his bed. She placed the tray on his bedside cabinet. 'We think your Uncle William is going out to the farm tomorrow. In the morning we'll ask if he'll take you.'

Frank sat up and pointed to the cigarette card propped on the mantelshelf. 'Why hasn't my grandma and granddad in America sent me anything like that? Why haven't they?'

Evelyn picked up the Babe Ruth card, looked at the picture and read the print on the back of the card. 'I don't think they know about you, Frankie. They haven't been told.'

'Why not?'

Evelyn carefully replaced the card on the shelf. 'All in the Lord's time,' she said. 'All in the Lord's time.'

William had indeed arranged to go over to the farm early the following morning, and he consented to take Frank in the van. Frank found his uncle in a somewhat brittle mood; preoccupied and inclined to say things Frank didn't understand.

'Not going to throw me one today are you?' William asked him a good while after they'd got underway.

'What?'

'Ar.'

That was it. That was all Frank's Uncle William had to say for the entire journey. But his Uncle Tom and Aunt Una made a huge fuss of Frank when they arrived. Una was looking much better and her own twins were thriving. She was said to be beating something called the baby blues. Una took Frank indoors as Tom helped William load some garden produce into his van. William came back into the farmhouse to say goodbye to Una.

'Going straight back then?' Una asked him.

'Got to call in at Rugby first.' William cupped his hands to light a cigarette, even though he was indoors and out of the wind.

'Business in Rugby?' Tom said.

'Ar.'

Tom agreed to take Frank home later and they all waved William away. Frank and Tom stood in the yard while Una shuffled in the doorway with the twins crawling at her feet. 'Not awful chatty these days is he?' Una said.

'Not awful. Wonder what business he's got in Rugby?' Then Tom remembered Frank standing beside him. 'Well now, schoolboy. You going to help me move some hay this morning?'

Frank helped his uncle Tom shift hay around in the barn. At the back of the barn stood some old crates, plus a rusting bicycle that had rested for so long in the same place it was sheathed in cobwebs. The cobwebs had coagulated with black dust. It looked as though if you touched it the whole thing would disintegrate in a spectacular rust and dust shower. Behind the bicycle was the tail fin of a German Luftwaffe bomber brought down in Tom's field the night of the Coventry blitz. A black swastika with a white border was emblazoned on the grey paintwork of the tail fin. The wreckage of the plane had been spread over three acres of land, and Tom had removed the tail fin as a souvenir before the Ministry had carted away the important parts of the wreckage. When Frank asked about the plane, Tom told him that another piece of the twisted metal had been melted down and cast into a 'peace bell', and that the bell sat on the altar of St Mary's church in the village. He'd promised to show Frank the peace bell, one day.

171

After a while Frank tired of helping Tom shift hay bales from one end of the barn to the other, and started chasing the bantam hens. When the moment was right he asked if he could play in the field.

Down at the stream he was surprised to find how overgrown the makeshift footbridge had become. The hollow underneath was hidden by grass and purple-flowered thistles. Careful not to disturb the ground too much, nor to draw attention to his activities, it took him some time to make himself an entrance. He found it more difficult to wriggle inside, not realising how much he'd grown during the past months.

His den and his shrine were undisturbed. The sunshine filtering through all the new growth cast everything in a green light. It made the Man-Behind-The-Glass difficult to see, but as Frank pressed his eye against the smeary, webbed glass he breathed a sigh of relief. The jaw of the Man-Behind-The-Glass hung open and the hollow eyes stared back at Frank. 'Where have you been?' he seemed to say.

'Sorry,' Frank whispered. 'I have to live with my aunts. They're always cleaning. Dusting. Sweeping.'

'Lonely.'

'Sorry. I can't get here on my own. I've brought something for you.' Frank pressed one of Clayton's American trading cards to the glass. It was a picture of a woman in a cowboy hat with a rifle. She was called Annie Oakley. Allowing a moment for the Man-Behind-The-Glass to see it, Frank propped the card alongside the feathers and horseshoes he'd placed there earlier.

'Rita. Rita. Ritaritaritaritaritarita brrrrrrrrrrrr-rrrrrrrrrrr brrrrrr-pppppp brrrrrrrr,' said the Man-Behind-The-Glass.

Frank was sympathetic. He knew how difficult it must have been all this time with no one coming to see him. He got close up and peered through the glass again and was surprised to see the man had acquired a tongue. It was never there before, and now the tongue was vibrating and waggling between the permanently open jaws. Or perhaps it was a white moth fluttering its wings where the tongue should be. Whatever it was, it spoke.

'Brrrrrrrrrrrr brrrrrrrr Frank get me getmegetmeget the bell. The bell.'

'Oh,' said Frank.

When Tom drove him back to his aunts that evening Frank asked if they might stop at the church and look at the peace bell. Tom wrinkled his nose but obliged by drawing the van up outside the church. St Mary's was a fourteenth-century greystone church with a Norman tower and spire, resting on a great sloping green burial sward populated with Victorian headstones. The wrought-iron gate squealed as it swung open. Tom kicked his muddy boots against the wall outside before going in.

The church was empty and silent. Tom led Frank to the altar. There was a golden cross, a pair of candlesticks and a silver-grey bell. 'That's it,' Tom said, his voice unusually subdued. 'Peace bell.'

'Can you pick it up?' Frank asked.

173

'No.'

'Why not?'

Tom wasn't sure why not. He wasn't a church-goer. But he knew there was something about approaching the altar. 'You don't touch.' He craned his neck over the bell to read the engraving. 'I'll tell you what it says. It says: "This peace bell was cast from metal plucked from the wreckage of a German bomber brought down in this parish." Then it gives the date it was made.'

'What's plucked?'

Tom rubbed the back of his neck. 'Come on,' he said. 'Or we'll be late getting you home.'

A loss of vibration had occurred, it was observed, and not just by Evelyn and ma. How was it, they wondered, that the spirits could find their house welcoming on one day and then inhospitable the next? So disappointing! Just when Ina and Evelyn were developing something of a reputation amongst spiritualist circles as running a house of splendid ingress. Naturally they discussed the matter, wondering what might have changed, but without fathom. A house once busy with activity from spirits invited or otherwise had become neutral again. Ina it was who suggested they should put their question to the Other Side; Evelyn it was who decided to put.

So it was that on the Sunday evening after spiritualist church, with two other ladies from the congregation, Frank was allowed to sit in on the questioning. Frank still carried something of his own reputation as a splendid prospect for the spiritualist cause, and he was not blamed in the least for any diminishing of the vital contact. On the contrary it was upheld that his presence would help.

A somewhat reluctant Frank was called down from his bedroom, where he'd been playing with his cigarette cards. Ina drew the curtains, lit a candle and dimmed the electric lamp with a silk scarf as the small company gathered round the lounge table. When she took her place at the table Evelyn reached out so that those to right and left might join hands. Frank too was recruited into this circle.

Evelyn led neither by dint of extra experience nor authority, but simply because someone had to take on the job of addressing the Other Side. Frank had already noticed a wide range of tones and styles among the visiting spiritualists when addressing the dead. There were those who seemed formal and lugubrious; those who spoke in archaic terms referring to spirits as 'thee' and 'thou'; and those who seemed by contrast jocular, slangy and irreverent.

Evelyn, with her heavy face and her large nose, favoured the formal and the archaic both. She let her head loll in the manner of Mrs Connie Humbert. 'Beloved,' she announced in a slightly quavering voice, 'we come to thee in a spirit of love. We welcome thee. We open ourselves to thee. We ask thee to make thyselves known in the disposition of light and love.'

Nothing happened. Frank looked from his Aunt Evelyn to his Aunt Ina, but her brow was furrowed as she squinted through her tortoise-shell glasses at her sister. Mrs Tull and Mrs Palm from the spiritualist church wore expressions on their faces which made him want to snigger. He knew better.

'Come hither, beloved. Come hither in vestments of love. We would ask thee whether there is anything leading thee away, or withholding thee from our love. We ask this in good faith.'

Still nothing. At least, Frank thought, Aunt Evelyn isn't a fake, pretending to have a conversation. He remembered his mother in the house telling him that Mrs Humbert was a fake.

The electric lamp flickered off and came on again. The four women round the table stiffened visibly. Frank could almost smell their sudden excitement. It streamed off them like perfume.

'Art thou with us?' Evelyn asked.

'Ask again,' Ina whispered. 'There *is* a presence.'

'Art thou with us, beloved?'

Nothing. Frank wished his mother were still there with him. She had no fear of these sessions, and yet these odd ladies seemed crouched over the table in a mixture of terror and rhapsody. He felt much better when she was there to explain these meetings to him, or to laugh about them afterwards. He thought of Cassie laughing. The electric light blinked off and on again, and he felt a frisson chase round the circle of hands.

'I'm getting a name,' Evelyn said decisively. 'It's coming through.'

The other ladies gazed back at her with brimming eyes and half-open mouths, willing Evelyn on.

'The name is Ruth. Does anyone here know of a Ruth?'

Mrs Tull shook her head but Mrs Palm said she did know of a Ruth, a young woman who lived across the street from her.

'Ask if there is anything blocking the spirits,' Ina suggested.

'I'm getting something else. Something about a... That's it. A babe. You'd better tell this Ruth she's going to have a babe.'

Frank wrinkled his nose.

'There's more,' Evelyn said excitedly. 'It says ... it says ... it says ... "Watch my dust".'

Frank scratched his knee. The light bulb flickered out, this time permanently. There was a gasp from the ladies as they stared hard at each other in the candlelight.

18

Cassie was creating a 'psychic disturbance' at Ravenscraig. So said the eminent scholar and famous anarchist Peregrine Feek, privately, to Beatie, just a few weeks after Cassie's arrival at the communal dwelling. Feek, a red-faced fellow-traveller with fizzing white eyebrows and a great snowy mane of hair, had invited Beatie into his room for a quiet word. He was the owner of Ravenscraig; though only nominally, since he knew that property is theft and had declared the house to be owned by all those who lived in it. The title deeds and the utility contracts only remained in his name because of the accident that had originally allowed him to inherit Raven-scraig from his wealthy parents. He was a professor of philosophy, teaching at Balliol College, Oxford, where he had rooms in which to stay when he wasn't at Ravenscraig. Indeed so great was Feek's reputation as a scholar that he was often in demand in Paris, where he kept an apartment for his spring visits, and in Florence, where the family Tuscan villa often proved useful for summer retreats whenever he was working on a new book. All of these extra properties were useful in accommodating his children and their mothers, who had moved out of Ravenscraig over some dispute never made explicit shortly after Cassie had moved in.

'What do you mean by a "psychic disturb-ance"?' Beatie asked. 'You mean that all of the men want to sleep with her.'

Feek had a habit, when talking about difficult subjects to members of the commune, of pretending to peruse one of the heavy books from his groaning shelves. 'All of the men and several of the women as far as I can gather.'

'And that's a psychic disturbance?'

He finally returned the volume to its shelf. 'Beatie! No one is doing any work!'

'Ah!' said Beatie. 'Then there's no change there then.'

Feek smiled. Beatie's remark addressed what he referred to as a hidden agenda. 'I mean academic work.'

'Yes. The more important academic work.'

'She's your sister. Just ask her to … to…'

'She hasn't done anything, Perry! Everyone

178

keeps propositioning her, that's the problem. The whole house has gone fuck mad, and that had happened long before Cassie came on the scene. I wouldn't be surprised if you've tried her yourself!'

Feek blushed slightly. He looked pained. 'Beatie my darling, what has made you cynical, so combative? When you first came here you were a delight, fresh, open to ideas. Now there is such *reaction* in your soul. What happened?'

'Vigorous dialectic is not reactionary.'

'Ah! Throw my own words back at me would you? You are a charmer Beatie, a charmer.'

'They're just unhappy because she doesn't want to fuck any of them. She's my sister, I know. If she wants to, she will soon enough. If not, she won't. She'll decide for herself. She's a modern woman.'

'Just like you, eh dear Beatie?'

'Just like me. Only more so.'

Feek checked his wristwatch. He was already moving. 'I have to be at Balliol. Tender young minds are calling.'

'You'll be back this evening for the house meeting?'

'Sadly I must stay over at Balliol. I know you'll manage without me.'

Then Feek was climbing into his gleaming Ford, and was gone. He knows, Beatie thought, he knows this evening's meeting is going to be a stinker.

Cassie came over to her. She wore shorts and a blouse knotted around her midriff, making the most of the Indian summer. October of that year saw a late flourish and some unseasonably warm days. Beatie had told her to make the most of it, as living at Ravenscraig could be pleasant in the summer but hard in the winter. 'Has he gone?' Cassie said. 'I stay out of his way cos he keeps trying to feel me up.'

'Best policy,' Beatie said grimly.

On arrival at Ravenscraig Beatie, too, had to get quick at dancing out of Peregrine Feek's lascivious grasp. So did Bernard. For the first six months or more Beatie pirouetted, swivelled, pivoted, shimmied and dodged all advances. She was flattered, and anyway not at all naïve and she was tough-minded enough not to be upset by any of this. She even laughed about it with Bernard. They discussed it. Sexual liberty, was closely tied up with Feek's philosophical anarchy and economic egalitarianism, so it was not as if in this matter he could be said to profess one thing and practise another. Then one day Feek came up behind Beatie while she was in a savage, pre-menstrual mood and she'd bared her teeth and called him some flavoursome things. Feek crept away and had never bothered her since, except for the moments when he claimed to be in need of a reassuring hug, on which occasions Beatie followed the house pattern and obliged.

It had been difficult to work out the values at Ravenscraig. Not the stated rules, which were pinned up in the kitchen, but the concealed mores and the hidden codes. There was sexual licence, for sure. When Beatie and Bernard had moved in there were three other couples and two single women, and it took Beatie a fortnight to work out who was with whom; and this was

180

further confused by the fact that *who* and *whom* were not necessarily married; or that they may be married but nevertheless went to different partners at night-time. And once you'd managed to figure it out, it didn't stop someone approaching you from behind while you were in the middle of the washing up, or on your hands and knees doing a bit of scrubbing in the filthy place. And that the one coming at you from behind might just as likely be one of the women as one of the men.

Bernard and Beatie had managed to survive as a couple because they'd had a pact to get them through the first weeks. They agreed to tell of each pass, of every approach and even of what might be described as nothing more than a twinkle. They shocked each other and made each other laugh, and their relationship hardened in the heat of the unrelenting Ravenscraig assault, and that way they managed to remain loyal. Except for one occasion Beatie would rather forget.

Because it wasn't all laughs. Occasionally jealousies would explode and there were casualties. The Ravenscraig personnel changed frequently, either because of career developments or inability to resolve disputes, but sometimes because of the carnage witnessed in this temple of Eros. In the two years Beatie had been at the commune she'd seen one young man trash the house and a young married woman taken to a mental asylum. If psychic disturbance hawked the commune, it hadn't been brought there by her sister.

'It's a queer run here at Ravenscraig,' Cassie had remarked to her sister more than once,

181

where 'a queer run' was something just this side of Tom the farmer's 'rum do'.

And it was a queer run all round. Even though the house was much grander than anything the sisters had ever lived in, and was owned by a gentleman with sub-aristocratic connections who spoke in a frightfully cut-glass accent, the dwelling was primitive. The wallpaper in most of the rooms was fungal and peeling from the walls, the paint-work was kicked and scuffed and the fixtures in poor shape. Yet the house had a telephone and an indoor lavatory, luxuries the sisters had never pre-viously known. When Beatie had commented on the poor state of hygiene and the uncleanness of the place, someone had used the 'B' word on her.

'Bourgeois?' Beatie had said, confused. She'd only been in the commune for a couple of months. 'Bourgeois? What do you mean?'

'Dear Beatie! This obsession of yours with fussiness and tidiness. It's simply bourgeois!'

It was the first occasion that Beatie had squared up to anyone else in the commune. 'So then, comrade, it's working class, is it, to want to live in squalor? Proletarian, is it comrade, never to stick a bog-brush down a toilet, is that it? The working classes like living in shit, do they? Prefer it do they?'

The company had been rather thrown by Beatie's intemperate outburst; especially the young man who had patronised her five minutes earlier. There was a silence until one of the other women shouted, 'Well said, Beatie!'

That had happened almost two years ago, and was the first outburst in a slow process of

182

learning and disillusion, but one which had never shaken Beatie's faith in the idea that a commune could, with effort, be made to work.

When Beatie and Bernard had arrived at the commune they had found a list of rules pinned to the kitchen wall. The list read:

1. Everyone is responsible.
2. Those with incomes contribute half to the household.
3. House meetings compulsory.

Over the time she'd been there, Beatie and some of the other members had added to that list, though it had been hard work since anarchists were notoriously resistant to rules. Two additions she'd fought for and of which she was proud were:

4. Men also share in the cleaning.
5. Pressure of academic work does not justify evasion of Rule 1.

But she was particularly pleased with:

6. Wash all your dishes, plus at least one other.

Not one of these additions had been easy to achieve, because it wasn't merely the sexual mores that were difficult to adjust to or understand. It was as if everyone else at the commune operated on a set of standards that were always implicit, as if they'd been born into them, whereas she and Bernard had to learn those standards.

When political matters were discussed, for

example, she and Bernard did so in the traditional Trade Unionist fashion, with fire in the belly and anger in the eye. Everyone here had a way of talking in a detached, intellectual manner, as if it were all academic rather than a genuine matter of pounds, shillings and pence to the people who did the counting. Here they seemed to regard caring too much as some sort of a transgression. The other thing people here didn't like was confrontation, in the eyeball-to-eyeball sense. Family life and factory work punching rivets during the war years had given Beatie a sense that if you didn't like something or someone then you should bloody well tell them, and they should tell you back. Here there was disagreement and dispute and varied opinion, but it was never resolved. It always seemed to go by default, or by hint or suggestion or implication, as if passionate conflict was somehow vulgar.

'Yes, it is a queer run,' Beatie said, turning back to Cassie.

'It's not how I thought it would be,' Cassie said. 'It's not that I don't like it here. I just thought it would be different.'

'Like what?'

'More ... like a family. A big family, where everyone looks out for each other. Here everyone just wants to feel each other up and talk into their sleeves. And squabble without looking like it.'

'Come off it Cassie. At home we squabbled all the time with our sisters!'

'Yes, but we didn't mean it. Not really. Not most of the time anyway. And here they do it behind everyone's back.'

Beatie sighed. She couldn't dispute it. She had the evening's meeting on her mind, where she was about to confront one or two individuals who had no stomach for a proper row. Matters tended to get nasty early in the proceedings and nothing could ever be sorted out.

'Oh!' Cassie said, stamping a foot. 'I wish we could have Frank here with us! If there were children here then other people would have to be a bit more grown-up!'

Beatie looked at her sister. 'Cassie, you're a genius. Make sure you are on time for tonight's house meeting.'

Beatie had learned enough about politicking to know that most decisions are made before a meeting and not during one. She gathered what support she could prior to making her proposal. Not counting herself, Bernard and Cassie, each of whom had a full vote as residents, there were only four or five others to talk round. Everyone else had excused themselves from Rule 3 on the get-out of 'pressure of academic work', which might mean anything from punting on the river to romancing the Dean's daughter.

Everyone in the house belonged to some kind of political slate defined when dragooned into standing for election at some hastily called left-wing conference. Beatie had a wise friend in Lilly (Syndicate of Lesbian Artists) and could generally count on George (Marxist-Leninist 4th International). A clear enemy would be Philip (Maoist) who was still stinging from her rebuke about working-class cleanliness. Then there was Robin

185

(Radical Vegetarian and Anti-Vivisection League) who would never make up his mind until the last minute. Tara (Unaligned Anarchist Tendency), too, had supported her along with Lilly on feminist issues, but had lately and mysteriously taken against her. Tara helped out in a left-wing bookstore in town and had told Beatie, coldly, that she would try to cycle back for the meeting in time. Before Tara left Beatie did the head-count and fiddled with the valve on Tara's rear bicycle tyre. Such was the politics of Ravenscraig.

Decisions in the house were made by consensus, though no one person was allowed to wield the heady power of the veto. Thus to effect change, unanimity less one vote was required and this often had the result of maintaining the status quo.

'Comrades,' Beatie said, first on her feet (there was no chairman at Ravenscraig). 'This house urgently needs the presence of children.'

The men looked up. If they had been gazing beadily at the floor it was because they had suspected that Beatie was about to harangue them on the importance of domestic responsibility, arguing that no one who repeatedly failed to clean their own toilet pan once in a while had any right to propose political solutions for the future economy and social policy of the nation. It was always a tricky premise to out-argue. But although they had been initially correct, in that Beatie had originally been planning a make-or-break issue of this running sore, her new position had taken them by surprise.

'It's not as if,' Beatie continued, 'this house has been exclusively adult in its recent history. When

Bernard and I came here there were the three Spencer children; and for a short while Jessie Conrad stayed here with her niece. The place would be more civilised with kids around, and the educational objectives of this commune could be more informally realised.'

Philip the Maoist put on his wire-rimmed spectacles, the better to see through the smoke-screen of capitalist running-dog trickery inherent in this proposal. 'What?' he said evenly. 'Are you suggesting we just go out on the street and kidnap the first passing infant?'

Beatie compressed her lips, but Bernard dived in to save her. 'No, that would be a little extreme even for we radicals, comrade,' he said jovially. 'Though before we talk about the specifics we need to see if the comrades are broadly happy with the idea of children being around the place.'

'Is this really a suitable place to have kids under your feet?' Philip said. 'Ask yourselves. You all know the honest answer.'

'Might cheer the place up a bit,' Lilly said. 'Might make one or two people behave like grown-ups, too.'

'My thoughts exactly,' Beatie said. 'There's a psychological argument to be made that adults can't explore their roles as adults unless they can define themselves against childish behaviour.'

'What?' Philip said.

'She's saying,' said George, 'that an adult can only be an adult in a dynamic relationship.' George blinked happily at Cassie. He'd been thunderstruck ever since her arrival. 'Having kids around helps you to be grown up. Like the

187

communist states of Russia or China keep people as children, so the powerful can maintain their status as the only adults.'

Philip the Maoist let out a deep, deep sigh.

'Let's stick to one subject at a time,' said Robin the Vegetarian Anti-Vivisectionist.

Some two hours later the matter had still not been resolved. Lilly was for, George couldn't see any problem with it, Philip was passionately against and Robin couldn't make up his mind. At Ravenscraig an abstention was a vote for the status quo.

'If you're so keen on children why don't you have your own?' Philip said airily.

Beatie looked furious and compressed her lips a second time.

'That, comrade, is no one's business but Beatie's,' Lilly retorted.

'Anyway,' Robin said, 'whose brats are we talking about?'

'Mine.' Cassie spoke up for the first time. 'And he's not a brat. And his name is Frank. And it's not about capitalism or communism or syndicalism or any other kind of ism. It's about me wanting him here.'

While Cassie spoke a shadowy figure slipped into the room unnoticed, waiting at the door, listening.

'It's about love. I want him here because I love him. And you'd all love him too. You could learn to love him. He's just a little boy. But you are all so busy with what you've got in your heads with this ism and that ism and isms I can't even say that you've forgotten that looking after a little

188

child and being part of his life counts for more than any of your tub-thumping. You ought to remember that it's all about love and if it isn't then it should be.'

'Well spoken Cassie!' said the figure at the back of the room. It was Peregrine Feek. He stepped forward. 'A fire-in-the-belly speech. I don't think there's any answer to that. Perhaps it's time to put this issue to the vote, and I say let the little fellow join us here at Ravenscraig.'

Bernard said, 'Well then. The vote. Those in favour of welcoming Frankie into our commune.'

Everyone but Philip and Robin raised their hands. Robin seemed to be writhing in protracted agony. Feek raised his own hand an inch or two higher. Robin looked at Feek and decided to join the majority.

'Against?'

Only Philip, from the Maoist position, raised his hand against little Frank.

'Well, that's it then,' Bernard said brightly. 'Meeting adjourned. I do so love a democracy.'

Beatie looked out of the window and saw Tara, red-faced, wheeling her bicycle towards the house. Her rear tyre was flat. Beatie suppressed a snigger.

19

Some days later Martha dozed by the fire. The wall clock over her head ticked heavily and each leap of the second hand was prefigured by a tiny drawn-out thump that could still the heart. The fire was low in the grate and the smudgy, sulphurous fumes of low-grade coal had almost suffocated the air when Martha heard at the door not a knocking, but a scuffle or a scrape. She blinked her eyes open, looked at the clock and guessed it to be the postman making his second round of the morning.

Martha waited for the rattle of the letterflap and the flutter of an envelope on the mat, but it didn't come. There was more scuffling outside and a kind of pawing at the door, but no delivery. She waited, but there was nothing. She blinked again, and rose out of her chair too quickly, and for a moment the room swam.

Steadying herself against the back of the chair she allowed the giddiness to subside and then made a slow path to the door, resting her hand against the dresser along the way. 'Gettin' old, my gel,' she whispered to herself, 'gettin' old.'

At the door she reached up and pulled back the draught curtain and felt the stab of rheumatism in her shoulder, too quick to confirm her earlier remark. The bolt whispered as she drew it back and her fingers slipped slightly on the brass latch.

When she'd finally got the door open she found no one there.

Or so she thought. For when she stepped outside she became aware of a brown figure to her left, at the periphery of her vision. She turned and her heart knocked. Sitting on the windowsill was an old woman, squeezing a shopping basket and an umbrella under her arm. On her head was an unfashionable hat stuck through with a pin, of the kind that Martha might have worn when she was a young woman. Her skin had a yellow, jaundiced tinge and her lips were painted with lipstick of a blackcurrant colour.

Martha was taken aback. The woman sat on her windowsill in a posture that might be more appropriate for a girl of eight, not a woman of eighty. There was something immature in the way the old woman held her body and squirmed slightly on her uncomfortable seat. 'What are you doing on my window?' Martha said.

'You want to get yourself down to that spiritualist church,' said the woman on the sill. 'And give that boy a chance.'

And though she was trembling and her heart was still knocking, Martha pointed aggressively at the woman and said, 'And you should bugger off! You hear me? You go and BUGGER OFF!'

The brown figure on the windowsill disappeared like a match flame in a high wind. Martha staggered to the gate and leaned against the fence-post, clutching her heart. She looked up and down the empty street. There was a single sheet of newspaper standing stiff and upright on the pavement, balanced on one corner. Martha

191

went back inside, banging the door behind her, shooting the bolt into place.

'Don't you be coming here,' Martha muttered, agitated but resolute. 'Don't come to *me*. I don't ask you to come. You come here and I'll give you your marching orders. I've got your measure. I'll tell you to bugger off. I damned well will, and every time. Who knows it?'

It was an old trick, and one taught to Martha when she was a little girl by her own mother. 'You tell 'em,' her mother had said. 'You cuss 'em out because they don't like that at all, oh no, and they'll leave you alone. Cuss 'em out. Give 'em a mouthful, bad as you like. They have to learn to leave you alone. So you stand up to them.'

'You hear me? You bugger off!' Martha said out loud again, in case any out there had any lingering doubt. It was an old trick to liberate oneself of spirits and shades and apparitions; and Martha had found in her long life that it generally worked.

She sat back in her chair and rested her face in her hands. But then she heard the gate swing outside and there was another scrabbling at the door. Martha got to her feet for a second time, and had the door open in seconds. It was Eric, the postman.

'Oxford postmark, Mrs Vine! That'd be Beatie wouldn't it? Oxford postmark?'

Martha pushed past the postman and looked up and down the street again. The newspaper standing on end had gone the way of the old woman.

'Are you all right, Mrs Vine?' said the postman, still trying to hand her the letter. 'You look

192

proper turned over!'

'But he's settled, Mother! He's settled!' Evelyn had her dander up. This wasn't happening without a combat.

Ina on the other hand had taken off her spectacles and was dabbing at her eyes. It wasn't that Ina had none of the fight shown by her twin sister; she just had a shrewder sense of what was worth the powder and shot. Still, it didn't stop her from saying, 'And just as he's doing so well at school. And just as he's doing so well at church.'

Ina might have done better than to mention the spiritualist church. Ina and Evelyn didn't know that Martha had that very morning received what they called an 'inspirational message', the very message that had brought on a bout of inspirational cussing. Though Martha knew how to despatch apparitions, she was never so confident in how to deal with their messages, or in how to interpret them.

She knew, incontrovertibly, that the message was about Frank. She also understood that he was passing into some unspecified danger. What it was she couldn't tell, and what Martha knew from repeated experience was that it was very easy to make a mistake in the interpretation. The messenger may have been malign, benign or plain neutral for all she cared. She just didn't like the messengers getting at her all the time, whatever their intentions. But some warning concerning Frank had to be observed, and Martha had already decided that it had something to do with the church. The boy was safe, she knew, with his twin aunts, who had no more capacity for dealing with the spirit world than a pig had for dancing the polka. But she sensed dark birds gathering, and this morning's emissary had come to tell her, however brusque was her reward. That she had the sharp end of Martha's tongue wasn't at issue. Martha had to act to disjoint the steady flow of events, and the wherewithal came in the form of Beatie's letter.

If Martha thought, Beatie had written, that it was timely to rescue Frank 'from the fog of unsavoury spiritualism' (her daughter had picked up some fancy phrases during her time in Oxford, Martha had noted), then everyone at Ravenscraig was ready for him. Cassie was 'in the best of health and in good mental spirits' (Beatie had underlined the word 'mental', quite unnecessarily) but was pining for her boy. He could have his own room and would be exposed to 'some of the finest minds in the country'. (Martha would never guess at how Beatie had had to bite her lip to write that; Beatie had consoled herself with the notion that if Feek and all the others at the commune were not *fine* minded they were at least *high* minded, and she was still at that time ready to confuse these two things.) It would, she promised, broaden the boy's outlook and experience at a time when he could be most influenced to raise his sights. Beatie also wrote a lot of other stuff about Jesuits and psychology; how the child is the man at seven years old; and how this would therefore be Frank's last chance 'before his legs would be forever encased in the concrete of ordinariness'. Martha had to read this last flourish twice,

194

and with raised eyebrows.

All this fanciful language had no effect on Martha. It just happened that the letter coincided with the apparition of that morning. Martha had always been uneasy about the idea of Frank growing up in the spinsterish, cloying, pot-pourri and beeswax spiritualism of the twins, and the apparition had today put bizarre clothes on her anxiety. Above all she felt that Frank needed a man's example: that there should also be a masculine presence around him as he made his way through the world; and that though the twins were irreproachable and for kindness and care could not be bettered, Frank needed about him the savour of the male.

'You're forgetting,' Martha said to Ina and Evelyn. 'You're forgetting that he's Cassie's boy, and that she's calling to him. You've done a good turn by that lad. No one could ever say you've not. But it would be a bad day's work if you tried to hold him back from his natural mother.'

And how, in their tender hearts and in their incomparably sweet natures, were Ina and Evelyn ever going to find an argument against that? Though their chins quivered, and though they brought up the issue of Cassie's incompetence and challenged the wisdom of constantly disrupting the boy's place in the world, when Martha said those words, and with such a tone of moral authority, they knew it was over and that Frank was on his way to Ravenscraig.

It was just a question of when. Martha was easily persuaded that Frank should at least see out his first term at school, and what with Beatie and

195

Cassie coming home for Christmas it would make more sense if they were all to return to Ravenscraig together. They also agreed not to tell the boy of his impending move until after the holiday.

Christmas then was a little more strained than usual. Olive and William remained at odds. Evelyn and Ina were still hurting, choosing to see Frank's imminent move as a rejection of their best efforts; meanwhile recognising each moment as precious they tried to smother Frank with love, whereupon his natural shyness caused him to cringe and retreat from them. Aida's husband Gordon had had a dose of influenza and looked more cadaverous than ever. On the upside, postwar rationing was beginning to relax, and Una was back to her old self but now sporting two healthy, bruising, noisy children.

After Christmas, when Beatie and Cassie took Frank aside to tell him what the near future had in store, he received the news silently. In his head he was conducting a profit-and-loss account. Above anything else he would be back with his mother. He also liked Beatie and Bernard and he understood they would all be living together. He loved his maiden aunts but lately he'd felt suffocated by their overweening affection and their pink face-powders. But he would also miss the company of his exciting new friends at school. Then there was the farm, and what lay hidden.

'Can I go out to the farm before we go?' was how this all reduced down.

'Blowed if we can't!' said Beatie. 'I've learned to drive since I've been in Oxford. I'll ask William if we can borrow his van one day.'

It was a snowy Saturday morning in January when Beatie, Bernard, Cassie and Frank squeezed into the front of William's van and drove out to the farm. William generally didn't need his van on a Saturday but asked Beatie to bring it back by mid-afternoon so that he could make a few deliveries. The snow gusted and drifted against the hedgerows but it wasn't strong enough to settle on the road.

Una was thrilled to see them all, and though Tom was out attending to his beasts, she made them all tea and put out sandwiches, and regaled them with stories of how she hadn't coped with the arrival of her twins. Frank found it easy to drift away from the laughing, chattering adults. He told them he was going into the fields. Cassie made him pull on a scarf and gloves and instructed him not to stray too far from the yard.

When he got outside, Frank immediately started walking. He could see the spire of the church in the near distance, so he just dug his hands in his pockets and made for the village. It took him no more than fifteen minutes before he drew abreast of the mediaeval church. He was about to pass under the lych-gate when a figure bustled out of the church, clutching bags and cloths and a sweeping brush: an odd little woman who looked rather familiar. Frank ducked back, but as she emerged from the gate, the woman spotted him.

'Hey, I knows you!' Raggie Annie said brightly. 'You'm the cousin of they twins up at Tuffnall's Farm, aintcha? What have you to say, hey? Well

197

ain't it cold this morning, ain't it? You'm all wrapped up for it, though. Ain't you all wrapped up? Ain't you got anything to say? Forgotten me have you?'

'Tell it to the bees,' Frank said.

Annie cackled with joy. 'You ain't forgotten me! You lovely!' She dropped her bag and reached over to pinch his cheek, hard. 'No you ain't forgot! That's right.' She stooped to pick up her bag. 'Well I've done me bit of cleaning in the church and earned me bones for the pot so that's me set for the day and now I'm off home, cos I can't stand here freezing all hours.' Annie was already walking away as she said all this, talking almost to herself, leaving Frank to nurse his reddened cheek. He waited until she was out of sight before passing through the lych-gate and into the porch. Checking that he was unobserved he raised the giant iron latch on the huge oak door and passed inside.

The church was so different to the sparse, functional hall used by the spiritualists. Where the spiritualists had to call to the ghosts, it seemed to Frank that this church lived and breathed them. They hung over the pews and hovered at the mullioned windows; they breathed on the stained glass and tried to sip without mouths from the ancient stone baptismal font. Though the church was otherwise empty it was busy with this other-worldly traffic and for a moment he thought that he couldn't do the thing he'd come here for.

He shivered. The place smelled of wax polish and he remembered of course that Raggie Annie was the church cleaner and that she'd only just completed her duties. Frank slowly made his way between the pews and the sometimes leering man-like figures carved into the varnished wood. On reaching the altar rail he paused. He looked back, nursing an uncanny suspicion that someone was watching. Then he stepped forward to the altar, reached up and took the peace bell Tom had showed him. The bell fitted snugly in his coat pocket. There was a small golden plate on the altar, too. A beam of light through the stained glass lit up the plate. Motes of dust danced in the beam. For good measure he took the plate, too. This did not fit into his pocket – he had to hide it inside his coat. He turned and walked quickly between the pews, out through the door and under the lych-gate, and back in the direction of the farm.

On reaching the farm he climbed through the fence and headed for the footbridge across the brook. The early morning snow had drifted among the tangled brambles and the straw-coloured winter grass. He was afraid of muddying his coat if he were to squeeze under the footbridge, so instead he lay down on the icy grass and pushed his head underneath the wooden bridge. Though he couldn't see the Man-Behind-The-Glass from this position, he could hear his teeth chattering.

'C-c-c-c-c-c-c-c-cold.'

'It is cold,' Frank said. 'It's bloody freezing.'

'L–l–l–l–l–lonely.'

'I know. But I've brought you what you asked for. Look.' Frank produced the peace bell and pushed it right up to the glass, so that it could be appreciated. 'Oh-oh-oh-oh-oh,' sighed the Man-Behind-The-Glass in gratitude.

'Is that better?'

'Better better better bbbbbbbbbbbbbbbbbbbbb bell bbbbb–'

'Oh and I got you this, too,' Frank said, producing the gold plate. 'I thought you could eat your dinner off it.'

The Man-Behind-The Glass stopped talking, and his teeth stopped chattering.

'Don't you want it?' Frank was disappointed. Perhaps only the bell was required after all. Frank thought for a moment, and considered taking the plate back to the church. 'Well anyway I've come to tell you I'm going to a place called Ravenscraig which is a place where people live without having to put on a stuffed shirt my aunt says, and where there are scientific minds. We'll be making a better society. I'll be helping them. Which is why I got you the bell. If things get too bad for you, just ring it and I'll probably hear it. Though it's a long way, Ravenscraig. Near Oxford. Though I expect you know that. I expect–'

'Frank! Frank! What the hell are you messing about at down there!' It was Cassie. She grabbed him by the collar and dragged him from under the bridge. 'I've been looking all over for you. Look at you! You're soaking wet! What were you doing under there? Beatie has to get the van back to Uncle William this afternoon and we're all waiting for you. Come on,' said his mother. 'Really Frank, sometimes I think you're away with the fairies. I really do.'

20

School at Ravenscraig was nothing like school in Coventry. In Coventry there were lots of children seated behind tiny desks while the teacher stood at the front of the class and yelled. At Ravenscraig there were only two or three other children, who were brought in by people not living at the house. And every day, and sometimes seven times a day, the teacher changed.

Frank was not party to a resolution that had been passed that every adult at Ravenscraig should take equal pedagogical responsibility for every child presented to them. This meant that Ravenscraig had somehow catapulted itself into the business of offering an 'alternative' to the state-sponsored education available to all. Given Feek's contacts and the educational qualifications washing around the commune, the set-up somehow acquired official approval, and one or two anarchist-minded parents were prepared to offer their tender charges up to the great experiment. On some days, however, these anarchist-minded parents liberated themselves from the responsibility of bringing their kids along, and so Frank might find himself in a class of one, and at the mercy of whichever scientific method of teaching was preferred on that particular day.

His favourite teachers were Lilly, who referred to herself as a 'dyke' but who wouldn't let anyone else call her that, and who taught him to write by painting huge letters on the side of a ramshackle stable-block; and George, the Marxist-Leninist (4th International). Frank couldn't understand a word the excitable upper-crust George said, but seeing what the day's lesson had in store was fascinating and always worth waiting for. Together George and Frank hunted the huge, neglected gardens of Ravenscraig, uncovering earthworms and tree roots and spoors and rich composts. Robin and Tara and others also took a turn, but their idea of a school lesson was to take Frank to some café or to a bookshop where he might be shown the coins in the till as a prelude to understanding the iniquities of the capitalist system.

Other afternoons Philip might take a lesson. Philip didn't seem to want to be there at all. 'Go and look around the house,' he would say. 'Find something interesting. Don't come back until you have found something very interesting.' Philip would then stick his nose in a book. Frank might come back with a piece of string. 'Is that the best you could do? Right then, tell me what it is.'

'It's a piece of string.'

Philip would stare hard at the object. 'No it's not. It's a commodity. What is it?'

'It's a commodity.'

'Good. And what's the value of a commodity?'

One afternoon when it was raining outside, Philip did his usual trick of sending Frank to find 'something interesting'. 'And don't come back with your usual rubbish,' he shouted before parking his nose in the same old book.

Frank wandered the house, never sure if he was

allowed to go into other people's rooms. Most of the communards were out, teaching, shopping for the house or were otherwise engaged. Tara's room was always fascinating. The door was ajar so he poked his head inside. It was empty. He went in and found, on the floor by the bed, what he took to be a balloon. It was an unusual balloon, and someone had put some milky stuff in the bottom of it before tying a knot in the neck.

Philip looked up from his book at the object Frank had carefully laid on the table before him. 'What's that?'

Frank knew the rote. 'It's a commodity.'

'Where did you find it?'

'In Tara's room.'

Philip looked strange. He gently laid down his book, stood up and, staring straight ahead, walked out of the classroom. Frank never saw Philip again.

Occasionally, and with great trumpeting and theatrical airs, Peregrine Feek himself would take on the mantle. Frank's sessions with Feek would be conducted in Feek's study rather than the makeshift classroom of the stable block. Feek called these sessions 'seminars'. Frank would sit in a chair to be bombarded with questions from Feek, who, at a certain point in the proceedings, would get up and stroll about the room wringing his hands, talking at length about some tiny detail encased in one of Frank's muted responses.

Frank wasn't at all sure that he liked these sessions. Feek had a habit of standing behind Frank. Then he might place a hand on the boy's shoulder, gripping tightly. Or he might bend down, whereupon Frank would smell tobacco on the man's tweed suit or feel a soft breath on his neck. One time Feek rested a hand on Frank's knee and the old man's breathing became shallow, and his eyes glazed, until a sound from elsewhere in the house seemed to bring him to his senses, whereupon he suddenly announced that the 'seminar' was over. Frank understood from his mother and from Bernard that he was enjoying a tremendous privilege in personal sessions so decided to say nothing about the incident.

But the huge compensation in all of this was that Frank was close to Cassie. They shared a room. Some nights she even let him in her bed.

'I'll help you sort out a separate room for Frank,' George had told Cassie, with an involuntary twitch of his eyebrows.

'It would be no trouble,' Robin assured her. 'There's a nice room at the front of the house he can have.'

'No need,' Cassie sang merrily. 'Frank will be fine with me.' And, she failed to add, it stops you two from scratching on the door every night. That had been fun for the first few nights at Ravenscraig, but of these Ravenscraig men she preferred George, whose demonstration of interest was always inept.

'We could find Frank a room of his own,' Feek had also said to her.

'Not necessary,' she sang again. Feek himself had never seriously troubled her, apart from a few avuncular pats to the bottom, and if it occurred to her to wonder why he would be making suggestions about re-locating Frank, she put the thought away.

Frank loved the freedom. He was allowed to keep an irregular bedtime – so unlike the strict regime at the twin aunts' house. Though Ravenscraig was a cold, draughty place to live, he could snuggle up with his mother and they would talk and giggle about the strange antics of other members of the commune. Or Beatie and Bernard would drop by at any hour, drinking tea and chatting late into the night until Frank felt his eyelids droop. Bernard or one of the others would lift him into his own bed, and he would feel a kiss planted on his forehead, before the animated whispers of the adults receded as sleep closed him in. The terrific thing about Ravenscraig was that anything could happen, and any one of the communards could go off like a firework at any time.

Usually these explosions were directed at each other, but the evening after Philip had walked out of Ravenscraig, Tara stormed into the kitchen, where Frank was smearing his face with bread and jam. Tara put her freckled face up close against his.

'You little shit!' she screamed at him. Her spittle hit the side of his face. 'Don't you ever, EVER go in my room again, d'you hear me? If I find out you've even been NEAR my room again I'll knock your nasty little head off your shoulders!'

It was too much for Lilly, who pushed Tara away from the boy. 'And you, lady, don't EVER talk to that boy like that again. He's not to blame, so you just shut it!'

'He damned well is to blame! Snooping about in people's rooms!'

'If you want to blame anyone for why Philip left

then blame yourself. Philip left because of something YOU did with Robin, not because of something Frank did. Now get out of here and go and cool down.'

Tara shrieked and stamped her foot. Then she stomped out of the kitchen and slammed the door behind her so hard it rocked off one of its hinges. Frank was left holding a piece of bread close to his jam-smeared mouth. Lilly smiled at him. 'Women, eh Frank? Can't figure 'em.'

Peregrine Feek sauntered into the kitchen to see what the commotion was all about. Seeing Frank there he just made signs with his eyes. Lilly in turn made a sign back with her eyes. Nothing was said. Feek scratched the back of his neck and turned to examine the sagging kitchen door.

Later, Cassie and Frank were relaxing with Beatie and Bernard. Frank loved being in his aunt's room. Bernard usually had the radio playing jazz music softly in the background, and he always paid the company more attention than he did the book resting permanently in his lap. Beatie illuminated the room with candles poked into the necks of wine bottles, and Frank liked to chip the multi-coloured frozen wax fountains that shaped themselves around and obscured the bottle within. Plus the walls were covered with slogans raided from poets, philosophers and politicians. Unable to read them he would pick one at random and ask Bernard or Beatie to tell him what was written there. *'The great only appear great because we are on our KNEES'*. Or *'Beware the radish communist!'*

It was always Cassie who would say, 'What does

that mean? The radish thing?'

'Red on the outside, white on the inside,' Bernard explained.

'I see,' Cassie said, not seeing anything.

Beatie sighed that evening and said, 'I don't know. I really don't know how much longer I want to put up with all of this.'

'But the experiment!' Bernard said, dismayed.

'Sod the experiment. I feel like the white mouse on the wheel here. The wheel is going round with no purpose.'

'What wheel?' said Cassie.

'It's an evolving thing, Beat,' Bernard implored. 'It would be reactionary to give up just because it got tough.'

'But nothing is changing!' Beatie cried. 'It's not really an experiment in communal living, because people leave when they can't hack it, only to be replaced by new people and then we have the same old arguments about who is going to do the menial jobs! There's no progress! It's a radish experiment.'

'You want to go back to life and two vegetables?' Bernard said.

'What?' said Cassie.

'He means like meat and two veg, Cassie. Well, maybe. Perhaps that's what I want. My own house and my own–' And here Beatie stopped. But Bernard knew why she didn't finish her sentence, and though Cassie had never discussed the matter with her sister, she intuited it anyway. Beatie had wanted to add 'and my own children' but she didn't, to spare Bernard's feelings. She and Bernard had been trying for some time to conceive. They'd worked hard at it. They'd even enjoyed working hard at it. It just wasn't happening, and it hadn't been happening for a long time.

Partly they were trapped by their own ideology. Marriage, they had avowed on several occasions, was an outmoded institution configured by an oppressive church and state apparatus dedicated to the subjugation of the individual in the interests of first feudalism and then capitalism. Fidelity to one's partner was an existentialist choice not a social or moral precept. This clarity was only complicated by the presence of children, in which the securing of dedicated emotional bonds had utilitarian value.

Such was the language they used, which was a shame for two young people who deeply loved each other. But what they'd managed to convince themselves it meant was: no kids, no marriage.

Cassie second-guessed all this. She once came close to suggesting to the couple that she have a baby for them. She was convinced that if Bernard stuck it in her just once – and Cassie thought that could be fun – then she would click into pregnancy. She just knew it. Then she could happily bear the child and hand it over to them knowing that she could be with the baby as often as she wanted. For once in her life, however, some resonation in the dynamics of sisterhood stopped her from articulating this thought out loud.

'I don't think it's so bad here,' Cassie said. 'Sure, all the fellows try to feel you up – not you Bernard, you're the only one who doesn't – but at least every day is different.'

Frank had been listening to all of this, not

208

understanding too much of it, but suspecting that important things were being said. The three adults suddenly became aware of how focused he was on their talk. It was Bernard who turned to him and said, 'So what about you, young Frank? Do you like it here?'

Frank had a sense of having been given a giant lever. Three pairs of eyes stared down at him and he dimly understood that they were all looking not at him but to him. Looking to him, that is, for permission to make a decision of significance for all their lives.

''S'all right.'

'Yes, it's all right,' Bernard said. 'But do you *like* it?'

Once again three pairs of eyes burned into him. He was being offered a burden he found too heavy to carry. So he shrugged.

21

Martha kept a packet of wooden spills by the fender so that she could reach over and light one from the fire before touching the flame to her pipe. Only after she'd got her pipe billowing nicely did she accept one of Una's twins on her lap. She was very happy to see Una back to her cheerful self, and even though the twins were a double handful, Una was coping again. Martha's anxieties were always her children's, and those related to her children's children, never her own.

She had enough ailments to make her complaints if she wanted to – arthritis, rheumatism, lumbago, varicose veins and an overactive thyroid gland just for starters – but her concerns were always for the happiness of this child or that. It seemed that there was a finite pot of well-being and it was drunk from in unequal measure. Her matriarchal instinct was to try to even out, wherever she could, by intervention, help, or manipulation. Una was back on course, and with that worry over she could let her mind whittle at another cane stripped from the willow.

In this case her thoughts turned to the deepening rift between Olive and William, and she was only partly attentive to Una's gossip. 'You see,' Una was saying, gamely fighting off the feeding instincts of her own daughter as the other twin blinked through the blue cloud of pipe tobacco smoke, 'it's the National Health Service and all the regulations they are bringing in with it. Hygiene for this and sterile that and disinfected the other. Well that's it. They've told her she can't get her permit or whatever. Said she's not fit. Well, I've never seen her so upset.'

'Yes, that would knock her. Poor old gal. That's what she is, ain't it? I mean that's all she's ever done.'

'Forty years she's been a midwife, Raggie Annie, and do you know she's never lost more than two in any year in all that time. Two babies in any year. Now I'll bet there's not a midwife in the land could claim that. And she were so good with me, Mam.'

'Poor old gal. Is there something to be done?'

210

'Well that's it: she needs a permit. You don't have to be employed by the state but she still needs her licence.'

'But what business is it of anyone if you or your neighbour wants to have her in again?'

'Breaking the law, Mam. She'd be breaking the law.'

Martha puffed thoughtfully on her pipe, shifting the other twin from her left arm to her right. 'She's a funny little dame, there's no doubting that. But I agree with you: she must be the best midwife in all the county.'

'And if that wasn't enough she's just lost that bit of cleaning work she used to do in the church and the hall. Some things went missing out of the church and though nobody's said it direct – that new vicar at St Matthew's, he's a worm you know Mam – the finger has been pointed and they've stopped her doing that bit of cleaning.'

'Raggie Annie? She'd not pinch anything!'

'That's what I say. But they reckon she's going senile.'

'She ain't senile! She's always been that way. But how's the poor old gal to live?'

The question went unanswered as another daughter appeared at the door. 'Hello,' Olive said gloomily.

'Now then!' Martha said. 'Why the long face?'

'I told you not to come back. I told you it would just be the once.'

'So why did you let me in the door, then?' William said, tamping a cigarette on the box before lighting it and sitting back in the armchair,

211

crossing his legs, trying to look more relaxed than he felt.

Her back to the window, Rita stood with her arms crossed. 'I told myself I wouldn't. Not after the way you rushed off that last time.'

'Sorry about that. I just...'

Rita blinked. 'You ought to go. You should, you know.'

'Can't stop thinking about you, Rita.'

'Don't tell me that.'

'Can't stop. I think about you last thing at night and you're on my mind first thing when I wake up. I think about you when I'm at work. If I smoke a cigarette I can still smell you on my fingertips.'

'You're such a dirty bugger.'

'It's hell for me. It ain't fun, Rita, I'll tell you. I used to think that blokes who did this were having a good time. Now I know different.'

'How do you think it is for me, Mr Married-with-kids? I'll tell you something that will put you off me. I thought I'd got over Archie. I thought I'd manage and never have to think about another man. Pushed the thought aside, I did. But then you came along all moping and staring at me with your big brown spaniel eyes – yes, I know what you do – and you started me off again. So I went up town one night and I said to myself, Rita tonight you're going to sweat whatever happens, and I found myself a decent-looking bloke and went down an alley with him, a dark alley behind the bombed-out cathedral, and all because of you. There, has that put you off me? Mr Know-it-all? So don't tell me it ain't fun for you because it's not a picnic for me, neither.'

'I'm sorry, Rita.'

'You can't just start a woman off, you know. You just can't do that.'

'I know.'

'Do you? Do you really know? Women don't switch it on and off like you blokes do. You paw us and you wake up what's in us and then you rush away or you don't come back or you get yourself killed–' Rita fell on to the sofa, sobbing, her face in her hands and her knees pressed together. William glanced up at the framed photograph of Archie smiling down at him.

Rita quickly stopped her sobbing, brushing her eye with a thumb. 'Anyway, you're not coming here to upset me.'

William moved across to offer her a cigarette. She accepted it and he sparked his lighter for her. Then he sat down again. They sat in silence as she smoked her cigarette.

'I can smell you from across the room, Rita. You have a lovely smell.'

'Oh stop! Don't you ever stop?'

'Really. I think I have a highly developed sense of smell. I'm working with fruit and vegetables every day and I've got so I don't even need to handle the produce when I go down to the markets. I can just stand over them and I know what's ready and what's over-ripe and how many days it's got, or if it's a bad crop. Maybe it's a talent I have. Maybe it's my only talent.'

'No it's not,' Rita said, looking at him.

'Anyway, I can stand over it and catch a scent of it, and I know. And I like the scent of you, Rita. It hasn't left me since that last day I was round here.'

'What are you saying, William?'

'I'm just saying that the smell of you is on me, and it won't go away. It hangs on me like a ... like a ... ghost. Keeps calling me back here.'

Rita stood up. She folded her arms and crossed her legs slightly, putting one foot in front of the other, so that she looked like a caryatid carved into the stone portico of an ancient temple. 'You must go. You must.'

William got to his feet, stepped over to her and put his hand into the rich mass of red hair tied at the back of her neck, and he pressed his lips on hers. She didn't resist him. Then he pushed her back against the wall next to the mantelpiece, and she prickled as he kissed her neck.

'I don't believe this is happening again,' Rita said.

A moment later he had his hand between her thighs and was parting her knickers from her skin and pressing his fingers deep inside her. Then he sank to his knees, yanked her knickers to her ankles and pushed her skirt up around her hips. She grabbed the hair at the nape of his neck, twisting his head back so that he had to look up at her. Then she let him go and he plunged his head into her muff, sinking his tongue inside her as far as he could, withdrawing only to find the spot, and when he did she went into a spasm, flinging her arm back so that it knocked over a brass candlestick on the mantelpiece. The candlestick toppled over, dislodging the centre-piece clock, which in turn nudged the framed photograph of Archie off the shelf.

William heard the clatter and glanced down at

214

the photograph, relieved to see that the glass in the frame had not broken. Archie only smiled up at him, pleased to see what a virtuoso performer William had become on the calliope of the pink kazoo.

22

'Now then young Frank, what shall we talk about today?' Feek was in an ebullient mood, the gloom of the cold season briefly relieved by a spell of winter sunshine. Sunlight poured through the south-facing windows of Feek's cluttered study. They could see other members of the commune moving back and forth across the yard. Cassie and Lilly were paused not far away to chat.

Frank liked some things about Feek's study. The oak desk had a huge globe that the eminent professor allowed him to spin; a skull he was permitted to touch; and a gyroscope that Feek sometimes set in motion for the boy. The walls were lined with books from floor to ceiling, opened out only by the large, ornate mirror hanging over the mantelpiece. It was a nice place to sit and have lessons, but there were other things rendering the study less than flavoursome.

Perhaps it was the smell of the study that he found discouraging. Or rather, since he couldn't separate the two, it might have been the smell of Feek himself. That same smell had got into the fabric of the chair Frank had to sit on; it drifted

215

from the row upon row of dusty books, on the shelves; it nestled in the weave of the rug and was triggered whenever the rug was walked upon; and it lodged in Feek's tweed jacket whenever he got up close to Frank.

'I have an idea,' said Feek this sunny afternoon, 'that today you're ready to face a little of what we call philosophy. Do you know what that is, Frank?'

'No.'

Feek had taken an increasing interest in Frank's education. Beatie remarked to Bernard that they actually saw more of the old man at Ravenscraig since Frank's arrival, rather than less which had been the original fear. She had wondered if the presence of the child might keep him away. But Feek claimed to have been impressed by the boy's 'enquiring mind' and stimulated by his 'freshness of thought'. So much so that he now freely offered two sessions a week to the lad. What better education could a boy possibly have? Frank's gain was Balliol College's loss, surely.

'Philosophy,' Feek opined, digging his thumbs into the waistband of his trousers and addressing Frank as if he were a crammed lecture hall, 'is the search for wisdom. It's a treasure hunt.' Then he beamed, disconcertingly, pleased to have found the right metaphor to appeal to a six-year-old. 'It is not, as some people have claimed, the love of Sophie.'

Frank blinked.

Abashed at the feebleness of a joke that normally garnered a few sycophantic laughs, Feek fell back on elaboration. 'Yes indeed, well Frank, philosophy is an enquiry into the ultimate reality of things, or with the general principles of causes of things, of ideas, of human perception, of ethics even.'

Frank looked out of the window to where his mother chatted with Lilly.

'Perhaps I should just spin the globe again Frank? And you can stop it with your finger?' Feek smote his own brow. 'No, come on let's not give up so easily. Let's not. What about this: philosophy is the hunt for truth. Do you know what truth is, Frank?'

'It's always hidden.'

Feek's eyes blazed open. His white eyebrows levitated. 'Good! Very astute!'

Frank wasn't being astute. He was merely parroting one of his grandmother's lines, that the truth is always hidden until it slaps you in the face.

'And what is it that lies hidden?'

Frank blinked.

'Come on Frank, dig deep for that treasure. What secrets lie buried?'

Frank looked at the mirror above the mantelpiece, through which he could see the reflection of Cassie and Lilly, talking outside. 'The Man-Behind-The-Glass.'

Following Frank's gaze, Feek turned to look at the mirror, seeing only the boy reflected there. 'Curioser and curioser! How extraordinary! The lad is a metaphysician. And how does life appear through the looking glass?'

Frank turned his gaze back to Feek, suddenly embarrassed by the intensity of the professor's interest. Feek leaned forward, twisting his lower lip between thumb and forefinger. Frank blinked again.

Feek cleared his throat. 'I mean to say, what does the man behind the glass look like?'

Frank got up off his chair and moved across to Feek's desk. He pointed to the human skull grinning behind the pen-and-ink stand.

Feek's snowy eyebrows jiggled in excitement. 'Good lord! The boy is a genius!'

Cassie had followed Lilly out of the yard and up the stairs to her room, where Lilly was brewing a pot of tea. She was the only one who had a small kitchen in her room, partitioned from her living quarters by a curtain. Lilly, a clinical psychologist in waiting, had offered Cassie some free counselling sessions since her arrival at Ravenscraig. Cassie did her best to participate with an open heart, but she found the interrogation a little intense, and was inclined to make excuses for not keeping the thing up with the commitment and regularity Lilly seemed to want from her.

Lilly handed her a steaming cup of tea. 'You seem to have something on your mind today, Cassie.'

'Oh, it's Frank. I glanced through the window of Perry's study and I didn't think he looked very happy.'

'Do you worry about Frank?'

'I do! I do! All the time! Well, not at all the time and that's the problem. I mean when I have one of my blue periods as Beatie calls them, then I forget I'm even his mother; I mean I know that must mean I'm not a good mother oh damnit

Lilly! You've started me on one of your sessions already, haven't you, and I was just talking!'

'That's all we are Cassie. Two friends talking.'

'I know but is this a counselling session or a cup of tea?'

'I can put on a white coat if you want.'

'I don't mean that.'

'Yes you do. I'm trying to be a friend to you, I'm trying to be a help to you. The job of asking what you are and why you do things doesn't stop when the hour is up. I also take the view that no one has a problem that is not everyone else's problem. Talking about life is part of life. And it seems best if you talk about the things you do when you're *not* having one of your blue periods as you call them.'

'Oh I can't remember what it is I do at these times. That's just the problem.'

'I think you can, Cassie. I think you do remember. I think you can go there if you want, but you shut it out. And if you remembered it, then maybe it wouldn't need to happen to you so often.'

'What wouldn't?'

'Whatever it is.'

'Do you think Frank is all right?'

Lilly sighed. 'I thought we were going to talk about you.'

'It's just that Perry ... well, sometimes he seems a little bit creepy.'

'Perry is ... in control. Shall we talk about you? Last time you were telling me of the ECT they gave you at the hospital.'

'I still get bad dreams about it. And the smell of rubber I can't stand. They put a rubber gag on me.'

219

'Do you recall the shocks?'

'The shocks were not painful. At least not in the way you would think. It was what was inside the shocks. You would be strapped down with your gag and you would feel a bump and a wheel would turn, a wheel as big as the seasons of the year and that would release a wind blowing from the inside of your soul, but a wind with teeth and it rips out a small part of you, and off it goes, carrying that small something in its jaws; and I always feel sick afterwards, and I never want it again.'

'They shouldn't do that.'

'They shouldn't. They shouldn't be allowed to strap people down and gag them and turn that big wheel. They shouldn't.'

'Stay with me Cassie, and I'd never let them do that to you again.'

Cassie looked at Lilly to see if she was joking; saw that she wasn't; chose to behave as if she was. 'Gosh, what a handful that would be for you!'

'Where do you go, Cassie? On these strange, dark flights of yours? Where do you go and what do you see?'

Bernard came home that afternoon, exhausted from teaching at the local secondary school. His initial enthusiasm and fire for the job was being blunted by reluctant pupils and obdurate colleagues. He sank into a chair nursing his old dream of becoming an architect as Beatie helped him off with his boots. 'Where is everyone?'

'Tara is fucking Robin, Lilly is counselling Cassie, Perry is teaching Frank,' Beatie sang in a rote voice.

'Only Tara and Robin doing any work, then,' Bernard said.

Beatie loved Bernard for his humour. He knew what she was thinking. 'I've decided to stop doing the cleaning, the cooking, the shopping and all the thinking like a mother. I've decided to stop being like Mam.'

'The only difference between you and Martha,' Bernard said, 'is that Martha is successful at getting everyone to take their share.'

'Well I'm going to stop. We'll see what happens. Tonight. As usual, nothing has been done.'

'Oh,' said Bernard. 'Well that will be fun. What about Frank? Perry's spending a lot of time with him lately. Do you think he's all right?'

Frank was not feeling terribly comfortable. Peregrine Feek's disconcerting habit of stalking the room did not abate. He prowled slowly about the place as he spoke, at great length, of things Frank couldn't even dimly understand. Feek walked behind Frank's chair and placed a hand lightly on each of Frank's shoulders. 'There is a point you see, in which the truth will insist on breaking through the surface of things and speaking to us, often in a contradictory voice, Frank. It's a kind of alchemy, philosopher's stone if you like, in which a union of opposites snaps into place, male and female, young and old, until' – and here Feek put his mouth very close to Frank's ear and whispered the word – *'Bang!* The world as we know it falls away, the surface of the earth peels back and even rationality – *rationality itself, Frank* – is revealed as no more than a construct, a useful tool which will aid us so far and then no further. Oh why is it Frank that we must live out our lives by the lights of lesser men? Can you tell me why?'

Frank shook his head. He couldn't.

Feek walked back around to his chair opposite Frank and pulled it closer, dropping into it so that their knees almost touched. 'It was a rhetorical question, Frank. That means one that needs no answer. Frank, you know if you were to stay with us here at Ravenscraig, we could train you up to be the finest mind in the country. Of that I have no doubt. How would you like that Frank, eh my boy? What would you say to that?' Feek grabbed Frank's bare knee, just below the hem of his short trousers, and shook it slightly.

Frank looked at the hairy, slightly clammy, liver-spotted hand and wished that Feek would remove it. But Feek didn't. The professor's eyes were half closed and his eyelashes fluttered slightly. His breathing was short, and he exercised his fingers under the hem of Frank's shorts.

'The shocks, you see,' said Lilly, 'they would make you forget. That's how it works. But I think you need to remember.'

'It's true. I couldn't even remember my sisters' names after they'd done that to me.'

'So why won't you remember? Why is it I think you are lying to yourself?'

'Get on with you, Lilly!'

'Don't be insulted Cassie. We all do it. Lying is an emblem of our humanity. We lie and we pretend we don't lie. Look at this place. Isn't it a

222

lie? They're all subscribing to notions of progress and a better society, and that's good if it helps people carry on and do good, but here it's a joke.'

'So why do you stay if it's so bad?'

'I didn't say it was bad, or that the people here are bad. At least not all of them. But they allow me to be myself, which I can't be in other places.'

'Oh! You mean being a dyke and all?'

Lilly offered a late smile.

'No offence Lilly. I've thought about that, and it's true some girls are so drop-dead pretty that you'd like to just rip their blouses off and give their titties a suck, but they're no substitute for having a man inside you, are they? I mean, when your legs and arms are wrapped around a fellow and he's just like a little baby and his eyes turn gooey, well God! I love that! I really do. Don't you really prefer that?'

'We're supposed to be talking about you, not about me,' Lilly said sadly. 'You know, you're so beautiful Cassie. I can see why the men go mad for you. I think it's your wildness. They want to be touched by that. It's enough to wake a dead man, this thing that you have. I hope they never find a "cure" for that. If they do, a light will go out of the world.'

'Now you're teasing me,' Cassie laughed.

'No I'm not. Give me a little bit of that thing, Cassie. Tell me where it is you go. Tell me what happened on the night of the Coventry blitz. Can't you tell me?'

23

Everyone suspected that the big storm was coming, but Cassie seemed to know exactly when. There had already been numerous raids on the city between June and October of 1940, when bombs had rained down on Coventry. Factories, shops and cinemas were left twisted and smoking. There were even incidents of German planes machine-gun strafing civilians in the street. The civilian injury list was high, and almost two hundred people were killed outright in these early raids.

After all, Coventry was located exactly at the heart of the country and Adolf Hitler wanted to show what a surgeon he was: show how the heart could be cut out. Coventry was a beautiful mediaeval and Georgian rosette town, boasting resplendent cathedrals and picturesque antiquarian buildings, a heritage showpiece of the English Midlands. And after all again, Coventry had manufactured the Armstrong-Whitworth Whitley bomber, the first plane to penetrate German airspace, and the main instrument of the torment of Munich. No, not surgery. The Fuhrer wanted to show he could bring his fist down on it and turn it to dust. The storm *would* come, but if only the city might know *when* then the fatalities might be minimised.

But Cassie knew. Sixteen years old, going on

seventeen, exactly how she knew is unspeakable, but she knew it in her water, in her bowels. Her blood coursed differently. Perhaps it was the moon fattening in the night sky which spoke to her; whatever it was she knew better than to tell. She'd already learned that if she did try to tell, no one would believe her; and that after they'd failed to listen they would call her a jitterbug. So she knew with certainty, but did not speak.

Like the dead.

'The dead can hear you,' Martha had said, 'but they can't get their words out.'

It started when she woke early one morning with music playing in her head. Her sleep patterns, already disrupted by the nights spent in the Anderson shelter at the bottom of the back garden and by the sirens, had broken like an egg yolk, spilling something of her. She felt a mild flow inside her and put her hands between her legs. The wetness she found there made her think of the residue of sleep, a slippery vernix left behind by her dreams. While Beatie and Martha still slept in the other rooms she pulled on her dressing gown and went downstairs.

The haunting music was still playing in her head. It was a piece she'd heard several times, familiar, comforting. Cassie switched on the radio. It was tuned to the BBC Home Service, and the same piece was playing, perfectly segued with the version sounding in her head. She switched the radio off and although it was fainter, she continued to hear the music, without it missing a beat or dropping a note. After switching the radio back on again she sat on a chair and stared hard at the radio until the piece had finished playing. When the music stopped on the radio, it stopped inside her head, too.

Cassie went upstairs to her room, dressed hurriedly and reached under her bed for a tin tea caddy painted Japanese lacquer-style. In it were her savings. After emptying the caddy into her purse she went downstairs again, put on her coat and allowed the door to click quietly behind her as she let herself out. The morning was cold and sharp and there was a rime of frost on the ground. She walked into the city.

Up Trinity Street to the top of the town and directly to Paynes music shop. Too early: it was closed. She stood in the doorway and waited.

It was an hour and a half before the manager of the store arrived to open up.

'You're keen,' he said, producing his glittering bunch of keys. He had to wave his hand at Cassie to get her to stand aside for him.

'I want a record player,' Cassie said as soon as they'd got inside the shop. 'A new one.'

The store manager switched on the lights. 'Let me get my coat off,' he said. 'Where's the fire?'

Coming, said the voice in Cassie's head.

He took her over to the latest box players. Cassie was mesmerised by the little explosions of hair in his nostrils and ear holes. 'This is a HMV gramophone. It has a Bakelite playing arm and it comes in this attractive beech cabinet–'

'Yes.'

'Yes?'

'Yes. I'll have it.'

'You haven't asked me how much it is.' The

226

manager eyed this slip of a girl suspiciously. 'How much can you afford?'

Cassie emptied her savings out of her purse. The manager sighed. 'I've got some second-hand cabinets over here. Let's see what we can do.'

Cassie could just afford one of the machines on offer. It took her last penny. Then she said, 'I want a record. I don't know what it's called. But you'll know it. It goes like this.' She hummed the music that had been playing both on the radio and in her head that morning.

'"Moonlight Serenade". I've got it in stock but how are you going to pay for it? I've just let you off a few shillings on that cabinet and that's cleaned you out, hasn't it?'

Cassie merely fixed her eyes on the man and crossed her legs at the ankles. She swayed, very slightly.

The manager seemed cross, but he stepped behind his counter and sorted through the discs until he found the Glen Miller recording. 'I'll let you have it, but you're going to have to bring the money in when you've got it. Understand? I don't know why I'm doing this.'

It's because I've got power over you, thought Cassie.

Cassie lugged the record-playing cabinet home by its carrying handle. It was heavy and she had to keep stopping to switch hands, but she was unwavering. On the way home an ARP officer in a tin hat, hands on hips, interposed himself on the pavement before her. 'Oi girlie, where's your gas mask?' he shouted in a bullying tone.

She stepped round the ARP man, leaving him

to gaze after her.

Martha and Beatie were up and about when she got home. Cassie bustled into the sitting room and squeezed by them without a word. 'Where've you been?' Martha called. 'Do you want some breakfast?'

'Whatever have you got there?' Beatie said, eyeing the record player. Cassie only bumped upstairs without a word. 'She's getting to be a proper moody girl,' Beatie complained.

'Not like someone I could name,' Martha said.

Beatie was about to fire back an answer, but there came to stop her the strains of 'Moonlight Serenade,' drifting from Cassie's room. The sound filled the house like a dew-backed mist.

In the next few days, Cassie played the piece over and over and over. She would lie on her bed, sometimes naked, listening. At first, Beatie and Martha were merely irritated. Martha had already quizzed her daughter about why she'd blown her savings on the record player without getting an answer. Beatie had actually gone out and bought Cassie two more Glen Miller hits, and an armload of stuff a friend at the bomber factory had found too sad to keep because it had belonged to a brother in the navy killed at sea. But Cassie didn't play any of it. She sat upstairs in her room, spinning 'Moonlight Serenade'. And if Martha or Beatie complained too aggressively, then she merely went out, and stayed out, for long periods of time.

At night, wide awake with whatever it was that had broken her sleep and when her mother and sister absolutely would not tolerate any sound coming from her room, she huddled in a blanket on the edge of her bed, watching the moon fattening slowly, maturing, feeding her with more energy as if on a silver umbilical cord. If the sirens came she was ready, and would help the others pull a few things together for the shuffle to the Anderson shelter; have the kettle boiled for a flask of tea while they were still blinking and complaining; especially helpful to Beatie who was doing ten-hour shifts on the bombers and who needed the sleep, unlike Cassie.

Most of the sirens at that time were false alarms, and Cassie knew it; knew they might as well sleep on, that it would be Birmingham or some other Midlands city catching it that night. But even in the shelter she couldn't nap. One night some time before dawn Beatie got up to relieve herself in the tin pail. Martha, blinking, dozy, said, 'Hark! Is that the all-clear?'

'No Mam, it's Beatie pissing in the bucket. Go back to sleep.'

Beatie was having a hard time for sleep. Like many of the women of Coventry she was under pressure to work ten and sometimes twelve-hour shifts for the war effort. *Buck up girls! Let's bomb the hun!* This she did readily, and since the pay was good she'd never had so much money in her pocket; but the sirens going off on so many nights like this left her exhausted and irritable.

One evening Cassie heard her sister calling up the stairs, 'Cassie if you play that bloody thing one more time – just one more time – I'm coming to sort you out! You hear me Cassie?'

Cassie didn't answer. She lay on her bed in her bra and pants. 'Moonlight Serenade' played on. When it stopped, Cassie languidly reached over and put it on again. After a moment came the thundering of shoes on the stairs. Beatie threw open the door, made straight for the record player, lifted the stylus arm, plucked up the record from the turntable and broke it over her knee. Then she turned to look Cassie in the eye.

Cassie didn't flinch. Beatie screamed and thundered back down the stairs. Cassie didn't mind. She'd got the music in her head, and perfectly, note for note. She could switch it on or off any time she wanted to.

What's more she could repeat that trick with the radio over and over. Many times she heard music playing in her head, and would go to switch on the Home Service to find the same tune broadcasting loud and clear. Without saying anything she tested this ability scientifically. It was clear to her that she could somehow 'hear' radio broadcasts in the thin air. She didn't need radio receiving equipment. She somehow *was* the equipment.

Though she was not so stupid as to try to tell anyone else about this.

Other things were going on in her body. Her breasts had plumped slightly, and her nipples were tender and sensitive. The lips of her vagina, too, were swollen, and she felt an itch or a trickle deep inside her. She needed to masturbate often, and before Beatie snapped the slate disc she would lie under a sheet on her bed stroking her clitoris and squeezing her nipples while 'Moonlight Serenade' teased her on. And in the street,

230

too, it was obvious all this wasn't just one way. Even as a virgin she could calculate the effect she was having on men. Off-duty soldiers and sailors and airmen would be burning for her, it was plain from the way they sized her up. Plus she could make men's heads turn – not in the usual figure of speech but literally: all she had to do was focus her gaze on the back of the neck of a man somewhere in her vicinity, perhaps on the bus or while waiting in a queue with her ration-card, and after a moment the subject would have to turn and look at her. It worked without fail. She was accreting powers to herself, she knew that. What powers they were she had no idea, but they were extraordinary. She'd used them on that man in the record shop, but he didn't know it. They never did know. They were easy. Men were easy.

And that was just part of it. It was knowing that the storm was coming that most excited her. Terrified and excited her.

On the night of 12 November she went to a dance with Beatie. Martha had stopped worrying about what the girls got up to a long time ago. Though Cassie was only sixteen she could easily pass for a twenty-year-old, and Martha had given up trying to keep her in. Though she'd been stricter with her other daughters, something about the incidence of death all around had relaxed her with Cassie; and she'd learned early that Cassie would go her own way whatever obstacles were placed before her. But she did extract a promise from both her daughters that they would seek proper shelter, and *not* to try to find their way home should they get caught in a raid.

Cassie was in a highly excitable state as the two stepped into town together. The moon was moving into its fullness, like a silver autumn gourd, and though it was a clear and rather frosty night, the searchlights sweeping the starry sky passed across the three spires of the city, prickling the night. Beatie was trying to get her to calm down.

She might not have bothered. As soon as they got into the dance hall Cassie heard the band and broke away from Beatie's side. When Beatie caught up with her she was already jiving with an airman, his hair slicked back and his eyes dripping with ardour. 'Don't give it all away too quick,' was all Beatie could whisper, but Cassie was spinning and waving her hands in the air.

That jitterbug.

Within the hour Cassie was in the shadows of the cathedral in Bayley Lane, her back against the cold, damp mediaeval wall and her skirt around her waist. There were no streetlights because of the blackout. 'Wow, you're in a hurry,' said her airman as she fumbled with his belt.

'We might never see each other again,' Cassie said, clinging to the fleecy collar of his leather flying jacket. 'Imagine that. And then we'd have missed the chance to fuck.' *And I'd never lose my cherry*, she thought.

'Hey, you think like a bloke,' he said.

'Does it put you off?'

'No, no ... it's just ... and oh you smell good.'

'Stop talking. Let's do it.'

A siren began moaning, very close. 'Fuck and damn.'

'Ignore it,' Cassie said. 'It's not tonight.'

232

'What?'

'Maybe tomorrow night. Or the next night. But it's not coming tonight.'

'Hey, and they ought to have you down at Bletchley, if you know all that. You know, intelligence service. I'm sorry, I can't do much with that siren going off in my ears. How old are you anyway?'

Cassie dug her hand into the airman's trousers, stroking the bell of his cock with her thumbnail. He flinched, and settled back into her arms again. 'Can't do what?' Cassie shouted. She was having to bellow to make herself heard above the siren. Someone ran past them on their way to a shelter. Then she put her tongue in his ear.

'Christ!'

Cassie glanced up at the cathedral spire and at the crisscrossing searchlights raking the sky overhead. She knew the airman wanted to get himself off to the nearest air-raid shelter, but with his cock fattening in her hand he couldn't tear himself away. 'Do it,' she said.

He tugged his trousers down and he hooked the back of Cassie's leg over his arm. He had to push her knickers out of the way and come at her from the side, almost lifting her from the ground as he made to enter her, their eyes locked together in that ancient place, under the sky-pricking spire, under the crossbeams of the searchlights, inside the demonic and melancholy howl of the siren. He fell back. 'It's no good. I can't – not with that thing going off right in my ear.'

'What's the matter?'

The airman fumbled. He looked up at the sky,

at the searchlights raking the clouds. Then he looked down again. 'It's just not happening for me. Can we please go to the shelter? My arse is getting cold.'

Cassie pulled up his trousers for him. Hand in hand they strolled towards the shelter on Much Park Street. An ARP man standing outside the shelter said, 'Don't 'urry yourselves, will you?'

'It's all right,' said the airman glumly. 'It's not coming tonight.'

'Another bleedin' know-it-all,' the ARP man said sourly.

The airman whispered as they went down into the basement of Draper's Hall, 'Don't mind him. He just needs to get laid.'

Not the only one, Cassie's voice said.

They spent an hour in the shelter together before the all-clear came. His name was Peter and he was a navigator. He was twenty, and seemed worldly and mature to Cassie. She was cold so he pulled his leather flying helmet out of his pocket and put it on her head. He walked her all the way home and they kissed again in the alley running between the houses. He put his hand on her forehead. 'You've got a fever.'

'I'm all right,' Cassie said. 'Really I am.'

But the moment had passed. Cassie sighed when she knew it wasn't going to happen. She made to give him back his flying helmet. 'You keep it,' he said.

'Won't you get in trouble for losing it?'

'Yeh. Goodnight Cassie. You're too lovely, you are. Too lovely.'

And he went back to his war.

The next day Cassie lay in bed late, touching herself, thinking of her airman and other handsome men, sleeping fitfully. Now as well as the music her head was full of other sounds: high frequency whistles and intermittent morse signals and snatches of foreign language. When she rose the house was empty. Beatie had gone to work and Martha had left a note on the kitchen table to say that she had popped out to do some shopping.

Munching on the remains of Beatie's cold toast Cassie switched on the radio, fiddling with the tuning dial. The frequency whistle rose and fell, throbbed and hummed. There was morse code. There was guttural language. She didn't need an interpreter. It was going to be the following night for sure. Last night the moon had been almost full. Tomorrow night it would be complete. Cassie shook with excitement. It was plain. Adolf Hitler would send his bombers to Coventry tomorrow night. That is what he would do.

'There you are,' Martha said, letting herself in, pulling off her hat. 'Sleeping the sleep of the dead. It'll do you no good, all this lying in.'

'Tomorrow night. They're going to bomb us tomorrow night.'

'Eh? What's that?'

'More than before. More than last month. The big raid. It's tomorrow night. I know.'

'Know? How can you know?'

'It's a full moon tomorrow night. It's coming. It's going to rain fire here in Coventry Mam.'

Martha walked over and put her hand on Cassie's forehead. 'You're shivering. You're burn-

235

ing up. Do you want to go back to bed?'

Cassie hadn't even known what the airman had meant in his reference to the intelligence mansion at Bletchley, the government code and cypher school. Its very existence was supposed to be top secret. But the day before Cassie met her airman at a dance the Bletchley school had succeeded in decoding a recent German transmission. The transmission laid down the signal procedures for an operation codenamed not Moonlight Serenade but Moonlight Sonata, implying that a three-pronged attack would be launched against a British city on the night of the full moon. On the same day a captured German pilot was overheard telling his cellmate that a three-phase raid would be made on either Coventry or Birmingham on or around 15 November.

The Germans had invented a radio navigational system known as the X-Gerat, guiding a plane to its target and automatically triggering the bomb-release on arrival. The X-Gerat used four radio transmitters sending radio beams from different locations. It comprised one main beam aligned on the target and three intersecting beams. The German pathfinder pilots flew parallel to the main beam until they hit the first intersecting beam. That was their instruction to change course and fly directly along the main beam. Twenty miles from the target they passed through the second intersecting beam, a signal to press a button starting a clock. Five miles from target they crossed the third beam, an instruction to press another button that stopped the first hand of the clock and started a second hand ticking. The bombing run had begun. When the two hands came together, the bomb load was automatically released on the people below. It was an efficient system for obliteration bombing.

Bletchley had also uncovered signals to special bombing units, all starting with the code-word Korn. They also decrypted information revealing that special Luftwaffe calibration signals would commence at one p.m. on 14 November.

Among the brilliant mathematicians, linguists, logisticians, chess-players and crossword specialists was a brilliant Oxford philosopher and philologist named Peregrine Feek. Though Feek can't be blamed for the clumsiest of errors committed by Air Intelligence, which calculated that the full moon rose on the night of 15 and 16 November rather than the night before, at 03.23 hours. Air Intelligence also indicated to the authorities that possible raids would be directed at London.

At 13.00 hours on the afternoon of 14 November the German calibration signal was detected. Two hours later British Fighter Command were satisfied that the X-Gerat beams were aligned on Coventry. The Air Ministry warned the RAF home commands that Coventry had become a special target.

They might also have warned Coventry. The city's anti-aircraft batteries and barrage-balloon units might have appreciated the tip-off; not to mention the Coventry Fire Brigade, the Chief of Police, and the local ARP. They might have tipped the wink to the mayor of the city, or rumoured it at the Coventry and Warwickshire hospital.

They chose not to. Cassie was the only person in Coventry who had been informed.

At one o'clock that afternoon, Martha and Cassie were about to sit down to lunch. Martha switched on the radio for the news. Just as it came on Cassie felt something click in her head, like a switch being thrown. 'It's started,' she said.

'Yes yes,' Martha said, bringing the teapot to the table, thinking Cassie referred to the news broadcast.

'I don't mean the news. Do you think we should all go out to the farm? That would be best. We should go out to Wolvey where Tom and Una are. Safer, Mam.'

'I can't be bothered with that game,' Martha said. 'If Adolf wants me he'll have to come and get me.' When the early raids had started in June they had, like many other Coventry citizens, all gone out together to stay in the country. But what with the small aerodrome at Bramcote so close to the farm, they had found the concentration of bombs denser and somehow more immediate than when they stayed shivering under the stairs in the days before the Anderson shelter was erected.

'Well I'm glad. I don't want to go to the farm. I want to stay. Stay and be here. Stay and help. That's it. I want to help.' Cassie spoke rapidly. Martha had seen it before in her. A repetitive but cheerful chatter. 'But you and Beatie, Mam, I want you and Beatie to stay in the shelter. While I'm out. Helping.'

'Is it your time of the month?' Martha said.

Some time after six o'clock that evening Cassie changed from her dress into a pair of slacks, pulled on a pair of Beatie's work boots, donned her coat and scarf and went out without telling her mother. She stopped by the park to light a cigarette and to look up at the night sky. A Harvest Moon, they had called it before the war. The moon was indeed loaded, and one great thing about the blackout, Cassie thought, was the restoration of the stars in the sky. The evening was crisp and cold and the cigarette smoke reared up like white horses' heads briefly painted on the air. And if she swung her head the black night ran with tiny beads of colour, and she knew that these were radio signals that she could not just hear but could see tracking across the sky, and it was no point trying to fix your gaze on these tiny iridescent parabolas because they would be gone in a twinkling anyway and the only way to apprehend them with the human eye was to acknowledge the brevity of the leap they made into and out of the visible spectrum, and it was an extraordinary thing how few people understood that.

Cassie was chipped out of her reverie by a burn on her hand. The cigarette wedged between first and second fingers had burned down to a stick of ash, unsmoked. The stub sparked as it fell to the flagstones, and she stamped it out under her shoe. She took her compact out of her bag and reapplied her lipstick, blind. She combed her hair and returned her comb to her bag. 'And the night,' she said; though she didn't know why, because her mind was racing. Turning her collar against the chill of the evening, she proceeded to

239

walk slowly towards Coventry city centre.

At around seven p.m. she developed a strange feeling in her stomach, or perhaps in her bowels. A vibration. Then it spread across her body to her ears, until she understood that the vibration was not inside her, but was the familiar air-raid warning sirens. She'd somehow anticipated it by several seconds. That sour, almost forlorn howl dragged up from the lowest place on earth, fattening and rising into a despairing moan, climbing at last until it wails, fighting to live at its uppermost note until it falls back, uselessly, defeated, and then climbs again, wanting to infect with its own panic. Cassie heard the whistles of nearby ARP men as they went through their drill. Soon, she knew, there would be more urgency. Within ten minutes she was right. The throbbing of incoming aircraft could be heard like a great rumour in the distance, behind the moan of the air-raid siren. The ARP men began to whistle more spiritedly and shout along the streets, some of them jocular, 'Run rabbits, run my little rabbits!' The searchlights were thrown on, criss-crossing the night sky from points in the centre of town.

Cassie pressed on. Then something beautiful illuminated the sky. It was a parachute flare, strontium-white and blazing brilliantly, hanging in the air. Then more, several parachute flares hanging in formation, dropped on the east side of the city and floating west in the light breeze. Ack-ack guns replied from ground placements in nearby villages, uselessly thumping rounds into the sky; then Bofors guns from nearby, louder.

In Swan Lane a voice from the dark said,

240

'Come on girlie, let's have you off the streets.'

'Hello Derek,' Cassie said. 'Where've you been these past weeks?'

Derek was an old friend of Beatie's. He'd been turned down for active service because his right leg was three inches longer than his left. 'Cassie! What are you doing? Why don't you get home? This one's for real.'

'I can see that. I'm out to help. Official, like.'

Derek squinted at her. 'Official?'

'Go and do your rounds. Get some rest. It's going to be a long night.'

Derek snorted at this sixteen-year-old advising him. But she was already gone. Derek put his whistle to his lips but merely stared after her.

Cassie took Thackall Street alongside the football stadium. There was a cut-through alley behind the football ground, and she hoped that route into town would help her dodge most of the ARP men. As she slipped through the alley towards Hillfields, Cassie could see families getting into their Andersons, and she thought she heard a snigger. Then another, and another, and she realised the sniggers were coming from the air. They were incendiary bombs, producing an eerie sound as they twisted in the air. They thumped the ground without exploding, but spread fire where they fell, and they began to rain down in great number. Someone saw her from a garden by the light of one such flame and shouted, beckoning. But even when a different type of incendiary dropped with a flaring, phosphorescent flash, Cassie wasn't going to be deflected.

Why am I unafraid? she said to herself. This

241

isn't natural. It's because, she told herself, it's because I am *meant* to be here.

Isolated minor fires broke out around her as she moved along King William Street, still set on getting to the heart of the town, and as she moved away from Hillfields she left behind her some of the sniggering rain of incendiaries. But there came another sound in the air, like a fluttering of leathery wings. It raised the gooseflesh on her arms, but she hadn't time to think what had caused it because the incendiaries were followed by the crump blasts of high-explosive bombs falling all over the city.

A fire engine with its bell ringing sped past her on Primrose Hill and she turned into Cox Street, making her way towards the cathedral. Some incendiaries around her were burning in the middle of the road without effect; others were spreading their fire. One licked at a gatepost in Cox Street and she tried to kick the flames away with her toe before a man rushed out of the house, smothering the small fire with a blanket. The man grabbed her arm and tried to drag her inside but she pulled free of him.

The drone of planes overhead got louder, and it occurred to Cassie that there must be many, many bombers in the air above her head, other-wise the throbbing noise would have passed. She looked up and she could see them. Hundreds of them, in beautiful geometric formation. Some of them near enough to reflect the light of their own flares, others, tiny specks caught in the cross-beams of the searchlights. She could see tracers, and the brief orange puffball explosions of anti-aircraft fire, and still around her she heard the sniggering and the unexplained bat-wing flutter. In the sky she could also detect – briefly visible, now gone – the iridescence of radio waves, sparkling but following an undeviating route across the sky and she knew that the bombers were somehow following this rainbow bridge. Another parachute was falling behind her, in the Swan Lane area where she'd been. It had something dangling on the end. She thought it was a paratrooper, that the Germans were actually going to land. The parachute swung hither and thither in perfect time to the beat of 'Moonlight Serenade'. But then she saw that the parachute carried a cylindrical box, and after it disappeared behind the houses it rocked the earth with a fantastic blast that left Cassie's ears ringing. She reached in her pocket and found the leather aviation helmet her airman had given her two nights ago, and she put it on, tying the strap under her chin.

It was also plain to her by now that each new cascade of incendiaries and explosives was coming down at approximately thirty-second intervals. That must have been the distance between each bank of planes, half a minute. She began to punctuate her movements accordingly.

By the time she got to the cathedral there were small fires burning everywhere and crews of firemen putting them out. No sooner would they extinguish one small fire than another packet of incendiaries fell within yards. Cassie saw four men on the roof of the cathedral trying to put out the flames. She stood behind a policeman who stared up at the roof.

The policeman glanced at her and, seeing her in her aviation helmet, took her to be a messenger. 'Son, get down the Command Centre and tell 'em we need firemen up here if we're going to save it.'

She was gone. She knew that Command Centre for Civil Defence was in the basement of the Council House. A Home Guard soldier stopped her at the door and said he'd pass the message along. 'Don't hold out much hope. The phone lines are gone already. Try to get a crew along yourself.'

Cassie ran up Jordon Well. Another fire engine was active in Little Park Street, where a small factory was alight. A fireman was screwing his hose to a hydrant. Then another wave of bombs landed and three buildings went up like matchwood. An empty double-decker bus was turned on its nose to come crashing down, belly up, in a great groaning and splintering of metal. The fireman stopped what he was doing and stared at the destruction. Cassie had to tug his arm. 'Cathedral,' she said. 'They need you.'

The fireman's face was streaked with soot. Pink furrows stood out on his brow. 'I can't leave this,' he shouted above the thudding of anti-aircraft fire. 'The entire block'll go. Tell 'em I'll come if I can.'

Cassie ran back up Jordan Well. A crater had appeared in the road and an ambulance had driven into it. The driver was climbing out of his cab. Back at the cathedral the policeman was gone. There were still men on the roof, but acrid, yellow smoke writhed off it like fat worms making their escape from the conflagration. The men tore up the lead to get to the incendiaries that had fallen through to the timbers beneath. Cassie knew they were wasting their time. She looked up in the air again and saw the sky was still filled with planes. *They are riding on a secret beam*, she thought. *They can't go anywhere else.*

More incendiaries came sniggering, metal clanging or thumping depending on where they hit, all landing on the roof above the north door. Nearby was a massive, vibrating explosion. The men on the roof turned from their work to see where the newest parachuted land-mine had hit. Then they went back to the scrabbling job of tearing up the lead. But the new basket of incendiaries had gone through and took hold. 'Where's the fucking firemen?' someone screamed.

'Putting out the other fires,' Cassie screamed back.

The men on the roof looked down at her. Then one said, 'We're coming down. Help us save what's inside.'

The interior was choked with twisting yellow fumes. They all went in and saved what they could. Everything on the altar, some paintings, a couple of tapestries. But the cathedral was a museum of priceless mediaeval artworks. No one knew where to begin. Cassie rescued a gilt-framed painting of Lady Godiva. Within half an hour the smoke was overwhelming. One of the men put an arm out to stop Cassie going back in again. 'It's all over,' he said. 'We don't want to lose you as well.' One of the others, a young man, broke down in tears. They all stood together at the south porch and they watched the flames grow higher. Outside more explosions rocked the city. Inside, history burned and the jewel of the city melted.

At about nine-thirty a group of firemen from Solihull battered their way through the rubble-strewn streets and set up hoses. When they trained water on the interior of the burning roof, violent billowing geysers of steam howled back at them in a reverse draught. There was a moment of hope before, without warning, the hoses stopped running, dribbled. The water mains had been hit. An exploding incendiary injured a policeman still involved in salvage. 'It's gone,' a voice said quietly.

Another policeman put a hand on her shoulder. 'Look sharp,' he said firmly, 'the phones are down and they need more messengers over at central.' Then he squinted at her. The giant red flames from the cathedral roof illuminated Cassie's face. 'Are you a lass?'

'I'm a messenger,' Cassie said.

'You're a bloody angel.'

She skipped away.

The entire city was aflame. The fire crew on Little Park Street had given up and moved on, leaving the street burning, a row of three-storey scooped-out front walls. Cassie could see that Broadgate, the heart of the city, was spectacularly aflame. At the Council House Command Centre the soldier on duty recognised her this time and waved her through. She went down the stone steps to the basement. Three men and half a dozen women were chalking on blackboards or conferring. The telephone lines were still dead. They worked away under insipid yellow emergency lighting.

'Who the hell are you?' said one bespectacled, sweating man, shirtsleeves rolled. He had a cigarette squashed between his fingers but it had gone out.

'Messenger Vine,' Cassie said.

'Right then messenger Vine, get down the fire station – speed of light – and take this list of water hydrants. On you go.'

'First I've got a message for you.'

'Let's have it then.'

'The message is: we will win through this.'

Everyone looked up from his or her task. The man took off his spectacles. He grimaced. His lips twitched and his mouth shaped to speak but no words came out. Then he said, 'Who is the message from?'

'From me. Messenger Vine.'

The man put his cigarette to his lips, took a drag on it, then remembered that it had gone out. Then he started laughing, and within a moment everyone in the basement was laughing. The man stepped forward and crushed her in a bear hug, and he kissed her cheek. 'You beauty!' he shouted at her. 'You little beauty!' Then everyone in the basement was applauding her. 'Somebody please give her a tin 'at!' the man shouted. One of the women found her an oversized ARP helmet and squashed it over Cassie's flying cap. Cassie ran back up the stairs, clutching her note, flushed and embarrassed by the applause. People are strange, she thought.

But when she got into Broadgate she was shocked into paralysis by what she saw. The height of the town was in flames. Fire crews were fighting uselessly. The fires and the bombs had stripped department stores. Steam genies rose from the water directed by the hoses. Bible-black smoke, underlit by fire, belched and roiled. It was too hot to pass through Broadgate. She stood back and watched the flames and the vile beat of leathery wings at her ears returned. She swatted wildly at the small tormenting demons in the air about her. Then she saw her first corpse.

It was propped against a shop doorway. The glass from the shopfront had blown out and crystalled the street before her, and every winking shard of glass reflected the red flames. The sparkling rubies crunched under her boots as she approached the figure, its face and clothes white with plaster dust, eyes wide open, worms of blood glistening at ears, nostrils and mouth. It was a man, middle-aged, in uniform, though she couldn't tell which uniform because it was caked in dust. He looked like one who, exhausted, had squatted down in the doorway for a moment's rest. Cassie thought she should try to close the staring eyes, not out of respect or religious practice but because she thought that was what you should do. But the eyelids wouldn't stay closed. She tried again and said, 'You can go now.' The eyelids sprung open again. Cassie shivered and walked backwards from the staring corpse, and turned to run, prepared to take her chances amidst the flames of Broadgate.

The flames were climbing. Not one building in Broadgate seemed untouched, and still the bombs and incendiaries were raining down, and for a moment Cassie lost the centre of herself and the unassailable confidence that had so far been guiding her. She retreated to the white stone steps under the portico of the National Provincial Bank and looked down at Broadgate aflame. The drone of the bombers, the snigger and the howl of bombs, the leather wings, the roar and crackle of the flames was not going to go away. The planes in the night sky became demons, exulting, stretching their wings in effortless displays of aerial prowess, gloating, making merry. They fanned winds with their wings to make the flames dance higher. Was this hell, then? Cassie thought. Is this what they meant? If it was, she knew she must walk through it. Wasn't that the only way to move about in hell, to be defiant?

Snigger. Another stick of incendiaries falling.

Cassie turned to see the beautiful globe of a parachute, its silk reflecting pearl and pink, moon and fire, waltzing low in the air currents, tugged down by its land-mine basket. It dropped in Broadgate and the blast punched Cassie's ears and the black wind that followed flung her on her back. Then came a shuffling sound, almost like water, like the sound of someone taking a loose shit in a backyard outhouse, and Cassie lifted her head to see a four-storey building shredding itself into the street.

She got to her feet and moved away from the swirling, hot dust. She clapped her ears. She hadn't been deafened, but all sound had become muted. The roar of fire had become a low surf. The blast of further bombs had become the crackle of sticks on a fire.

Someone appeared at her shoulder. It was her

249

father. 'Dad, are you here?' Her own voice was muffled, dislocated. Her father shaped his mouth to speak but all he could deliver was a thin smile. Cassie was unperturbed by his appearance, even though he had died two years before the outbreak of war. She'd once seen him two weeks after the funeral, while she still grieved. 'The air tastes warm and bitter, Dad.'

But he gestured wildly at another figure hunkered in the corner of the portico of the National Provincial Bank. It was another corpse: a young boy of her own age, about sixteen. He was also a messenger: she saw the insignia on his epaulette. This time the eyes were closed in death and his face was pancaked with white masonry dust. More red worms of blood soaked into the dust from his ears and his nostrils. Cassie reached out, very, very slowly, her forefinger and second finger extended in a probing V, and touched the boy's closed eyes. His eyelids shot open, and his blank, bloodshot eyes stared back at her.

Snigger in the air. Another stick falling. Flutter of leather wings.

She leaned forward and put her lips very close to his. 'You can't go,' she said. She exhaled a kiss into him. *Still a virgin, like me.* She took dust and ash on to the moistness of her own lips. The boy shivered.

His eyes were now wide with terror and he cowered from her touch. She peered hard at him. His teeth chattered. Cassie moved very slowly, squatting next to him, and put her hand on his head.

He moved his mouth, saying something, but

with the recent blast muffling her ears, Cassie couldn't make out what he said. She remembered the fire hydrant list, still clutched in her hand. 'Come with me,' she said. 'We'll help each other.'

He twitched slightly, grimacing, making an effort to stir. He spoke again but Cassie couldn't hear it. She guessed from his lip motion that he said, 'I can't move.'

'Dad!' she shouted, looking round for help. 'Dad!' But her father had gone. Then to the boy she said, 'Are you injured?' Still she was barely able to hear her own words.

Perhaps he said something like, 'No. I just can't move.' There was a sound in her head when he tried to speak. But it was out of sync with his lip movement.

'If you stay there you will die of shame. You must get over your fear and come with me now. What's your name?'

Something. Again he moved his lips, but no clear sound came.

'I can't hear. My ears are damaged.'

'Michael.' Maybe, he said his name was Michael.

Cassie placed her hands either side of his face, and she leaned into him, kissing him full on the mouth once more, sucking more dust and ash from his lips. He trembled and his teeth continued to chatter, so she kissed him harder. 'Coventry boy,' she said at last. 'Coventry boy. Are you coming with me?'

The boy wept and tried to hide his eyes from her. She stood up, as if to go, and he scrambled to his feet.

'Which way to the fire station?' Cassie asked.

He pointed that they would have to go along Broadgate.

'Cut through Pepper Lane?' Cassie said, putting the tin hat back on the boy's head. 'No, we won't get. Hold my hand and we'll find a way through.'

Together they moved into the inferno of Broadgate. Though St Michael's Cathedral was lost, Holy Trinity Church was untouched. They ran down Broadgate between the blazing shops and into Trinity Street. When they got to the fire station it had been abandoned. The roof had completely collapsed.

They passed the twisted skeletons of double-decker buses and clambered over the brick and broken plaster and melted girders. The bodies of two women ARP workers spilled from an ambulance. They stepped over the corpses. The tyres of the ambulances had liquefied in black puddles. The women too had blast-blood leaking from eyes, nose and ears. Everywhere there were corpses, there were worms or eels of blood.

They managed to find the relocated Fire Service headquarters and deliver the message. An air of numb resolution gripped the emergency services now. They worked fiercely but blindly. The need for messages was giving way. No one stopped working but there was a sense that planning, strategy, co-ordination in the face of these odds was useless. There was just the need to fight the fires and ferry the wounded. So they went back to the Command Centre to see if they could be useful.

On the way Cassie heard the fluttering of leather wings again, and one of her aerial

252

tormentors clanged on her tin helmet. 'They give me the creeps,' she said.

'What does?' At first she thought her hearing was coming back, but it just seemed that she was better able to intuit Michael. He spoke and she heard his words in her brain, and the words came before his lips moved.

'These bat things. These creatures fluttering around. Listen.' Michael strained his ears. The thirty-foot flames lighted the perspiration on his face. 'There! Did you hear it?'

Michael pointed at a piece of smoking metal on the ground. 'Shrapnel. Spinning to the ground. From our own ack-ack guns. What do you think happens to the shells after they burst?'

Cassie felt stupid.

A man ran past them, very fast, with his hair on fire and the soles of his boots smoking. They watched him run into a side street.

Together they spent the night running messages for the Command Centre. They were given tea and cigarettes, and told to rest for ten minutes. One of the workers there pulled Cassie aside. 'Are you all right?' he said. Cassie could hear him more clearly than she could hear Michael.

'Yes. We're all right.'

'We?'

'Yes.'

'I think you're in shock.'

'Well, we're all in shock.'

'Blown if that's not true. But get someone to look at you if you get a chance.'

The news of the city's losses couldn't be kept from them. Hundreds dead. Wounded incalculable. The library destroyed, churches burned out, shops obliterated, monuments smashed. History had been pulled from the town like a set of back molars. Seven hours after the raid had started it was still going on. The German planes, it was calculated, had had time to go back to their bases, reload and return.

When they went outside again, it was obvious that there was nothing to be done. Roads were blocked and ambulances couldn't get through. Fire engines had no water. Buses and cars lay tossed around in the streets like toys. There were the bodies of policemen in Cross Cheaping and a dead messenger boy in Pepper Lane. They had to leave them. Fires on either side of the streets were joining up in the middle, like theatre curtains closing on some hideous show. The heat sucked oxygen from the air and made the mouth taste of ashes and plaster dust and charcoal. And there was the smell of sewage and corruption. Rats ran squeaking amongst the rubble. Still the buildings burned. Coventry was going to be punched into powder. Even the ack-ack guns were giving up.

'Why aren't the guns firing?' Cassie asked Michael.

'Out of ammunition,' she thought he said.

'Shall we bring one down. Michael? A Nazi plane, I mean? You and me? We could do it!'

'You're mad, Cassie.'

'Do you trust me?'

'Somehow.'

'Then hold my hand and follow me.' She led him down Cuckoo Lane and into Priory Row, perilously close to the burning cathedral. All attempts to put it out had ended and the roof had collapsed entirely. Only the smoking gothic shell remained, a pulsating ruby of vile heat. Every prayer to hope in half a millennium spitting and roasting and smoking. But the tower and the spire were untouched. The door to the tower had burned off. She beckoned him in.

Michael laughed bitterly. 'Not up there.'

'It's the safest place in the city,' she said. 'That's why it's still standing. Trust me, Michael. More than anything I need you to trust me.' She took his hand and pulled him towards the base of the spire. Though it stood apart from the dense smouldering and smoking at the other end of the cathedral it was like walking into an oven. The spire acted like a chimney, sucking up heat, but after the first few twists of spiral steps the updraught blew out of the open mullioned lightwells and it became cooler. Together they climbed the one hundred and eighty spiralling, echoing stone steps.

When they stepped out on to the parapet of the tower the wind whipped at Cassie's hair, and she realised what a cold evening it was and how the fires raging below had made an oven of the city. The sky overhead glowed rust-red. She poked her head between the crenellations of the gothic spire and looked down.

From below she could hear nothing, and up here only the wind, and that muted, like a sad murmuring at her ears, like the whispering of an inconsolable, defeated angel. The city was a broken bowl, spilling fire. It was like looking into the heart of Satan. Rivers of flame, grinding sparks, belching black puffs of smoke. Miles of red glowing earth at all compass points. She ran to the other side. A filthy strand of smoke, twisting up like a giant snake. Silvery tongues of flame. Crimson jaws working away. Sudden flares. Puddles of combustion. A writhing, as if the flames were a maggoty infestation on the underbelly of the city. For a moment it seemed to Cassie that the tower too dropped away beneath her; she felt her stomach flip, but she was borne up by hot currents of air and she went flying over the inferno, over a city of three hundred thousand burning souls. Then she was back again, her feet planted firmly on the stone parapet of the mediaeval tower, with the wind in her ears. She heard a new drone.

More German aircraft coming in from the south-east, ten, no twenty, no twenty-five or so, flying in perfect formation. She put her hand out behind her and found Michael's hand, drawing her to him. He was shivering uncontrollably.

'My God you're freezing,' Cassie said.

Michael's teeth chattered wildly. Cassie unbuttoned her coat and wrapped him inside. 'Come here,' Cassie said. 'Take some of my warmth.'

Michael tried to say something, shaped his lips, but he was unable to speak. He was unbearably cold, his fingers like frost. She took his hand and put it inside her blouse, on to her breast. He stared at her in anguish.

'Look at them Michael,' Cassie said, indicating the incoming bombers. 'They think they are beautiful. They think their engines are keeping them in the sky. We know different, don't we? Don't we? Smell that? It's aviation fuel. Close enough to smell aren't they? Look! It's almost possible to see the pilots in the cockpits, isn't it? If you imagined him a little closer you could talk with him Michael. Which one? Pick one for yourself. Which one will you choose? Which one must pay? Which one shall we say will not be going home?'

Michael didn't answer. Cassie drew his other hand under her skirt and placed it between her thighs, rubbing his icy fingers against herself. 'No one should die a virgin, should they Michael?'

Michael shivered as she unbuttoned his trousers and massaged his erection, stroking her thumb over the head of his cock, whispering to him, encouraging him, as if she were expert. 'We'll have to fly to him, Michael. Scare him. Fly at him like a demon from out of the night.' She hoisted her leg over the crook of his elbow, just as the airman had taught her. Michael was wide-eyed, shocked, but yielding. As she guided him inside her they both gasped, grabbing each other to steady themselves against the surpassing pleasure of the penetration. All words had gone. They were paralysed and the sky was ripping open in a fire-breathing ejaculation. Cassie tipped back her head and tried to look up into the moon-flooded fuel-drenched sky. And they fell, upwards, soaring, locked together, the wind streaming in their hair, Cassie's jet-black curls lashing behind her, making a banshee of her, swooping on the incoming aircraft.

Oh Michael. Let's choose one. Let's choose one for you. For you and for the city. Don't be afraid and you mustn't feel guilty. After all, they have chosen us. This one? This one coming in a little lower than the others?

Shall we punish his beautiful daring? Shall we? He won't know how it's done. He'll have no idea.

And they swooped on one of the German aeroplanes, arcing through the night, burning silver moonglow in their wake, coming upon the cockpit, and they fastened upon the glass nose of the aircraft with their sucking fingers and mouths, seeing the bombardier look up from his controls inside the glass nose of the plane, seeing his hideous smile of bowel-loosening, uncomprehending fear.

That's it. That's it Michael. Fly to him. See his face. Look at his eye. Fix your eye on his. It will be like glue. Our eyes. Will be glued. Iris to his iris. We'll be angels. In his cockpit. Or demons. Look at his terror. Look at the terror in his eye. That's it. That's it. That's it. It's done, Michael, oh it's done. He won't get home. That one. No way home for him. It's done. You can let go.

Back on the parapet of the spire Cassie watched the targeted plane, saw it bank and turn and climb, and head north-east of the city. A single puff of ack-ack fire burst in the air nearby, but not close enough to damage the plane. The defensive ack-ack guns were depleted and exhausted now, offering only token fire. The plane disappeared safely into the darkness.

But she knew it made no difference. The plane was doomed. She knew in the same way she knew what song was playing on the radio even before she switched it on. The plane was locked into its course. It would come down seven miles from the city. Only Cassie knew that it wouldn't return home safely. Only Cassie and Michael.

258

'Michael,' Cassie whispered. 'Michael? Where are you?' She walked around the parapet, twice, calling softly to him.

He was gone. Cassie felt the wind at her ears. She buttoned her coat around her and descended the tower, feeling the heat return to her as she spiralled down the steps of the tower. Back on the ground the hot air was like a reeking and bitter pepper.

She knew where to find Michael. She retraced her steps, through the dripping fire and the acrid fog of smoke, dodging the fluttering airborne cinders and the maggoty cascading sparks, to the white stone steps under the portico of the National Provincial Bank. She found him hunkered in the corner of the portico, his face white with dust, dried blood in his nose and ears and eyesockets. She put a hand to his neck. His body was cold. This time she didn't touch his eyelids, and they stayed shut. 'You can go now,' she whispered.

More fire crews and emergency teams were finding their way into the city, but it was all over. Desperate salvage jobs were collapsing. Men were weeping or consoling the weeping. Cassie passed a pile of archaic manuscripts someone had pulled from the smoking ruins of the library but had then abandoned on the pavement. Gothic script and illuminated letters, handwritten by an ancient monk, left to char and blow along the street.

Cassie drifted through the streets with the surety of a sleepwalker, passing fire crews hosing mechanically and without hope. One fireman nodded to her, with a blackened face and with an insane grin twisting his mouth, as if he wanted her to share in some joke. It was all over. It was burning, and everything was gone. A fine, cold drizzle started to descend, mixed in with the swirling ash and soot and dust, mixing a warm smog that brushed the face like hot cobwebs. The reek was one of cooked filth, of cracked drains and broken sewers, the spices of hell's kitchen.

In Trinity Street she recognised one of the stretcher-bearers. It was Gordon. He stopped when he saw her. 'Cassie darlin' whatever are you doing here?' His atrocious stammer had disappeared. He tried to adjust a tarpaulin so that she might not see what was on the stretcher beneath it.

'Helping,' Cassie said.

Gordon nodded, as if he understood perfectly. Then his partner prompted him to move on. 'Bless you Cassie,' Gordon said. 'But you should get home my wee darlin'.'

No more raids came in, but it was not until six-fifteen that the all-clear sounded, mournful and hollow in the grey light. The drizzle made for steam, and where black smoke wasn't belching from the rubble, white smoke added to the dense, evil pall draped over the city. Cassie wandered without purpose, feeling herself like smoke, thinning, vague, unable to remember her purpose. Almost a ghost.

The city itself was a spectre. The steam and the mist and the smoke rendered the remaining walls and angles of broken buildings like vague pencil sketches, or photographic negatives, or perhaps they were only after-images of toppled buildings. Unrecognisable shells stood on weird stilts. Landmarks had vanished into rubble. Millions of bricks, splinters of wood, twisted girders, clumps of plaster and shards of glass spread in huge barrow mounds across the streets. Cassie wandered down Cross Cheaping, alongside the remains of a department store and saw a tailor's dummy hanging from a window. Amid a pile of rubble an ironwork lamp stand boasted an untouched sign reading 'Buses for Keresley Stop Here'. Beneath it was the twisted, melted skeletal frame of a double-decker.

And the people began to emerge. They picked their way over the bricks and the rubble, and they didn't speak. Cassie watched them, saw them making an internal inventory, trying to orient themselves. They moved about in huddles. They touched their faces a great deal as they moved, silently, through the desolation.

Some business proprietors and shopkeepers arrived, bent on getting into the remains of their stores. Brief arguments broke out with police and ARP men. One tobacconist, finding only a single wall remaining, had salvaged a few bales of tobacco. He found a piece of card and wrote on it: 'Tobacco sale, slightly smoked. Half price'. Then he sat down on a timber joist and waited for trade.

'I'd like a smoke,' Cassie told him.

The tobacconist looked up at her. 'Been at it all night, have you?' he said brightly. 'You look all in. Here help yourself. On the bleedin' house.'

'Would you roll one for me? My fingers are numb.'

'I'll tell you what I'll do. I'll roll one for you, and one for me. And we'll sit down here together and we'll smoke 'em, and we'll say we're glad to be alive. How about that?'

'Sounds good.'

'Right then.' The tobacconist made a big show of finding Cassie a spot on the timber beside him, dusting it off for her before she sat down. 'Shouldn't have a problem finding a light,' he said. Cassie smiled. He rolled two neat cigarettes, lighting them both before handing one to her. They sat and smoked, each in honour of the other, and not taking their eyes from the other until the cigarettes were done. And during that time Cassie hummed a tune, very softly.

'"Moonlight Serenade",' said the tobacconist. 'Funny. I had that tune going round in my head afore you sat down.'

Cassie grinned, as if she knew something. People stopped to look at them, and everyone cracked a thin smile at his sign. 'You need to go home, darlin',' said the tobacconist. 'If you've a home to go to.'

'Hadn't thought of that,' Cassie said.

She trudged through streets now thronged with people. Incredibly, most of them seemed to be up and dressed and on their way to their places of employment, as if they thought the morning ritual in preparation for work might change the events of the raid. They wheeled their bicycles through the rubble, they carried their knapsacks or their bags and gas-mask cases. A large number of houses outside the city centre had been demolished or damaged, and as she approached home Cassie's footsteps quickened.

The house was untouched. The front door was

slightly ajar. Martha stood inside with Beatie. When they saw her come in, Cassie with blackened face and filthy clothes and with her tin helmet, they peered hard at her. Then Martha screamed and ran to her and hugged her and howled and beat her child's back and head with her fists, hard, so hard that Beatie had to pull her away, before letting their mother hug Cassie to her.

'Cassie,' Martha wailed. 'What are you, Cassie? What must we do with you? Wherever have you been?'

'I've been helping the dead,' said Cassie. 'Beatie, you can have my record player.'

And she sat down and slept.

24

The rubbish was piling up at Ravenscraig. Plates, dishes, cups, saucers, pots, saucepans and kitchen utensils festered unwashed in the sink. The waste bin went unemptied, the floors unswept. The communal rooms were littered with books, newspapers, notepads and other reference material, not to mention beer flagons, wine bottles and overflowing ashtrays. The normal shopping errands were neglected and toilets were not attended to.

And no one said anything.

This parlous condition of the house could be blamed on the caucus of Beatrice, Bernard, Lilly and Cassie, all of whom had undertaken to do no further domestic work, absenting themselves on the grounds of serious academic study. Frank too was sworn not to tidy, repair or otherwise set back in order the domestic chaos of the house. Frank had been an eager convert to the do-nothing campaign. But the do-nothing campaign was met with a say-nothing campaign. George, Robin, Tara, Feek and the many casual visitors Ravenscraig attracted at that time all behaved as though the campaign was directed at someone other than themselves.

Naturally hygiene was a problem, and when Bernard found a rat in the kitchen he killed it but left the corpse for others to enjoy. Meanwhile the do-nothing caucus was secretly admitted to the cooking and toilet facilities hitherto privately enjoyed by Lilly, and were thereby spared the depravations of the communal areas. Peregrine Feek chose to rise above this unseemly tussle by retreating to his college rooms at Balliol, where there were plenty of servants, porters and bedmakers to take care of domestic duties.

He'd seen it all before and he knew the issues would resolve eventually.

Meanwhile Feek had been good to his word, and had found Frank a room of his own just along the corridor from Cassie's. The room was originally piled high with books, but Feek had two liveried men from Balliol come and take them away and replace the books with a bed and a few sticks of college furniture. Frank wasn't terribly keen on the room, which had only a small window. Neither was Cassie pleased with this new arrangement, but she had been persuaded by Feek and others that it was unhealthy for a growing boy to be sleeping with his mother; particularly by Robin who assured her that the lad's homosexuality was but a short step away from this morbid, extended attachment to the maternal bed. So Frank pinned up his Babe Ruth card and placed one or two other modest possessions around the room and tried to look happy. But he started having nightmares, and would occasionally drift back to Cassie's room, where she would let him into her bed.

Not long after the new arrangement Robin, under cover of night, tried the handle of the door to Cassie's room, standing outside while making cooing noises. This surprising mode of courtship gave Cassie the giggles, but she affected a stern look and chased him away. Another night George came to her room, but Cassie was aware that Frank might want to come into her bed, so she kissed George and sent him away with greater hope than she'd given Robin. Not an hour later than she'd sent George away did Lilly come along, weeping and apologising, but she made no more progress than had either Robin or George.

It's a wonder, Cassie thought, that they're not all cracking heads in the dark. It was not an immodest thought. The night corridor was a thoroughfare proper. And one night Frank woke up to find someone perched on the edge of his bed stroking his hair. It was too dark to see who it was but the figure placed a finger on his lips and Frank went back to sleep, thinking he was still dreaming.

Meanwhile the garbage piled higher and got

more rancid, and if nothing was spoken there was plenty of raw feeling at large. Indeed it was the main topic of conversation amongst both the do-nothings and the say-nothings so long as none of the opposing party were present. The do-nothings were adamant that they would not lift a finger; the say-nothings were determined not to let themselves be manipulated. Neither of the groups was prepared to call a house meeting to discuss the worsening situation, since that would present the other group with the advantage of not attending. They were deadlocked.

Frank, who was nominally outside the dispute, noticed how conversation would dry up whenever a member of the opposing faction drew near, and then would suddenly start up again in too high a gear, and about remote intellectual subjects.

'I say Beatie, have you seen Schulman's latest review of *The Turning-point of History?*' Robin might venture.

'No Robin. Is it worth reading?'

'I should say so, and though it's full of the normal self-regarding eclat one always associates with him he does make some pretty pertinent points about dialectic consensus.'

Or Bernard, unable to bear the fracture, might try to find common ground. 'Well Tara I see your friends from the PPR are finally merging with the syndicalist rump, which is pretty smart. Now if they could only get lined up with the ITA broad left alliance we might see some real progress.'

'Wouldn't that be good? But I can't see them coming on board while the executive is mainly

AMG members.'

'True. Very true.'

Frank thought it rather odd that they all smiled so ferociously while they said these frigid things. He wondered if they were speaking in code, and even if they were the room seemed to fill, when they spoke, with a breath that might match the rancid and curdled odours of the kitchen. This sourness pervading the house started to creep into Frank's dreams. He dreamt of corpses in the kitchen and rats in his bed. One time a rat with human hands was sitting on his bed and Frank screamed himself awake. It was a recurring dream.

Two doors away, while the rest of the house was sleeping, Cassie heard her door open. 'Who is it this time?' she whispered.

'It's me. George. I say Cassie, can I come in?'

'What do you want?'

'Code of courtly love.'

'What?'

George let himself in and gently closed the door behind him. Cassie was up and out of bed, pulling on her dressing gown. George, in striped pyjamas, threw himself to the ground and kissed her feet.

'Get off me you clown!' Cassie giggled. 'What are you up to?'

George looked up. 'Code of courtly love, Cassie. It's the only way, what with this stupid fight going on. I'm yours to do whatever you want with. You can have me as your slave. Anything. But you've got to let me have you in return. You have to take pity on me. That's the code of courtly love.'

'Have you gone soft in the head?'

267

'I demonstrate my utter devotion for you until you take pity on me and let me have you. That's how it works. You can't say no.'

Cassie thought she heard a floorboard creak in the corridor. She didn't want Frank to find her with George. 'Let's go to your room,' she said. 'We'll talk about it.'

But Frank was already awake. He'd had another terrifying nightmare about rats with human hands. He sat up in bed, hyperventilating, clammy with perspiration. After climbing out of bed he pulled on his dressing gown and padded along the corridor in search of the comfort of his mother's bed. When he got to her room he was dismayed to find her bed empty. He stifled a sob.

Too afraid to return to his own bed he turned to Beatie and Bernard's room. He pushed open the door and wandered in. Beatie and Bernard were both asleep. Frank stood close to Beatie willing her eyes to open.

'Who's that?' Beatie said, waking with a start.

'It's me,' Frank sobbed. 'Mummy's gone. I had a bad dream.'

Bernard groaned and tried to bury his head under his pillow. He had to be up early for school in the morning. He hated to teach after a bad night's sleep.

'Get in with us,' Beatie said. 'Come on. Jump in.'

Frank climbed in between Bernard and Beatie and they all settled down again. Pretty soon Frank had dozed off. But then he twitched in his sleep. Bernard pushed him away, trying to rescue the pillow Frank had somehow stolen from him in the dark. Bernard gave up on the pillow and eventually sank back into a doze. After a while Frank's hand came up and fetched an impressive slap on Bernard's ear. Content, Frank turned and snorted into the pillow seemingly deep in sleep. Bernard almost managed to claim a moment's slumber, but Frank twitched again, before starting to snore. Finally his knee came up in an involuntary jerk and cracked Bernard on the hip.

'Where are you going?' Beatie hissed at Bernard, seeing him get out of bed.

Bernard grabbed the torch from his bedside table and wrestled a pillow from Frank. 'It's like trying to sleep with a combine harvester going up and down the ruddy bed,' he growled. 'He can stay here with you. I'll have his bed.'

Even after settling himself in Frank's small bed Bernard didn't find sleep easy to come by. There was giggling from another room to distract him. He thought it sounded like Cassie, and possibly George. There was also the sound of a door opening and closing and someone else shuffled along the corridor. It occurred to Bernard that there was more activity in the house at night than there was in daytime. He considered all of the romantic permutations – just the ones he knew of – that had passed through Ravenscraig. He sorted them into categories: confirmed, probable, possible, denied but confirmed, denied and unconfirmed, claimed but improbable and so on. The taxonomy helped him to drift off to sleep.

It was perhaps an hour later when Bernard was stirred by a slight pressure on his head. Someone was stroking his hair. He was half-drugged with sleep and thought it must be Beatie. He made a tiny noise of pleasure and tried to go back to sleep. Then in his dazed condition he thought it wasn't Beatie because the pressure of the hand was rather lighter. It occurred to him, after everything he'd heard, that it was Cassie. His eyes were half glued together with sleep, and in any case the room was pitch-black. He made to speak and then reconsidered what he might tactfully say to Cassie. A part of him was not entirely surprised at this approach by Cassie; he was determined to turn her down tenderly but firmly.

The hand was withdrawn, and there was a rustling. Bernard felt his blankets being peeled back and heard the bedsprings groan as the visitor bounced into bed beside him. 'Look, Cassie...' Bernard began.

The figure next to him stiffened. Something was wrong. If it *was* Cassie, she didn't smell right. Bernard fumbled for his torch on the bedside table. He switched it on and shone it into the aghast face of Peregrine Feek.

25

Martha Vine dozed by the fireplace. The fire in the grate had built up a nice hot bed of red embers. A small coal crackled and released a wisp of sulphurous yellow smoke. It drugged the air. The clock over Martha's head ticked louder, and

270

there came a knock at the door.

Martha got up to answer. It was the postman, cheerful, chatty, red face, bad teeth. 'Oxford postmark Mrs V. That would be from the lovely Beatie then would it?'

'Are you wanting a cup of tea with your idle chatter?' Martha offered, good-natured beneath the gibe. She was relieved to see Olive heading towards the house with her three girls in tow, confirming what she needed to know about the nature of the knock at the door.

'No thank you Mrs V! I'll be on my way. And good morning to you Olive. How's your William? Haven't seen him for weeks.'

Olive brushed the postman aside and stepped into the house.

'Rude of you!' Martha said after the postman had gone. 'Not to say a word like that. Just bad manners!'

'He's a chatterbox. Haven't the time for it,' Olive said, filling the kettle.

'There's some as would call you a chatterbox,' Martha said. 'No need to be frosty with the postman just because he mentioned William.'

The distance between Olive and William was expanding. Martha trembled to intervene. But she hated to think of Olive's marriage running the same way as had her own, into silence and hostility.

Olive compressed her lips. Martha sank back into her chair and fumbled for her reading spectacles before tearing open the letter. 'It's from Beatie!' Martha said. 'She's coming home! All of them! Beatie, Bernard, Cassie and Frank.

They're all coming back to Coventry!'

Rita, returning from town that same morning, turned her key in the lock of her front door. As she pushed open the door she felt a rushing behind her, like huge wings, and a force bundled her inside the house. The door slammed as she was pushed roughly against the banister of the stairs in her hallway.

Rita giggled. 'You silly bugger! You frit me to death! Where have you been hiding?'

'Sat in me van,' William said. 'Waiting for you to get home.' Then he grabbed the coils of her gleaming chestnut hair. The light streaming through the circle of glass in the front door played on her hair, and it enraged him. He pulled her hair to him to stop her head from moving and he kissed her, mashing his lips against hers until they were both gasping for breath.

'Stop it!' Rita giggled. 'I've just come back from paying the gas bill.'

William held her head between his two hands. He was panting, and looking at her strangely, deep into her eyes.

She stopped giggling. 'What? What is it?'

'I don't know. It's the taste of you when we kiss. It's the smell of you. No, it's something in between, like the taste and smell of you. I keep trying to think what it's like.'

'What is it like?'

'Honey. But burned. Like something you know won't be there for ever.'

'I wish you'd stop looking at me like that.'

William kissed her again, and put his hand up

her skirt.

'Get off you dirty bugger!' Rita was giggling again. 'Who's looking after your shop? You're going to get caught out you know, and it won't be my fault.' She shuddered as he pushed a finger inside her. William fell to his knees and tore her stockings. 'Dirty bugger,' Rita said, more quietly. William made Rita come very quickly. Then he stood up and unbuttoned the rest of her clothes until she stood, still breathing heavily but now staring hard at him, naked in the hallway, leaning against the wall. He unbuckled his trousers and pushed his cock inside her and they fucked hard and up against the wall.

They leaned together afterwards, his head on her shoulder, mixing their perspiration, saying nothing.

After a while William said, 'I've got to get back to the shop.'

'You're mad coming here.'

'Well.' William buttoned up his trousers and ran a hand through hair gleaming with sweat. Then he gave her a quick peck on the cheek and was gone.

The door slammed behind him. Rita reached for the cigarettes in her handbag. She lit up, and, blowing a plume of smoke, looked at her nude self in the hallway mirror. 'Christ,' she said to her flushed image. 'I only went out to pay the gas bill.'

The following day Martha took a bus from town out to Wolvey, to visit Una and Tom at the farm. The farm lay a short walk from the bus stop. She could see Tom driving his tractor in the field, while Una trailed her non-identical chicks around the muddy yard down at the buildings. Martha shouted and waved, but they didn't hear her. She drew up and watched her daughter and grand-daughters moving about the yard, letting go an involuntary sigh of satisfaction. Una was over her spell of depression, and Martha could devote her energies elsewhere. But this wasn't what made her sigh with pleasure. It was the complication.

Martha had a mathematical turn of mind. She added numbers up and down and from side to side. She was perpetually involved in the task of evening out and reconciling discrepancy. If one equation was solved, she moved on to the next. That there was no end to life's problems in general and her own and her daughters' equations in particular did not daunt her in the slightest. That was life: in the busy shadow between perfection and the chaotic human ebb and flow that made perfection impossible. She had an eye for perfection but never expected to find it, indeed never wanted to find it. For Martha, perfection was something approaching death. Her sigh of pleasure, when she breathed it out into the crisp air of the farmyard morning, was simply that of the beads shuttling back across the abacus frame.

This complication was for Martha not another name for difficulty, but life itself; and she welcomed it.

She raised her voice, making a curious hailing sound, high-pitched and sing-song. 'Ooo-ooo! Ooo-ooo!'

Una and her daughters looked up. Martha could see Una's smile, broad and pleased, right across the yard.

Inside the farmhouse kitchen Martha balanced her teacup as Una filled it, and expertly cradled one of the twins with her other arm. The one thing she had learned from life, she often remarked, was how to hold a child and a cup of tea without spilling a drop. Una and Martha exchanged gossip, and Martha told Una about Beatie, Bernard, Cassie and Frank coming back to Coventry.

'Why so sudden?' Una wanted to know, trying to stop the other twin from twisting off her eyebrow. 'Ouch! You little monster!'

'Don't smile when you say that. They don't know what way to take it. I don't know why so sudden. Just the letter saying we're coming and get ready for us. That's all I know and they're here tomorrow.'

'And you're going to ask us to have Frank and Cassie back here,' Una said, thinking she'd seen to the bottom of Martha's surprise visit. Seeing to the bottom of Martha was a favourite pastime amongst the daughters.

'Hadn't thought of that at all. Is that teapot empty? No, that's not what I'm here for. I've come over to visit that Raggie Annie.'

'Raggie Annie? What do you want with her, Mam?'

'I was thinking of what you were saying. She's been done a bad turn and I collected a bit for her. She delivered Aida and Evelyn and Ina all those years ago when I was over here. And she delivered these lovely two o' yourn. Well I went around a few and told of her plight and we collected a bit.'

'Well you'll not see her. She's shut herself up in

that old cottage of hers and won't come out is how I've heard it.'

Martha struggled from her chair and lowered her twin to the floor. 'Well we'll see. I'll be on my way because it's a fair step.'

'Shall you have your dinner here? Tom will drive you back to Coventry, you know that. And here, before you go.' Una reached up to take down a biscuit tin from a shelf. It was her savings. She twisted the lid off the tin and put her hand in. 'Let me put a bit in for the old girl. I feel so sorry for her.'

Martha rapped the brass knocker, fashioned in the shape of a hare's head, for a second time. A small dog somewhere inside offered a muffled and pathetic bark but there was otherwise no response. Martha stepped back to survey the cottage.

It was as derelict as a cottage might be and still be called a domicile. The red paint on the door had peeled back to reveal an unassailable coat of thick dark green paint that might have been slapped on three generations earlier. The guttering over the door had leaked and streaked the grey walls with rich rust stains. A rainwater barrel leaned against the corner of the house, full to the brim. The wooden window frames had rotted and split and though the small panes of ancient glass were clean, drawn curtains obstructed the view inside.

Martha knocked again, vigorously this time. 'Come on young Annie, let's be having you.' Martha was Raggie Annie's senior by two years.

'Leave me be!'

276

'I'll not leave you be. Get and open this door.'

'Who is it?'

'Who is it? It's Martha Vine come a-calling on you Annie and you should know better than to leave an old woman standing on your threshold like this.'

'Never heard of you. Leave me be.'

'You delivered three of mine and my daughter Una's two, so don't be making out you never heard of me. And if I get cross it will not go well for you, so don't insult me by making me stand here Annie for I shan't think well of you! Now there.'

Martha's tone betrayed that she was already cross; and perhaps the old woman within detected it, and was moved by something in it or by a veiled threat hidden in Martha's words. After a moment there was the rattle of a bolt drawing back on the other side of the door, followed by another. Then the door opened a crack.

Annie's tiny, downcast voice pretended at defiance from the other side of the door. 'I'm not beholden to you or anyone.'

'No one says as you are.'

'What you here for then?'

'I needs your help Annie.'

'No one needs my help any more. They all done with it. They all–'

'You can stop that! You can stop feeling sorry for yourself right now. You've been done a bad turn, but I'm here to give you your due and to ask for a little help, so you can buck up and start by telling me you know who I am.'

Annie opened the door a little more and peered

277

round at Martha. Then she lowered her eyes. 'I knows who you am.'

'Then you'll know I mean you no harm and you'll let me in.'

Once inside, Martha took off her hat and sat down without being asked. Annie, more stooped and spine-curled than Martha remembered, went about the unconscious ritual of basic hospitality, getting chipped tea cups and saucers out of a cupboard, finding a loaf of bread and a pot of jam. Martha looked around. The cottage was untidy and exhibited a depressed air, but Martha wondered how much different it would have been before Annie's misfortunes. There were piles of rags heaped in the corners but the hearth was swept and the pots were washed and stacked. The beams overhead were pinned with herb and hedgerow bunches dried or drying. The shelves were filled with old stone and glass jars.

There was no gas ring or stove, only an iron pot on a swinging bracket in the hearth and the low embers of a wood fire. It reminded Martha of the house where she'd grown up. 'You needs water, Annie. I shall fetch it.' Without waiting for a response, Martha picked up the pot and took it out into the back yard, where she knew she would find a water pump. She levered water into the pot and returned to hang it on the bracket, swinging the arm so that the pot settled snugly over the embers to boil.

Annie sawed laboriously at the stale loaf of bread, setting it aside until the tea was ready. Then she took a seat opposite Martha. 'Want to know how many?' Annie said angrily.

'Go on,' Martha said.

'I made a record. Right from my very first. Scratched every one in a book.' Annie got up and rummaged in a drawer to produce a grubby, ancient notebook. She advertised the pages to her visitor. 'Seeing as how I can't write I could never make a note of the names but I made all these marks, see, this for a boy and like this for a gal. And I count 'em up, I do. It's my pride, Martha Vine, even if I'm to be punished for a bit of pride. Well I never could have my own, you know, never could, but I counts all these little ones up. All these little birds. And look at that. You know how many they is?'

'I'd like to know.'

'Yes. There's my first, look, more than forty years ago. There was people as would call me from thirty miles away for a difficult one. And here's my last. Twelve hundred and twenty-nine souls. And here, look, marked here in black is the few as I've lost. Them little ones. Them few marks in my book. And I've cried for them, I have. Not in my eyes but in my heart, Martha Vine. And here they are and they tell me that I'm no good for any of it.'

'My dear.'

And at Martha's last words, Annie's defiance and anger collapsed into a fit of sudden, exhausted weeping. And though Martha didn't go to her, preferring to wait it out, she had to lift a handkerchief to her own eye, because as she sat there she thought how it was much worse to see an old woman crying than a young one.

When the sobbing had subsided, Martha said, 'Never mind the bloody tea Annie, haven't you got anything better?'

Annie got up, sniffling, and pulled a bottle of dark liquor from a creaking cupboard. Finding a dusty glass apiece she splashed a measure for each of them.

'Sloe gin?' Martha said, sipping. 'It's good. Did you make this?'

'Aye.'

'You've been done a bad turn Annie. That's for sure. But you ain't to take it personal. It's all changed, all of it. Have you been into Coventry? Have you seen how it's changed?'

'Not since they bombed it to nothing I ain't.'

'It's all changed. Everything. There's buses and cars everywhere. There's television. And the kids have all got new ideas, some bad some good. It's not about you and me Annie.'

'It feels about me when they snatch my livelihood off me. They say the state will give me a dole but I don't want to make a dole, I want to fill out my book, Martha. That's what I do best.'

'What's this about the church?'

'A nonsense. I cleaned there, too, for fifteen years, and now this new vicar comes in and he takes a dislike, well I don't like him neither, but he says I've been pinching stuff from the church. What do I want with no bell and a gold plate? Well they paid me next to nothing anyway so I don't miss it, or I wouldn't if I had my true work back but the regulations this and the regulations that. What regulations? I say, I know how to wash my hands don't I?'

Martha placed her envelope containing cash on the table. 'This might help a little. I talked to a

280

few people as you've assisted over the years and they was all glad to give a bit. It's not much but there it is.'

'I want no charity. I'll not take it.'

'It's not charity Annie, it's recognition. People who have appreciated you have said you've been done a wrong turn. And anyway there's a payment amongst it from me.'

'Payment, what payment?' Annie was glad to have the matter turned.

'There's a small matter I need some help with. In confidence. And I know you'll keep it to yourself.'

'Who do I see to tell anything? What's it all about?'

'I had nowhere to turn but to you Annie. Pour me another glass o'that sloe and I'll tell you.'

26

Rita dozed by the fireplace. The embers had sunk low in the grate, and Rita was not quite asleep yet not awake either when there came a knock on the door. At first she couldn't seem to stir, experiencing a moment of paralysis and a constricting of the chest. But when the knocking came again, louder, she managed to break out of her lethargy.

She knew it must be William. No one else visited unexpected. She could see the figure at the door through the circle of frosted glass. Her response was ambivalent as she checked herself in the hall mirror, her cheeks flushed and her eyes slightly puffed from dozing by the fire. She knew what he would do as soon as he got inside the door, and that excited her; she knew she would feel empty after he had gone, and that made her not want to open the door. But she did.

It wasn't William. It was an old woman, dressed in shapeless black. She wore a broad-brimmed hat stuck with a hatpin, something that might have been fashionable in the 1930s. The old woman carried a small potted plant. Rita felt momentarily dizzy. The street roiled, like the sea. Rita thought she might be dreaming, then recovered. 'Yes?'

'Rita?'

'Yes?'

'I'm Martha Vine.' When Rita offered a quizzical shake of the head, Martha added, 'William's mother-in-law.'

Rita closed her eyes and moaned softly.

'I haven't come to give you trouble, Rita. I want to talk.'

After a long pause, when it appeared she might faint clean away, Rita opened her eyes, looked up and down the street and asked Martha to step inside.

In the lounge, Martha placed the small potted plant on the mantelpiece, beside the photograph of Archie. 'I brought a little gift for you. It's pretty isn't it? It scents the air. Is this a photo of your husband?'

Rita looked at the plant as if she wasn't so sure it was pretty at all. It looked like something dug from a hedgerow. 'Yes. Why don't you sit down Mrs Vine? Shall I fetch you some tea?'

'No don't. I can't stay more than a few minutes.

Fighting in France together weren't they? William and your husband?'

Rita sat down. She covered her mouth with her fingertips. When, she spoke it was through her fingers. 'Yes.'

'William has spoken of him a great deal. I think he misses him an awful lot. Just as you must miss him.'

'Yes.'

'Do you want him? William, I mean? Do you want him for yourself?'

Rita got up and went to the window, turning her back on Martha. 'I don't know. Sometimes I think I do. Then I think I don't. I didn't chase him, you know. He came here. I never once chased after him.'

'Look, I'm not judging you Rita. I've done it myself in my time.'

Rita turned back to look at Martha.

'Yes. There was a cost though. My husband and I didn't speak for all the years after. I was so stupid. I let it go on and then he was dead and then it's too late isn't it? Not that he wasn't to blame. But then blame is not worth bothering with, is how I've come to look at it. It's what you do that matters.'

Rita sat down again, hugging herself.

'You have to decide if you want him for yourself. If there's no stopping it then there's no more to be said. He will have to pay the price, along with Olive and his children. But if you don't want him then you've got to end it.'

'I've told you, he comes here. I never invited him. I never tell him to come back. But then

283

when he comes I can't stop myself.'

'You can. It's us women who stand at the gate, Rita. Us women. We control the gate. We hold the gate open or we keep it closed. You're a handsome woman; you'll not be short of men at the gate. But you've got to be precise.'

'How did you know where I live?'

'For goodness' sake Rita! Everyone knows William's van. It's got his name on the side of it.'

'It's just not so easy as you're painting it. I feel like I've been bleeding my life away these five years. Then he comes and the bleeding stops.'

Martha got up to leave. 'It's both as easy and as difficult as I'm painting it. I only said you have to decide. And I've given you something to help you.'

'Help me? What will help me?'

'You'll see. Now will you show me out?'

At the open door Martha said, 'It's up to you whether you say anything to William about my coming here. I certainly shan't. But if he wants to tackle me about it, I'm ready for him. Otherwise I'll keep my mouth shut. There's another thing.'

'What's that?'

'The little plant I gave you. If you don't take to it you can throw it out. But not before a week has passed. It's bad luck to throw them away before the week is out. Mark that. Very bad luck. Goodbye Rita.'

Rita closed the door on Martha and leaned her back against it. She'd been holding her breath. Then she ran through to the lounge, pressing her nose against the glass to look up and down the street after the old woman, but she was gone. Almost as if she had never actually been there.

Rita looked at the fireplace. Then she looked at the mantelpiece, and there was the small potted plant. Rita couldn't identify the rather scrawny plant, what with its bright green, herb-type leaves. She sniffed at it. The scent was unusual, sharp but sweet, and quite pleasant. Rita didn't like the idea of leaving the plant there. She thought about tossing it out immediately. But something in Martha's parting shot made her reconsider. She decided to leave the plant where it was.

27

Beatie, Bernard, Cassie and Frank all rolled up together and there was great rejoicing. They might have returned not from some place fifty miles away but from war and conflagration in the Far East. All the sisters weighed in, tins of salmon were turned out, sandwiches were buttered and filled, joints of ham and tongue were sliced, beetroots and red onions were chopped and bottles of stout and brown ale were handed round. And if Beatie were the Prodigal Daughter, none felt at all envious.

Except that Aida, the eldest of the sisters, somehow felt her nose had been pushed out in the preparations. Olive had taken charge and had ridden roughshod over everyone else in trying to make the party special. Una had offered to make a cake, but Olive hadn't heard her so had gone out and paid for one. Evelyn and Ina had come by a leg of pork but Olive had asked Una to bring the ham. Aida had undertaken to provide a bottle of sherry but Olive had sent William out for beer.

'It's all the flippin' time,' Aida protested to Martha, who tried to defend Olive in that she was having a difficult time of late, but Aida wasn't having any of it. 'She listens to no one but herself, and you stick up for her and her misery. All the flippin' time.'

Martha made to answer, but then the prodigals had arrived. William had driven down to the bus station to pick them up and there they were frothing at the door like a high tide, rolling in, all smiles and there were kisses and hugs and some small tears.

'Whatever have you done to your hand Bernard?' Martha said. 'Here, let me take your coat. Come on Frank, give your grandma a kiss cos I've missed you. There, look how you've grown! He's grown Cassie, he's grown!'

'He has grown,' Tom said. 'You'll be ready to kick a football won't you?'

'Now there's ham, and there's tongue, and there's–' Olive tried.

Aida said, 'Let them get in the door Olive, for goodness' sake!'

'Have we got enough chairs?' Evelyn asked.

'Give Bernard a beer,' Una said. 'What's that bandage on your hand, Bernard? Get those chairs from the lean-to, Ina, I'm sure we'll need them.'

'There's salmon, there's cheese...'

'A lovely spread,' Beatie said. 'Come here Tom and give us a kiss!'

'You put him down!' Una shouted.

'Oh look at the twins!' Cassie said. 'Aren't they beautiful! Give 'em here, God let me kiss 'em! Give me both! I want both.'

'Have you ... eeeeeeeeeeee ... been in the wars, Bernard?' Gordon said, pouring a nut-brown ale. 'Here you...'

'There's plenty of beetroot...'

'For God's sake stop fussing Olive!' Aida went, red in the face.

Everyone's coat was off and put aside, all had found a chair, everyone was talking and drinking and Martha sat in her chair under the clock feeling that all might be well with the world. She picked up the poker and stabbed at the burning coal with a zealous pleasure. To be all under one roof. These were moments she savoured as one might sip a vintage brandy.

'Tell me all about this place then Frank,' Tom said. 'Sit here and tell me about Ravenscraig. Did they have any animals there?'

Frank sat on the arm of Tom's chair and told him, 'Only capitalist running-dogs and imperialist hyenas.'

'Eh? What?'

'Ravenscraig was set up as an experiment against Capital. We were an important alternative.'

'Were you? Don't spill your ginger beer, Frank.'

'Sorry. Yes. You see, all the best minds of the country were gathered there including me and we had to arm ourselves against the onslaught of shoddy materialist goods which will comp ... comp–'

'Compromise,' Beatie said, kneeling beside him to listen. 'Compromise the working classes and

287

debase their social values.'

'Goodness me,' Tom said. 'What does it all mean?'

'I don't know,' Frank said, 'but now everyone has left Ravenscraig for a while, for logical differences.'

'Ideological differences,' Beatie corrected, looking at Tom. 'We had a dust-up.'

'I see,' Tom said, swallowing a mouthful of brown ale, not seeing anything. 'Did you learn anything else Frank?'

'Yes. There was too much shagging going on.'

Beatie winced. Tom put his finger in his ear and fetched out a tiny piece of wax. In all the noise no one else had heard the remark. Beatie said, 'Frank, I don't think we'll be able to be quite so open about things here as we were at Ravenscraig.'

'Why?' Frank asked reasonably.

'Different places have different rules. That's all. Isn't it Tom?'

'Oh yes. Apparently. When are you coming out to the farm again, Frank?'

Elsewhere in the room, Cassie was also being quizzed about the dreaming spires of Oxford and the exotic mystery of Ravenscraig. What sort of place was it then? Una and William wanted to know.

'All posh types,' Cassie said, 'with nothing in the cupboard.'

'Ha! That's bloody left-wingers for you!' William said.

'I'm a left-winger, I've decided,' Cassie said. 'I'm a hell-bent radical. That's me. You can stuff your grubby capitalist values for all I care.'

'Stone me! They've got to her!' William laughed.

'But what was it like?' Una exclaimed.

'Sex for breakfast, dinner and tea. If you wanted it. With readings from big fat books in between. But they were strangers to soap and water so I didn't much fancy any of them, except one called George, and I made him go and wash himself before I'd let him touch me and just as he was doing that it all happened.'

'What happened?'

'The reason why we came home. Are there any more of those tongue and pickle sandwiches? Are there any more? I'm going to get some.'

William and Una were left nursing empty beer glasses, looking at each other.

'Well,' Una said after a moment, 'don't sit there like a capitalist lackey, go and get some more ale.'

In another corner, Bernard was very patiently explaining things to Aida, Evelyn and Ina. His hands measured an exact eighteen-inch gap, as if he were describing a length of wood. 'It had its virtues and its vices. No social experiment is without difficulty, that's why it's an experiment. We were blessed with some penetrating intellectual minds at Ravenscraig, but sometimes with that kind of genius a certain temperamental disposition can be tricky to contain. Though we did make progress with establishing certain rules for the community–'

'Have to have rules,' Aida avowed. 'Can't live without rules.'

'Quite so Aida, and Beatie would be the first to agree with you, as she succeeded in setting up some of those rules, and let me say–'

'Another sandwich, Bernard?'

'Thank you Olive.'

'Shall I take your glass? You can't use your other hand with it all bandaged up like that can you?'

'*We* were talking!' Aida snorted.

'I'm only commenting—'

'And we were talking so stop being so rude all the time. What were you saying Bernard?'

Olive, white-faced, shrank back with her tray of sandwiches.

More beer bottles were opened, the sherry was uncorked, the sandwiches eaten and the cakes consumed. Ravenscraig continued to be a subject of enquiry but somehow, after all questions had been put and all answers weighed, no one in the room who hadn't been there felt any wiser about the place or its populace. The erstwhile Ravenscraigites might have been reporting back from a mystical plane beyond the veil, for the summaries were no more concrete than reports from those who had gone before at one of Ina and Evelyn's spiritualist sessions.

But Ravenscraig was already history. It was a strange event in the family that had passed, like the war had passed. And the pleasure of the party was to show that they had survived Ravenscraig just as they had survived the Coventry blitz. They might be marked, or scarred, but they had come through wiser and stronger. Once again they had earned the right to celebrate with a brown ale and a ham sandwich.

Frank played with Olive's children and with Una's twins, and it was a treat for everyone to see the children get along so well. Cassie in particular was relieved to be home, and to see Frank back in the bosom of the family. Ravenscraig had been fun, thrilling at times, alarming at others, and only occasionally deadly dull. Sometimes it had even been a relief to be among people who were clearly madder than she was but who seemed to be able to function perfectly well in the world. Nevertheless, the unpleasant business with Peregrine Feek had brought the adventure to a suitable stop, and anyway Bernard had given him what he deserved, and the professor had recourse to philosophy to explain his black eye to his students.

Though she'd been furious around the event itself, and had almost broken her own hands and her toes, too, on Feek's back as he'd crawled on all fours out of the grounds of the commune, now it made her smile. And as she smiled and looked up she saw her father grinning back at her. He was sat cross-legged on the draining board next to the kitchen sink. She gasped, and then smiled wider, because it had been so long. Cassie looked up and round, to see if anyone else had seen the old man. She couldn't help but look to Martha; and Martha, even though she was engaged in a conversation with Ina, looked up at Cassie because nothing, but nothing, was ever lost on her.

'What?' Martha said. 'What is it Cassie?'

'Nothing,' went Cassie.

Martha wasn't easily put off the scent. She was about to quiz Cassie further when the storm broke.

'Get my coat!' Aida screamed. She jabbed a finger at Frank. 'Go in there and get my coat!'

'You tell her to get it herself if she wants her coat!' Olive screamed back at Aida, glaring at her but not addressing her.

Everyone else in the room stopped talking instantly, all turning to watch the confrontation.

'Go and get my coat! I'll not stay here a minute longer with this stupid meddlesome woman. I shan't!'

'Don't you move, Frank!' Olive shrieked.

'Let's be calm,' Tom said.

'Calm?' Aida spat. 'How can anyone be calm when you've got this stupid silly fusspot setting everyone's teeth on edge at every turn. She wants a good slap so she does.'

'Steady on,' William said. 'Don't talk about Olive like that. She's no more stupid or silly than you are Aida.'

'Will somebody get my coat? Gordon are you going to let William talk to me like that?'

'Aye, watch your tongue William.' Gordon had lost his stutter, and finished a sentence.

'Watch my tongue should I? I didn't say anything different than she did about Olive. And what will you do?'

'We'll see,' Gordon said.

'This is getting daft,' Bernard said.

'We'll bloody well see what?' William shouted. His blood was up and his eyes were moist. 'Like when you were hiding when the rest of us were over in France?'

'Don't bring that up,' said Tom.

'Hiding! Playing bloody toy soldiers in the ARP because he was too bloody scared! So what's he going to do now?'

'He wasn't scared,' Cassie tried to put in. 'Cos I saw him on the night of the blitz.'

But no one heard because now everyone was shouting. Martha banged her stick on the coal scuttle, but where this might normally be expected to bring everyone to order, it only added to the, din.

In the commotion Aida managed to get her coat. She and Gordon left by the back door and were gone before anyone could bring them back.

After a decent interval of silence the adults in the room tried to analyse what had happened while the children played with toys on the floor and pretended not to be listening. Olive, in fits of weeping now, was comforted by Evelyn while Bernard and Tom tried to talk William out of the silence into which he'd retreated. Martha sat in her chair and said nothing. She'd seen it all before, and many times over, when the sisters were girls; and at six, sixteen or sixty, was there any real difference in a bust-up of this nature? A pity, only, that it had to occur at the homecoming, but then Martha had a pretty shrewd idea of why that had happened, too.

Cassie, not wanting to join in the general enquiry, went outside into the back garden to smoke a cigarette. From the garden she could see the three spires of the city, and of those the spire of St Michael's she had climbed (or thought she had climbed) on the night of the blitz was the highest. She sat on a bench slab her father had raised there years before and gazed into the weed garden, and as she did so her father took shape, out of the background of the brown earth and the green weeds and the distant, spires. He looked at Cassie fondly, but his grin had gone. He shook his head sadly, and then he disappeared, and though she had seen this apparition of her father many, many times, this time it made her cry.

After a while William came out of the house and saw Cassie sitting in the garden.

'Budge up a bit,' he said.

Cassie shifted to make room for William. He was about to light his cigarette when he said, 'You been crying Cassie? Don't worry. It don't mean nothing. I didn't mean the things I said and I'm sorry for it.'

'I haven't been crying about that,' Cassie said.

'About what then?'

'About my dad. He was so sad. Always so sad. I think he's still sad now.'

William puffed out his cheeks and pinched the knees of his trousers higher. He always felt out of his depth in conversation with Cassie. 'I don't know that the old boy was always so sad, from what I remember of him.'

'Are you happy, William?'

'God Cassie, what a question!'

'Are you?'

'No, I ain't. Though I have been thinking about it lately. I'm coming round to the idea that there's no shame in not being happy. I'm coming round to the idea that it ain't about being happy all the time. This life.'

'What is it about then?'

William smiled thinly. 'I haven't got that far yet. No shame in not knowing, either, is there?'

'No. William, what you said about Gordon? In

the war? It isn't true, you know. I saw him on the night of the blitz. I saw what he did.'

William stubbed out his cigarette. 'Tongue ran away with me. Been feeling mithered lately. I shall apologise to Gordon when I see him. Shall we go back in?'

Cassie got up and followed William to the house, but before she went inside she looked back for signs of her father. He was long gone.

Indoors, Evelyn and Ina were getting ready to leave. Olive was stacking plates, Una and Tom were dressing the twins.

'A funny homecoming party,' Beatie said to Martha.

'I'm just glad to have you back amongst us,' Martha said. 'And anyway, Beatie, a homecoming party is not always about those as are coming home.'

28

Frank and Cassie stayed with Martha. Beatie and Bernard billeted for the initial few weeks, but before the Christmas of that year decided to rent a flat in Paynes Lane, nearer to town. Both found teaching jobs with the Workers Education Association, where they felt dedicated to replenishing the opportunities that had been afforded to them. Though they were unlikely to direct their charges to Ravenscraig, they were both committed to the notion of an educated proletariat. After all, someone was going to have to lead the revolution which would inevitably follow the crash of capitalism.

Capitalism, however, wasn't yet done with Coventry. The wartime factories beat swords not into ploughshares nor spears into pruning hooks, but into civil aviation and Standard Eight saloon cars. The rebuilding went on unabated, though not always in line with the master-architect's vision.

'It's not right.' Bernard said. 'They're not doing what he said.'

They stood in the new precinct in the town centre, shivering in their winter coats. A compromise had been made on the vision of a pedestrianised shopping garden in the centre of the city, and a new road had been cut through what was supposed to be a traffic-free area in Smithford Street.

'We should have stayed here,' Beatie said bitterly. 'We should have stayed and got on the Council and fought like mad. We shouldn't have been wasting our time playing silly games at Ravenscraig.'

'Would have taken more than you and me fighting like mad,' Bernard said sadly. 'Looks to me like a few wallets got lined.'

'A few palms got greased,' said Beatie.

'A few pockets got picked,' Bernard said.

'A few faces got licked.'

'What? I don't get that one.'

Beatie shrugged. Then she laughed. 'Let's go and get a beer in the Golden Cross.'

And it was in that ancient pub adjacent to the bombed cathedral, over a couple of warm beers, maundering over the mess that compromised architects, businessmen with vested interests and corrupt councillors were making of the rebuilding of Coventry, that Beatie and Bernard decided they would stand for election to the City Council.

A few days after the home-coming party William made another call on Rita.

'I haven't got long,' he said.

Rita led him into the lounge. When William went to hug her she pressed the flat of her hand against his chest and then stepped back. 'William, I don't like it when you come round here and then just as quick you go again.'

William collapsed on to the sofa. He scratched the back of his neck. He looked up at her and his nostrils twitched. He glanced at the photo of Archie on the mantelpiece above the fire. 'I don't blame you. I don't blame you at all.'

Rita sat down next to him and put a hand on his knee. 'I cry at night.'

'Do you?'

'I do. I cry because I still miss Archie and I cry because I miss you, too. You're with me but you're not with me. We're together but we're not together. You've made it so that I keep thinking about you but I can't be with you.'

William's nose twitched again. He glanced round the room as if trying to puzzle it all out, looking for inspiration about what to say. 'Rita, something smells a bit off.'

'Aren't you the romantic one!'

'I'm just saying.'

'I hope you don't mean me!' Rita laughed.

'Of course I don't mean you. Something in the house.' He glanced round the room again. There was nothing to comment on. Only the usual ornaments and the picture of Archie and a potted plant on the mantelpiece. 'Come here, come close.'

Rita let William hug her this time, snuggling against him. He buried his nose inside the collar of her blouse, inhaling that intoxicating Rita-scent, the natural perfume of her body that chained him to her. This was what he'd come for. He took a deep draught of her. It was heady and awesome. It turned all this madness into a kind of sanity. It was an oasis. An island in the dark. You could fall into that scent and never want to come up for air.

But William did come up for air. He sat upright and his nostrils twitched again. Something bothered him. He glanced again round the room. 'What is it?'

'I should go,' he groaned. 'I really should go. Look Rita,' he said, standing up. 'Christmas is coming. I'm not going to be able to see you for a few days. Holidays. Kiddies and everything. You'll be all right, won't you? Christmas, I mean.'

'I'll be all right,' Rita said softly. She knew William was saying goodbye.

William bent down to kiss her. She offered her cheek for him to peck. Then William was gone, letting himself out through the front door. It clicked softly behind him. Rita looked thoughtfully at the potted plant on the mantelpiece.

That Christmas of 1951 was difficult in other ways. Customarily each sister's home was visited by all of the other sisters, and where possible all together. But Aida and Olive were Not Speaking.

Not Speaking being particularly difficult when in the same room, the engineering to ensure this didn't happen was a more delicate and exact process than the bomb-making many of the sisters had become trained in during the course of the war. If they might all be going to another's house on the same day then they made a point of finding out what time the one might be leaving so that the other might arrive, and the two warring sisters colluded with this without ever admitting that was what they were doing.

'She can do what she bloody well likes,' one said.

'She can please her bloody self,' said the other.

They were all careful not to appear to take sides, even though their sympathies might lean one way more than the other. Evelyn and Ina had always found Aida overbearing, whereas Una and Beatie readily confessed to being irritated by Olive's fussy and neurotic controlling nature. Cassie was swayed by whoever was arguing the point.

'But she's a heart of gold, Olive has,' Cassie told Beatie.

'She is, Cassie, but it's all a means of making you feel beholden to her,' Una argued.

'I suppose you're right.'

Then Cassie would say, 'But Aida is nothing but fair with each of us.'

'Yes Cassie,' Ina might answer, 'but she has *so* got to have her own way in everything.'

'Yes, you have a point.'

Martha kept out of it, and told both Aida and

Olive point-blank that they were behaving like schoolgirls. Whatever happened, the cake had always been cut eight ways equally, and still would be now.

'Grandma,' Frank asked Martha, 'why aren't Auntie Olive and Auntie Aida speaking to each other?'

'They've sent each other to Coventry.' Frank blinked at that. Martha had cleaned out her pipe and was packing it with fresh tobacco. 'It's what people say when they're not speaking: sent to Coventry.'

'Was it something that happened at the party?'

'Well they say as it is, but it isn't. When people stop speaking to each other, it isn't for something that happens in a minute.'

'Why would anyone stop speaking?'

Martha lit her pipe, shook out the spill and slung it on the back of the fire. She puffed up a cloud of blue, sweet-smelling smoke. Frank peered at her through the smoke. It appeared to make her eyes water. An answer was a long time coming. 'Ghosts,' Martha said.

'Ghosts?'

'Yes. You can make a ghost out of a person by not speaking to them. It's a way of killing them, do you see, turning them to stone, but still having them around so as you can go on and on punishing them. So don't you ever do that, will you Frankie?'

'No Grandma.'

'No Grandma. Now can you go and play in your room as I'd like to have a bit of peace.'

29

The feud between Aida and Olive lasted all through 1952 and well into the summer of 1953. It was a nuisance for everyone, having to work round the feud without overtly taking sides and without treating anyone less favourably. Though Martha was fond of saying that she'd gone down on her knees to get the two sisters to behave sensibly, her arthritic joints would never allow such a gesture and anyway Martha wasn't given to theatrical display. In fact she'd pleaded and remonstrated for a while, but to counter-productive effect. Then she'd stopped. After all, she knew a thing or two about lengthy silence in her own life, and had a pretty shrewd notion of what might and might not break it.

Cassie and Frank lived with her, and without bringing a great deal of trouble or shame to her door. Frank was old enough to walk to and from school along with a gaggle of local children; Cassie was enjoying a period of life untroubled by the blue funk. Whatever else had happened at Ravenscraig, something of her time there had given her an extra confidence to the way she carried herself, and to the way she might argue a point instead of turning to a pout or a sulk. She was even visited occasionally by the young man from Ravenscraig called George.

Martha liked George. He made her chuckle,

even though she could see he was charming her to get to Cassie. Frank liked George too, and the three of them would entertain Martha with abridged stories of what folk were like at Castle Ravenscraig, as it came to be called. George stayed over some nights. They made him a bed on the floor of the living room. On those nights Martha often heard the creak of floorboards, or of whispering, or of light footfalls on the stairs, but said nothing, even though the other sisters would have been scandalised at her tolerance. Martha had come to the conclusion where Cassie was concerned that it was not sex that got Cassie into trouble; it was roaming the streets looking for it. She'd ruled out the notion of Cassie ever finding a husband who'd stick by her through the times she became a faun in the woods or started seeing spirits. It was just too much to expect of any fellow. So if George turned out to be a steady interest (if not quite a regular boyfriend) then it was all to be encouraged.

Bernard and Beatie had always maintained good relations with George, and they were glad to see him. And when on occasion Lilly came to Coventry to join them, usually staying at Paynes Lane with Beatie and Bernard, it seemed that Ravenscraig, or at least the radical rump of Ravenscraig, was drawn to Martha's house and offered her a kind of second family.

'Anyone who doesn't mind plain bread and butter and who has no objection to soap and water,' Martha said more than once, when asked if she minded having all these unusual visitors, 'is welcome.'

But it was during the summer, when Martha mentioned that Tom and Una wanted Frank to spend some time over at the farm, that Aida made an unexpected offer herself.

Cassie was horrified. 'Oh no! We shan't go there! It's really not right! Why ever has she offered, now, of all times when we don't need it?'

'It doesn't seem suitable,' Ina and Evelyn agreed. 'Not with that awful back room of his!'

'Ugh!' said Una.

'The top and bottom of it,' said Olive, who'd lately taken on her mother's most decisive figures of speech, 'is that she's offered it to nark me.'

'How does it nark you?' Martha said. 'Not everything is about you.'

But Martha knew that there was some truth in Olive's words. Olive and Aida were the only two of the sisters who had not taken their proper turn in the original pact to share the burden of raising Frank. Olive and William had come through a difficult patch and their marriage was – mysteriously – vitally restored. Something had happened one Christmas to give Olive a girlish spring in her step and knowledge in her eye. Consequently the feud hadn't hurt her as much as it might have. But it did indeed 'nark' her to think that Aida's surprise proposal would leave her, Olive, looking like the only sister who had failed on a point of serious family duty.

Beatie was on hand to talk it over with Martha. 'Seems to me you've got to let Aida have her turn, Mam. Whatever her motives are. I mean Frank came to us when everyone thought Ravenscraig was a den of vice, and you allowed it.

303

How's it going to look if you say a den of vice is all right for Frank but not your house? You'll be the one she's not speaking to next.'

Martha knew Beatie was right. Beatie talked more sense than any of them put together. Frank was going to have to have a short spell with Aida and Gordon.

'Let him have the rest of the summer with Tom and Una,' Beatie said. 'Then when the new school term starts he can go with Aida. Cassie can stay here if she can't face it, and that way she can bring him back every weekend.'

Martha sucked on her pipe, melancholy and thoughtful. 'Yes. That's how it shall have to be.'

'Not that I fancy it much for the lad,' Beatie said. 'Not with Gordon's back room and everything.'

So Frank was allowed to enjoy the deep summer at the farm. Cassie was pleased because she could renew her devotion to horse riding. Frank was also able to check that the Man-Behind-The-Glass was exactly where he'd left him. The plank bridge across the stream was a dense, overgrown tangle of nettles and brambles, foxgloves and fireweed. He found it difficult to worm his way under the bridge to get to his old shrine, and when he did the Man-Behind-The-Glass, though undisturbed, didn't have anything to say. 'Have you sent me to Coventry?' Frank asked him. But the lack of response confirmed only that the answer could have been yes or no; and on retreating from under the old den, Frank got his head stuck, experiencing a few moments of dreadful panic.

He didn't put his head under again for fear of a

repetition, though he did try to hail The-Man-Behind-The-Glass from a distance, just to let him know he was still around. The rest of the summer passed in a hallucination of lush green meadows and haymaking; of barley fields and harvesting; and of humid afternoons and sudden thunderstorms. Frank had such little impact on his environment, and the passage of day into night and back into day again made life seem so ephemeral and indiscriminate, that he might just as well have been a brilliant blue damselfly skimming the water of the pond at the bottom of Tom's fields.

For pass the days did, and when summer that year turned to autumn, it was not with the slow swing of a hinge or the nudging of a vast wheel: it was as if one day the door on summer had slammed shut. Suddenly the hedgerows were spilling a seasonal store of blue sloes and ruby elderberries, of scarlet haws and blackberries, and of deadly nightshade.

Frank was returned initially to his grandmother's house, where he was serenaded with the news that he was to go to live with his Aunt Aida and Uncle Gordon for a 'week or two' until his grandmother's health recovered a little.

In fact there was nothing wrong with Martha's health beyond the regular catalogue of ailments of ripe age. It was put that way so that Frank wouldn't argue, and Frank didn't. He'd come to accept this eternal shuttling back and forth between his aunts as a natural condition of childhood, assuming that most people lived in the same way. He never once asked himself why his Aunt Olive's three children or his Aunt Una's twins were not shared around. He'd already learned to pack the things he wanted to take rather than leave it to someone else's judgement. When he brought his small battered case downstairs with him on the day Gordon was appointed to collect him, Cassie cried all over again.

'Chin up!' William said to Frank. William had called in at that moment with a delivery of vegetables. He turned to Cassie and said, 'He'll be all right: he'll frighten them spooks to death!'

This only made Cassie sob louder.

'Enough of that,' Martha said. 'He's only going three streets away.'

That was a slight understatement, since Gordon thought it was far enough to get out his Coventry built Standard Eight and have it purring outside the front gate, ready for the boy. Gordon's parsimony kept the car garaged except for very special occasions and bank holiday weekends, and Frank enjoyed the sense of privilege as he was driven to his new home with slow, careful and obsessive precision.

The fact remained that in matters of space alone Gordon and Aida were the best disposed to take Frank at any time. They owned a comparatively stately house on the Binley Road, a lugubrious pebble-dashed and slate-tiled property set back from the road and half-hidden behind conifers. Even as Gordon eased the motor into the drive Aida was waiting in the doorway, hands clasped under chin, her lips mobile without actually speaking, as if about to ask for the answers to three riddles before admission to the house might be granted.

306

Gordon made Frank wait in the car until he came round and opened the door for him, as if he were a young prince. The rictus – the raw, gum-exposing smile – never left Gordon's mouth as he daintily carried the boy's suitcase to the door. 'Ayeeeee, well missis,' he said at last. 'Here's our boy!'

Aida wobbled her head slightly and with disconcerting pride pressed the palm of her right hand to her breastbone and intoned the words, 'Welcome, Frank, to our home.'

Whatever Aida's motives for inviting Frank to stay might have been – and Olive's jaundiced view was not wholly inaccurate – she was pleased and oddly excited to receive Frank, and Gordon was, too. To say that they knew nothing about small children was not entirely true. Aida's youth had been plagued by the arrival of so many younger siblings, but she was well out of practice. Gordon had been an only child, and as such had inherited enough money to give Aida and him a good start in this superior property. Frank was to learn just a little about superiority on the Binley Road, starting with the principle that Aida was determined to give Frank the best; or at least better than any of the other sisters had managed.

To begin with he was shown his room, and a very fine room it was. Like Evelyn and Ina before her, Aida had made an *effort*. As before the *effort* included a picture of a football team hung on the wall. This one was not so superannuated as the picture still hanging at the twins' house. It was a recent team photograph of the Coventry City Football Club, with ruddy-faced soccer players

307

smiling toothily at the camera. In addition there was a Sky Blue rosette pined to the wall, and with it a promise that Gordon would take him to see a match on a day when the rosette might be worn. There was also a brand-new full-sized match ball, inflated and laced and balanced on the top of the cupboard. Other boyish paraphernalia had been specially imported: a model aircraft hung from the ceiling; a ship in a glass case. Splendid things for a boy but all, including the football, which Frank suspected he might not be allowed to touch.

This impression was re-enforced when Aida drew his attention to a bookcase filled with mostly pristine reference books. Aida said that the books had been put there especially for him to help with something she called 'his studies'; and that he might consult them at any time but that he might think to wash his hands first. This injunction came in direct contrast to his experiences at Ravenscraig. Peregrine Feek had told him that a book was merely a commodity of low value containing ideas of high value which themselves resided elsewhere. That the ideas contained in a book and the book itself were different things, Feek had proved by lighting a fire one day with pages torn from *Das Kapital* which everyone at Ravenscraig seemed to think the best book ever written. Frank looked at the gleaming books shelved in his new room and had an early notion that Aida might not on all matters agree with Peregrine Feek.

When tea was served it was at a polished table draped in crisp linen and loaded with silver cutlery and china plates so fine Frank thought they might tinkle to bits if he tapped them with his silver fork. Soup was served as a first course and Aida showed him how to tilt the soup bowl away from him rather than towards him; fish was offered for the main course and Frank encountered a flat boning-knife for the very first time; dessert came in the shape of a small peach and he observed that though it didn't need to be peeled, it did need quartering while still on the plate.

New rules came in the smallest things. During dinner Frank listened as Aida complained that a tradesman had that day appeared at the front door rather than the back. From what was said this terrible reversal had been brought about by the war. The war had created a decline in standards in general, and the public wearing of trousers by women in particular. Frank wondered what might happen to Aida if a *female* tradesman wearing *trousers* came to the *front* door. It was a long way from Ravenscraig to the Binley Road.

'Now then,' Aida said, 'have you had sufficient?'

'Yes thanks.'

'Yes thank-you, Frank, yes thank you. Thanks is common. Isn't it Gordon?'

'Eeeee... If you say so.'

'I do say so. Where are you going Frank?'

Frank was arrested in the act of climbing down from his chair. 'Nowhere.'

'Well before we go nowhere we usually ask if we may get down from the table, don't we Gordon?'

'Aye ... eeeeeee ... Aida, don't be going on at the laddie!'

'I am not going on and Frank will be grateful when he's out in the world to have learned good manners. Frank I'm not telling you off, I'm trying to help you after this disaster at ... what was the name of that awful place?'

'Ravenscraig.'

'Yes. We can guess at what the manners were like there, can't we?'

'Yes Aunt Aida.'

Then Aida picked up her serviette and dabbed at her eye. 'I'm sorry Frank. I'm not being very nice am I? When I'm like this your Uncle Gordon calls me an old trout. Am I being an old trout?'

Gordon laughed heartily. Then Aida laughed too. Suddenly the pair of them were red in the face from laughing. Frank looked from one to the other and manufactured a smile of his own.

'You must tell me if I'm being an old trout. You will won't you Frank? Won't you? Say you will? What will you say? What will you say I am?'

Frank looked wildly at Gordon, who, displaying more of that livid gum-matter, bared his teeth and nodded encouragement. The laughter had stopped as the two waited for Frank to say it.

'Old ... trout.'

Aida nodded with grim satisfaction and put down her napkin. Gordon too seemed satisfied with that. The brief uproarious laughter had ended and now it was time for everyone to get down from the table with or without permission.

Gordon excused himself, saying he had one or two things to attend to 'out the back'. Frank watched him over his shoulder. He'd heard more than a few things about Gordon's activities 'out the back'. The rear section of the large house had been given over to Gordon's funerary occupation.

310

Though not an undertaker (Gordon's haggard visage was for the public too eerily close to that of a long-dead corpse to allow him to don the black serge and top hat of the funeral attendant except in cases of dire shortage) he was a skilled embalmer, dating back to his sudden induction into the business after the air raids on Coventry.

At that time, when the need was pressing and there was urgency about processing the huge number of corpses in the city, he had quickly learned the art. He had set up the rear premises of his house, a former dentistry, as a temporary mortuary as he quick-packed the mortal remains of the blitz casualties on their way to hasty burial. He'd found something he was very good at, and the temporary soon became the permanent, and he was licensed. He had an arrangement with two nearby funeral parlours. Fresh corpses would be brought to him for preparation and afterwards collected by the undertakers for presentation to the grieving relatives in a proper chapel of rest.

Frank knew all this, in the abstract sense. He'd heard Evelyn and Ina object to his coming here because of his special empathy with the spirits. 'He shouldn't be in a place while the spirits are still passing,' they argued. 'Not with his special sensitivity.'

'Tosh!' Martha had said to that.

'It'll be creepy for the lad,' Olive had said.

'It's where we all go. It's a fact of life,' Martha had countered.

'It's too creepy for words!' Cassie had complained.

'Oh get and grow up,' Martha had said, losing

patience in having to defend the decision.

So Frank was left looking over Gordon's shoulder as his uncle let himself into the shadowy room at the rear of the house. Gordon closed the door behind him with a click so gentle but so decisive it seemed ominous. The spell was broken by the sound of Aida's voice.

'Now as a special treat,' Aida was saying, 'you can go through to the lounge and watch television.'

Television! Frank had heard about Aida and Gordon's television! They had a TV set long before anyone else in the family could consider the thing anything other than a fabulous luxury. Frank had witnessed a house discussion about TV at Ravenscraig. Everyone had agreed that the coming of television was a reactionary hyena, because it would be used to exploit everyone's softness for shoddy material goods and low forms of entertainment in order to divert them from political education. They'd also agreed that they must eventually get hold of the reactionary hyena and regulate its use. More importantly, Frank remembered it was said that television could even broadcast live events, like football matches.

The reactionary hyena stood in the corner of the room, a silent but ominous presence. Its single eye was closed. It looked like a large cabinet with a green window in it. For a moment Frank wondered whether Beatie and Bernard ought to be told that it was here, in Aida's house, and that they could just walk in and get it and regulate its use. He sank into a chair in front of the set, giving it the sort of respect one might

312

accord an unexploded bomb.

Gordon reappeared from 'the back', smiling broadly. He went behind the set and plugged it in. 'Eeeeee, it takes a few moments to warm up. The valves, you know.'

Eventually a picture faded up on a man in a studio putting a lot of small animals through their paces, but in a few moments the programme was over and a very presentable young lady was making an announcement. They had caught the tail end of BBC Children's Hour.

'That's Jennifer Gay,' Aida said, her voice breathy with admiration. 'Doesn't she speak beautifully?'

Frank listened to her. He'd heard other people speak like that. 'She speaks exactly as they did at Ravenscraig!' he spluttered. 'Exactly like that!'

'Oh!' Aida said, not certain she wanted to sully the spotless image of Jennifer Gay with the prejudices she'd come to associate with the lawless commune.

'Yes,' Frank said listening. She says "children's are" where we say "children's hour". And she says "prips" where we say "perhaps".'

'Oh?' said Aida.

'Yes. And she says "hice" where we say "house". Just like they did in Ravenscraig.'

'Yes.'

Frank had a good ear for this. 'And where we say "now" she says "nah".'

'Yes.'

'And she says "Sutton Kewlfield" where we say "Coalfield".'

'I think that's enough examples, Frank,' Aida

313

said, 'to give us an idea of how they speak at Ravenscraig.'

Chastened, Frank turned back to the television. They'd reached an interlude. Flute and strings music played over a picture of a pair of hands fashioning clay on a potter's wheel. It went on for a few minutes. When it was over Frank said, 'That was good.'

A bat-wing clock counted down into the next programme, helped along by the plucking of harp-strings. It commenced with footage of a tractor harrowing a field and it was called *Farming*. It also had a helpful sub-title: 'For those who live by the land'. It was also a very good programme, Frank thought, though he did remark that it would be good if Tom and Una were there to see it.

Just when it seemed to Frank that there were plenty of good things to be said about the reactionary hyena television, he saw something that disturbed him. The farming programme contained a section where a farmer talked of problems he had in ploughing a field full of bits of rusting shrapnel and the broken fragments of an aircraft that had exploded across his field during the war. The buried metal wreckage kept damaging his plough equipment, though the Ministry of War had helped with the loan of metal-detecting apparatus. The report made Frank thoughtful.

'He looks tired,' Aida said to Gordon.

'Perhaps a little longer,' Gordon argued. Frank noticed that his terrible speech affliction wasn't nearly so pronounced when in the comfort of his own home. 'You like the television don't you, Frank?'

314

'Let's not spoil his first day,' Aida said with authority. 'A hot bath, a glass of milk and a ginger biscuit. All right Frank?'

It seemed a trifle early to Frank, whose bedtimes had fluctuated wildly over the years, but he'd been schooled by Cassie not to argue. Gordon sighed and snapped off the television. Frank had his bath, and the milk and ginger snap that was to become a staple of life on the Binley Road, and crawled into bed. He was kept awake for some time, however, by thoughts of Gordon's activity in the back room directly below Frank's bedroom; and by images of vast ploughing machines turning the earth of the black-and-white fields.

30

The smell Frank had always resisted, the odour clinging to Gordon's clothes, was one that permeated the house. It was the reek of a formaldehyde-based embalming fluid. It got into his dreams on his very first evening in the house. It was the rat-man who sat on his bed in the middle of the night, and it wore rubber gloves on its human hands and in place of the rat head was the head of the Man-Behind-The-Glass chattering in a language he couldn't understand. The formaldehyde-smelling gloves were placed over his nose, preventing him from breathing, until he woke up.

On the following Monday he was taken back to school where he made joyful reunion with his

315

two friends, Chaz and Clayton. Chaz's squint was worse than ever. Clayton had a suntan. His American grandparents had paid for Clayton and his mother to sail over to America for a holiday in a place called Cape Cod. Frank felt the familiar pang of envy, assuaged when Clayton flicked cigarette cards at him. More gifts.

'What are these?'

'Movie stars,' Clayton said.

'Why are their faces screwed up like that?' Chaz wanted to know.

'They're just smiling,' Clayton said. 'That's how movie stars smile.'

Chaz distracted them with a different kind of collection. Cuss words. He had spent the summer replenishing and increasing his supply of cuss words, mostly gleaned from his older brothers who were scattered across a number of families throughout the city, and from his equally widespread cousins. Chaz collected cuss words the way he and other boys might collect birds' eggs. He lined them up in size order and prized certain obscenities for their rarity. That day he had some good ones for them.

Frank returned from his days at school to an established routine: wash hands, tea, television, bed. Aida pronounced that such routines were good for a growing boy. Why they were good she didn't elaborate; but here again she would be at odds with the Ravenscraig philosophy, where Frank had been taught that routine and habit were a kind of mind-weakening disease. Not that Frank was about to argue with Aida across the crisp linen and the salmon-paste sandwiches.

316

And not that Frank was disaffected from a routine that included television. Even though the potter's wheel and other interludes dulled somewhat on multiple viewing, there were plenty of other programmes of interest, whether they be *Muffin the Mule* during Children's Hour presented by the charmingly well spoken Jennifer Gay or the more adult *What's My Line?* It did seem to him a trifle odd, however, that Aunt Aida and Uncle Gordon were somewhat less interested in the programmes than was he, such that he was often left alone for the evening's viewing. Gordon would insinuate himself into his mysterious, reeking back room, and just as frequently Aida would join him, returning at Frank's regulation bedtime, carrying the same scent of formaldehyde with her, to usher him to bed. Frank assumed that Aida helped Gordon in his work.

But one evening per week Aida put on her hat and went out for an evening with the Women's Institute. Once during this time, Frank was left alone by Gordon who, obviously immersed in his work, had forgotten about the boy. Frank on that occasion put himself to bed.

But the following week when Aida put on her hat and left Frank to enjoy *What's My Line?* the same thing happened. This time, on hitting the potter's wheel interlude, Frank rose out of his chair and made slow steps towards the rear of the house.

The door to Gordon's workroom stood slightly ajar, but not open enough for Frank to see much of anything. Frank set one foot softly in front of the other, afraid that he might betray himself. He put his eye to the crack of the door, and what he

317

could see was a big toe.

It was a very big big toe; and it had a ticket tied to it. The kind of ticket or label you might have attached, with similar string, to a parcel for the post office. Something was written on the label but Frank couldn't quite make it out.

He could hear Gordon humming from inside the room. It was the sound of a man enjoying, or rather totally absorbed in, his work. It was a tuneless humming, but one which swelled occasionally in small bursts of unsustained enthusiasm. Frank put his eye closer to the crack, and his nose nudged the door slightly. He froze. The humming went on undisturbed and Frank sighed with relief, though he'd gained no advantage since the door had instantly swung back.

Again Frank fixed his eye to the crack. Suddenly the door was yanked open and Gordon was bearing down, eyeball to eyeball with Frank. 'Eeeeeee ya stinker! Ya wee stinker you! Spying on me you were! Eeeeeeee!'

Frank was paralysed. There was a brilliance to Gordon's eyes, hitherto unwitnessed by Frank. He was, evidently, highly amused.

'Come on in then, come on little stinker, in you come. That's it. You may as well see what Gordon's got behind the door. Nothing to be afrit of, son. Here, sit you down in your Auntie Aida's chair, go on son, sit you down, that's it. Your aunt likes to park herself there and she'll no mind. I know what a boy wants to know and you may as well find out from Gordon as from any other ignorant body, hmmmm? Hmmmmm?'

Frank slid his bottom on to the upright chair

318

Gordon had indicated as belonging to Aida, though he couldn't take his eyes from what was attached to the big toe glimpsed through the crack in the door. It was a big woman, naked, her skin puffed and speckled, grey-white, the colour of a field mushroom, lying flat out on a table of white enamel tiles. She was surrounded on three sides by the instruments of Gordon's art. Frank had an uninterrupted view of the dead woman's sagging flesh, the floppy mounds of her breasts and a tangle of dark pubic hair that made him think, inexplicably, of the brambles, nettles and deadly nightshade overgrowing the plank bridge across the stream at Tom's farm.

Gordon got straight back to work. 'Eeeeeeeeee, well, aye, just before I caught you at the door there I was just fixing this lady's jewellery for her. Look at these gold and diamond rings, son.' Gordon held up the corpse's swollen left hand for Frank to see, before replacing it, with great delicacy, on the slab. 'Aye, there's a few buggers as would have those off before the lid is nailed down, so there are, so I give 'em a wee surprise. Glue them on, son. Glue. They're going nowhere. Glue them on, then I pump a bit of extra fluid into the fingers. Swell 'em up. Not that she's taking the ruddy things with her. But it's family wishes you see, son, family wishes. And we don't want one of your rum buggers down at the crematorium coming between us and family wishes do we son? Eh? Eh?'

'No.'

'Bit of strong adhesive. Same as I use to keep the eyes closed. Only way you can keep 'em shut.

Unless you put a stitch in but why bother with that sort of mess? There, that's done it. Did you want a glass of lemonade while you're sat there Frankie?'

'No.'

'No lemonade? Milk? Do you want a glass of milk, son?'

'No thank you.'

'As you wish, son. Now we've cleaned her up and I've to make a note of these rings, do you see? For the family. Now we have to close the mouth, and that's just as important. Your Aunt Aida always advises me on this because it's a fine thing, Frankie, a fine thing. If I was to close her mouth up too slack now, well, you cannot get a pleasant look at all' – here Gordon turned to Frank and modelled for him a startling, closed-eyed slack-jawed expression – 'and if I was to close it up too tight this bit of skin under the nose puckers up and twists the upper lip and you'd have her scowling at her family. Well, she may well scowl, and you may think what does it matter, but there's the Calling Hours, you see son, that's really what I'm here for, to get her ready for the Calling Hours. So I'm just going to widen her lip a little with this scalpel, and, that's got it. When I've cleaned her mouth up a bit you can come and tell me what you think.'

'Who is she?'

'Eh? What?' Gordon looked startled. He let the hand holding the scalpel fall to his side. 'She's nobody, son. She isn't anybody. She was somebody, but not any more. Whoever she was, this isn't her. She stopped being what she was several hours ago, Frankie. I want you to know that, ken? If there is anything after all this, well she's long gone; and if there's nothing, well she's still long gone. This is just the packet she came in. But she's not here now, see?'

Frank must have looked startled, because Gordon set down the scalpel and came across to him, stooping and putting his face uncomfortably close to Frank's. Gordon's normally dead eyes were still aglitter; the rawness of the gums withdrawing from his teeth, revealed even now as he smiled, seemed to glisten with vitality and not with the usual necrosis; and Frank noticed that Gordon's animated talk was punctuated with none of the usual stammering, whining or piping noises.

'You see, son, even though you're a wee boy I'm going to tell you why I'm here to do these things. I'm a little fairy, yes, yes, tee-hee, a wee fairy sent here to wave a magic wand over these old packets, to pretty them up. Why? Because even the grown-ups, the adults, they can't abide to see what's true; they can't abide it. It's the decomposition. We'll do anything to pretend that the end has not really come in this way. So I'm here to get out my wee wand, and wave it over this old packet of meat. And they pay me, that's my job; but I do it because I love the people, Frankie, whoever they are. I do it for the love of those left behind. Because I don't want them to suffer when they see their loved ones. So I get out my wand and I do my work, ken?'

Frank nodded. Gordon nodded too, and then stood up again to return to the cadaver, the Fairy of Death waving his miraculous wand. He splashed a small sponge into a solution in a tin dish and began vigorously sponging the body.

'Disinfect and preserve, Frank, that's what we do, disinfect and preserve. You wouldn't want to look at this within a very short time. No one would. I've got to make it look presentable, so that the loved ones can come during the Calling Hours and pay their respects. So I'm preparing it, that's what I'm doing. Now someone else has already laid her out this time, which makes my job easier, but if they come to me all twisted and mangled' – here he lifted an arm, sponging under the armpit, gently lowering the arm again – 'then I have to massage and bend them all back into shape. But now I can get on with the embalming.'

Gordon put down his sponge and picked up his scalpel, waving it at Frank. 'Water and air, Frank, water and air. The two things that cause the decomposition; and mark you that it is with their opposites, fire and earth, that we dispose of the dead. But if we can keep water and air away we buy ourselves a bit of time.' Here he turned to the body and made a sudden deft incision on the right side of the lower neck. 'Always right side, son, always right. Carotid artery and jugular vein. We're going to drain off the blood and replace it with formaldehyde-based fluid, aren't we? Yes.'

It occurred to Frank that Gordon was talking as much to himself as he was to Frank. Chattering, always chipper, Gordon hoisted a small drum with tubes attached and inserted one tube into an artery. He inserted a second into the jugular and set up a drain. Then he went about pumping the fluid from the drum into the artery, pumping vigorously. Frank could see the veins flexed in Gordon's arms, though his uncle looked up from his exertions to encourage Frank with a tardy smile. Frank could not see but could hear the blood draining into another drum behind the table.

'Three gallons does it,' Gordon said, as if he'd been asked. 'Or thereabouts. Of course if you've got a fatty, well, you'll need more. But generally speaking the three will do it. This one's a fatty.'

After a while Frank recovered the faculty of speech to say, 'She's turning pink.'

'Pink? Yes, there's a wee bit of dye in the fluid. Give her a bit of colour. And it lets me see where we're up to, ken? And if this part goes well and there are no clots or breaks, well, we're laughing aren't we son? Laughing.'

Frank grinned to indicate that they might, hopefully, be laughing with this particular subject so monstrously laid out before him.

It was a long process, and at some point Aida returned. When she put her head round the door, Frank was taken by surprise and thought he might be in trouble for delaying his bedtime.

'A little helper?' Aida said, seeming not at all displeased. 'Have you found yourself a little helper?'

'I have,' Gordon called cheerily from his work. 'And a grand wee helper he is too.'

Frank swung his legs, pleased at being so described but unable to see quite how he'd earned this accolade.

'This has gone beautifully,' Gordon trilled, 'beautifully. You're just in time for the cavity embalming.'

323

'Oh good,' Aida said. 'I'll put the kettle on and we'll watch together.'

Aida left the room and returned shortly with a pot of tea and a glass of milk for Frank. She went out again and returned with another chair, drawing it up alongside Frank's chair. Gordon set down his mug of tea so that he could sip it while still working. Aida and Frank drank their tea and milk respectively while spectating.

The cavity embalming was a little more complicated. Gordon made another cut with his scalpel just above the navel and he pushed a long needle inside the abdomen. He had a water-powered suction pump, which he used to remove blood and other fluids. Then he used the same needle, the trocar, to pump full-strength preserving fluids into the organs. 'Stronger disinfectant,' he muttered to Frank, 'for the organs. Right that's it. Then we suture up these little cuts and we're laughing.'

While Gordon was doing all this Frank learned that Aida generally helped with what she called the 'washing, grooming, dressing and casketing'. Normally they said they would complete the process in one session, but Aida noticed the time and insisted that Frank should, finally, go to his bed. On seeing Frank's disappointment Aida promised that he could see the rest of the process on another body, since, she pointed out, there were always fresh ones coming in.

'Yes, yes, away to your bed wee man,' Gordon said. Then he added, 'Sweet dreams,' before swallowing the last of his tea.

Reluctantly Frank said goodnight and made his way to bed, past the lounge where the reactionary hyena was still broadcasting feebly. And as he dragged his feet up the stairs Frank concluded that despite the fun of *Muffin the Mule* or the comforting repetition of the potter's wheel, or even the well-spoken prettiness of Jennifer Gay, what he'd seen on Gordon's slab was far superior to any television.

31

Cassie was awoken in the middle of the night by a bad dream. The dream was about Frank. In it Frank was surrounded by the dead, and the dead were calling to him but he couldn't hear them because he had no ears. His ears had been taken away by government officials in bowler hats. The dead were becoming frustrated, even angry, with Frank, and Cassie had wanted to tell them it wasn't Frank's fault; it was the fault of those in government. Then one of the dead, a large red-headed woman recently deceased, asked quite reasonably why Cassie could hear them since she had no ears either. Cassie felt for her ears and they were gone, and this had made her wake up.

When she got downstairs she was surprised to find Martha in her dressing gown, making cocoa on the stove. Martha had some time ago taken to sleeping in the downstairs front room of the house, to spare her arthritic bones the nightly climb up the stairs. William and Tom had carried down her iron bedstead and set it up for her there.

'It's cold down here,' Cassie moaned.

'Fetch a blanket off my bed and put it round you. I'll make you a drink.'

Cassie told Martha about her dream. Martha nodded and said nothing. She'd been woken, too, by an almost identical dream, but chose not to say. She stirred the cocoa before handing it over.

'Do you think Frank is all right?' Cassie wanted to know.

'You mean with Aida and Gordon? They won't let him come to any harm, Cassie.'

'I was wonderin', Mam. Just wonderin'. Do you think I'll ever be right enough to have my own place, you know, to give him a fixed home? Do you think I will?'

'That all depends on your wherewithal, Cassie, don't it? If you want a home you'll have to hold down a job or find a husband, or both. What about this chap from Oxford? He's nice enough but as far as I can see he's got no work either. He's a tag-along, isn't he? Well he's decent enough, but you can't tag along with a tag-along.'

'He's a writer, Mam.'

'Yes, a tag-along.'

'But he said he would get a job for me. Said he'd teach, like Bernard.'

'Well, then, get and bite his hand off. You're not getting any younger. You shan't have good looks to go on for ever.'

'Not fair to him though is it, Mam? The way my head is. Not fair. I just wish it was different. It seems odd when Aida and Ina and Evelyn and Olive and Una are all so level-headed and have all got homes of their own.'

Tell her, a voice seemed to speak in Martha's ear. *Just tell her she can't have what the others have.* But she couldn't. Not at that moment. Instead she changed the subject and said, 'Cassie, what do you think we can do about Olive and Aida? You know I've tried not to interfere, and to let nature take its course, but now I'm worried about those two.'

'I'm sure I don't know Mam. If you can't pull them together no one can.'

'It weighs heavy on me, it does. I know what happens when people stop speaking. I know how it happened with your father. At first it's an attitude, and it could be broken with a few words, but before you know where you are it's hardened, the silence has gone like bone, and then it's all the harder to break. And it grieves me that I allowed it with your father. It grieves me every day.'

Cassie was shocked to see a tear squeeze from Martha's eye. A lifetime of stoicism, a lifetime of not showing, a life of containment, and now the pitcher was broken. 'Oh Mam!' Perhaps for the first time Cassie saw the frailty in her mother's age. For so long she had been used to Martha making and mending, sorting and separating that it had never occurred to her that her mother might be tired. But now she saw it, and she felt a sense of shame for her own weaknesses that only added to Martha's burden.

'I'm useless to you Mam.'

'What? What?' Martha bucked up. 'Don't ever let that be said. You're a joy to me every day of your life Cassie. You may be a black swan but you're a joy. And though I'd never treat any one of you any different from the others somehow you've always been my favourite. Now come sit on the floor and drink your cocoa while I stroke your hair.'

They talked a great deal that night. They talked about Aida and Olive, and whether they might break the feud of silence, the hardened heart, the old Coventry weapon of ice and stone. They also talked about Frank and what the future might hold for him. Cassie jokingly said he'd make a good psychic; but that had made Martha put her straight. She told Cassie that when Ina and Evelyn had the boy they'd thought the same thing, but they'd overlooked one important thing.

'What was that, Mam?'

'Who was with him at that time?'

'Only me, Mam.'

'Exactly. Frank has got a bit of it. He's a lovely boy, but he ain't got it like you have. Do you think I would have let him go to Aida's if he could make the dead sit up like you can? No. It's you Cassie. Things happen around you. Ina and Evelyn want to see it but they don't even know what's under their noses. It's you Cassie. You make things happen. You always have.'

The two of them passed into a silence after this speech of Martha's. Cassie because she was unnerved to hear Martha talk openly like this. It was as if she was signalling something to Cassie, some intimation that Martha knew her own time was running out. A coal shifted in the grate, and Cassie gazed hard into the fire.

The next day Cassie set off on her bicycle to see Aida, with the intention of talking about the feud.

She couldn't do it. When she got to the house on Binley Road she developed a powerful migraine. The nearer she got to the house the worse her headache became, until at the front driveway it seemed to her that a hundred or more voices were shouting for attention inside her head. As she dropped back from the house, the disturbance abated. Approaching a second time, the crescendo built again. She pedalled away, and felt better as she put a distance between herself and the house.

Instead she went to see Olive. Olive made milky tea and gave her a slice of Dundee cake but didn't stop talking to draw breath. She chattered with neurotic zest about the many things on her mind, about William's business, about the children, about their mother's health and a dozen other things, ultimately talking Cassie into silence.

Dispirited by the failure of her venture, Cassie pedalled home on her bike.

'Mam,' she said when she got in, 'I think I'll cycle up to the farm tomorrow. I shall stay with Una and Tom for a couple of days. I could do with the fresh air.'

'What ails you then, girl?'

'Don't rightly know. I'm going up to my room for a sleep. I'm tired.'

Martha watched her go. She could read her daughter like a barometer. If she's set to go into one, Martha thought, then at least she can do less damage out at the farm.

Meanwhile at the house on Binley Road, television had been displaced by a nightly ritual in which Frank and his Aunt Aida sat alongside each other, perhaps the one with a glass of milk and the other with a cup of tea, and watched Gordon at his work.

It was the gentleness; the tender grace with which he worked that made both of them want to spectate the process over and over. At a certain point in the proceedings Aida would put down her cup and saucer and join her husband for the post-embalming routines. She would stand by the corpse, hands clasped together in a gesture of infinite patience, and on some minute signal from Gordon would commence the grooming of what she always referred to as 'the remains'. There was a lot to do. Male and female cadavers alike were to be shaved and plucked; hair was to be washed and combed; the bodies were to be dressed in clothes provided by their families; 'the remains' had to be casketed – a difficult enough job if the corpse was weighty; and finally there were the cosmetics, the make-up to be applied, again to both genders.

Frank only threatened his own position of high privilege on one occasion. He had daily reported the things he'd witnessed to his two close pals at school. Under pressure, one evening, while Aida washed the blue-black hair of one recently deceased, he'd blurted, 'But can my friends from school come and watch one day?'

Gordon dropped his scalpel and Aida let the soapy head fall from between her hands. It thumped on the porcelain tiles of the embalming table. They both looked at Frank with open mouths, quite aghast. Frank lowered his eyes. Nothing was said, not a word. He never asked again.

At the end of each job, with the casketed remains waiting for transportation to the chapel of rest or in some cases the home parlour for the Calling Hours, both Gordon and Aida would step back and survey their handiwork. This moment was always rounded by Aida's, 'Well, I for one think he/she looks *lovely*.'

'Aye,' Gordon would say. 'Aye.'

And with that Frank would know that it was time to climb down from his chair to be the first one to file out of the room, always followed by Aida, and then by Gordon, who would switch off the embalming room lights, and who would close the door behind him with the gentlest of clicks.

32

In the late September of that year, with the giant golden leaves fluttering to the ground, life for Frank was full. In the midst of death there was abundance. It didn't matter how many cadavers were pumped full of Gordon's pink formalde-hyde, it didn't seem to stop the seasons turning nor did it stop babies being born. Una at the farm fell pregnant again. And so did Beatie.

The joy was unbounded, but celebration amongst the Vines was never precipitate. All the sisters knew what Martha knew, that nine months was a long time in matters of politics, payment and pregnancy. No counting until hatching. But the delight all round was difficult to disguise, and

Una and Beatie could be seen to exchange looks of especial intimacy. And the sisters who had no progeny of their own, Aida and Evelyn and Ina, were also delighted. 'That'll quieten Beatie down a bit,' they said with a chuckle. 'She'll see!' they avowed. And, 'It's what she wanted all along, you know,' secretly meaning that if only Beatie had conceived earlier, then she wouldn't have been so taken up with these wild politics of hers.

They were wrong about that. The idea of off-spring only put fire into Beatie's ambitions. If she was going to bring children into this world she was damned well going to improve it first. The health, education and welfare of the common people were a disgrace. Beatie and Bernard had long since joined the Labour Party with a view to them both standing at election as local council-lors. The pregnancy changed that. Now only one of them would stand.

'Madness!' said Aida. 'You must be yampy!' Una said. 'You want both your heads looking at!' Olive added. 'Criminal!' echoed the twins.

Only Beatie, Bernard had announced, would be standing for election, rather than both of them.

It seemed at times to the Vine family that Bernard and Beatie deliberately went out of their way to do the contrary thing; to say black when everyone was saying white and tartan when all were saying both; to upset apple carts; to cause commotion. It made no sense at all that a nursing mother would want to enter politics.

'But who will look after the baby when you're off to the council chamber?' Martha wanted to know.

'I will, obviously,' Bernard said proudly.

When the campaign started properly, though the sisters all agreed they would vote for Beatie (even though William and Olive and Aida were arch Conservatives), they would not assist in the leafleting, door knocking and canvassing associated with local politics. Not that this was any great loss; both Bernard and Beatie were popular in their local ward, and the Party drafted in plenty of helpers in the week before the election. From the Vines, only Cassie weighed in, cycling back from the farm with a mad-eyed evangelism, ready to stuff leaflets in the letterbox of hell if it would help. Bernard wasn't sure if her presence wasn't counter-productive: she talked to people on the doorsteps as if her sister were Joan of Arc, and her stammering, wild-eyed intensity disturbed the electorate. So they persuaded her away from doorstep canvassing to concentrate on leaflet stuffing, and for that task she took Frank with her.

Frank also enjoyed darting up the paths of the terraced houses to deliver the Vote Vine handbills, even though he was snapped at by a dog and scowled at by an unshaved man in a yellowing vest. He understood that he was doing something very grown up and that it was all to help Aunt Beatie make the world a better place.

Not everyone thought Beatie was set to make the world a better place. While out targeting one neighbourhood with Bernard, Beatie, Cassie and a few other Party members, Frank took a leaflet to the letterbox of a pub – closed at that particular time – called the Axe and Compass. The letterbox was set on a stiff spring, and as Frank tried to negotiate the flimsy leaflet through the difficult flap, the door opened and the pub landlord snatched the leaflet out of his hand. The landlord, a burly, bald-headed bruiser with tiny iron-grey wings of hair nestling behind his ears and bushels of grey nostril hair, glanced at the leaflet, screwed it up, made a fist of his hand and punched Frank so hard on the side of his head that he toppled back into the gutter.

Only Beatie saw what had happened. She immediately ran over to Frank and picked him up. Frank was too dazed even to cry. Beatie looked up at the pub landlord. 'You vile, ugly coward! You wart! Scrotum! Scum!'

Bernard was over in a second, quickly calculating what had happened. Beatie was still railing at the landlord. Bernard pushed himself between Beatie and him. 'You're standing for election,' he whispered, 'you can't get involved in this.'

Bernard turned to the landlord. 'You're good at hitting boys. Now try and hit me.'

In sizing up Bernard the landlord sneered. Bernard was almost a foot shorter, but with a powerful stocky frame. After a moment the landlord stepped back inside and slammed his door shut.

'Have we got his vote?' Cassie said.

Beatie was returned to Coventry City Council by a substantial majority. Though by no means Coventry's first woman councillor, she was certainly the youngest ever. She, Bernard and a few close friends from the local ward staged an early meeting to plot as to how Beatie might 'make a difference'.

A victory party was held, naturally at Martha's house. It was crowded out with the sisters and local Labour Party activists, all drinking beer and eating sandwiches. Even Lilly had come up from Oxford to join in the festivities. In the fun and the singing and the raised voices, no one seemed to miss Cassie, who spent much of the party upstairs, gazing out of the window. The strains of 'Moonlight Serenade' from a replacement disc on her old box record player were barely noticed.

Cassie was disappointed on two counts. Firstly, on hearing of Beatie's political victory, she had called on Aida and Olive in turn, imploring them to end their mutual hostility and to break their silence. They had refused, and the careful engineering of times at which they might each appear at the party without embarrassment or confrontation proceeded as usual. Cassie's second disappointment was that George, who was also expected from Oxford along with Lilly, failed to show up. When Una and Tom and their twins left the party relatively early, Cassie went with them.

During the celebrations Martha, who had heard about the episode outside the Axe and Compass, produced an article in the Coventry *Evening Telegraph*. The landlord of the Axe and Compass had been put out of business. The pub had been closed on grounds of hygiene. A local authority inspection of his cellars had discovered a number of festering rat carcasses. The authorities rejected the landlord's wild claims that someone had broken in through the pavement-level delivery hatch and put them there the night before the inspection.

Martha fought through the celebrating party activists to draw Bernard's attention to the article. 'Well,' he said, 'we shan't be shedding any tears over him, shall we?'

'Sometimes Bernard,' said Martha, 'I can't tell whether you're a dark horse or a piebald pony.'

'I can't think what you're talking about Mrs Vine.'

'No,' Martha said, folding the newspaper. 'I can't either.'

The following morning at the farm, Tom rose early and went down to the kitchen in his socks to make a pot of tea. A super-fine, icing-sugar mist had settled on the morning fields, and the farmyard cock crowed languidly. Tom glanced out of the window into the yard and noticed that his cattle truck was missing.

Tom owned a rattletrap lorry for transporting up to half a dozen beasts to and from market. He used it for no other purpose, and consequently it stood mouldering in the yard many more days than it saw use. But Tom's eye registered its absence at once. He took a cup of tea up to Una. 'Do you want to get up?' he said gruffly. 'Someone's pinched the cattle lorry.'

Not waiting for a reply he went back downstairs, slipped on his boots and went out to see whatever else the thieves had taken along with the cattle lorry. It was not uncommon to hear of thieves who would steal farm equipment, or even the animals, in the dead of night. Tom kept a shotgun locked in a cabinet under the stairs should he ever have to confront prowlers. Right at that moment, however, he was more irritated that his collie hadn't barked to alert them during the night.

On first inspection he couldn't see anything missing. None of his British Whites nor his Friesians seemed to have gone; nor his pigs; he wouldn't know until later if they'd been after his sheep. Then he noticed something else missing.

Back at the house, Una had come downstairs in her nightshift. 'You won't believe this,' Tom told Una. 'They've taken the grey cob.'

'I'll wake Cassie,' Una said. 'I'll get her to go down the police station on her bicycle.'

33

In the narrow cobbled street that was Bayley Lane, between mediaeval St Mary's hall and the fractured gothic window arches of the blitzed cathedral, a factory watchman was returning from night shift. He regularly signed off at six a.m., handing over to the charge-hand who would in turn prepare for the workers clocking in at eight. The nightwatchman always made his way to his home in Gosford Street by slipping between Holy Trinity and the bombed-out shell of the old cathedral, looking forward to a fried breakfast of bacon and mushrooms and tea so strong it might stand a spoon upright.

The morning of 7 October 1953 was blanketed in a myth-hatching thickness of fog. The swirling mist had been banked up into a yellow-streaked smog by coal-burning home fires across the city after the temperature had dropped quite suddenly following a mild few days of early autumn. The oyster-grey and sulphur-yellow mist roiled over one of the few remaining narrow mediaeval streets of Coventry, and it tumbled through the stark, blackened sandstone windows of the fractured cathedral. The nightwatchman coughed, and the bark of his cough hung in the mist.

But as the sound of his cough did recede it gave way to another sound, one that seemed to the nightwatchman to be both out of place and yet familiar. It was the strike of a horse's hooves making uncertain progress along the cobbled lane before him. He stopped, peering into the fog, waiting for a horse to emerge from its mysterious folds. The passage of the horse was slow and unsteady. A few steps echoed through the fog, but then it stopped again. Whatever it was, wherever it was, it failed to manifest out of the drifting grey shroud. Straining to listen, almost a little afraid, the nightwatchman seemed unwilling to go on.

A moment later the sound of metal striking on cobbled stone rang out in the lane once more, and this time the jerking head of a white horse emerged from the mist, reigned towards the nightwatchman by the hazy outline of its rider. As the rider came into view, passing close by him, the nightwatchman's bowels turned to crystal. His flesh crawled, the hair on his neck bristled, and his tongue stuck to the roof of his mouth. He had never before seen a ghost but he knew in his blood and his bones that he was seeing one now.

The horse rider was a woman. She was naked.

She showed no awareness of his presence as she passed by. Her head hung low and she held the reins limply in her hands, letting the white horse pick its way through, the swirling mist of the cobbled lane. The horse appeared to breathe smoke as it passed, tossing its head, snorting, assaulting the cold morning air with its billowing breath. After a few moments this apparition was swallowed up by the dragon mist, with only the slow, steady ring of iron on stone to convince the nightwatchman of what he'd seen.

'My life,' he whispered to himself. 'My life.'

In Broadgate a double-decker bus in corporation livery of claret and dirty buttermilk growled up the incline of Trinity Street to Broadgate, collecting drivers and bus conductors to be relayed on to the bus depot for the commencement of the morning shift. The drivers and conductors, some still sleepy, some exchanging banter, were aroused when one of the conductors, hitherto gazing glumly from the window of the bus as it lurched into Broadgate, suddenly became excited.

'I just saw a naked woman!'

Cheers, whistles, cries of, 'You're dreaming!' and, 'Someone slap his ear!'

'Over there! Going into Hertford Street! She were on a norse! Over there! Naked!'

Because of the equestrian statue located in the centre of the garden island of Broadgate no one took this claim remotely seriously. Why wouldn't their colleague see a naked woman on a horse? But when he scrambled to his feet trying to get another glimpse through the moisture-beaded window, they just shook their heads.

A policeman at the crossover of Market Way and Smithford Way also saw the apparition. He'd found the door of a tobacconist's standing ajar and, suspecting a break-in, was inside the shop when he heard the clopping of horse's hooves. He'd looked through the store window, past the samples of Red Burley and Marlin Flake and Rough Shag to see what looked very like a naked woman on a horse. By the time he'd got himself out of the shop, she was gone. He would have given chase but for leaving the tobacconist store unshuttered; and by the time he came to his senses, he wasn't even certain about, what he'd just seen.

He chose not to report the incident at the time.

There were several other sightings. In Ironmonger Row a man working for the Water Authority, taking advantage of the early morning quiet to listen for underground leaks, saw the ghost of Lady Godiva pass by. So did a cleaning lady on her way to work in Priory Lane.

By midday the diffuse October sunshine had burned off the smog and the city was abuzz with reports that the ghost of Lady Godiva had paraded the streets that morning. An early edition of the Coventry *Evening Telegraph* ran a front-page article about the reappearance of the city matriarch. It reported seven eyewitnesses' accounts, and even though there couldn't have been more than two or three dozen people at large in the city centre at that time of the morning, it reported that over a hundred people had claimed to have seen her. She was 'beautiful'. Her hair 'cascaded down her back'. Her steed was 'milk white'. She looked 'sad' and 'downcast'. But above all, in the swirling mist, she was 'radiant' and 'golden' and even 'dressed in an aura of light'.

In the afternoon of the same day, Beatie Vine was due to make her maiden speech in the Earl Street City Council chambers. It seemed for a while that her thunder had been stolen by the swelling rumour of the ghostly apparition of that morning. Though she needn't have worried. Her reputation as a good-looking firebrand had preceded her, and the lofty debating chamber was full to capacity with her mostly male fellow councillors from across the parties.

The agenda for the day was the subject of the setting of the Coventry rate, the system of local taxation that determined on whom and on where should fall the burden of municipal financing. Some said it should be the responsibility of householders. Others said that local businesses, those that profited most from municipal organisation, should bear the burden. The matter had been in contention for a very long time, and Beatie was scheduled to speak on the question.

In the chamber she had both her natural supporters and her automatic enemies in the opposition party, and the latter were determined, if at all possible, to humble Beatie on her first day. If they could somehow cause her to trip on her words, to stammer, to stumble or to lose her way, then indeed they would. Since she was one of few women in the chamber, they had an additional reason to indulge in this sporting tradition of

341

baiting the maiden speaker. That she was young, attractive and clearly oriented to a Marxist position gave Beatie's opposition extra impetus.

When the Chairman of the Council called her to speak, Beatie rose, a little shakily, to her feet. There were murmurings and not a few wolf-whistles, and one shameful cry of, 'Get home and make the dinner' – suitably reprimanded by the able and impartial Chairman. Beatie drew herself to her full height, and waited for absolute silence to descend. Then she began.

'Comrades,' she said, in a clear, steady voice.

This single word was followed instantly by cheers, catcalls and howls of derision in equal measure. Catcalls from the political Right because this opening salutation excluded and dismissed almost half the chamber. Cheers from the political Left because it was an unequivocal statement that, maiden speech or not, Beatie was neither about to submit to the patronising sympathy of false friends nor court the indulgence of anyone. More than that, she was baiting them in turn.

It was some minutes before this noisy reaction to her first word as a city councillor had died down. Through it all, Beatie stood aloof, patient and unmoved by the commotion. At one moment she did allow her eyes to stray to the public gallery, where Bernard stood, his hands clasped above his head in triumph and exhortation.

The Chairman thumped his gavel and called for order in the chamber, but not until she had absolute silence did Beatie continue, whereupon she said, 'There is a spectre haunting Coventry.'

342

This time the cheers and the howls were even louder. This reference to the famous opening line of the Communist Manifesto had the deliberate effect of enraging her opponents and galvanising her allies to her side. The Chairman banged his gavel and complained that the debate would not get underway if councillors on both sides were determined to act like over-excited schoolboys at Councillor Vine's every word.

Once again, not until the commotion had subsided and everyone had sunk back in their seats did Beatie continue. 'The ghost of Lady Godiva,' she said, and here she paused for effect so that everyone present might absorb the allusion to the day's spectacular rumoured event, 'is stalking the streets of this city. And everyone in this room knows why. Lady Godiva rode naked through this city to protest an injust taxation. And she has appeared again. Because the local rate of taxation set by the last council is iniquitous and injurious – not just to the weakest and those least able to defend themselves, but to every member of our community. The local tax rate is a bodge of a job cobbled together by corrupt, pernicious and devious-minded men who have made no contri-bution to this city other than to disgrace this evil assembly.'

Uproar in the chamber.

Another strange event took place that very afternoon on the Binley Road. Frank came home from school to find Gordon, assisted by Aida, commencing work on a fresh cadaver. Gordon prepared the body – a hefty male in his late forties

343

– sponging it in the usual way. Meanwhile Frank regaled Aida with the small stories that made up his school day.

Frank was still deeply fond of his two school chums Clayton and Chaz, and though he knew enough to edit the stories he brought back, he often reported the difficulties Chaz would get into with his teachers.

'I'm not sure I altogether like the sound of this Chaz,' Aida said. 'What do you say, Gordon?'

Gordon was more concerned with adjusting the smile on the dead man's face. He raised his scalpel and said, 'Aye, well, he does sound a bit of a wild thing.' Then he nicked the corner of the mouth of the cadaver with his scalpel.

'Ow!' said the cadaver, sitting upright, holding the freshly cut corner of his mouth. 'What the hell are you doing?'

Aida fainted. Frank ran from the room screaming. Gordon, quivering, held up his scalpel in defence, like a cross before a vampire. 'Eeeeeeeeeeeeeeeeeeeeeeeeee!'

Though the dead were said to be riding through the centre of Coventry, and corpses were sitting bolt upright on the Binley Road, events at the farm were more muted. Before Beatie's provocative speech to the Coventry city councillors, before the startling events on Gordon's embalming table, Tom had opened the farmyard gate to allow his cattle lorry to be eased back into the yard.

Tom and Una had not gone to the police on discovering the missing lorry. When Una had

344

hurried to fetch Cassie that morning, she'd found that her sister was gone from her bed. On hearing this, Tom had checked the lorry keys he kept hanging on a hook by the kitchen door. They were also missing. Tom and Una decided to wait.

When before midday Cassie returned, Tom and Una had no notion of the rumour sweeping the city. Tom did ask Cassie where she had been and why she'd taken the lorry, but, getting no intelligible reply, he let the matter drop. Cassie had been distant, even remote for the past days, and both Tom and Una knew enough to recognise the signs. After Cassie had stabled the grey cob and hung up its saddle and bridle she went back to bed, complaining of tiredness.

'Your sister is off on one,' Tom said.

'That's plain,' Una had snapped back at him.

But by mid-afternoon, the news had reached Wolvey and beyond. A wagoner delivering cattle feed told Tom what he'd heard. Tom still didn't put the two things together. The story of a milk-white steed and a woman with lustrous hair flowing down her back didn't register in his world. After all, his cob was … grey, and no woman in his family wore hair any longer than much below their shoulder blades. But by late afternoon the story in Coventry had complicated, and another farmer who had dropped by to loan Tom a roller to run across the bottom field reported this complication to Tom. It seemed that the appearance of Lady Godiva might not have been spectral after all, since two witnesses had spotted a woman, fully dressed this time, loading a horse into a lorry in Priory Street shortly after the time of the last sightings.

Tom did this time connect up what he knew; though he said nothing to his neighbour. After uncoupling the roller and seeing his friend away, Tom went back up to the house.

'No,' Una said. 'It can't be!'

'Is she still sleeping?'

'Yes. But I mean no, Tom, honestly, no. What time did they say this was?'

'We'd better get her down here.'

'No, Tom, for goodness' sake. She wouldn't. She couldn't. Where did you say? In town? In the city centre?'

'Go and get her, Una! I don't care if she is asleep. Go and bloody well fetch her down!'

34

The following afternoon Una paid two visits, first to Aida, then to Olive. At Aida's, the household was still in some distress what with one of Gordon's charges coming alive on the embalming slab. There was a lot to be done. The coroner had to be alerted that a local GP – a notorious alcoholic – had erroneously pronounced death on a victim of a stroke. Gordon was in no way culpable: he wasn't after all responsible for determining whether someone was actually dead or not, merely readying them for the despatch when they were; though the unfortunate citizen was not best pleased about the slit made to his lip while he lay unconscious on the slab. Since the event, Gordon had been busy with paperwork and the enquiry that was already underway.

Frank didn't seem too scathed by the experience, and had returned to school with a story to tell his classmates, though it was clear from his early remarks that his enthusiasm for watching Gordon perform these funerary duties was somewhat reduced.

Aida was still slightly tremulous, and bruised from her fall when she'd fainted. She told Una she'd quite lost her appetite. Where she looked to Una for sympathy, she was surprised when she got none. Una had other things to talk about, namely Cassie's ride.

'Cassie says it was because you and Olive are not speaking to each other.'

'Nonsense!'

'It's not nonsense our Aida. It's why Cassie did it. She *says* she'll do it again, once a week, unless you and Olive sort out your differences. And I've no doubt as she shall. You're to come over to Mam's house tonight, and Olive will, too. This silliness has got to be put to one side.'

'I've got nothing to say to Olive. I'll not be in the same room as her. I don't care if Cassie does the same thing all over again, I shall not–'

'You don't care?' Una got up to leave. 'No, sit down Aida. I shall fetch my own coat. Seven o'clock tonight. You please yourself because I shan't argue with you. Aida, I hope this isn't the last time I see you today. But if you're not there this evening, sharp, you'll have to suffer the consequences. So Frank had better be there, too.'

At Olive's house, Una met a similar, stony resistance. Olive made sandwiches and spoke without pause about the children's ailments and William's store and the hundred small trials that Olive had somehow overcome. She also had some good hand-me-down clothes thoughtfully parcelled for Una. But when Una put it to her, she froze.

'Look, Cassie's hurting. Cassie's grieving because of you two. This is her way of telling you how much.'

'I'm sorry Una, I love Cassie as hard as any of you but I shan't have anything to do with Aida. She's not my sister any more and – where are you going?'

Again Una had got up halfway through a speech. 'I've been to Aida's and I've told her exactly the same. I'm not listening to silliness. If the pair of you don't come at seven, then the rest of the family have decided what they will have to do and it's up to you to accept the consequences of your own actions.'

Then Una was gone.

Wise of Una, it was, to make only the veiled threat, the dark talk of unspecified 'consequences'. She knew well enough that any specific sanction would only have the effect of making the sisters dig in. Precise threats would produce only the deeply stubborn reaction common to all the Vines. Far better to leave it open, to let Olive and Aida speculate about what those dark consequences might be; Una knew that their minds would each turn to the thing they were both most afraid of, which was the

348

same treatment they were currently dishing out. Their worst fear was to fall out of speaking terms not just with one sister but with all six and the mother as well. The old Coventry curse, the sister to malediction – that was the worst scenario. Banished to the emotional winterland. Cut off from the family root they would shrink. They would parch. They would wither.

And they both knew that all of the other Vines were routinely capable of delivering this cold promise.

Tom, Una and a subdued and dishevelled Cassie ate supper at Martha's house. At six-thirty Beatie and Bernard appeared. Beatie was still buoyant from her debut in the council chambers. She looked as though she had grown six inches, and if anyone was bruised by the experience it didn't appear to be her. By now, however, she knew what she couldn't possibly have known when she was invoking the ghost of Godiva in her maiden speech.

She nodded at Tom and Una. 'Hello Cassie,' she said.

'Hello Cassie,' went Bernard.

Shortly afterwards the twins appeared. Where they had thin smiles for everyone else, they addressed the wayward sister directly.

'Hello Cassie,' said Evelyn.

'Hello Cassie,' echoed Ina, but softly.

By seven o'clock no one else had arrived. Martha took the iron poker and cracked it across the back of a huge, smoking lump of coal in the fire. Then she sat back. The clock over her head ticked on. At seven-fifteen they had all fallen into silence. At seven-twenty they heard a car pull up in the street outside. Beatie went to see if it was Gordon's. It wasn't.

The pendulum over Martha's head clicked back and forth, and she too seemed diminished by each swing. Una looked crestfallen. Beatie and the twins looked thoughtful.

Then at seven-thirty the back door crashed open and Frank came in. Everyone except Martha and Cassie stood up, as if he were the prince royal. 'Mam!' He ran to Cassie, who stirred from her trance to embrace him.

'Where's your Aunt Aida?' Martha wanted to know.

'Sitting in the car. She said she'd be along in a minute.'

Waiting for the other one to come first, Martha thought. Within moments Olive appeared, trailed by William and her three moon-faced girls. Olive made directly for Martha, kissing her mother, fussing around her before turning to Cassie. 'Hello Cassie,' she said sternly.

'Hello Cassie,' said William.

It was only a minute or two before Aida and Gordon came in. Silence gripped the household again. Someone found a hardback chair for Olive, and another was dragged across the room for Aida. It was Aida who broke the silence. 'Hello Cassie,' she said.

Then Gordon, wild-eyed and smiling his hideous old carrion smile, walked directly up to Cassie and took her cheeks between his large white bony hands.

'Eeeeeeeeeeeeeee aye eeeeeeeeeee Cassie, you're a wee wild flower so you are. A wild orchid. A bloom on the mountain slope.'

'Do you really think so?' said Cassie, gazing up at him, eyes cloudless now.

'Eeeeeeeeeeeeee I do! I do! Heheheheeeeeeeeeeeee! Let me kiss you, you wee wild flower! Cos I know why you did it!'

This is a fine thing, Martha thought, if Gordon is the only one who can crack the ice on the pond. Then Gordon took a chair. All of the adults present were seated. All of Martha's grandchildren stood, limp and attentive, sensing the imminence, the proximity of fracture, silenced by it while the adults preferred a round of small talk to cover it over. Martha grasped the poker and clanged it on the side of the coal scuttle.

'Martha is in the chair!' said Bernard. 'Could have done with you at the council chambers, Martha.'

Bernard's attempt at levity fell flat. Martha spoke up. 'Aida, you're the eldest. You'll speak first.'

'Speak?' said Aida. 'Speak on what?'

'You shall speak to Olive and she shall speak to you.'

'Speak to Olive?' Aida said, looking directly at Olive, 'I've no more of a problem with Olive.'

'Then you shall say it to *her*, and not to *us*. Shan't you?'

Aida's breast rose and fell. At last she lifted a hand saying, 'Olive, I've no more of a problem with you. And that's the end of it.'

Olive had to wipe a tear from her eye. 'And I've

351

no problem with you, Aida. I've never given you any trouble.'

'Just don't be so bossy,' Aida said.

'I'll not be so bossy if you'll not be so bullying,' Olive said.

And it was about to start all over again, but Frank remembered the sherbet lemons. Aida had brought each of Olive's children a packet of sherbet lemons and had entrusted them to Frank. He sprang forward to hand his cousins a packet apiece, and that act caused William to remember he'd brought a large pumpkin and two pounds of conference pears to give to Aida. He passed the bag of fruit and vegetables to Beatie, who handed it to Una, who in turn passed to Aida.

'A plump one,' Aida said of the pumpkin.

'It had better be,' Tom said.

'Now then Aida,' Martha said when the stiff, gift-giving, hatchet-burying ritual was over, 'tell Olive about that corpse what sat up on your slab the other night. That will give us all a laugh.'

'What a family,' Bernard said under his breath.

Not under his breath enough for Martha, though. 'Hoi! We'll have less of that! And Cassie, what are you crying for, now?'

'Happy, Mam.'

'Good. And can we say that the horse is to be kept in the stable?'

'Yes, Mam.'

'Right then, Aida, on with telling your tale.'

35

Out at the farm on the following Friday afternoon Tom was rolling the field below the brook, trying to level out the pits and gullies left after the haymake. As he turned his tractor at the top of the field near the brook, the roller snagged on a jagged flange of rusting metal in the ground. He stopped his tractor and got off to inspect it. He tugged, but the flapping metal wouldn't come free. Tom cursed because he knew he would have to dig it out. He switched off his tractor engine and made to cross the plank footbridge over the brook, to fetch a spade, but on the bridge his foot dropped through the edge of the rotting plank.

Tom swore a second time. He looked up to the farmhouse and he saw Cassie, Frank, Una and the twins in the yard. Cassie and Frank were staying with them for the weekend. He made his way across to the buildings.

It took him an hour to dig out the great sheet of rusting metal, and even when he'd pulled it free of the soil he couldn't identify it. After dragging it over to the ditch at the side of the field, he climbed back on his tractor and finished the task of rolling the earth. When that job was done he returned to the building to fetch a sledgehammer and some new planks of wood, intent on repairing the footbridge.

First he stamped down the withered autumn

remains of brambles and nettles clumped around the footbridge. Then he swung his sledgehammer and brought it thumping down on one of the rotting planks.

There came a single thump at the door. A thump so heavy it seemed to shake the house. Martha was dozing in front of the fire, alone in the house since Cassie had taken Frank to the farm for the weekend. Though everyone had enjoyed Aida's tale about the corpse sitting upright on the embalming table, the story had cemented in each of their minds a fear of morbidity and the notion that Frank might be getting just a little too interested in embalming as an evening's entertainment. Martha had already been engineering ways of drawing Frank's Binley Road phase to a close. She'd been mulling over the problem and gazing into the fire when the knock came.

Martha struggled to her feet. Her breathing was coming harder these days and by the time she had tugged back the draught curtain and got the door open she was already slightly dizzy. She had to take a step back.

An airman stood at the door. His heels pressed together and he held his arms stiff at his sides, carrying himself proudly erect. He wore a padded leather aviation helmet and flying goggles, but his eyes were clearly visible, magnified even, behind the goggles. Martha knew from his insignia that he was a German airman.

The German airman looked hard at Martha. Then he said, '*Wir, die wir einst herrlich waren. Wir fallen immernoch aus den Wolken.*'

'I didn't understand you,' Martha said.

The airman looked confused, lost, and he began wringing his gloved hands. He glanced quickly over his shoulder. Then with sudden movement he saluted her and turned back down the path. Martha was afraid. She knew that she was seeing a ghost, so she made no attempt to follow. Instead she closed the door, bolted it, drew the draught curtain back in place and returned to her seat by the fire.

Tom swung his sledgehammer a second time and the plank splintered. He flipped the plank over and tossed it up on the bank. Since the other planks looked in no better condition than the first, he came round about and swung his hammer from beneath. Two or three blows were enough to dislodge the second plank from the earth into which it was wedged, and his final blow sent it skyward. On seeing a pile of chicken and bird feathers revealed, Tom guessed that a fox had used the bridge for cover. He thought he might even have found the fox's earth. As well as chicken feathers there were kestrel, pigeon and crow feathers. Then Tom realised that a great number of feathers had been stuck upright in the earth, and in neat rows. There were other things, too. Conkers, acorns, hazel-nut shells; pebbles, lumps of shiny tarmac and small rocks; bits of green bottle-glass, shards of pottery and fragments of broken mirror; cow horn, rubber lambing teats and other bits of missing farm equipment.

Tom swung his sledgehammer again, breaking the third, and then the final plank, exposing all.

There were rubber balls, toy soldiers and dinky cars; there were cigarette cards and children's comics; there were chicken bones and rabbit skulls. There was a bell. There was a small gold plate. There was something else, glass and metal. Tom tried to pull it out of the earth but it wouldn't come. He stooped to take a closer look. 'Hell's bells!' Tom whispered to himself. 'Hell's bloody bells.'

Perhaps half an hour after her encounter with the German airman Martha woke up in her chair beneath the wall clock and blinked at the embers of the fire. She got to her feet and emptied the coal scuttle on to the fire. Then she filled the kettle and set it to boil.

The vision of the airman – and she was convinced it was no more than a vision, even though the verisimilitude of these apparitions could sometimes still have her guessing – had disturbed her more than most. While the kettle was boiling she went to check the front door. The draught curtain was drawn, so she pulled it back. The door was bolted. She drew back the bolt and opened the door.

It was late afternoon and a dilute, brass-coloured sun was sinking over the slate rooftops and glowing dully on the redbrick terrace of houses. Upon hearing a curious, high-pitched engine Martha looked up the empty street. An odd three-wheel contraption came combusting around the corner. It was tiny, and it seemed to be neither motorbike nor motor car, but some improvisation in between, a kind of aeroplane cockpit on three wheels and driven by a hunched figure. It coasted to a halt outside Martha's house.

The hunched figure flung back a canopy and stepped out. The driver of the machine wore a flying jacket and goggles. His teeth were clenched.

'Not again surely,' Martha whispered to herself.

But the figure was beaming stupidly at Martha. Neither did he wear a full uniform, unlike the earlier apparition. This one wore denim jeans. 'The admirable Mrs Vine!' the man shouted jovially in a cut-glass accent.

'Hello,' Martha said evenly, remaining on guard.

Dragging off the aviation helmet and goggles the man said, 'Don't you recognise me, Mrs Vine? George. Cassie's friend from Oxford.'

Martha was greatly relieved. She did recognise George after all. She jabbed a finger at the contraption he'd arrived in. 'What's that?'

'That? Why it's a Messerschmitt Bubble, Mrs Vine. Dandy little thing isn't she? Look here Mrs Vine, I've driven up posthaste. I want to marry your daughter if she'll have me.'

'What?'

'Cassie. If she'll have me. What do you say? Is that your kettle whistling Mrs Vine? Cup of tea, marvellous. Good timing, what?'

'Frank,' Tom said, 'you come down the field with me. You too, Cassie, there's something you need to see.'

'What is it?' Una said.

'You stay here with the twins for the moment. I'm not sure they need to see it.'

357

'See what?'

Tom didn't answer. Frank looked wistfully in the direction of the footbridge. He knew where Tom had been working all afternoon. When Tom turned and walked back in that direction, Frank simply fell in behind him, as did Cassie, Una and the twins, Tom's injunction notwithstanding.

When they reached the brook, Tom said to Frank, 'Is this your doing?'

Frank nodded. He felt oddly relieved that his old den had been discovered. 'I didn't put that there, though,' he said, pointing at the large bubble-like glass and steel frame. 'That was already there.'

'I know that,' Tom said.

Cassie got down on her knees and put her eye against the exposed part of the glass bubble. 'Good God,' she said.

Una wanted to look. She also dropped to her knees and peered through at the Man-Behind-The-Glass. 'Ooh ya!' she said. 'I don't like that.'

The, twins craned their necks. They also wanted to take a look. Tom had to be sharp with them. He sent them to play back up by the barn. They trudged away, looking over their shoulders.

'I used to speak to him,' Frank said. 'Though I haven't in a long, long time.'

'So that's where he came down,' Cassie said.

'What?' Una said. 'What are you talking about, Cassie?' Cassie never answered. She just gazed down at the glass bubble.

'Explains why there were never any bodies found,' Tom said.

'What will you do?' Una wanted to know.

'It's got to come out. I shall have to tell Snowie.' Snowie was the local ruddy-faced, white-haired police constable who patrolled the neighbourhood on a bicycle. He'd been on the scene during the war the morning after the plane had come down. That day he'd told Tom to keep his shotgun loaded in case the crew had survived.

'All this time,' Una said.

Tom reached over to pick something out of the debris of feathers and coins and pebbles and glass. It was the bell. 'And what shall we say about this, young Frank?'

It was not known, in the Vine family, which was the most extraordinary event: that a German HE 111 bomber that had crashed and burned in Tom's field the night of the Coventry blitz had buried its plexiglass nose and part of its bombardier under the footbridge; or that Frank had stolen the peace bell from the church; or that George had come up from Oxford determined to marry Cassie Vine.

'You don't know what you are taking on,' Martha had said to him.

'But I do Mrs Vine, I do!' George had cried. 'I've heard all about Cassie riding around town and–'

'Hush up you soft ha'porth! Do you want the neighbours to hear?'

'I was told about that,' George continued more quietly, 'and that did it for me.'

'Did it? Did what?'

'That's what I want. Cassie! She's the girl for me. Anyone who would do that is amazing! I'd give a month of misery for an hour of the kind of excitement Cassie can give a chap. She's the one I want, and at any cost.'

'You want locking up! And her along with you!'

George held out his hands for the manacles. 'Lock me away with her! Lead me to the prison of matrimony!' Then he flung himself full length on the floor before Martha and tried to grab her foot so that he could place it on his head. 'Look Mrs Vine! I am supine! The code of courtly love, Mrs Vine! I abase myself! Instruct your daughter to marry me! Put me out of my misery!'

'Get off my foot, you silly posh twerp! What would your mother say if she could see you?'

'Silly posh twerp that I am, I must have Cassie!'

Martha reached down to grab the poker from beside the fire and let George have a vital crack on the ribs. Groaning, George released Martha's foot and rolled over.

'Now get off the floor and stop making a fool of yourself!' Martha slumped back in her chair, flushed from the exertion. 'If you really must have her, then for God's sake let's talk o' this properly! Look at the state you've got me in.'

While these dramatic scenes took place in Martha's sitting room, some rather more sombre discussions were going on at the farm. Snowie came wheezing up to the farm on his bicycle, scratched the few remaining white hairs on his head, and declared he'd never seen anything like it and admitted he didn't really know what to do. Who should they tell? There wasn't a local war office to inform any more like there was on the night that the plane had actually come down in the field. He wasn't sure, he said, who should be notified exactly, though he felt *somebody* should be told.

He and Tom decided to dig around the glass and steel nose of the aircraft to get a good look at the remains inside. The cockpit was broken away, and when they managed to lift the glass nose they saw that the skull, with its flying helmet, was the only part of the airman fully intact.

'Well,' Snowie said, gently excavating with his spade, 'it ain't a whole *skelington*.'

'Look, he's still wearing his dog-tag,' Tom said. 'Are you sure we should be doing this?'

'I've no idea,' Snowy said. 'I don't normally dig up dead German skelingtons for a living, do I? Look, it's just a bit of ribcage and nothing else.'

'We can't leave it here,' Tom said.

Snowy sniffed, and thought for a moment. 'Can you keep it in the house or the barn until someone comes to look at it?'

'No, I bloody well can't.'

'A German skelington ain't going to hurt you none, is it?'

'Bugger off, Snowie.'

Snowie scratched his head again. 'Right then, let's put the glass back over it until I can get someone here. Help me lift this.'

The two men walked steadily back up to the house. Tom poured them both a nip of Scotch while Snowie, after licking the stub of a pencil, made laborious notes on his pad. He reminded Tom that when the plane had crashed bits of metal had been flung everywhere, some of it landing several acres away from the main fuselage. They concluded that the cockpit had been sliced in two, along with the airman's torso, and had embedded itself in the mud bank of the brook. The rising and falling water had excavated part of the buried nose until Frank had found it. Snowie snapped his notepad shut, concluding that he'd have to tell both the local council and the Home Office. He pushed his empty whisky glass across the kitchen table, looking for a top-up.

Snowie was not informed about Frank's theft from the church of the peace bell. Instead Frank was marched off by Cassie to Raggie Annie's cottage and forced to make a confession and an apology to her. Whether the police were to be told, it was decided, was a matter for Raggie Annie.

'But why did you want to get an owd gal like me in trouble?' Raggie Annie said to him inside her cottage. 'What did I ever do to hurt the likes of you?'

'I didn't mean it!' the tearful Frank said. 'I didn't mean to get you into any trouble!'

'That's as may be. But you did. And they thought as I was a thief. But it's you as is the thief.'

'Una says to tell you,' Cassie said, staring about her, fascinated by Annie's bottles and jars and vials and dried herbs, 'that it's up to you if you want to tell the police.'

'What, and get that useless old Snowie to stick his big shiny nose into our affairs? What good would that do? No, let me think on it.'

And while 'thinking on it', Annie cast a bird-like stare at the snuffling Frank, and so fierce was her gaze he had to look down at his shoes. 'No,' she said at last, 'we'll not tell the police. We'll tell the bees, shan't we son?'

Frank looked up. Cassie said, 'What's that?'

Annie tapped her nose at Cassie. 'The boy knows. Una can say as she found the bell in a ditch and take it back to the church. But as for you Frank, for what you've put me through you'll have to repay me, and I've no wood chopped for the winter. You can chop me a pile of wood for my fire. What do you say to that?'

Frank said nothing. He merely stared at Raggie Annie, as if she were an elf from out of the woods.

Cassie said, 'If I were you I'd say yes, and quick.'

'Yes,' said Frank.

'Big pile, mind you,' Annie said. 'Long winter ahead. It'll take you many a Saturday afternoon.'

'If I were you I'd still say yes,' Cassie put in.

'Yes,' Frank said.

'Well, there's an end to it. Know how to use an axe, Frank?'

'No.'

'No? A big grown-up lad like you? Time you were shown then, weren't it?'

36

'Where are we going, Mam?' Frank had asked Cassie the same question several times without receiving a satisfactory answer.

Cassie had only told him that they were going to the 'top of the town' and that she had something to show him. So they'd taken a bus ride into town and walked up Trinity Street to Broadgate. Frank thought there was something altered about his mother. To begin with she wore a different perfume; there was a new spring to her step; and she looked like she couldn't hide a smile.

Cassie steered Frank across Broadgate. His eyes swept across the lovely grass island, laid out in a cross to echo the transept of the blitzed cathedral, to the thrilling Lady Godiva statue that had come to speak of the city's sacrifice. The resolute modernity of the place – that statue, that green traffic island at the head of the pedestrian precinct – had come to be the town crest, and in that crest a kind of covenant after the years of disaster.

Cassie then ushered Frank up the white stone steps of the pillared portico of the bank. 'Are we going in here?' Frank asked.

'No, we're not,' Cassie said at last. 'I've brought you here to tell you something Frank. And I hope you will understand.'

Frank blinked at her.

'Frank, not quite thirteen years ago I stood on these steps one day and I had a little baby girl in my arms. You see, everybody knew that I wouldn't be the best mother in the world for that little baby. So they found somebody kind to take the baby away and look after it and give it a good home. Even though it broke my heart. Even though it breaks my heart every day.'

Cassie had to stop to open her handbag. She rooted round for a handkerchief, and blew her nose. Then she clasped her bag shut, and continued with her story.

'Then Frank it happened all over again a few years later. Here I was with another baby, a little boy this time. And I was supposed to give him away. But you see that spire up there? St Michael's? I looked up there and it was like a needle pricking the sky. I thought I could hear the clouds tearing themselves on that spire. Well, it was my heart tearing, that's what I could hear. And you know that little boy was you and I couldn't give you away. I just couldn't do it again.

'So your grandmother found a way for me to keep you, which wasn't easy on anyone because I'm so scatty and, well, as I say, not the best mother in the world.'

'You are Mam! You are!' Frank protested, alarmed now more by his mother's emotional state than by anything in her confession.

'No, I'm silly and I'm a fathead and I have blue funks but you know what Frankie? I love as hard and as fierce as anyone on this earth. I love you and I love my sisters and I love my mam, your grandma. I do. And I'd never do anything that you really didn't want me to do. So I've brought you here today to ask you something. It's about George, from Ravenscraig.'

'Yes.'

'You like him don't you?'

'Yes.'

'Well Frank, he's asked me to marry him.'

'Yes.'

'George said he would marry me and look after us both. He said he doesn't mind that I'm a ninny. He said we'd have our own home here in Coventry near the rest of the family and that he'd be a proper dad to you and that he'd love you too, just as if you were his own.'

'Yes, I know. I know all that.'

'What do you mean? What do you mean by saying you know all that?'

'George asked me for my permission to marry you.'

'He did?'

'Yes. When we were at Ravenscraig. He was supposed to be teaching me about Karl Marx but he kept going on and on about being in love. He said he was writing a book and he said if he sold it he would ask you to marry him so we could all live together, and I said yes that would be all right so he must have sold his book.'

'So you don't mind if I marry George?'

'I'd like it. He's a decent person. So I gave him my permission already. He asked me to keep it quiet though. It's all right, Mam. I like him.'

'Really and truly?'

'Really and truly.'

Cassie wept and flung her arms around Frank. Frank shrank slightly, feeling the gaze of bypassers. He didn't much like being a public spectacle on the steps of the bank at the top of the town. 'Mam,' he complained, 'everyone is looking at us.'

While Cassie was weeping and hugging Frank on the steps of the bank in Broadgate, Martha was enjoying her regular glass of stout, her daily dose of the black stuff courtesy of the National Health Service. Not all GPs were so wise, but Martha's was, and what with her compendium of ailments he often repeated how remarkable it was that she could keep going so well.

Martha slurped at the black beer and wiped away with the back of her hand the buttery foam it transferred to her upper lip. The stout settled her stomach and it stopped her mind from racing. She'd been short of breath lately, and the daily round had become tiresome to her. She set down the glass of stout on the low table beside her and eased herself back in her seat.

The house was quiet. Now that Beatie had gone and now that Cassie had accepted an offer from this strange but decent and funny oddbod from Oxford, she knew she'd have a lot more quiet to look forward to. Martha wasn't sure that quiet was what she wanted.

She sat back in her chair, hearing the steady whisper of the clock pendulum from over her head. She gazed wistfully into her stout, at the tiny bubbles of air still popping at the surface. Then there came a knock at the door.

It wasn't a loud knock. Not one that shook the door. It was a light tapping, a bony knuckle laid against the wood, slightly musical, *rap-de-raprap*. Martha sighed and struggled to her feet.

She was slow getting to the door, and before she'd had a chance to pull back the draught curtain, the light knock came again. 'All right, I'm a coming,' Martha said.

Even though it was deep autumn and there was a winter chill in the air there stood at the door a man in his shirtsleeves. He wasn't a particularly impressive figure: short of stature, unkempt and in need of a shave. His skin was tanned, leathered even. Martha took him to be a gypsy or travelling tradesman.

His manner was friendly enough. 'Down your way,' he said with a smile. 'I've come to cut the grass.' He had with him an old and rusting push-me-along lawnmower. It was a sorry looking piece of equipment. Martha thought the man must be hard-pressed. He nodded at the lawnmower.

Martha did have a tiny apron of grass above the back yard, but it was almost winter and the grass had anyway stopped growing. 'Lawnmower is it? It's the wrong time of year for a lawnmower. Where have you come from?'

He was a sad little man with gentle eyes. 'Just looking for work.' His smile was served up and dropped too quickly.

'I've no need of you,' Martha said.

The little man took a tiny step closer. 'No charge.'

The hair on Martha's arms bristled. 'Oh no,' she said, stepping back. 'Oh no. I'd have much rather you didn't say that.'

'Sorry,' the man said. 'I had to mention it.' Again the man took the tiniest of steps closer. 'Sorry.'

Martha quickly closed the door on the man. Her breath came short and the room was spinning. She had to fight her way back to her chair, into which she collapsed heavily, knocking the table and spilling her glass of stout. The thick rug next to the hearth soaked up the foamy black beer.

37

Cassie's wedding to George was – to everyone's surprise and delight – doubled with Beatie's wedding to Bernard. It made economic sense just as it made emotional sense: George was best man to Bernard and vice-versa. Only one new suit apiece; and only one reception, since the guest list was almost identical, with only one marathon round of buttering cucumber and salmon-paste sandwiches.

There was some controversy over the ceremonial venue, which was the city registry office. Aida, Ina, Evelyn and Olive were all scandalised that their sisters had opted against a church wedding. Una explained it to them over and over, 'Look, they're all bloody communists, what would they want with a church?'

'Excuse me Una,' George corrected. 'I'm not a bally communist I'm a syndicalist.'

'And we're democratic socialists, thank you,' Beatie added.

'Well Cassie what are you then?' William wanted to know.

'I,' Cassie said airily, 'am a neo-anarchic free spirit, George says.'

'I see,' William said with a wink at Tom. 'That's all right then.'

But the argument went by, mainly because it was sensed by everyone that some important – if dimly understood by others – principle had been compromised in Beatie and Bernard getting spliced *at all*. The two had been so publicly outspoken about the hypocrisy of marriage and the uncertainty of monogamy that this sudden capitulation to bourgeois values had amazed the whole family. But then the whole family was not party to a conversation Martha had had with Beatie.

It was not long after Martha had had the 'funny turn' in which she'd collapsed into her chair and spilled her glass of stout. Beatie was sitting with Martha, telling her of the antics of certain councillors in the city chambers.

'Pigs getting their noses in the trough, Mam, that's what some of them are. It's not about politics half the time. It's about how can I line my pocket.'

'Yes,' Martha said with a tug on her pipe. 'It's hard to keep the personal and the political apart.' Then Martha said, 'Getting a lot of attention aren't you Beatie?'

'Too bloody much.'

Beatie was the darling of the press. To have a young woman on the council who was both attractive and incendiary made for wonderful copy, and suddenly the reporting of local politics had become sexy. She was known variously as Bolshie Beat, Beatie Boadicea and Valkyrie Vine. Her speeches and interventions were written up in the Coventry *Evening Telegraph* by a doting young reporter.

'It's just as well this baby is coming along,' Martha said. 'That'll take the heat off.'

'Why do you say that, Mam?'

'When they find you're not married, I mean. With a baby. That'll send the balloon up. But you're doing the right thing. Have your say now, while you're young. No one wants to be in politics for the long run. Can you help me out o' this chair, Beatie? My back's all seized up.'

Beatie went strangely quiet as she helped Martha stand up. She went away that evening looking quite distracted. Within a couple of days Beatie and Bernard had made their announcement.

The double wedding was a great day. The reception was held in the party room of the Working Men's Social Club. In addition to family, the guests included a few city councillors and other friends from the political scene. Lilly came up from Oxford. Frank got to sit on the top table, between Martha and Cassie.

There was sherry, a sit-down buffet lunch and speeches where Bernard and George got to make *both* a hilarious best man's harangue *and* a humble salutation from the groom. Bernard called George a 'futurist in syndicalist's clothing', which made at least two people laugh and caused William to narrow his eyes at Tom. George's speech was the funniest. He told the guests he was aware of how curious they all were about what went on in those days at Ravenscraig, but admitted that he was so busy having sex with everybody that he couldn't remember. This earned uproarious laughter, but of the kind that drops suddenly when everyone realises that the joke was probably true.

Beatie quite naturally broke with tradition, hauling herself to her feet to give a short speech from the bride. Cassie, not to be outdone, followed suit. She challenged George's account by saying she couldn't actually remember if they'd had sex at Ravenscraig. George retorted that he was surprised if she could remember anything. Bernard chipped in by saying how glad he was that they'd started off married life with an argument; whereupon George swept up his new wife in his arms and kissed her, publicly and passionately, to wild applause from the guests.

Jazz music was supplied by a six-piece band paid for by William, Tom and Gordon. There was dancing, and beer on tap, and the guests were intent on drinking the bar dry. At some point while everyone else was up dancing, Tom whisked a glass of stout and an orange juice over to Martha and Frank.

'Well Martha, that's the last of your chicks all nested for themselves.'

'Ar. And with Cassie I never thought I'd see it.'

Tom leaned forward. 'No, it's Beatie is the one as surprised us. You going to tell me how you pulled that one off?'

'Nowt to do with me, Tom.' Martha lifted her glass of stout to Frank. 'Cheers.'

'Cheers,' said Frank.

Tom could only gaze back at Martha with admiration. 'All of us. Played like a bloody banjo. Cheers.'

When Tom had gone, Martha glanced at Frank sipping his orange juice, and was thunderstruck. 'Long trousers,' she said.

'Gran?' Frank said.

'You're in long trousers.'

'Yes Gran. George brought them for me, for the wedding. Now that I'm ten. Nearly.'

'My word, we've seen you through to your long trousers Frank. The blink of an eye and here you are, nearly a man, and with it all before you.' Martha wiped away a moustache of foam from her upper lip and leaned back, as if to examine Frank in this new light. 'Frank my dear! Suddenly I've no fear for you. No fear at all. And you were such a worry to me, you were, not for anything you'd done, no, but for the rest of us. But here you are and with it all before you.'

Frank drained his glass, blushing under Martha's sudden reappraisal.

'I think you'll be all right. You're cleverer than we are, Frank, aren't you? Why? Because you know you don't have to listen to them if you don't want to, isn't that right Frank? You know what I'm talking about.'

Frank nodded.

'Not like your mother and me. Pulled this way and that when they try to get our ears. Not you. You choose which of them to listen to, Frank, don't you? Was it that business with the bell? Was that what told you they don't always steer you the right way? Was that it? It was, wasn't it?'

'Yes Gran, it was. It was exactly that.'

'And you're cleverer than us! Now I see it. You pick and choose! You've got it Frank. And whether it's a blessing or a curse, I don't know but you've got it, and you shall do better than us. And now I have no fear for you, now we've seen you through to long trousers.' Martha seized Frank's hand. 'You'll look after your mother won't you Frank?'

'Yes Gran. I won't let her come to any harm.'

Someone came up behind Martha. 'You bending our Frank's ear Mam?' It was Una. 'I want him to come and dance with me seeing as how he's such a good-looking chap. Are you coming Frank?'

Frank looked to Martha. He knew that in Martha's words he was being given some extraordinary permission, and he wasn't sure she was finished. But she was.

'Go and dance,' Martha said. 'Go on.'

The celebration went on until early evening. Noticing the fading light outside Martha announced she was ready. She let Aida and Gordon know, since Gordon had promised to run her home when she got tired. While Gordon was fetching his car Martha made her way, under pressure of an excess of stout and leaning heavily on her stick, to the toilets in the corridor. Before she got there the band struck up a version of 'Moonlight Serenade'. Martha turned to see her newly wed daughters move in to embrace their husbands for the slow, sensual dance. Both Beatie and Cassie spotted Martha watching from the doorway. They waved and smiled lazily to her from the pool of circling dancers. A sigh of pleasure passed through Martha's ancient body. She felt her eyes swimming so she pivoted on her stick and made to move through the door.

But she pulled up with a gasp. There in the corridor was her husband Arthur, dressed in a wedding suit. Martha recovered quickly. 'Are you talking to me now, then?'

'It wasn't me,' Arthur said, 'who stopped talking to *you*. It was you as stopped talking to *me*.'

'Whichever way it was, we haven't got time, have we Arthur?'

'No,' he said gently. 'Gone before you know it.'

There was a slight scuffle behind her. It was Cassie. 'Are you all right Mam? Who were you talking to?'

Martha turned to Cassie. 'Can't you see?'

Cassie looked past her mother's shoulder. 'See what? Who were you talking to?'

'Help me through to the lav, will you? Has that Gordon got his car ready?'

Beatie, Bernard, Cassie and George all came to see Martha into Gordon's car and to kiss her goodbye, since they were shortly to leave for their separate honeymoons. Beatie and Bernard were going walking in the Lake District, while Cassie and George planned on spending a few days on the Isle of Wight. Frank was to stay at the farm while they were away.

'Where's my Frank?' Martha shouted before allowing Gordon to drive her off. Frank came out. Martha kissed him and whispered two words in his ear.

They waved the car away and gaily turned back to the wedding festivities. 'What did she say?' someone asked Frank.

'"Long trousers".'

On the third day after the wedding, Martha made to fill a kettle with water when she suddenly felt overburdened by exhaustion. Instead of boiling the kettle she opened a bottle of stout, poured herself a glass and sank into her seat beneath the old clock. She lit a pipe and puffed away thoughtfully. She drank her stout. When both that and her pipe were finished she set down her empty glass and shuffled back in her chair, listening to the easy whisper of the clock pendulum. Then Martha closed her eyes and went to sleep; and in her sleep she passed over into the inevitable.

38

Gordon undertook to deal with all the funeral arrangements for Martha, and one of the first things he did was to ask Frank if he would like to help. He drove out to the farm to talk to the boy. Una had to direct Gordon to Raggie Annie's cottage, where Frank was swinging an axe. He'd already been told of his grandmother's death.

Gordon asked him to assist with the embalming and preparation of the body. If we help Martha now, Gordon explained, we help the others later. Frank understood perfectly. He said he would help, and off he went back to Gordon and Aida's house and embalming studio on Binley Road.

This time Aida did not watch proceedings. She went to be with the twins while Gordon and Frank prepared the body for the Calling Hours. Gordon said, 'Remember now son. This is not Martha. This is just the packet she came in.'

Frank was solemn and diligent in everything he did. Together he and Gordon worked away, mostly in silence. Gordon was pleased at how much the lad had picked up during his stay there.

'You'd make a good mortician,' he observed.

'No,' Frank replied. 'I wouldn't want to do this all the time.'

Gordon thought for a moment, then nodded. 'Aye. It's not everybody's cup of tea. Look, laddie, I'll do any cutting. Will you start the sponging?'

Frank didn't need asking twice. It was a loving act. He was the Fairy of Death, waving his wand. Gordon had to use his wand to nick the corners of Martha's mouth to take off a twist in the upper lip. Then Gordon hoisted the drum of chemicals and they got on with the embalming. Frank pumped vigorously. Gordon set up the drain.

'Three gallons,' Frank said.

'You've remembered laddie. You've remembered.'

Gordon took care of the cavity embalming while Frank brushed his grandmother's hair and took on some of the tasks Aida would normally have dealt with. He applied Vaseline to her face and a smear of lipstick to her mouth. He touched up her lashes with mascara. He applied a little blusher to her cheek. Gordon looked up from his own task and nodded approval. 'You've got such a gentle touch Frank. That's better than I could have done it. And don't tell your Aunt Aida but it's better than she could have done it, too.'

Together they dressed Martha in the clean clothes provided by Aida. Frank polished her shoes and slipped them on her feet and laced them. Finally they lifted Martha into the casket. Frank thought her surprisingly light. Gordon intuited his thoughts. 'Seemed bigger in life,

377

didn't she? All that power in such a small woman. We'll not see the like of her.'

It took them a long time but Gordon concluded they'd done a good job. He had a trolley on to which they slid the casket. Then they wheeled Martha into the lounge, ready for the Calling Hours. Gordon said they had a while before the family would come, and that Frank should run himself a bath and change into his best clothes, because he had to cross over from being Martha's embalmer to Martha's mourner.

Aida covered the mirrors in the lounge and she took away the clock from the mantelpiece. The family members started to arrive from six o'clock that evening. Only the immediate family was invited to come: Martha's seven daughters and their husbands, and Martha's six grandchildren. The funeral the next day would extend a wider invitation, but for the Vines the Calling Hours were restricted and private.

Ina and Evelyn arrived first, closely followed by Una and Tom and their children and thereafter the house filled quickly. Cassie and Beatie had to face Martha fresh from their respective honeymoons. Beatie took it the hardest of all the sisters, and Cassie tried to comfort her.

'She was ready, Beatie. Mam was ready.'

'I know that,' Beatie said blowing her nose into a handkerchief provided by Tom. 'But I wasn't.'

They each made a point out of touching Martha's cold body, because she'd told every single one of the girls that if you touched a corpse it would never come haunting you. It was not that they necessarily believed in this superstition, but they did it because that was what Martha always told them to do. Then Ina took off her glasses and asked if they could sing 'Abide With Me' even though the proper place for singing was at the funeral. So they did that.

I fear no foe, with Thee at hand to bless;
Ills have no weight, and tears no bitterness;
Where is death's sting? Where, Grave, thy
   victory?
I triumph still, if Thou abide with me.

Though they didn't sing it well, and some couldn't sing it all. Beatie couldn't make her voice break through her grief; and William's voice seemed to collapse entirely halfway through; and Frank's voice cracked on the high notes. The tune was too hard for them to hold. And when they finished singing they placed their arms around each other, and at that moment the family tenderness was almost harder to bear than the bereavement.

EPILOGUE

It was in the following spring of 1954 that Frank happened to be visiting at Wolvey along with Cassie and George, when the farm received an unusual caller. George had rented a cottage for the three of them at Withybrook, quite close by, and Cassie often came out to the farm to ride. Raggie Annie had discharged Frank at Christmas from his reparation duties, but he still called on her to help with chores. An unusual friendship had developed between him and the old woman, and not merely because he still felt guilty about the peace bell.

Frank had just returned to the farm to see a motor car turn into the driveway. The vehicle carried a tall, elderly but dignified man. A white-haired woman remained inside the car while the man climbed out. He approached Frank, and, without a word, produced a name and address written on a scrap of paper. The name was certainly Tom's and the address was indeed that of the farm.

'This is it. Tufnall's Farm. Yes.'

From the kitchen Una saw what was happening. She came out, carrying her baby in her arms and trailing the twins behind her like a mother goose. 'What is it?'

'I from Germany,' the man said at last, in a heavy accent. He gestured towards the car. 'This my wife. We want to see where came the plane.'

There followed an extraordinary moment where no one spoke. The man bowed his head for a moment, then squinted up at the diffuse yellow sun. Then he looked back at Frank.

'I think this must be the man's father,' Frank said.

'Can you go and call Tom?' said Una, flustered.

Frank hurried along to the cowsheds and brought Tom back with him. Tom, in overalls and wellington boots, nodded at the visitor.

'I want to see where came the plane,' the man said again. 'My son it was, in the plane.'

'I see.' Tom rubbed his chin and looked at Una. She raised her eyebrows by way of reply. 'Well,' Tom said, turning towards the lower fields. 'There's not a great deal to look at.'

The German gentleman smiled sadly.

'I'll take him down to the field,' Frank said.

Tom said to the man, 'This lad will show you. He found the cockpit.'

'Thank you,' said the German gentleman. 'I bring my wife.'

He opened the passenger door of the car for his wife to get out. She was a little frail, leaning on his arm as they made to follow Frank.

While they were out of earshot, Tom said to Frank, 'Show them, but don't go into detail.'

'I know what he needs to know,' Frank said.

As Frank and the German couple made their slow way down to the field, Una said to Tom, 'Well, what do you make of that?'

'I don't know what to make of it. The authorities must have got in touch with them.'

'One minute they're bombing you, next minute they're calling on you.'

'Odd, ain't it?'

'I'll say it's odd. We lost a lot of people that night didn't we? And then they come here.'

'But what can we do?'

Una sighed. 'In the past, isn't it? I'll put the kettle on. We'll give them a cup of tea and a slice of cake. That's what we'll do.'

Within half an hour Frank returned with the elderly couple. They were grateful to him for having shown them the scene of the crash. They were shy, but they allowed themselves to be coaxed into the farmhouse kitchen, where they drank tea and allowed the twins to stare at them with bulging eyes. They revealed they were visiting Coventry as part of a church reconciliation project involved in the building of the new cathedral. They had hoped to get a glimpse of the landscape in which their son, a Luftwaffe bombardier, had met his fate. The British authorities had returned the pilot's dog-tag and other information to the German administration, which was how they came to know where to look. They relaxed a little in the farmhouse kitchen, but remained at all times formal and polite. Translating for his wife, the man said that she too had been brought up on a farm that could almost have been the same one, so similar did the land seem to her.

After they had gone, Una said, 'Well,'

'What about that then, Frank?' said Tom.

'Strange,' Frank said. 'But I'm glad you gave them a cup of tea. Costs us nothing to be kind, does it?'

Tom smiled at his wife, because it might have been Martha talking.

This Large Print Book for the partially sighted, who cannot read normal print, is published under the auspices of

THE ULVERSCROFT FOUNDATION